In the Shadows

In the Shadows

An Outsiders Mystery

A Novel By

Susan Finlay

This is a work of fiction. Names, characters, places, and incidents either are products of the author's imagination or are used fictitiously, and any resemblance to actual persons, living or dead, events, or locales is entirely coincidental.

IN THE SHADOWS. Copyright © 2014 by Susan Finlay.

All rights reserved. This book or any portion thereof may not be reproduced or used in any manner whatsoever without the express written approval of the author except for the use of brief quotations in a book review.

First Edition

Cover Artwork by Samantha Finlay

Cover Design by Susan Finlay

Paperback ISBN-13:978-1493544639

Published in the USA

AUTHOR'S NOTE

This is a work of fiction, and all the characters and places and events are inventions. The troglodyte village of Reynier, France, does not exist, although some may recognize different aspects of the cave system and cave homes, since caves and troglodyte villages are not uncommon in France. I did a significant amount of research for this book and series, but I've never actually been to France, and therefore used author creativity to fill in the gaps. The Trizay River and the other small villages, such as Belvidere and Saint-Julien-du-Tarn are also fictitious.

This book is dedicated to my husband Will (having provided support and patience during my good times and doubts), our children Scott and Samantha, my mother-in-law Pat, and my stepmother Linda.

CHAPTER ONE

MAURA BARRINGTON PULLED back the curtain and stared out the second story window of her shabby hotel room in Paris' 18th arrondissment. A young couple strolled by, pushing a pram. They stopped and the woman bent forward to check on the baby. When she straightened, the man with her reached over and tucked a loose lock of her hair behind her ear.

Maura let the curtain fall back in place. She turned to look at the bed where her new clothes lay strewn about, waiting to be packed away in her duffel bag. Two days ago, her first day in Paris, she'd spent all her time observing people and figuring out what she needed to wear to blend in. Yesterday, she'd gone shopping.

She picked up one outfit, a blue-and-green flowered blouse and coordinating skirt, and took it into the bathroom. After she got dressed, she copied the woman's hair style—a classic French twist. Lastly, she stuck her feet into the stiff high heels, put away the rest of the clothes, and zipped up the bag. On impulse, she reopened her duffel bag, lifted the false bottom, and verified everything was still there. She hid the bag under the bed and left the room, locking the door carefully. Following the worn red carpet down the creaking staircase, she stopped at the next to last landing, where the musty darkness mixed with a smell she couldn't quite identify. The hotel felt abandoned. Continuing, she reached the ground floor and was about to step into the dingy hallway when a door directly across from the stairs swung open, startling her. In the doorway a big-bellied man with greasy hair stared at her. His deep-set eyes swept over her, and he grinned widely. Maura hurried past him along the corridor, her footsteps echoing on the cracked tiles, but not loudly enough to cover up the sound of his laughter. A brown mouse darted in front of her and ran under the sofa in the lobby.

Outside, she rushed down the worn steps, but had to stop at the street curb to wait for a string of cars to go by. A ragged-looking dog wandered up to her and sat down beside her as she waited. When the light changed, Maura lifted a foot to step off the curb, but the dog barked loudly, causing her to hesitate. In the next instant, a bus zoomed through the red light and past her, sending a gray plume of exhaust spiraling into the air. Maura swore under her breath. She whirled around toward the dog, but it was already gone.

She crossed the street and walked two blocks, rounded the corner onto bustling Boulevard de Barbès, and continued on to Chateau Rouge train station. It was one of the poorer areas, populated by African and Arab immigrants, yet it was vibrant and alive. As Maura walked through the train station, the frequent train announcements, clatter of metal, and odor of dust and rubber brought to mind London's underground system, a place she practically knew by heart. She stopped and closed her eyes, savoring the vision of what she would never again see for real, until someone bumped against her. Her eyes popped open. Instinctively, she wrapped protective hands around her handbag, and scanned the area.

Maura proceeded to the platform and found her train already

waiting. In the process of rushing aboard the train, something snagged one of her heels causing her to stumble. She almost fell into a man's lap. "Pardon," she muttered as she pulled herself together, trying to hide her embarrassment. Once seated near the rear of the train, she glanced cautiously at the people around her. Everyone was busy reading papers or typing text messages on their mobile phones. She removed her shoes and checked the heels to make sure they weren't damaged. Thankfully the shoes were intact. High heels might be fashionable, but she despised wearing them.

When the train eased to a stop at the Montparnasse station, she exited and climbed the stairs, emerging into the pleasant air of early evening. Ten minutes later, she stood in front of Le Bistro du Nord, an attractive restaurant occupying the ground floor of a tall brick building. On the outside patio, customers sat at silver tables shaded by the building's dark-green awning, enjoying their dinners and drinks. Her French, though not good enough to pass as a native-speaker, was good enough for a bar job. But she was far from confident in her ability to wait tables well enough for Paris. She took a deep breath, steeled herself, slid past the tables, and entered the bistro. At the hostess station, she greeted the attendant.

"Table for one, or are you meeting someone?"

"Oh, I'm not a customer. I saw the advertisement for a waitress position. I'd like to apply if it's still available."

The hostess, a slender blonde woman with tanned skin and shimmering lip gloss, looked her over critically. "Of course." She bent down, and pulled out an application from a drawer at the station. "Please have a seat in the bar area and fill this out. Be sure to return it to me when you've finished."

"Merci." With the form in hand, Maura turned, and stepped right into the path of a waiter. His quick reflexes avoided a crash, but Maura felt heat rise up her neck, instantly embarrassed.

Fortunately, other than the grumbling waiter, no one else seemed to notice.

She stood for a few moments and surveyed the dining room. Judging from the customers, it was classy enough to lure in couples wanting a romantic dinner and business men and women wanting a neutral place to meet with clients, and yet relaxed enough to bring in families with young children. A waitress breezed past her, expertly balancing a tray of several attractive plates of food. The aromas made Maura's stomach growl, and reminded her of her meager lunch that had consisted of a stale roll, a chunk of cheese, and tea.

Overall, the bistro was rather dark, lit only by its lovely ornate stained glass lamps hanging over each table and by the light bouncing off its mirrored walls. Shouts and raucous laughter drew her attention. Against the farthest wall, illuminated by dozens of candles, was a gorgeous sculpted wooden bar, so highly polished that it shimmered in the candlelight. Glasses of all shapes and sizes lining the wall behind the bar sparkled like stars in the flickering light. A group of at least a dozen men and women were gathered around the far end of the bar, the apparent source of the shouting and laughter.

Moving to the bar area as she was instructed, she selected one of the few empty tables and sat down with her back to a large television screen. After spreading out the three-page application form, she withdrew a pen from her handbag and began filling in the form. For her name she wrote Anouk Allard, and gave the hotel's address.

Meanwhile, more people arrived nearby, after which several explosive bursts of laughter firing in machine gun fashion, distracted her. Maybe she should move to the dining room, she thought. But when she glanced toward the hostess who had specifically sent her to this area, she squashed the idea.

Halfway through filling out her application, she took a break and glanced around her. Her attention fell onto the back of an English newspaper that the man sitting next to her was reading. She scanned the page and stopped abruptly, recognizing a photograph of herself. A gasp escaped her. The man turned and glanced at her. With her heart pounding, she folded up the application and tucked it inside her handbag, scooted back her chair, stood up, and as quickly as she could manage without drawing attention, walked tall and confidently toward the door.

Near the exit, the hostess stopped her. "Are you finished already?" she asked, extending her hand to take the application.

Maura shook her head. "I—I'll have to fill it out at home and bring it in later."

Frowning, the hostess said, "Is there a problem?"

"No, no," she said. "I just need to look up my references. I bought a new handbag yesterday and forgot to put my address book inside. You know how it is."

"Yes," she answered. "I do that sort of thing all the time."

Once outside, Maura paused and looked around. Her heart fluttered, making her lightheaded. She pictured the newspaper, and her stomach twisted in a knot. She started walking and making plans. She would leave the city from the Montparnasse station on the first departing train. Moments later, she faltered. Her duffel bag with all her belongings was in her hotel room. If she lost those, especially her cash, she might as well give up. At best, she might have enough cash to buy the train ticket, but then what would she do? She would have to make a quick stop at her hotel.

She didn't bother changing clothes, but covered her blouse with a loose-knit green woolly, grabbed her duffel bag, and left the hotel without checking out. Outside, she decided to take one last precaution by donning her dark glasses and a scarf over her hair.

By nightfall she was back at Gare Montparnasse. She rushed

inside the glass building and purchased a ticket to Angers in the Loire Valley. Her mother had vacationed there for two weeks many years ago, while Maura was away at school, and it was the first familiar name she saw. When the boarding announcement came over the intercom, Maura climbed aboard the TGV and carefully made her way to the back of the carriage. She had barely sat down in an aisle seat and made herself comfortable when she noticed three police officers enter the carriage at the front. Craning her neck, she tried to make out what was happening. She turned her head and looked behind her, thinking she might need to sneak out that way, but a train conductor stood in the aisle, his arms folded in an intimidating stance.

"May I be of assistance, Mademoiselle?" someone asked.

She noticed a gray-haired gentleman dressed in a business suit sitting across the aisle from her. He was leaning toward her with a friendly smile.

"Oh," she said, trying to sound nonchalant, "I was wondering why those officers are here. Is that normal?"

"I see them on the train occasionally. I make this trip at least twice a week, you see." He smiled, showing tobacco-stained teeth, which surprised her. "It may be a random check, or perhaps they are looking for someone. Either way, they will ask each passenger to show their identity card."

"What if we don't have one with us?"

"By law, anyone without ID is subject to arrest in France. That law is rarely enforced, I've been told. But—"

She felt a knot in her stomach. "I forgot my identity card. Is there a way off the train?"

An uncertainty crept into his expression and her hope sank.

In the seconds that followed, he winked. "I'll create a diversion. Hopefully, that will distract the conductor. If you're quick, you might manage to dash out through the back exit."

She nodded.

The man stood up and looked toward the officers. "I need help. Can somebody help me please? I think I'm having a heart attack." He clutched his chest. In that instance, the officers rushed forward, and Maura slipped past them. She ran out onto the platform, began walking quickly back to the main concourse, and then onto the next platform with a train waiting.

CHAPTER TWO

LIFE IN A small French village is certainly different, Dave Martin mused as he gazed out the front window of his date's apartment above her café. Reynier, a village of approximately six hundred residents, didn't exactly have a bustling nightlife—not like back home in Chicago. But there weren't shootings every day either. No graffiti, no gangs, no corruption—only gossip and meddling. After only ten days here, he'd already gotten an earful of that. As a kid, he'd loved coming here for summer-long visits with his grandparents. As an adult who'd outgrown his interest in the area's caves, and who didn't care for gossip, it was often boring.

His days were split between tending to his seventy-seven-year-old maternal grandmother, Fabienne Laurent, working on his novel, hanging out at the local café, and going on occasional dates with Simone Charbonneau. He was in Reynier because Fabienne had called him and more or less told him she was dying. She'd begged him to come to stay with her until the end. Although he'd dreaded the emotional pain he knew he'd have to face, he couldn't say no. Not when he was Grand-mère's only remaining family—if you didn't count his mother, who hadn't spoken to her in thirty-four years.

In spite of everything, he was mostly enjoying his stay. This evening, though, after a phone call had interrupted his date with Simone, he was finding it difficult to hide his impatience. He tried to focus on the scenery outside while Simone gabbed with her own grandmother, Jeannette Devlin, Fabienne's oldest and closest friend.

The view from this hillside vantage point halfway up the hill on the main side of town included a black-roofed Romanesque church peeking through the trees and extending its spire upwards, and right in front of it, the Trizay River, a dark ribbon shimmering in the moonlight at the base of the hill, or at least what he could see of the river since the businesses on the main street partially hid it. The river separated the hilly side of Reynier from the flat side. Sometimes, it seemed to Dave that the village had tumbled down the hill, jumped over the river, and spilled out. It could have continued that way, because the land on the other side of the river was wide-open, but the nearby town of Belvidere, with its alluring traditional town square, dozens of shops, and ample parking had taken over the growth spurt, leaving only one business street and five residential streets in Reynier's newer section. The rest of the valley, for as far as the eye could see, consisted of farms, vineyards, woods, and unused meadows. The village and valley were by day a brilliant green, and peaceful—starkly different from Chicago's tangle of high-rise buildings of glass, metal, and concrete. Even Reynier's chalky limestone hillside on the north bank of the river, though barren during winter, was now shrouded by leafy bowers of trees, vines, and shrubs that made the creamy-gold bluff and white tufa houses and cave entrances all but vanish if you looked at them from the south bank.

Dave impatiently glanced at his watch. Fifteen minutes on the phone.

Simone, standing in the kitchen, covered the phone's mouthpiece. "I'll try to keep this call short. Why don't you pour yourself a glass of wine?"

Short? It was a bit late for that. She seemed more interested in her phone conversation than in spending time with him.

He poured wine into both of the wineglasses on the coffee table and handed one to Simone. He carried the other with him, and went back to staring out the window, watching kids kicking a ball in the moonlit street. The lamppost in front of the café provided them with additional lighting, though occasionally the ball flew into shadowy areas, causing the boys to hesitate before going after it. After a time Dave checked his watch again. Twenty minutes. He glanced over his shoulder and tried to make eye contact, but Simone was too absorbed in her conversation.

"A dinner party? Oh, that sounds like fun. Who's going to be there? Of course Dave and I will come."

Tuning out the rest of the conversation, he studied the rooftops in the distance. He hoped he was wrong, but he suspected he'd have to replace the roof on his house when he returned to Chicago. He'd already replaced the heater two months earlier. Before that, it was the air conditioner. It was always something.

A young couple strolled by, arm-in-arm. They made the partial U-turn onto rue Corneille, which would take them downhill to the main street that ran alongside the river. So peaceful they looked. He and his ex-wife had strolled together like that on their visit here six years ago—before the divorce. He'd bumped into her and her new family at a Chicago mall two months ago. Seeing her holding her baby and watching as her husband and three-year-old son sat on a carousel, waving at her and laughing in delight, had reopened old wounds.

He drew his attention back to the phone call. Simone's grandmother, Jeannette, could talk anyone's ear off as her often prolonged calls to his grandmother attested. At first, he hadn't thought much about it, but recently he'd noticed how long

Grand-mère gabbed and laughed, without showing any signs of pain or fatigue. Grandma Ellen, his paternal grandmother, hadn't felt good enough to sit around talking and laughing when she had been terminally ill with cancer.

Simone's burst of laughter drew his attention back to the present. Her back was turned to him, and she was talking excitedly about some funny incident. A couple of minutes later, she finally hung up the phone. Holding out her arms to him, she said, "I'm sorry about that. Shall we go back to the living room?"

They sat together on the sofa, and Simone said, "This is wonderful. I wish we'd met years ago. If I'd moved to Reynier after I finished school instead of remaining in Paris—"

His kiss stopped her from talking.

THE NEXT DAY, back at his grandmother's house, Dave walked downstairs after his shower and heard music playing on the radio. He followed the sound into the kitchen and found his white-haired grandmother smiling and swaying to the music as she folded laundry on the countertop. He moved toward her, intending to take over the chore, but as he neared, she must have sensed his presence because she jumped.

"Oh, I didn't know you were still here," she said, wiping her forehead with the back of her hand. "I—I was just about to go upstairs and lie down. I'm exhausted."

Dave frowned. Not only was she working on laundry, but she'd apparently been baking. The smell of bread emanated from a loosely covered pan on top of the oven, evidently set there to cool. The rolling pin was still lying on the counter next to the stove.

As she hung up a dish towel, Fabienne yawned, and then said, "I need to lie down for my nap, dear boy. I should have done it an hour ago. You should go visit with friends. Now that she has an assistant at the café, Simone will likely have time to chat."

She stood by, waiting for him to leave, but he hesitated.

"I think I'll stay here today. I need to work on my new book. Can't keep neglecting my writing."

She shrugged, then nodded and left the room. She trudged up the stairs, making enough noise to awaken the dead.

Dave opened his laptop computer, which was on the dining table, then brought up his book file so he could work on the outline for his new mystery novel. The characters and setting were easy, but he still wasn't sure about some of the plot. Searching through his notes, he began making progress. Footsteps in the other room pulled him out of his thoughts. He glanced at the clock on the wall. Only three-quarters of an hour had elapsed.

Peering around the corner into the living room, he watched his grandmother put on scarf and shoes. "Where are you going, Grand-mère?"

She swung around. "Oh, dear, you startled me again! I'm going over to Jeannette's house. She invited me for an early lunch."

He kept his face blank, and nodded. After she closed the door, he pulled the front curtain aside and watched her walk up the street. As soon as she was out of sight, he strode up the stairs and into her bedroom.

He recalled the conversation with her when she'd called him in Chicago. She'd told him she had ovarian cancer, the same illness that had claimed Grandma Ellen. He'd asked if she was undergoing treatment, if there was any possibility of recovery. She said 'yes' to the first question and 'probably not' to the second, though the treatments might buy her a few months.

Dave glanced at her tidy bed with its pale green cover. Just as he'd thought. Not a single wrinkle or indentation. She'd probably paced her room until she thought she could sneak out of the house. He sighed. Time to get to work. He had plenty of experience, but this was different from the usual police search he used to do; this time he didn't want anyone to know he'd been there. He opened drawer after drawer. She must have prescription medications somewhere. Grandma Ellen's bathroom had been full of them. He hadn't seen any pill bottles in either of the bathrooms here. Finally, he found her appointment calendar underneath a book on her bedside table. He thumbed through it from January until today, the ninth of June. She'd scribbled dinner parties, meetings with friends, hair appointments—but not a single doctor appointment. No hospital tests. No radiation or chemo treatments. He set the calendar back where he'd found it and continued searching for her prescription pain killers. Coming up empty-handed but for a small commercially available packet of aspirin, he finally went downstairs to wait for her return.

NINETY MINUTES LATER, Dave looked up from his chair in the living room as the front door opened. Fabienne set her handbag and scarf on the table next to the door, and smiled.

He smiled back briefly, then said, "We need to talk, Grand-mère."

"Of course, dear boy. What did you want to talk about?" She sat on the sofa across from him and folded her hands in her lap.

Dave shook his head. She still thought of him as a boy. He was thirty-five. He closed his eyes for a second and took a deep breath. Questioning a suspect was second-nature to him, but when the suspect was a family member . . . .

"I don't want to have to say this, but you don't have any of the symptoms Grandma Ellen had and, well, you're energetic for someone dying of cancer. There have been no doctor or hospital appointments since I arrived. That got me wondering."

She averted her eyes, and fussed with a button on her cardigan.

The grandfather clock behind Dave ticked loudly and he tried to tune it out. Leaning forward, he said, "Are you really ill?"

"Oh, at my age, you know—"

"Are you really dying?"

Silence.

"Are you in some other kind of trouble? You can tell me. I'm here to help."

Still refusing to look at him, she focused on the button, twisting it back and forth until it came off. She let out a soft gasp, then stuck the button in a pocket of her cardigan.

He sat back and tapped his fingers on the arm of his chair. "Should I go back home?"

She shot him a look. "No! Don't go. I'll talk." She hesitated, then whispered, "It wasn't entirely my idea."

Dave's mouth twitched. Jeannette. He should have known.

"We just wanted you to spend the summer the way you did when you were young." She paused. "I wanted to see you, and, well, you're all alone, I thought it might do you good. Jeannette said you would probably enjoy the break, and I . . . well, I get lonely, too."

Dave leaned forward again and stared at her. "Explain to me why Jeannette cares if I come here."

She didn't answer.

He stood, his shoulders tensing, and closed his eyes as the question he needed to ask hung in the air, unspoken. Finally, he said, "So you aren't ill?"

She shook her head rapidly, while biting her lower lip.

"You lied about dying? I don't understand. Why would you do that?" He took a deep breath, let it out, and tried again. "It doesn't make sense for you to lie to me. All you needed to do was ask me to visit. I would have come. Why the pretense?"

"You wouldn't have stayed for months. What good would it do for you to come for a week or two?" She suddenly looked truculent. "You are enjoying yourself, aren't you? You always loved it here, and it seems like you and Simone are getting on well."

"Simone?" Almost under his breath, he said, "You and Jeannette wanted to play matchmaker?"

She looked away.

He stood and glanced at her, intending to say something, then closed his mouth and walked out the front door. Down the narrow hillside street he strode. Past several shops, past the hotel, straight to Café Charbonneau on the corner. He yanked open the door and the bells attached to it clanged so loudly that everyone turned to stare. He ignored them and walked straight over to Simone, who was standing behind the counter and holding a full coffee pot. "Can you get away for a few minutes?"

She raised an eyebrow, then looked around for her assistant, Isabelle Lambert. She motioned to her, set down the coffee pot, took off her apron, and then led Dave upstairs to the first floor of her apartment. After she closed the door behind them, Simone looked him in the eyes. "You seem angry. What's wrong?"

"I just had an interesting conversation with my grandmother. She lied to me to get me here. It even seems like there was some idea of getting you and me together, and—" He searched her face, then added. "You already knew about that."

"No, not really. I did wonder—you know, my grandmother's heavy hints. 'Oh, Simone, you aren't getting any younger, and how will you meet anyone?' But . . . ." She shrugged. "You know our grandmothers. Once they get an idea, there's no talking them out of it, and they would have denied it had I asked. When Fabienne said you were coming over, I got all the meaningful looks and the suggestions that it would only be friendly for me to help you settle in. I went along with it—but grudgingly. Until I met you, of course." She smiled, and raised her eyebrows.

He squinted at her and she broke their eye contact. A moment later she held out a hand to him, which he ignored. "You mustn't be angry with her. She only wanted to help you."

"I don't need any help." He strode over to the window, then turned around and faced Simone. "Why would she think that?"

Simone said, "You went through a divorce. I did too. I suppose our grandmothers thought we could help each other."

"I don't need their meddling. You shouldn't either." He ran his fingers through his hair. "I've been divorced almost five years. This is the first time she's done something like this. Why now?" He studied Simone. "Tell me something. What gave them the idea for their little plot?"

She shrugged again.

"It's rotten no matter who came up with it," he said.

"Please don't hold it against them."

"How would you react if you were told your grandmother was dying? How would you like to be tricked?"

"I understand your anger. But try to think of it this way—Fabienne's healthy and you'll have her around at least for a few more years." She patted the cushion, trying to get him to sit beside her. "My grandmother is probably the sneakier of the two. She's the instigator."

He snorted at that, and stuck his hands in his pockets as he paced.

"I'm sorry they tricked you, but I'm glad you're here. They were right. We do make a good couple."

He turned around and faced her. "Of course I'm happy she's healthy, but I can't just forgive and forget. How can you justify what they did—and what you went along with?" Dave frowned. Something more was going on here. What were they up to? And who exactly was involved – Fabienne and Jeannette certainly, but Simone?

He suddenly realized she was speaking again. "— You'll be going back to the U.S. soon. You might not get another opportunity to come back to France for some time. She might not be dying now, but she's getting up there in age. Try to make the best of the situation. Why not get away for a week or two? Give yourself a chance to cool down? We could go sightseeing. We could leave in a few days, after the dinner party. How much of this country have you visited?"

"We'll see," Dave said. He turned and walked out.

OUTSIDE THE CAFÉ, Dave took in a breath of the fresh air and tried to calm himself. Over the past year he'd considered moving away from Chicago plenty of times. Too many sad memories, too many lost relationships. He'd felt un-rooted for some time, as though he didn't really belong anywhere anymore. Certainly not in Chicago. Reynier, because of his ties with the village and because it was about as different from Chicago as you could get, had long been at the top of his list. Too bad it was now tainted for him. Yet, he could do worse than stay there. After all, in the end, what harm had been done? Still the annoyance—yes, and hurt—at being deceived rankled. Had Simone been laughing at him this whole time? He started walking to the far end of the town.

Ten minutes later, he sat in the living room at the home of his childhood friend, Jonas Lefevre, whom he hoped was a man who wouldn't go blabbing to the rest of the town. He really needed a man's perspective. Whether or not he could actually trust him, he hadn't decided.

"Nice home you have," Dave said.

"Haven't you been here before?"

"Don't think so. You and Lillian were out of town the last time I was in Reynier. The time before that—must have been twelve years ago—you weren't married yet. As I recall, you and Lillian were dating. How is she, by the way? I haven't seen her around."

"She works all the time over at the butcher shop."

An awkward silence ensued. Dave looked around the living room at photographs on the mantel—wedding photos, vacation photos, Lillian and Jonas with their dog, Jonas working on a clock, Jonas surrounded by clocks in various stages of production—a whole life that Dave knew little about.

Jonas poured them both some cognac. "Don't tell Lillian. I'm supposed to be cutting back both the amount I consume and the amount I buy."

Dave nodded. "Your secret's safe with me. But what if she comes home while we're drinking?"

Jonas took a swig of his drink. "She won't. Her boss never lets her go home early. He leaves early sometimes to do stuff with his boys. They're a handful. Speaking of boys who are handfuls, do you remember when we used to ride our bicycles down the hills and through neighbors' properties?"

Dave smiled. "How could I forget? The last time we raced down the hill, we almost caused a car accident. Mayor Rochierre phoned my grandfather and griped about our recklessness and I got grounded for a week."

"My father acted angry for a few minutes, but he was a softy. He didn't follow through with his threats of punishment."

"Yeah, as I recall you never got punished for anything—ever. Maybe that's why you don't have any morals. You could probably get away with murder."

"Hey, I resent that." Jonas squinted an eye at him, and then burst out laughing. "But it's so true."

Dave laughed for the first time today.

Jonas grew quiet. "What happened between you and Connie? Fabienne says you're divorced."

He shrugged, and then studied this older Jonas. Slicked-back brown hair and hazel eyes, and leaning back in his chair, his legs casually flung out, one arm bent and lying over the top edge of the chair back. The guy had always been laid-back, and lucky with women, but he seemed even more self-assured now.

"What about you? I've heard stories."

"Yeah, well, I tried to be faithful. And I did all right for the first few years. But Lillian and I, well, we don't have any sizzle left."

"Does that mean you have a mistress?"

"A mistress? Ha. That's an understatement. Women find me irresistible. What can I say? I try to keep my affairs a secret from Lillian. I don't know if she knows, or not. She doesn't say anything about it."

"What about your business?"

"Ah, come on, I don't want to talk about work. Tell me about you and Connie. I never even got to meet her. What happened?"

"There's nothing to tell."

Jonas raised his eyebrows a fraction, then nodded. "I heard you've been seeing Simone. How's that going?"

Dave shrugged again.

"She's certainly taken with you."

"Have you and she ever been involved?"

Jonas smiled, but instead of answering, he swirled the liquid in his glass. Finally, he said, "I'll tell you about Simone after you tell me what happened with you and Connie."

Dave moved to stand up.

"All right, I get it," Jonas said. "You always were closed-mouthed"

"Simone tells me you travel often. Paris, Orleans, Marseille,

Lyon," Dave said.

"Yes, that's one of the benefits. I'd go crazy if I was stuck here all the time. But what happened with your job? I thought you were still on the police force, and then I hear you quit. What happened?"

"I started writing."

"It takes time to build a writing career. How did you survive until the money started coming in?"

"I did all right."

Jonas studied him, then shrugged and gave a smile. "Ah. If you're staying in Reynier, I might be able to send a little something your way."

"Have you struck a gold mine with your business, then?"

"You might say so."

After a few more minutes of idle talk, Dave excused himself and walked toward his grandmother's house. His mood hadn't improved much, and he still couldn't believe he'd allowed the women to trick him. He'd sworn he would stay on guard, that he wouldn't let anyone use him or manipulate him ever again. Had he been deluding himself?

Why would his grandmother lie to him about dying? When he was a child, she'd occasionally been caught in a fib, usually by Grand-père. Nothing big. Nothing like this. Although he'd visited every summer throughout his childhood, he'd spent most of the time outside or playing in the caves—not conversing with his grandmother.

He sighed. Did he really know her? For that matter, did he know any of these people? Maybe it wasn't as lonely as Chicago, where you could live years in the same neighborhood without ever knowing your neighbors' names. But it made him wonder, all the same, if he belonged in Reynier any more than he did in Chicago.

He had almost called his parents in Missouri before he'd left for France, to tell them about the cancer. He'd hesitated because his mother hadn't spoken to Grand-mère since she'd moved to the U.S. when Dave was a baby. His father was the one who'd arranged the summer visits. No one would tell Dave what had caused their falling out. When he would return and try to tell his mother about his trip, she would stop him. "I don't want to know anything about my mother's activities," she would say. What had Grand-mère done to spark that kind of response?

It had always bothered him that his family was split—as a kid, he'd compared his situation to that of his friend, Billy, whose divorced parents had shuffled him back and forth between them. If something terrible had passed between his mother and grandmother, shouldn't he know what it was? What would his mother say about Grand-mère's lying and subterfuge?

He found Fabienne sitting on the sofa, her hair in disarray and her eyes slightly puffy. He sat down beside her and took a deep breath, then said softly, "How could you think that would work? It was only a matter of time before I would figure it out."

She turned away from him and didn't answer.

"Talk to me, please. You owe me a better explanation. Tell me what's wrong. I'll help you if I can."

Finally, she looked at him with sorrowful eyes that reminded him of himself as a boy, getting reprimanded by his dad. "Will you forgive me?"

He put his arm around her and sighed. "You can't lie to me again. Promise me that."

CHAPTER THREE

THREE DAYS LATER Dave found himself staring out the window again, only now he was not really looking at the scenery. Though he still loved the view, he was tired of it, tired of this place. On the surface, his relationship with his grandmother appeared undamaged. He had tried to forgive her manipulation, and told himself he was overreacting, but he hadn't really convinced himself and could not forget. He knew he didn't trust her as he had previously. He felt that her lie had been a smokescreen to hide something more—it was surely inconceivable that she had claimed to be dying simply to get him to stay. He wondered what had caused the fallout between his mother and grandmother. Jeannette would know what happened, and if she knew, there was a chance Simone knew. He decided he would go on the sightseeing trip with her and encourage her to talk. He sighed and shook his head. He realized he was growing impatient and edgy waiting around. That was one thing he'd always disliked about the village. At this time of year, most shops in France stayed open all day, foregoing the traditional two-hour lunch breaks, to accommodate the seasonal throng of tourists. Not so, however, in Reynier.

The shopkeepers claimed it was merely tradition, but Dave's grandfather always used to say it was because Reynier rarely drew in more than an occasional tourist. And it wasn't on the tourist route for one basic reason. The six hundred or so residents didn't want tourists invading their town. Dave understood and appreciated the peacefulness it provided. Reynier's layout, although lacking a town square, was fairly typical of French hillside villages, with homes and businesses spread out over multiple levels, connected by stairways, cobbled roads, and walking paths. Reynier's labyrinthine cave system in the hill, along with troglodyte cave dwellings sprinkled throughout, made it a bit more unique, although it wasn't the only such town in France. He'd seen several others, and had heard of more that he hadn't seen yet. It could have been a popular tourist destination and could have brought in some revenue for the locals. Apparently, the villagers had decided that the price of tourism was more than they were willing to pay.

The chiming clock in the corner drew Dave out of his thoughts. He glanced up. Two o'clock. The clock was fifteen minutes fast, but his grandmother was typically fifteen minutes slow, momentarily amusing him at the two being a matched set.

When he entered the kitchen, she was by the sink, talking on the telephone. She saw him, quickly said her goodbyes, and hung up. "Sorry to interrupt, Grand-mère, but if we go now, the shops should be re-opening."

"Thank you, dear boy. Let me gather a few things." She ambled out of the kitchen.

Dave followed her into the living room, where she searched the table beside the front door, sighed, and waved her hand. "What are you looking for?"

She ignored him as she flittered around the living room and foyer. She stopped and stared at the closet, raising her arms. A soft sound of exasperation escaped her and she stomped over to the coat rack, picking up her suitcase-sized purse that was hanging from a hook. "Never mind. I found them." She pulled out her bifocals along with her new pink and green flowered silk scarf, put on her glasses, and wrapped the scarf around her white hair, tying it underneath her chin. Reaching into the closet, she withdrew her new brown suede shoes, the ones she'd spent hours shopping for in the nearby town of Vendome yesterday. Dave shook his head in amusement as he watched her squeeze her thick feet into the dressy shoes to go walking along the sloping paved lanes.

Thinking that his grandmother was ready to go out, he strode over to the front door. But in the foyer, she again stopped and studied herself in the mirror. She made a clucking sound as she tucked wayward strands of hair under the scarf. She finally walked out the door.

Dave followed her and closed the door, not bothering to lock it since no one here locked their doors unless going away on a trip. Turning his attention back to the street, he breathed in the fresh summer air. The weather had changed in the few hours he'd been indoors. A wind had arisen and was swirling around the fine limestone tufa that covered the buildings. Though the air was still hot and dry as it usually was all summer long, the blowing wind carried with it the scent of flowers and the chatter of birdsong.

He entwined his arm with his grandmother's, and they strolled along rue de Rennes, the sloping lane on which she lived. They headed toward the intersection where the road would switch-back onto rue Corneille and down to the bottom, where most of the village's businesses were situated. They could have gone directly down the hillside, by way of a steep stone staircase, but Fabienne had tripped on them the last time they'd gone that way and ended up with a bruised leg.

Dave nodded politely when Jeannette strode up beside them,

but only half-listened as the two women chatted quietly, their heels clicking like horse hooves on the cobbled road, the thought momentarily providing a quiet chuckle. As they arrived at the end of the road, Jeannette waved and said her goodbyes, then disappeared into the town hall on the corner, across the street from Simone's café. Dave and his grandmother made the partial U-turn onto rue Corneille. At the bottom of the hill, they walked past the local drugstore and Dave started to cross the street, halting when he noticed the heel clicking had stopped. He turned around, backtracked to where his grandmother was standing, and waited as she reached into her purse and pulled out a piece of paper.

"If we split up," she said, handing the paper to him, "we can finish faster and return home in plenty of time to prepare the meal. I want everything to be perfect for our party."

He glanced at the flapping piece of paper before tucking it in the pocket of his blue polo-shirt and out of the wind's reach.

"Good," Fabienne said, not waiting for a response. "You'll find all of those things in the general store." She reached into her cloth shopping bag and pulled out another, smaller bag, which she handed to him. 'I'll get the cheeses, meats, and wine. We can meet by the town hall?"

"Okay," Dave said. "Half an hour, then?"

Fabienne flashed him a smile, waved, and then scurried down the street.

The main street was long and narrow with shops on both sides of the street. He watched her stop outside the cheese shop next to the post office across the street. The river was behind the businesses on that side, while the hill was behind the businesses on the side where he was walking. He reached the general store with its yellow awning flapping in the wind, the metal hangers creaking. It was still closed for lunch. On one side of the front door two elderly men sat on an old wooden bench, canes neatly propped nearby. They often sat there all day long. On the other side of the door, crates of fruit were displayed on a low platform. A small group had gathered outside the store, waiting for it to re-open. Dave nodded to Paul Lepage who was standing next to the store clerk, Robert Roussel, both smoking cigarettes.

Paul flicked ashes onto the sidewalk. "Bonjour. I'm looking forward to tonight's dinner party.

"Me too. She's planned quite a feast."

Paul laughed, blowing a plume of smoke towards the sky. "That sounds like Fabienne. I'm not complaining, mind you. She's the best cook I know. But don't tell anyone I said so."

Dave chuckled. Paul was Jeannette's grandson, and Simone's cousin; unlike Simone, he'd lived his whole life in Reynier, except for the time he spent at art school in Paris. He now worked as a handyman in order to make ends meet, though he'd told Dave a couple of days ago that he was talking with people who might help him get his art career going. His black hair was tousled and his face was dark and stubbled from not shaving. Dave knew he'd clean up for the party and out-dress him.

Someone rode past on a sputtering motor scooter as the store clerk opened the door. After he reversed the 'Closed' sign, the shoppers pushed their way in.

Dave pulled out the scribbled shopping list as he entered the store, reading the groceries listed for him to get: artichokes, aubergines, mushrooms, onions, bread, cream . . . .

He looked up from the list briefly and nodded as Robert passed by, then headed for the produce aisle in the back of the small store. As he proceeded across the old plank oak floor aisles, scrubbed spotless and shiny, but worn in the center from ages of use, the floors depressed and squeaked. It was clear that these aisles had remained unchanged from the time the store was created.

Starting in the produce area, Dave carefully picked through

the fruits and vegetables, knowing from experience that his grandmother was finicky and would complain if he didn't select perfect specimens. She had complained last week when he came back from a shopping trip with unripe fruit and undersized vegetables. Too bad she hadn't included a size-chart with her list.

He had been in the store for twenty-five minutes and had acquired most of the items on the list when he encountered the Cardin twins and their younger brother running around in the store. One bumped into him, then ran off. A few minutes later a crashing sound and a startled scream a couple of aisles over made him rush toward the source of the commotion, but he had to stop abruptly to avoid running over a young woman who was sitting on the floor, half covered in fallen cereal boxes. Dave looked from the apparent train wreck to the boys standing behind her, mouths gaping open. He turned his attention back to the dazed woman. She looked up at him, her diminutive face emerging from a dark cloak of long hair, revealing two of the most beautiful, most extraordinary, most mesmerizing eyes Dave had ever seen.

She was definitely not local, of that he was sure. He would certainly have remembered those clear blue eyes with little flecks of gold and green. Regaining his wits, he extended his hand. "Are you all right?"

She reached up and took his hand shakily, allowing him to help her to her feet.

"Yes, Monsieur. I must admit, though, this is quite embarrassing. I . . . I'm not sure what happened, really." She spoke the words breathlessly, as if pulling them out of the windy sky. Though she spoke in French, her accent sounded odd to him.

Dave, aware that he was staring, smiled and shrugged. "I don't think it was your fault. Those kids were clowning around. One of them ran into me a few minutes ago. I'm sorry you became a casualty as well."

She laughed softly, her cheeks growing pink. When she reached her hand up and tucked her hair behind one ear, the store's overhead light caught on an exposed earring, making its tiny diamond glitter.

"Thank you for your kindness," she said, lowering her eyes, her face suddenly closed.

Just then, Robert appeared, waving his hands excitedly and yelling at the boys who had created the mess. They took the hint and scurried out of the shop without looking back.

Dave shook his head as he watched the trio exit. He turned his attention back to the woman, only to find her gone. He searched through all the aisles in the store, and then went outside, looking in all directions. There was no sign of her. Giving up, he went back inside and helped Robert re-stack the cereal boxes. As they finished and Robert returned to his post at the checkout counter, Dave spotted something shiny on the floor at the edge of the aisle, half-hidden under the bottom shelf. He bent down, picked it up, and examined it. It was a silver necklace with a tiny-diamond covered heart locket—not terribly expensive, but nice looking. Its clasp was broken. He carefully deposited it into his shirt pocket.

When he left the store and strode back up the hill to the town hall, instinctively looking round for the young woman, his grandmother wasn't there. He checked his watch and realized that with all the commotion, he was fifteen minutes late. Maybe she'd walked home without him. He waited for another five minutes, debating whether to wait longer or go back to the house. Then he caught a glimpse of her trudging uphill toward their designated meeting place. She had seen him and was waving her hand. He started walking toward her.

"Oh, dear boy," she said, breathlessly as they neared each other, "I tried to get back sooner, but you know Brigitte over at the wine shop. She talks and talks to each customer. I couldn't get away." She paused to juggle her cloth shopping bags around.

He grinned. "I don't suppose you talked with Brigitte, huh?"

She faked being indignant and smacked him on the arm with her purse, then struggled to keep from laughing. "At least I was quick in the cheese shop."

"Are you ready to go home?"

She nodded, and they headed back to her house, their arms full of food and trappings for the party. When they were nearly home, Dave caught a glimpse of the mystery woman up ahead. He watched her inch her way down the stone stairs, the steps that passed Chateau de Reynier on the way down to rue Corneille. Though she could be heading to the road, he considered the other possibility that she might be a guest at the inn.

The rest of Dave's afternoon was taken up with dinner party preparations, leaving him no time to go looking for the woman. That didn't stop his mind from drifting though. As he helped his grandmother with food preparation and housecleaning, he tried to focus on the party and his upcoming trip, but images of the woman's face, and especially those eyes, kept appearing in his mind.

That evening, watching his grandmother and her friends, Dave wished he were somewhere else. He did his best to appear happy and at ease, and even whispered to Simone, "You look lovely." She wore a strapless red satin dress that displayed her perfect skin and sensuous figure. A sheer red scarf covered her neck. She smiled and wrapped her arm through Dave's. "I missed you today. Why didn't you come by the café?"

"My grandmother kept me captive. I had planned to stop in, but she was excited about this party and put me to work shopping. I suspect she has this need to out-do Jeannette's, which is no small feat."

Simone laughed softly. "For such good friends, they have a bit of a rivalry."

Throughout the evening Fabienne was in a splendid mood, which pleased Dave. And yet, seeing the intimate group of friends laugh and talk so easily while he remained mostly quiet and on the periphery left him with a feeling that perhaps he did not belong there.

CHAPTER FOUR

THE DAY AFTER the dinner party, Dave got up early to work for a couple of hours on his book and left for the post office on the main street. He stepped up to the counter and bought a stamp for the postcard he'd bought yesterday. His mother often complained that he didn't call or write to them enough and, thinking about it, he couldn't remember the last time he'd sent his parents a real letter. Leaving the post office, as he dropped the change into his pocket, his fingers brushed against the necklace he'd recovered from the floor in the general store.

He crossed the street and headed toward Chateau de Reynier near the far end of the village, not far from Café Charbonneau. The hotel was situated on a leveled-off section of the slope midway between the bottom tier and the next tier. It could be reached by walking up the winding driveway from the main street to the hotel's parking lot or by climbing halfway up a steep staircase that connected the two tiers, and then exiting onto a path, the staircase being the shorter of the two.

Dave strolled past several shops and cars parked along the roadway on his way to the staircase. As he reached the bakery, a scraggly terrier darted in front of him. He swerved to avoid it, stumbling backwards, and crashed into something. Disconcerted and embarrassed, he realized he'd careened into a woman coming out of the bakery. Following her gaze, he saw an empty coffee cup and a baguette on the ground near her feet, soaking up the now puddled coffee.

"Oh, no, I'm sorry," Dave said. He bent down and picked up the soggy bread and empty coffee cup, straightened back up, and looked at the dark-haired woman. "Are you all right?"

She nodded. Her hair was pulled back in a ponytail at the nape of her neck, making her look different than he remembered. But her eyes were unmistakable. It was the woman from the general store. His eyes locked onto hers and he again felt awestruck. Smiling at her and taking advantage of his unexpected good fortune, he said, "Why don't we go inside? I'll buy you another coffee and baguette."

"Oh, that's not necessary, really. Actually, I should be going." She took a step backward. Although they both spoke in French, he was more than ever sure she was not French.

"Of course it's necessary." Still holding the ruined items in one hand, he held the door open for her with his other hand. "I owe you that much. Besides, I wouldn't mind a cup of coffee myself. You'll join me at one of the outside tables, won't you?"

"No. I really shouldn't," she whispered.

"Please. It'll make me feel better about being such a big oaf."

She smiled and glanced down at her feet. "I'm not sure you're the oaf. I seem to be a magnet for accidents lately."

"Maybe we both are."

She looked up at his face and gave a tentative smile. "Well, I suppose it would be all right. To drink coffee with you, I mean."

"Good. By the way, I'm Dave Martin."

She didn't respond.

He frowned slightly, then said, "Do you have a name?"

"Oh, sorry. I'm Maur—" She blushed, then continued. "I'm Maurelle Dupre."

They went inside, where he disposed of the ruined bread and empty cup, and ordered two coffees and another baguette. He handed her the bread and carried the coffees outside to an umbrella-shaded table. After he set down the coffees, he pulled out a chair for her and they sat down.

They sat quietly for a few minutes, sipping hot coffee and enjoying the sunshine. Sunlight caught on one of her diamond earrings, reminding Dave of the necklace. He reached into his shirt pocket. "I have something I think is yours."

Her eyes lit up when she saw it. "Oh, it is," she said, accepting the chain. "Thank you. I thought it was lost forever. Where did you—" Her face flushed again. "The general store," she finished.

"The clasp was broken, but the locket didn't come off," he explained. "I fixed it."

"That was very kind. Thank you."

"Glad I could help." He smiled and watched her put the necklace around her neck, prepared to get up and help with the clasp if she needed it. She didn't. "What brings you to Reynier? You don't live around here, do you?"

"No. I'm on holiday."

He was about to ask her more, but she was watching something down the road. He turned to see what it was.

Halfway between the bakery and the post office, a gendarme vehicle was parked in front of a shop on the 'no parking' side of the street. Two gendarmes exited and stood in the street, looking around. If Dave remembered right, the nearest Gendarmerie was in Belvidere, the small market town three-and-a-half miles from Reynier. Dave waited to see where they were going. Perhaps there'd been a robbery. That would certainly give the locals something to talk about. When the gendarmes started walking toward the bakery terrace, Dave turned back to the woman. She had disappeared—again. He scowled. The gendarmes had stopped, and looked as if they weren't sure where to go. Dave approached them. "Bonjour, Messieurs. What brings you to Reynier?"

The red-haired man eyed him suspiciously. "Who are you?"

"Dave Martin." He extended his hand. "I'm a cop from the U.S. Here on an extended visit with family."

The gendarme smiled. "I'm Jacques Roland. This is Henri Du Bois."

"Is there a problem in our little village?"

"No. We stopped to buy coffees on our way back from Clairmont."

"Ah," Dave said. "Where is that? I don't think I've been there."

"Not far from here. A few kilometres," Du Bois said. "Where do you recommend for coffee?"

"I have a coffee waiting for me over at the bakery's terrace. Would you care to join me? I'd like to buy your coffees, if that's okay."

The gendarmes looked surprised, but shrugged and nodded. They followed him to the bakery and sat down at Dave's table while he went inside to buy their coffees. Dave returned a couple of minutes later with the beverages. "So, where are you headed now?"

"To Belvidere," Roland said.

"Ah, back to the Gendarmerie."

"Not right away. Officer to officer, we have reports of pickpockets and bag-snatchers in the area. We're investigating."

"What's being stolen?"

Roland said, "Wallets, handbags, watches, and jewelry."

The older officer nudged him, then said, "Thank you for the coffee, Monsieur. We must be on our way."

They got up to leave, but stopped when Dave said, "Any description of the pickpocket? Doesn't hurt to have another officer on the lookout, right?"

Du Bois, the younger officer, looked at the older one, then said, "A man and a woman in their mid-twenties, dark hair, nondescript."

"That makes it tough," Dave said.

They nodded, then shook hands once more and left.

Dave walked along the main street again, stopping now and then to gaze up at the hillside. The woman, Maurelle, may have gone into the caves or into a shop or into the hotel. While he was debating whether to climb up the stairs or stay down on the main street and check out some of the shops, he passed by one of the openings between the buildings on the river side and caught of glimpse of her. He ducked through the opening and followed the long path down to the river. Trees on the other side of the river blocked his view temporarily, and then he saw her again. She was heading toward the church. Unfortunately, to get to her, he had to cross the bridge which was in the opposite direction. By the time he crossed the river, she was out of sight. The tree branches began to sway and he looked up at the sky. Clouds were moving over the village.

He checked out the church and found it empty, then made quick stops at each of the shops on that side of the river. No one had seen her. Lastly, he entered the only restaurant around. "Bonjour," he said to the patron.

The man nodded, eyeing Dave suspiciously. "Can I get you something?"

Dave scanned the dreary room. Café Charbonneau, while not chic or fancy, made this place look like a dump. The walls were a dingy gray, and the tables were scratched and chipped. No wonder they only had one customer. Not wanting to appear rude, Dave ordered a coffee to go. While he waited, he said, "Have either of you seen a young woman around here, long, dark hair? I don't think she's local."

"Haven't seen her," the patron said.

The customer shook his head.

Dave left the restaurant and walked briskly along the residential streets. Fifteen minutes later and without any clues, he trudged back across the bridge, intending to go to the hotel and then the bed-and-breakfast inn. But with rather ominous dark gray clouds gathering overhead, darkening the sky and making it seem much later than it actually was, he expected rain was imminent. Just then, thunder cracked loudly overhead. As he arrived at the main street, a great flash of lightning lit up the sky. He raced toward the center of town as cold rain began pounding him.

Coming upon the shorter linking staircase near the bridge, Dave decided the hotel and inn would have to wait. He dashed up the stairs and along the gently sloping road back to his grandmother's house.

CHAPTER FIVE

DAVE CLOSED THE door quickly to keep the rain out. Drenched and shaking from the cold, he went straight to the bathroom, towel-dried his head, grabbed another towel, and then took the stairs two at a time to his bedroom, where he peeled off the clothing sticking to him, toweled himself dry, and changed into fresh clothes. Downstairs, he threw his soaked clothes into the dryer and proceeded to the kitchen to help his grandmother prepare lunch. While he worked, he thought about the stranger, Maurelle: beautiful, elusive, and quite possibly a criminal.

They ate lunch in near silence, on Dave's part at least. Fabienne alternated quiet munching with bursts of gossip to which he grunted and said "really?" automatically, his mind elsewhere. When they had finished, he carried his dirty dishes to the counter and left the kitchen. Rain still pounded against the roof. He picked up his laptop from the coffee table and sat down on his preferred chair in the living room. Fabienne didn't own a computer, which meant no internet. Without suffering much angst over the obvious piracy, Dave logged onto a neighbor's unprotected wireless internet and began searching for news about crimes in the area. After twenty minutes or so of browsing the internet and finding nothing of interest—not even the pickpocket reports—he returned to the kitchen for a cup of coffee.

Fabienne glanced at him, but said nothing. As she hung up a dishtowel, strands of coarse white hair strayed from her chignon, and her bifocals slipped down on the bridge of her nose. She picked up a stray saucer, put it away, and closed the cupboard door sharply.

Dave opened his mouth to speak, but hesitated when she breezed past him into the living room. Frowning, he followed her, sat down in his chair across from where she sat on the sofa, and waited for her to say something.

"You were very quiet during lunch," she said finally, laying her reddened hands in her lap. "Did you have a fight with Simone?"

"No. Why?"

"Nothing happened between you two?"

He shrugged.

"You don't seem yourself. Are you sure nothing's wrong?"

He looked at his computer lying on the coffee table in between them, closed and hibernating. Leaning forward, he said, "Have you heard about any problems in Belvidere or the surrounding area? Burglaries, pickpockets, vagrants?"

"No. I don't think so. Why?"

"You know I'm supposed to leave with Simone the day after tomorrow, right?"

She nodded.

"I need to check something out, first."

"What does that mean? Are you cancelling the trip?"

"No. I haven't said anything to Simone yet, but I might need to postpone it a few days. Something's come up."

Fabienne was silent for several moments, and then she said, "What is it? Something to do with your book?"

He took a deep breath before saying, "I met someone here

who puzzles me. I need to find out more."

"I don't understand."

"It's probably nothing. But you know me. I can't ignore a mystery."

She pouted and frowned, then looked as if a light bulb had been switched on inside her brain. "It's that woman, isn't it? The stranger everyone is talking about." She wagged her hand at him. "Even if she isn't what people think, you would be a fool to get involved."

"What have you heard about her?" he asked.

"She's a gypsy. That's what most people think."

He leaned back. Gypsies used to be a problem in this part of the valley. The police had even dismantled some gypsy camps because of similar problems. Okay, he supposed it wasn't impossible they were moving back into this area. And yet the gendarmes had told him about pickpockets and bag-snatchers, but said nothing of gypsies. "I bumped into the woman in the general store yesterday. There was a minor commotion. I didn't see it, but when I went over to find out what the noise was, she was there."

"You let me hear about it from Jeannette instead of telling me yourself." She folded her arms together. "She always knows everything before I do."

"I didn't think it was a big deal."

Fabienne pouted again for a moment, but then, in a sudden turnabout, she shrugged and waved her hand. "Well, go on."

"There's nothing to tell, really."

"Then I don't understand. Why do you need to find out more?"

"I saw her a second time."

"You did? And what happened?" She leaned forward.

"You haven't heard yet?" Dave said.

She shook her head.

"The woman was walking out of the bakery this morning. I bumped into her and caused her to drop her baguette and spill her coffee. I replaced the ruined purchases, of course, and we sat for a few minutes. She seemed, I don't know, almost afraid."

"Afraid of what?"

He shrugged.

"I may be an old busybody," she said, "but I know trouble when I see it. And this woman is trouble. Everyone thinks so. Why put yourself in the middle of it?"

"Look, I'm not saying you're wrong. All I was trying to say is that I want to find out what's she about. If you know something, please tell me. It'll save me time and maybe I won't have to postpone the trip after all."

"I don't know anything," she said. "But you'll tell me, before anyone else, if you find out something, right?"

He shrugged. She huffed at him, got up, and left the room. Dave sat alone for a few minutes, then followed her into the kitchen.

Fabienne was sitting with her back towards the doorway. He approached her, but stopped abruptly when he overheard her talking on the telephone about his accident outside the bakery.

He turned on his heels and walked out, slamming the front door. The sun had emerged from behind the rain clouds revealing sparkling beads of water on the leaves and flowers, reminders of the preceding rain.

CONTINUING WITH THE plan that had got dampened by the rain, Dave headed straight for the village's hotel. At Chateau de Reynier, he opened the heavy carved door and crossed the room to the reception desk on the far right. After waiting several minutes, Dave called out, "*Bonjour.*"

A tall man peered around the corner and upon seeing Dave

waiting, hurried forward. Simone had mentioned last week or maybe the week before that someone new had bought the hotel, and Dave guessed that this was the new owner. He had wavy hawk-brown hair, a curved nose that resembled an eagle's beak, and yellowish-brown eyes behind thick glasses.

"Welcome to Chateau de Reynier. How may I help you, Monsieur?"

"I haven't been inside this place since I was a young boy. Obviously it's been remodeled. I'm impressed. It's a beautiful transformation. The chandelier and grand piano really give it a luxurious feel."

"We try," the man said, shrugging.

"Are you the proprietor, then?"

"Yes, with my wife. I am Jean-Pierre Wickliff." They shook hands, and Wickliff glanced over at a woman who seemed to have appeared out of nowhere. She was no more than five-foot-four or five, slender, with a round face and straight fawn-colored hair draping past her shoulders. She, like her husband, was well dressed in a business suit. "Ah, this is my wife Camille," Jean-Pierre said.

"Bonjour," Dave said. He introduced himself, adding, "I'd love to stay here sometime, but I'm visiting my grandmother and she would be offended if I didn't stay with her. You know how that is."

Jean-Pierre nodded. "I do indeed understand, Monsieur Martin. For one thing, I know your grandmother. I've heard about you, of course. Fabienne is proud to have her grandson visiting."

"Yeah, she does love to talk."

"So, Monsieur Martin, what brings you to Chateau de Reynier?"

"Actually, I'm looking for someone. She's visiting the area and may be staying here. Her name is Maurelle Dupre."

"Sorry, Monsieur. She is not a guest here."

Camille looked up and exchanged a knowing look with Jean-Pierre, giving Dave the distinct impression that gossip had already been sowed and was spreading like weeds in a rose garden.

As he exited the hotel, Dave swore under his breath. He stood out front trying to decide where to go next. He glanced straight ahead at the partial view of the river, and then to his right he caught sight of Simone and her mother, Coralie, standing on the staircase that linked the levels, watching him.

CHAPTER SIX

DAVE WALKED TO the stairs where Simone and her mother stood waiting for him. There was a rundown bed-and-breakfast inn he still needed to check out at the outside edge of the village. He sighed. That would have to wait. He greeted Coralie with kisses on both cheeks as was expected, and then did the same with Simone. "You look lovely," he whispered in her ear.

"Come walk with me," Simone said, placing her hand on Dave's arm. "I'm on my way back to the café. I had to make a quick trip to see Maman and she was going to come with me. I guess she changed her mind." Coralie excused herself after exchanging an undecipherable look with Simone.

Dave and Simone made their way to Café Charbonneau in silence. As they entered the café, he nodded at Isabelle Lambert, Simone's employee who was chatting with two old men sitting at a table.

"Sit here at the counter," Simone said. "I'll be with you in a minute."

She stepped around the counter, brought out a self-serve basket of fresh croissants, and placed it in front of him. She then left to wait on another customer. Although Dave wasn't hungry, he took a croissant and slid the basket to the center of the counter. He broke the warm croissant in half and bit into it. Damn. He didn't need this problem with Simone.

A few minutes later Simone set down a steaming cup of espresso in front of Dave. She leaned forward with her elbows on the countertop and her chin propped on her hands. Her silky blonde head tilted to one side as she seemed to study him.

Dave took a long sip of the black liquid. He thought she looked beautiful in her flowing skirt and white blouse.

"It's all right, you know," she said. "Do what you need to do. Get it out of your system.

"I don't know what you're talking about," Dave said. "What is it exactly you want me to get out of my system?"

"You aren't the only person around here who has seen her. We've all seen her off and on for a week. She's pretty, to be sure, but she's not your type."

He raised his eyebrows, but didn't answer.

"I know you. It's in your blood to hunt for answers, to investigate, to solve mysteries. You may no longer be a detective, but you can't resist. I understand you better than you realize. You aren't really interested in the dark-haired woman, only the situation."

He cocked his head to one side. "So you're a psychoanalyst now. What other secret identities are you hiding?"

She pouted. "You mock me," she said, shrugging. "But I know what I know."

"Maybe you should be the crime story writer," Dave said, "since you think you have all the answers."

"She's a gypsy. That's what some of the locals think, and I agree."

He grimaced. "I've actually heard that theory already. You'll have to come up with something better."

She shrugged again. "You'll see that there's nothing mysterious. I can wait." She bit her lip, then leaned in and added,

"But don't let her trick you."

"I'll keep that in mind."

She nodded, then glanced away towards her customers, giving Dave the impression she was returning to her hostess duties. "I don't want to hurt you, Simone. I care about you. You do remember that I'm going back to Chicago, don't you?"

She nodded, but he didn't believe her.

THE CONTRAST BETWEEN the chateau and the bed-and-breakfast inn was stark. Dave grimaced at the peeling wallpaper, the mildew-splotched ceiling, and the spider-webbed furniture.

A man Dave vaguely recalled from his childhood appeared from a back room. "May I help you?"

"Well, actually, I'm looking for someone. A woman who may be staying here. Her name is Maurelle Dupre."

"Oh. The inn closed down six months ago. I'm the new owner. I'm going to remodel the building and turn it into a single family home."

Dave nodded. "Best of luck with the renovation. Sorry for bothering you. I didn't know." The new owner thanked him as Dave saw himself out.

Outside, he stood irresolute, debating what to do next. He'd already checked the Reynier hotels in person. He'd looked up all the hotels in Belvidere online and called those, without success. His grandmother and Simone had told him that locals were talking about the woman and that no one knew her, which made it unlikely she was a houseguest around here. He'd seen her in Reynier two days in a row and, according to Simone, other people had seen her around here for a week.

Back in Chicago it was common to see vagrants living on the streets, in cardboard boxes, or abandoned buildings. If this woman was a pickpocket, she might also be a vagrant. As he gazed up the hill, he remembered someone—he couldn't recall who—had told him that the older brother of one of his childhood friends had become a vagrant and was living in the caves and bumming food off the locals. Bruno—Bruno Houdan. If Bruno could live in the caves . . . .

Dave rushed up the nearby stairs to the second tier and back to his grandmother's house, where he found a flashlight in a kitchen drawer. He grabbed it, went back to the chateau area, and found the cave entrance behind the hotel. He hadn't been inside the cave system in years, but he had once known it well.

The caves had a long history of use—they had been mined for stone, used to house families, grow mushrooms, and store wine. They had even been used to hide members of the French Résistance during World War II. Because of that, electric lighting had long ago been installed throughout the main chambers, and if one knew where the switches were located along the walls, they could travel through most of the tunnels, or alleyways as the locals called them, in dim light. It was only in the lesser tunnels and unused caves that one had to rely on flashlights. If Dave remembered right, some tunnels led directly to the back doors of homes, others led to unused caves, and some dead-ended.

He explored each tunnel on the first level. As expected, some had access to chambers or tunnels on the next level. He climbed stairways, or in some places ladders, to get to those chambers and tunnels. Some tunnels weren't as easy to navigate as they had been when he was a kid, some because of the narrowness or low ceilings and some because of the increased bat population. For those, he would have to gain entrance from the outside. He finally decided to go out for a while and look around. He needed sunlight and fresh air. Later, he could come back inside, if necessary, and climb up to the next level.

For the rest of the day, Dave scoured the hillside the way he used to do when he was a kid. In those days, he would scavenge for treasures and artifacts, and his endeavors had usually produced fossils, animal bones, or collectible Neolithic polishing stones which the locals called polissoirs. But today, in the early evening, he came away empty-handed, frustrated, and with the suspicion that the sight of the gendarmes had sent the woman running from the area for good.

THE NEXT MORNING, Dave looked at the clock on his nightstand and groaned. He'd been awake for a while, thinking about his life, his poor choices, his failures. Simone had told him yesterday that he cared more about the mystery, not the person. There was some truth in that. The end of his career as a detective still rankled with him. He still felt the need to prove something. Writing mysteries helped a little, but the bitterness remained. He needed something real—and maybe that was at the heart of his dissatisfaction. And he had failed again this time.

He rolled onto his back and pictured Maurelle, her captivating eyes and shy smile, and then Simone's words intruded: "Don't let her trick you."

But Simone didn't know what happened in Chicago. No one here did.

He threw off his covers, pulled on a pair of navy trousers and a light blue polo, then ran a comb through his hair. Normally, he would shower and shave, but screw it. He jerked the door open and trudged down the stairs and into the kitchen. His grandmother was on the phone again. He listened for a minute. She was talking to Jeannette. Of course she was. He glanced at his computer that was sitting on the kitchen table and took a step toward it, but stopped when his grandmother mentioned the mystery woman. Apparently, Jeannette's daughter, Coralie, had seen her at the general store late yesterday afternoon buying a few grocery items.

Dave squinted one eye, then went into the living room, put on his sneakers, closed the front door behind him, and trudged toward the café. But he didn't stop there. He continued walking onto a pathway that led past numerous troglodyte homes; he must have missed something—she had to be there.

Half an hour later, while he was resting for a few minutes, he looked upward and spotted the outcropping of rock that hung over this lower level. The outcropping was visible even from the river because it stuck out like a wart on a thumb, but the secret swimming hole on that ledge was hidden between trees and shrubs. As a kid, he'd stumbled upon it and made the mistake of telling his grandparents, who scolded him and said he wasn't to go back. It was known to be dangerous because the trails leading up to the outcropping from this tier or down to it from a higher tier were steep and, in some spots, slippery, with loose stones and friable rock. That hadn't bothered him. He'd always been like a mountain goat when it came to navigating the hills, so of course he'd gone back despite his promises.

The rock wall looked more daunting than he remembered. Back when he was a detective, he'd kept in good physical shape. Five years out, and no longer in a fit physical regimen, he couldn't be sure he could still climb the rock, but by God he was going to try.

Pushing his way between overgrown bushes and getting his arms scratched in the process, Dave found the ragged path and started climbing. Halfway up, he lost his footing and had to grab onto a rock to catch himself. He stopped a moment, catching his breath, then scrambled upward again, exhilarated at the challenge. I've really missed this sort of thing, he thought. He felt loose gravel under his right foot, and it was too late. He slipped down a few feet and grazed his hand on the stone wall on the way. He examined the damage. It was bleeding slightly and ached like hell. Finally, on his third try he made it the rest of the way up, and stood on the ledge, looking out over the river valley below. It was still breathtaking. Against a backdrop of fat hedges of flowering Lavender bushes, the river glistened in the sunlight. Alongside the river, on the other side, he could see the church and businesses. Behind those were the houses. In the distance, trees and fields of dark green with squares of light green farms dotted the landscape.

The sound of splashing pulled his attention away from the view and moved toward the little alcove. The bushes, willows, and poplars were taller and fuller than the last time he saw them and took more effort to get through to the deep pond where he and his friends, Jonas and Paul, had occasionally gone skinny-dipping as children. He ran his head through his hair, remembering that even Michel and Bruno Houdan had gone with them once or twice.

In the alcove, he stopped abruptly at the sight of a naked woman sitting in the grass. Her eyes flew open and when she spotted him, a soft gasp escaped her, and she froze. Dave looked away, almost losing his footing as he turned. He glanced backwards and watched her. She grabbed her clothing, which was scattered on the grass near her and dressed quickly, casting glances at him every few seconds, like she was afraid he would jump her. Not that he blamed her. He'd known plenty of men who would take full advantage. When she finished, she stood barefoot on the grassy bank, in jeans and a pale green sleeveless blouse, shaking.

He moved toward her, and she backed up. Suddenly, she spun on her heel and tried to run away. Dave, expecting it, clasped onto her arm, preventing her escape. Then he reached around her head with his free hand and touched her chin, turning her head to face him. "I won't hurt you. Don't run, please."

"I—I have to go," she stammered, squirming and trying to pull free.

"Please don't be afraid. Remember me? We met before."

She looked up at his face and nodded, then looked away.

"If you're in some kind of trouble, I can help."

She cleared her throat and said shakily, "I'm fine, really. You just startled me." She smiled, and he released his grip.

Judging by the way she was looking around, he was sure she was going to try to bolt. He blocked her with his body.

"I looked for you here in Reynier, but I couldn't find anyone who knew where you were staying." He knew his words sounded accusing, but it couldn't be helped. He kept his expression and tone neutral. "When I was a kid," he said, continuing to watch her face carefully, "I was fascinated with the caves. I spent hours exploring, sometimes finding artifacts or animal bones. One day, inside one of the caves I found some fossils—carbonized leaves and small animal foot prints. Cool fossils. At least I thought so. I gathered them up and rushed outside, excited about my treasure." He paused. "I had barely come out of the cave when I came face to face with a wild boar. It was glaring at me, daring me to make a move. And I've got to tell you, that animal was the biggest damn pig I've ever seen. Had hairy black legs, grotesque haunches, and woolly grayish-black hair. Reminded me of bristles on a shoe-shine brush . . . but I think it was its huge tusks that terrified me most."

Her eyes widened in surprise.

"What did you do?"

"I did what any kid would have done. I backed up, right into the cave, hoping and praying that creature wouldn't follow. Unfortunately, in my frantic state, and walking backwards, I didn't see the large rock in the middle of the floor. My heel clunked into the rock and I lost my balance, landing on my ass in the tufa."

Maurelle smiled and seemed to relax. "What's 'tufa'?"

"Just a word for this kind of rock."

She reached down and picked up her shoes and then moved toward a large, flat-topped rock. She sat on the rock and put on her shoes. While she tied the second shoe, she said, "You made that up."

"Nope. I broke one of the fossils when I fell. Not only that, I sat in that damned cave all afternoon and well into the night before I had the nerve to come back outside." He laughed. "I always wondered whether that old boar was too fat and full to go in after me, or if he thought I wasn't worth the effort."

She laughed, and began running her fingers through her damp hair.

Dave reached into his pant pocket and pulled out a comb. He handed it to her. As he watched her comb through her long and curly tangled hair, he was reminded of a frightened wild colt that his former father-in-law had found near his ranch in Montana. That beautiful creature had skittered whenever anyone came close, and this stranger exhibited that same skittishness. Who was she? The pickpocket the gendarmes were looking for? She was certainly running away from something—perhaps an abusive husband or lover.

His grandmother's word 'gypsy' popped into his mind. That might explain her fear of the gendarmes, but nothing about her suggested Romany blood, except perhaps her dark hair. In any case, not only were gypsies not always as criminal as they were made out to be, as far as he knew, they travelled as families and clans, never alone.

She reached out to Dave to give him back his comb, but he motioned for her to keep it. He sat down next to her. Bending forward, he picked up a leaf that had fallen on the ground, held it between two fingers, and rubbed it absentmindedly while he pondered his words. He wanted her to feel comfortable with him, and he figured he had one chance to convince her that she could let down her guard.

"You can trust me," he said, finally. "I want to help you. Hey, I'm a nice guy! I know that you barely know me, but there are plenty of people in town who can vouch for me, if you need proof."

She shook her head. "Thank you, but that isn't necessary, really. It's not you. It's—it's just that I don't need any help. I'm on holiday from Le Mans. In fact, I'm heading to Paris this afternoon and then back home after that."

Dave cleared his throat. "Look, you are obviously not French. I speak it well enough, and even I can hear your accent—British, right?" She blushed, and opened her mouth to protest, but Dave continued. "What's more, I checked with the local hotels. They told me you aren't staying anywhere around here. I don't believe you're staying with someone either." Her head jerked up, and again she opened her mouth to speak, but Dave motioned for her to stop.

"If you were staying with friends, then you wouldn't need to bathe in the pond."

She blushed again and averted her eyes, making Dave regret what he'd said. But he couldn't think of another way to get her to talk to him. He felt her tense up, pulling away from him even further, consequently, when she stood, he was prepared. He reached out and grabbed her arm, drawing her back.

"I really do want to help you. Whatever the problem, let me in. Please."

"I don't need help." She sighed heavily, and then, in a barely audible voice, as if speaking to herself, said, "I don't need anyone."

He placed his hand under her chin and tilted her face up. Her eyes were clouded. He gently wiped away tears that had slid down her cheek. Tears didn't normally move Dave. He had been conditioned to them in his former line of work where he had seen victims and criminals alike break down into sobs.

"Let's go back to the village," he said. "I'm a guest at my grandmother's house. I'm sure she wouldn't mind having another guest." He paused, thinking back on his last conversation with his grandmother. "If that doesn't work, I'll rent a room for you at Chateau de Reynier or in a hotel in Belvidere."

She shook her head defiantly and pulled back. Her moist eyes showed fear and relief battling each other for control. She looked away, hiding her face as she reached up to dab at her eyes. When she finally spoke, her voice was so soft that Dave could barely hear.

"I can't go with you. I don't want to be a burden." She reached up and pushed wayward strands of hair out of her eyes, and then added, "And I have my own money."

Dave frowned. "Then why aren't you staying in a hotel?"

"It's—it's complicated," she mumbled.

He pursed his lips as alarm bells went off in his head. "Well, we can talk some more, later. For now, let's get you to a safe place, okay?"

She nodded, sighing deeply.

"Where are your things?"

She stared at the ground, not answering.

"Look, I know you must be staying in one of the caves. You might as well tell me which one."

Finally, she said, "All right. The cave is further up the hill. Not far from here." She looked up, shyly, and pointed toward a group of gangly bushes.

Dave scanned the area and spotted the twisting, winding trail of dirt weaving through sheets of limestone and dirt on the hill. He vaguely recalled that trail from his childhood. Now that he knew which way to go, he took hold of her hand and walked with her toward the trail. Climbing up was almost as difficult as when he'd climbed from the lower level to the outcropping.

Remembering his two falls, he let go of her, allowing both of them to use their hands. Maurelle was in front of him, which he didn't think much of, until she reached the top and started running. Dave made the final push onto the higher tier, scanned for her, and then rushed forward. Grabbing her arm, he looked questioningly at her. "Come on. Where is this cave?"

She took a deep breath and let it out slowly. "All right, I'll take you there."

Dave held onto her arm as they trudged through the woods of poplar, ash, oak, and alder. They came to the path that led upward to the ancient ruins of a church at the top of the hill. Maurelle went on past the trail. Did she even know about the church? Did she know about the tunnels leading to the other caves and to the troglos?

They continued through an area covered in wild shrubs, and then she stopped.

Dave raised his eyebrows.

"You'll have to let go of my arm," she said.

"I don't think so."

She moved toward one of the bushes and knelt down, making Dave bend over uncomfortably. Pulling back a thick branch, she revealed her cave, one of the few caves around that still had its original opening. It was nothing more than a four-foot high hole in the rock.

"You first," Dave said. He scrunched down and followed her inside. When he stood up straight again, he abruptly bumped his head on a low section of ceiling. "Damn!"

"Are you all right?"

"Yeah," he said, rubbing his sore head. "Now I remember this cave. My friends brought me here a few times when I was a teenager." He winced and stooped slightly to avoid another accident. His eyes adjusted to the low light and he watched Maurelle as she moved away from the entrance, closer to the narrow inner section that would eventually lead to the other caves if one could get through it. As he recalled, it was full of bats and was extremely narrow in spots. She might make a run for it into the tunnel-like chamber, but he doubted she would get far in the pitch blackness.

He waited.

She came back into the main room carrying a duffel bag and something that looked like a sleeping bag.

"Here, let me get those." He threw the duffel bag's strap over his shoulder and carried the other bag with his free hand, while he held onto her hand with the other. At the cave entrance he set the bags down and slid them through, then crept out and waited for her.

CHAPTER SEVEN

MAURA BARRINGTON WALKED alongside the tall stranger. He was far too quick and agile for her to escape from him at the moment. She would have to wait for a better opportunity. "May I ask you something?"

"Sure. What do you want to know?"

"How did you find me? I've never seen anyone in that area before. Near that pond, I mean."

"I was looking for you."

"Oh." She made a mental note to be more careful in the future. When she saw that they were approaching the inhabited troglodyte dwellings, she stopped.

"What's wrong?"

"I—I just . . . ."

"What?"

"This is private property, isn't it?"

His face broke into a grin. "Well, sort of, I guess, but I know the people who live here. They won't mind."

As they passed the first home, he waved to the white-haired man and woman sitting in rocking chairs on the veranda.

"Bonjour," the man said. He wore a blue and gray plaid shirt, and gray trousers, and kept a cane at his side. She recognized him. She'd seen him sitting on a bench outside the general store with another man on a few occasions. He never spoke to her, but he usually nodded when she had walked past. The woman, whom Maura hadn't seen before, wore a purple top and lavender skirt with purple flowers.

"Bonjour. How are you this fine day?" Dave said.

"Good. Taking a break. Nice weather for sitting outdoors."

"It sure is. Have you met Mademoiselle Maurelle Dupre?"

Maura glanced around for another person, but then remembered she was now Maurelle Dupre.

The man shrugged. "Seen her around."

"Maurelle, this is Jacques and Genevre Henriot. Oh, and the little girl on the swing is their granddaughter, Emelie."

She looked over at the girl on the swing and stared. The girl, she guessed, was around four year old. Emelie reminded her of herself at that age—long braids, skinny, swinging as high as she could, her legs kicking rapidly in sync with the motion of the swing.

Someone coughed, and Maurelle turned her attention back to the man. He was looking at her with his eyebrows raised. "Oh, I'm sorry. It's nice to meet you," she said.

"Likewise," Jacques said.

His wife didn't say anything.

Jacques and Dave chatted about mutual acquaintances, giving Maurelle a chance to study the troglodyte home. The face of the house appeared normal: wood structure painted light blue, with darker blue framed picture windows, and a white front door split in the middle so the owner could open only the top half for fresh air if he chose. The veranda in front of the door was tiled with white limestone. The rest of the house, however, was buried in the hill. She couldn't help but wonder what it looked like on the inside. Was it dark and dreary, or warm and inviting?

A few minutes later, once they were out of earshot, Dave

said, "Their daughter, Veronique, and her little girl, Emelie, moved here a year ago after her husband abandoned them. The grandparents are helping to raise the girl."

He led her down the narrow lane, turned, and headed west toward the center of the village, stopping at last in front of a two-story house. "Here we are. This is it."

She gazed at the old house. Dark green ivy blanketed the chalky white facade like a mother protecting her young, reaching out her arms gently and stroking the white shutters surrounding each window. Maurelle smiled at her romanticized depiction. She was getting carried away.

A sudden hint of perfume in the air drew her attention to the purple bougainvillea planted in a large pot next to the front door. She soaked in the lovely scent and shaded her eyes as she looked up at the top of the tall plant, where its vines entwined with the ivy near the top of the door.

Dave pulled open the arched front door and motioned for her to enter, but she hesitated. "It's okay. Go ahead inside."

She stepped inside and halted in the vestibule near the bottom of a walnut staircase. To her right was a cozy white and brown room. An imposing open fireplace edged with dressed stones was the focal point, surrounded by an old, upholstered chair, a sumptuous ivory sofa, a shiny walnut coffee table topped with a vase of yellow daffodils, and a gleaming rustic ladder-back chair. But it was the splendid grandfather clock between the fireplace and staircase that held most of her attention. The ornate wood carvings and the golden pendulum made her smile, calling forth memories of a similar clock in her own grandparents' house when she was a little girl.

The front door slammed, startling her. She turned swiftly toward Dave. He looked as surprised as she, and she guessed that he hadn't meant to shut it that hard. A minute later he dropped her duffel bag on the hardwood floor with a solid clunk and an elderly woman rushed out of the kitchen and stared at them.

"Bonjour, Grand-mère," Dave said, smiling warmly. "I'd like to introduce you to Mademoiselle Maurelle Dupre."

Maurelle smiled politely and extended her hand. "Bonjour, Madame. I am pleased to meet you. You have a charming home."

The elderly woman gave her a cool stare.

"And this is my grandmother, Fabienne Laurent."

Fabienne turned her attention to him, pressing her lips together for a moment. "How could you bring that woman here, into my home?" she demanded, nodding toward Maurelle. "You had no business."

"She had no place else to go."

Fabienne snorted. She raised her hands to shoulder level with palms out and upward. "Well, she can go back to where you found her. She is not my problem and she shouldn't be yours."

Dave moved closer to his grandmother and stood face to face with her. Fabienne didn't back away, but leaned in closer, staring angrily at him.

"She was living in one of the abandoned caves." He turned his head, glancing briefly at Maurelle, and then back to his grandmother. "She was all alone."

Fabienne stood like a marble statue.

"If you can't do this for her, then please do it for me. You owe me, Grand-mère."

"I don't know what you're talking about. I owe you nothing! How could you say such a thing when you are a guest in my home?"

"I'm a guest here because you wanted me here," Dave said flatly. "And now you have the nerve to act as if I'm freeloading. I'm the one who should be upset, considering how you got me to come here in the first place."

She pouted, then said, "Why don't you take her to Simone's house?" She placed her hand over her mouth for a brief moment, and added, tauntingly, "Oh, I'm sorry, you can't do that, now can you?"

Dave's face turned crimson. "I guess it's time I packed my bag, which is what I should have done the minute I found out you'd tricked me into coming to France."

When he turned and headed toward the stairs, Fabienne shouted, "Wait!"

He stopped, but didn't turn around.

"I suppose she can stay in the spare room," she murmured. "For a little while, perhaps."

With three quick strides, Dave stood back in front of his grandmother and placed his arms around her, squeezing her. When he released her, he kissed her on both cheeks and whispered, "Thank you", which made the elderly woman blush, though she shrugged again as though it was all nonsense.

Maurelle breathed a short sigh of relief—although she wasn't at all sure she really wanted to stay here.

While Dave and Fabienne discussed arrangements, Maurelle pondered her own problems. During the night she could sneak out and hike to Orleans or possibly down to Tours. She'd be far enough away by the time they noticed her missing. So preoccupied was she that she jumped when Dave placed his hand on her elbow. He smiled at her and she gave a nervous smile in return; then he led her upstairs, carrying her duffel bag over his shoulder. On the landing he gestured towards a door at the end. When he opened it, pink sun spilled out of the room into the narrow hallway. He reached inside and set her bag down, then smiled at her, and motioned for her to enter.

"If you need anything, you can find me in the room next door. There's a bathroom on the main level." He stared at her for a moment longer, then turned and walked back to the stairs.

Upon stepping into the tiny bedroom, Maurelle was greeted by sunlight radiating through lovely sheer pink curtains. She smiled and slowly appraised the room: hardwood floors, a dark green rug with pink and gold flowers, a twin bed covered in an ivory bedspread, and light green walls with a pair of paintings. One painting showed a Parisien boulevard at dusk, with the Eiffel Tower beyond. The tower was beautifully lit up in gold against a dark blue sky. The other showed a river and bridge, which she guessed was also in Paris— the Pont Neuf Bridge, perhaps. It was lined with street lamps that glowed green or gold in the foggy night and cast long reflections in the water. The hazy greens, grays, and golds gave a peaceful yet lonely feel to the painting. Wondering why images of Paris should be here in the country, she reluctantly moved away and ran her hand over the high-backed leather chair in the corner.

Moving past the bed and trying to avoid looking at it, she reached down and picked up her bag. She set it down on the chair and tried to focus on looking for her map while she fought the urge to check out the bed. Maurelle couldn't let herself be tempted. She needed to leave tonight while everyone was sleeping. But then she did look at the bed and thought about lying on a mattress, swaddled in a soft blanket. She moved forward and stroked the bed's chenille bedspread and its puffy pink pillows, imagining her head cradled on them. Her spirits lifted briefly. Perhaps she could lay her fears to rest for one night. She would wait until dawn to escape—before everyone awakened but after she had slept.

There was a quiet knock on the door.

Through the closed door, Dave said, "Sorry to bother you, but I need to tell you something. I hope you don't mind. I'm going to leave you here for a while. I won't be gone long. You can get settled and then go downstairs for lunch. Grand-mère is making lunch for both of you."

A wave of panic hit her at the thought of facing that woman alone. "I—I'm not hungry," she lied. "Please tell her she doesn't need to fix anything for me."

He opened the door and peeked inside. "She won't bite. And besides, you'll love her cooking. She can even make sandwiches that are out of this world."

Her stomach groaned, betraying her, and she reluctantly nodded her head. "Okay, thank you."

"Grand-mère wanted me to tell you to come down for lunch in twenty minutes. I'll be back in a couple of hours—maybe sooner. Okay?"

She nodded again and attempted to smile, though hearing that she'd be alone with a woman who didn't really want her here was already resurrecting her sense of danger, tensing her muscles, and giving her a knot in her stomach. "Yes, fine, thank you."

LATER, AS MAURELLE descended the stairs, she caught the sound of laughter coming from the kitchen and thought Dave must have decided not to leave after all.

She walked into the kitchen, expecting to see Dave and Fabienne. Instead, there was another elderly woman, with obviously dyed red hair. They sat across from each other at the table, and when they saw her Fabienne said, "Here she is. Come in and sit, Maurelle. Please join us for lunch."

She motioned to the chair beside her, where a plate with a baguette, another with salad niçoise, and a bowl of steaming soup were already set out.

Maurelle smiled politely and sat down, very much aware that the two women were staring at her.

"Bon appetit," Fabienne said. As Maura took her first bite of bread, Fabienne added, "Oh, I forgot to introduce you to my best friend, Jeannette Devlin."

"I'm pleased to meet you," Maurelle said.

Fabienne smiled smugly. "Jeannette is the grandmother of Dave's girlfriend, Simone."

Maurelle picked up her spoon and carefully put it into her soup, taking a small mouthful.

"Dave and Simone are leaving tomorrow on a sightseeing trip through France," Fabienne said. "Unless, of course, Dave has to postpone the trip because of you." She turned to Jeannette.

"Oui," Jeannette said. "That would be such a shame. They've been looking forward to it. The lovebirds will enjoy the sights, certainly, but we suspect that they'll enjoy being alone together more."

"Oui. C'est vrai!" Fabienne said. The two old ladies chuckled.

Through the rest of the luncheon, Maurelle listened only intermittently, digesting new information along with her meal. Of course Dave would have a girlfriend. He was a good-looking man. Didn't he know it was a mistake for a man in a relationship to invite another woman into the home where he was staying? What kind of man would do that?

She finished her soup and salad and began nibbling the crusty bread on her plate. During a rare pause in the older women's chatter, she complimented Fabienne on the food. And then, when conversation resumed, Maurelle retreated into her own mind again, this time going back to the day she'd caught her own boyfriend cheating on her. How could she have known how drastically her life would change after that?

"Are you all right?" Jeannette asked. "You look as though you've seen a ghost, dear?"

Maurelle looked up, embarrassed. "I—I'm fine. I'm tired, I guess. Would you mind if I went upstairs to rest?"

The two older women exchanged a look that Maurelle

couldn't interpret, then Fabienne said, "Of course you may. We'll take care of the dishes, dear."

Maurelle padded out of the kitchen, ran up the stairs and into her room, flinging herself on the bed.

CHAPTER EIGHT

DAVE LEFT HIS grandmother's house and walked to Café Charbonneau to see Simone about borrowing her car since Fabienne had never learned to drive and therefore relied on other people to take her places or to run errands for her.

The bell jingled on the door when he opened it, and Simone called out, "Bonjour."

He smiled and walked over to the table she was wiping clean.

"Sorry to bother you," he said, "but Grand-mère asked me to run errands for her in Vendome. Since she doesn't have a car, I need to ask if I can bother your car."

She tilted her head. "Isabelle is working today, and it's slow. I could drive you wherever you need to go."

"That's not necessary. These errands could take a while and they won't be fun."

She shrugged, handing over the keys. "No rush. Keep it as long as you need. You know where's it parked, don't you?"

He nodded. Simone always parked in the same space in the small parking lot behind the café. Finding the car wasn't the problem, but getting into the tiny car was a real challenge.

After traveling for half an hour to Vendome, the nearest large town, and spending an hour running errands, Dave drove back toward Reynier. During the drive, he thought about Maurelle. He couldn't imagine how she'd lived in that cave. How desperate she must have been to resort to that. What she was running from had to be pretty serious. Was it something she had done? Or something done to her? He instinctively felt the latter was the more likely, as she seemed to him to be honest and straight. He drove up the slight hill to the café, pulled into the parking lot, and turned off the engine. As he walked into the café and handed Simone's key back to her, he also reminded himself ruefully that his instincts weren't always to be trusted.

Simone slipped the key into her apron pocket while she waited on a customer. Dave quickly stepped outside before she finished and could engage him in conversation.

He rushed toward his grandmother's house.

"Dave, wait!"

He stopped and turned around to see Jonas Lefevre jogging toward him.

"I'm glad you decided to stick around here awhile," Jonas said.

"Me too."

"I've been hoping to meet up with you before I drive to Paris. I'll be leaving in about an hour. Have to meet some buyers. Do you know how hard you are to catch? I guess you've been too busy the last few days—and you've been holding out on me, from what I've heard. A new lady friend and you didn't tell me? I'm dying to meet her."

"Simone? You've met her." Dave started walking again. Jonas sped up to keep pace with him.

"Don't play dumb. You know I'm not talking about Simone. It's the mysterious stranger. Everyone is talking about her—and about you. You've made it to the top of the gossip chain. Quite a feat."

Dave shook his head. Just what he needed—to be the most

gossiped about. "Yeah, well, you shouldn't believe everything you hear."

"There is usually at least some truth in what the busybodies around here say. You and I both know that privacy isn't really possible here in Reynier."

"Yeah, you're right about that."

"So, tell me about her. I haven't seen her yet, but I hear she's pretty. Are you and she . . . ."

"No. I'm helping her temporarily. She's homeless."

Jonas tilted his head and studied Dave's face, then gave him a sly grin. "Aha. I guess that means you won't mind introducing her to me."

"Yeah, right. Lillian would skin you alive if you brought her home."

"So it's true she's staying at Fabienne's house?"

Dave nodded.

"I'll tell you what. She can stay there, and I'll help her out with whatever she needs. How's that?"

"I don't think so."

Jonas laughed, then patted Dave on the shoulder. "That's what I thought. The French blood courses through your veins after all."

"It really isn't like that. I'm not in a 'relationship' with anyone—not with Simone or Maurelle, okay?"

Jonas smiled. "Okay, okay. I won't mention it again. Let's get together for beers when I return from Paris."

"Sure. Call me when you get back."

As Dave entered Fabienne's house five minutes later, he was surprised by the silence that was pierced only by the ticking of the grandfather clock. He walked into the kitchen and then back into the living room. He took the stairs two at a time and knocked softly on Maurelle's door. When she didn't respond, he opened it and peered around the corner. The room looked as if she'd never been there. He checked the wardrobe, hoping she might have unpacked her bag, but felt a sinking sensation in the pit of his stomach. The wardrobe was empty. He rushed downstairs and this time noticed his grandmother asleep on the sofa—she had been hidden by the high back.

He rubbed his face with his hands, then began pacing as he considered what to do.

"Oh, you're home," Fabienne said, sitting up and looking at him bleary-eyed.

"What happened?" Dave asked, running his hand through his hair. "What did you do? Where is she?"

Fabienne's eyes widened and she gulped sleepily. "Upstairs resting."

"No, she's not there. And neither are her bags."

Fabienne shrugged, and lifted her arms, turning her hands palm upward.

"I know you didn't want her here. Did you do something to chase her away? At least be honest with me about this."

"I really don't know anything. She must have slipped out after I fell asleep."

"You had no idea she'd left?"

"Of course not. Why would she leave?" She looked up at him, batting her eyes innocently. This wasn't the first time he'd seen that look.

Shaking his head, Dave turned away and walked toward the front door. She'd let him down again—and so had Maurelle, for that matter. He reached for the door handle and then hesitated as another thought came to him: *Unless there was a good reason for her running away again.* He looked back and asked, "When did she go upstairs?"

Fabienne shrugged. "During lunch. She got up from the table and said she was going upstairs to rest. Such ill manners, especially for a guest."

"How long ago was that?"

She glanced at the clock. "I suppose it would have been an hour, maybe a bit longer."

"What did you do? Did you say something to upset her?"

She jutted her chin outward in her defiant way. Dave was losing his patience. "Tell me what happened, Grand-mère."

"I really didn't say anything. We were having a pleasant luncheon and then she got up and said she was tired. Jeannette and I really had no idea why."

"Jeannette was here?"

She looked away, then nodded her head.

"I'm guessing that the two of you intimidated her."

"No, no," Fabienne said, looking at him again. "We behaved perfectly."

"Right," Dave said. She was trying to give him a wide-eyed-innocent look, but her eyes were blinking rapidly.

"She doesn't deserve your help. That girl is trouble. You mark my words. You're better off not getting involved."

"But I am." He walked out of the house, slamming the door behind him. His mind raced. Where might Maurelle have gone? Unlikely she'd go back to the cave or even stay in the area. Thinking about his drive back to Reynier from Vendome, he didn't see a reason to search for her in that direction. He hadn't seen her. And, anyway, if his instincts were right, she would likely avoid that busy road. She might have hiked along a country road or cut through the fields. With any luck, she was doing the former, which meant he needed to borrow Simone's car again, something he really didn't want to do for this. If he'd stopped back here before he'd returned the car, he wouldn't have to bother Simone again. He'd rather borrow Jonas' car, but since Jonas was on his way to Paris, that was out. As he walked, he remembered Maurelle saying earlier that she was going to Paris and then back to Le Mans. Since he knew she was lying, and wasn't good at it, she was more likely planning to head in the opposite direction, south towards Tours or Blois, perhaps. On the other hand, he couldn't rule out the possibility of her heading due north to St. Calais.

"Bonjour, Cheri. Back so soon?" Simone said, eyeing him curiously as he entered the café.

Dave nodded, wondering how much he should tell her and how much she already knew. "Have you spoken to your grandmother this afternoon?"

Simone shrugged. "I know that you brought the girl to Fabienne's, if that's what you want to tell me. I'm not happy about that, but I do understand."

"I'm sorry, Simone. I know that I'm asking a lot of you."

She pouted for a moment and then offered him a forgiving smile. "You can't help wanting to help strays, and you see this girl as a lost puppy. I understand that."

He smiled and looked into Simone's eyes, saying, "I don't know all that went down during lunch, but the girl left. Grand-mère is so damn tightlipped about it." He paused, running his fingers through his hair. "It's probably hopeless, but if I could borrow your car again I might be able to find her."

"Of course. On one condition."

"And what's that?"

"Since our trip is postponed, I want us—just the two of us—to go to the theatre in Vendome. I'll take care of the tickets."

"That's fine," Dave said. "When did you have in mind?"

"I'm not sure exactly. I'll have to check the show schedules, but it will probably be in a week or two. I'll find out and let you know."

When Dave nodded, Simone disappeared for a moment and returned with her keys. "Take whatever time you need. I'll be here," she said.

A few minutes later, Dave again squeezed into Simone's Deux Chevaux and headed up the steep hill towards the ancient church ruins. At the top, he stopped on the roadside and pried himself out of the car. From this vantage point he could see the road stretching north for miles, all the way to the horizon. Except for the few village streets of the upper part of Reynier, directly behind the church, the landscape was mostly flat fields dotted with the occasional farmhouse. He scanned the view.

Turning ninety degrees, he looked down toward the river, hoping to see the whole river valley. But trees on the hillside and on the plain obscured much of the view. He decided that his best option would be to follow the southern route as he'd first thought.

Before long, Dave reached the bridge and crossed over the river. Driving slowly along the lonely country lane, he looked into green and gold fields on one side of the road and woods on the other side. After an hour, he was beginning to think it was hopeless. She could be anywhere. She could have hitched a ride or gone in a completely different direction. Coming to a junction in the road, he stopped, leaned forward, and tried to decide which way to go. Unfortunately, the choice was a crapshoot.

He turned to the left, onto a narrower road that headed into the woods. He drove another half hour without seeing anyone, not even another car.

Frustrated, Dave considered turning around and going back to Reynier. He could drive east toward Belvidere and Vendome. It was a long shot, but he was running out of options.

Still deep in thought, he rounded a sharp curve too fast. In that instance, something leapt in front of him. Startled, and not sure what it was, he instinctively swerved off the road and stopped in time to see a buck dash into the woods.

Shaking slightly, Dave gripped the steering wheel with both hands as he tried to calm himself. It was bad enough that he'd borrowed Simone's car twice in one day; now he'd nearly wrecked it. He yanked open the door and stepped out. Walking around the outside of the car, he inspected the tires and the frame. All looked fine. He climbed back inside and pulled back onto the road.

CHAPTER NINE

MAURELLE SAT ON a large boulder by the roadside, her elbows on her knees and her chin resting in the palms of her hands. Although she had been marching through the countryside for only two hours, she already felt crushed by her baggage and the ever-present burden of her situation, which both physically and emotionally weighed heaviest of all.

She hadn't intended staying too long in Reynier in any case, but hadn't worked out how she would manage with all her baggage. When she'd first left London, she'd carried only a small zippered bag containing cash, identification, and a few small items of clothing. Running had been much simpler. Then she'd bought the duffel bag and some clothing and shoes in Paris. Lugging all of that around had proven difficult but manageable. Over the last few weeks she'd added the sleeping bag, more clothing, snacks, and even several books.

Earlier today, immediately after her bath, she had toyed with the idea of purchasing a bicycle or motor bike, which seemed a great idea, and probably would have been easy enough if Dave hadn't found her. Now that she was stuck out in the woods, far from town, how was she supposed to make that work? She smacked her thigh in frustration and then straightened up, trying to think clearly. She could drag herself and her baggage back to Belvidere, the nearest place that might have a bike shop. But what if it didn't? And what if she ran into Dave Martin? She looked up at the clear sky and took a deep breath. Logically, leaving her belongings behind and running from here as fast as she could was her real best chance, but somehow she needed them, needed the reassurance of owning something, of having possessions and responsibilities. That brought her back to another option, one that she had touched on from time to time, but hadn't allowed herself to really consider until now, the option of going back to England and facing her problem head-on, of finding a way out of it there. She didn't want to live like this. The thought of returning, though, paralyzed her, and sweat beaded on her forehead. Until she could formulate a plan and know that it was her best option, she would have to keep moving further away from England.

It'll all work out, she told herself. God, she wished she could believe that. But this wasn't the first time she'd tried to convince herself of that, and she wasn't as naïve now as she had been a few weeks ago.

The sound of an automobile approaching made her tense. She looked away as though uninterested.

The car's tires crunched in the gravel on the side of the road as it came to a stop. The driver shut off the engine and opened the door. She turned casually to look.

It was Dave Martin. Relief and fear fought in her mind. She couldn't go back with him—but she was tired of running. And she really missed having someone to talk to. Maybe she could take a day to relax before she headed to Italy. Yes, that would give her time to make better plans and maybe even buy a bike.

She forced herself to stay still. He stood directly in front of her now, looking down at her with a grin on his face.

"I nearly hit a deer back there," he said, motioning down the road.

She stared at him momentarily, taken by surprise at his first words, then asked, "Are you all right?"

He nodded. "It scared the crap out of me though. Luckily, I swerved in time." He rubbed his hair. "I have to admit it really shook me up, but I feel better now that I've found you. I was afraid you might be nestled deeply in the woods by now, and that I might not see you again."

Shading her eyes from the bright sunlight, she looked up at his face. He smiled and she felt suddenly happy. She gave a weak smile back and then averted her eyes as she stretched out her legs.

"I don't know what my grandmother or Jeannette did, but I hope you'll forgive them."

She looked at him and shrugged.

"They can be challenging, to say the least." He chuckled, and added, "Anyway, why don't we go back to the house? I won't leave again. I swear." He paused, watching her intently.

"I don't need your help. I'm fine on my own. You should go back home."

She didn't want to spend the night like an animal in the woods and she didn't think she had the energy to make it all the way to the city. But getting involved with this stranger, with anyone, was too risky. She would manage on her own.

She stood up and reached for her backpack and sleeping bag to leave, but Dave quickly grabbed them up to put into the car. She rushed after him, intending to . . . to what? Kicking up a fuss could be dangerous, and he'd already proven his strength. She stopped and touched her throat. Her pulse throbbed erratically beneath her fingertips as she watched him stride over to the car, open the boot, and plop the bags down. At the slamming of the lid with a loud clunk, she jumped. He walked round and held the passenger door open for her.

She backed up. "No, I can't. Please give me my bags. I—"

He ignored her, strode around to the driver's side, climbed into the car, and started up the engine, drowning out her words.

She could run, but he was faster. Even the few seconds' advantage she'd have by already being outside wouldn't help. Besides, as much as she hated to admit it, she did long for human contact, if only for a few hours. She clenched her jaw and got in.

Dave said, "You'll be safe and fed, but you have to promise me that you won't run off during the night."

Unable to bring herself to say the words, to speak a promise she wasn't sure she would keep, she simply nodded.

Back at Fabienne's, Dave stopped in the street, near the front door. He got out of the car, removed Maurelle's bags from the boot, and led her into the house that she hadn't expected to ever see again.

"You can go settle in while I drop the car off. I will only be five minutes. Don't go away. Promise?"

She nodded, but alarm pulsed through her when he started back out the door.

Dave, apparently noticing her fear, said, "Damn. I promised you I wouldn't leave, didn't I? Sorry. I have to return the car. It's borrowed. I'll be right back, okay?"

Maurelle nodded. After he left, she took a deep breath, and turned back toward the living room. No one was in sight. She tiptoed around to see if either of the women were still in the kitchen; they weren't around. She went back to the foyer, picked up her bags, and walked over to the staircase.

Fabienne and Jeannette had told her that Dave and his girlfriend were leaving on a trip in the morning. She could go to bed early and get rested and then she could do an early morning escape before anyone else awoke. That would give Dave no time to hunt for her before he left.

As she reached the top of the stairs, the front door opened and startled her, making her jump. She turned around and found Dave grinning broadly.

"You're still here," he said. "I was half-expecting you to have slipped out through the window. I thought we were going to have to carry on playing a game of cat and mouse."

Maurelle laughed. "I don't have the energy to play anything."

"I can believe that. Grand-mère is going to eat dinner at her friend Jeannette's house, so I thought you and I could go to the bistro for dinner."

The crowded bistro in Paris—and the man reading the newspaper with her picture in it—flashed across her mind, and her first impulse was to decline Dave's offer. But it was true; she didn't have the energy, and a sense of 'what the hell?' overcame her initial fear. That left only the ever important question of what she should wear.

As if reading her mind, Dave said, "Do you have something dressy to wear?" Looking apologetic, he added, "The bistro is fairly casual, but . . . ."

Maurelle wiped her hand self-consciously over her rumpled shirt. "I have two skirts and a few blouses, but they have been stored away in my bag. They may be wrinkled."

"I'm sure they'll be fine. We have some time before dinner. If you want to take a nap or a shower, go ahead. Let me know if you need anything. I figure we'll leave in about forty-five minutes, if that's alright."

She glanced up at the grandfather clock. At the stroke of the hour, she needed to be ready. Dave took her duffel bag from her and carried it upstairs. She followed him. In her cozy bedroom, she sat down on the chair in the corner, removed her shoes, and rubbed her aching feet for a few minutes before opening her bag.

Fortunately, her clothes weren't quite as appalling as she'd feared. With a bit of smoothing, her pale-green blouse with its scoop neck and her flowing light green skirt with blue flowers and russet leaves would do fine. However, her face, she decided as she stared in the mirror above the dresser, needed work. A good scrubbing and a dab of makeup. And, God, her hair needed some serious taming. A shower, with warm water dripping over her body would be wonderful. But then she thought about trying to dry her hair.

She walked downstairs to the bathroom, washed and dried her face, and applied enough make-up to take away the shadows. When she finished, she returned to her room and sat down on the edge of the soft bed, stretching her legs out in front of her. With her hairbrush in hand, she worked on untangling her hair—a time-consuming task. Once that was done, she brushed her hair until it felt silky beneath her hand. Not so bad now. A sense of déjà vu washed over her; this was normality, getting ready to go for a meal with a good looking man. But it had not been her normality for quite some time now.

The grandfather clock chimed. Maurelle glanced at her dirty gym shoes, then frantically searched through her duffel bag for something better. She pulled out the high heels and the sandals she'd bought in Paris. She had almost forgotten about them. She selected the high heels. With one last check in the mirror, she headed down the stairs, feeling self-conscious, like a teenager on a first date.

When Dave saw her, the look of surprise on his face made her smile.

"You scrub up pretty well," Dave whispered approvingly as he intertwined his arm with hers.

"There was a fair bit of scrubbing involved."

Walking along the darkening streets, Maurelle stole glances at Dave, noticing how handsome he looked in his slate-gray suit, accented by a burgundy dress-shirt and a dark gray tie. He caught her looking at him once, and she turned away quickly, embarrassed.

Along the way, a group of boys, two on each side of the street, passed a soccer ball back and forth as they ran down the hill. Maurelle smiled at their simple pleasure. Dave apparently was watching them, as well.

"They remind me of my childhood summers visiting my grandmother. My friend, Jonas, and I, and sometimes Paul and Alain, would ride our bicycles down these steep, winding lanes, imagining ourselves as riders in the Tour de France or race car drivers in the Grand Prix. Back then, I loved that Reynier was remote and untouched. I thought I had a place I could always escape to, a place where my problems couldn't reach me."

"You don't feel that way now?"

Dave shrugged. "Reynier is still less 'touched' by all the problems of the world, but I'm not sure that one can escape the problems altogether."

As they strolled along, he waved to so many passersby that Maurelle felt as if they were in a parade, which was an odd feeling, considering she'd spent her entire life in London, where people passed each other in large herds without ever really seeing faces or acknowledging each other. She shuddered involuntarily as her fear of being recognized resurfaced. In her effort to take her mind off that, another thought thrust its way into her mind. Without intending to, she asked out loud, "Will she be there?"

Dave stopped abruptly and looked at her. "Will who be where?"

"I wondered if your girlfriend will be joining us."

Dave looked taken aback, but then seemed to pull himself together.

"So that's what Grand-mère and Jeannette talked about," he said, so quietly that Maurelle could barely hear.

"If you would rather have a romantic dinner with her, I can eat elsewhere. I know that you and she are leaving in the morning on a vacation together. I don't want to interfere with your plans."

"I've put that trip on hold. By the way, I'm already on vacation. This—my being here in France—is an open-ended vacation."

She didn't know how to respond.

"And no, Simone will not be joining us for dinner," he said in a clipped voice that contradicted his smile.

He motioned then for her to continue walking, but as she studied his face, noticing creases on his forehead and tenseness of his jaw, she sensed that something had changed between them. Her chance of actually enjoying this night out crumbled to dust.

CHAPTER TEN

THE BISTRO'S PATRON, Romain Chamfort, led Dave and Maurelle to one of the few empty tables, one located in the middle of the shadowy room lit only by faux antique lanterns. Even in the dim light Dave recognized every person here and every person in here was staring at him. By morning, the whole town would know he'd been dining there with the town's 'gypsy'. He scanned the crowded room for a less conspicuous location.

"If you don't mind," Dave said, "I'd prefer that table in the corner."

Romain followed Dave's gaze, then gave him a knowing look and a nod. As he seated them, he said, "It's nice to see you here again, Monsieur Martin. May I suggest a hors d'oeuvres? Our Warm Camembert with Wild Mushroom Fricassee is most popular."

"Thank you. That sounds good. I'd also like a bottle of your best wine."

After Romaine left, Dave sighed and rotated his shoulders, trying to ease the tension that had instantly appeared. He'd been looking forward to spending time with Maurelle, to having a real conversation. More than anything, he wanted to get to know her and find out what her deal was. He wished she hadn't brought up Simone on the way here.

When he'd spoken to Simone earlier in the day, both when he asked to borrow her car a second time, and when he returned it, he'd been open, telling her about Maurelle. So why was he now feeling guilty? Simone had acted as though she didn't mind. Her words even suggested that she thought of the girl as a stray puppy, instead of competition. But Dave wasn't so sure. Apart from that lay another issue. Despite the evidence of her desire to hide and her reaction to the gendarmes, he had instinctively trusted her. Had he made a mistake?

Romain brought out their wine and poured two glasses.

"Your fricassee will be ready shortly." He took their orders for the main course and departed.

Dave again focused his attention on Maurelle. The soft ambient lighting of the restaurant made her look even more enticing, adding sparkle to her bright eyes and a pinkish glow to her creamy skin.

She tilted her head at him the way Simone did sometimes.

Clearing his throat, he said, "I'm curious about why you were living in a cave. I have so many questions to ask you."

Maurelle nodded and set down her glass.

Dave asked, "How long did you live in the cave?"

"It doesn't matter. It was temporary."

"That's not a good enough answer."

"It wasn't long."

"How long?"

Looking a bit upset, she snapped back, "All right. A week."

"You need to understand something," he said, locking his eyes on hers and trying to explain himself to defuse her being upset. "I'm not a fool. You lied to me earlier. I don't like that. My own grandmother tricked me into coming here by telling me she was dying when there's nothing really wrong with her."

Her eyebrows lifted, and then she said, "That was a terrible thing to do. So that's what you and she were talking about when you first brought me to her house. I didn't understand."

He nodded. "While I'm thankful, of course, that she isn't dying, I'm disappointed in her. She tricked me. And she made a fool of me, which really hurt."

Maurelle bit her lip and looked round briefly.

"I have to tell you, you're a terrible liar," he added as she faced him. "I think."

She blushed and looked away again. When she looked at him again, he offered an apologetic smile.

"Why were you living like a vagrant? You told me you have money? Why not stay in a hotel?" he asked, then, after a moment, continued to probe, "Were you hiding from someone?"

Looking increasingly uncomfortable, Maurelle replied, "It . . . it's complicated."

Dave noted his last query had hit a nerve, but chose to divert from too quickly pursuing this line of questioning lest she go silent altogether or even bolt from the bistro. "How old are you? And don't lie."

"You think I would lie about my age?"

"Many women do."

"That's something I've not felt the need to do—at least not yet. I'm twenty-seven."

"Where are you from—really?" Watching for her reaction, he added, "I know your accent is British."

She smiled. "I gather you're American, or I suppose half American and half French since you have a French grandmother."

"Correct."

She lowered her eyes and paused. When she raised her eyes, she whispered, "I'm half French, as well. And half English."

Dave twisted his mouth slightly. Why had she hesitated to tell him that? He leaned forward. "Please, Maurelle, tell me who—or what—you're running away from?"

She reached for her glass and nervously took a deep gulp of wine.

"As I said, it's complicated," she said, trying to look casual, but failing badly. "I can't tell you. Not yet. Please give me some time. I barely know you."

He tapped his fingers on the table, thinking. She could be playing with him, trying to appear mysterious to make him more interested. No, that wouldn't explain her living in a cave. More likely, she was in some sort of trouble. When they'd met outside the bakery, she'd seemed willing to sit and drink coffee with him until the gendarmes arrived. He picked up his wine glass and stared into the liquid. If it was the gendarmes that made her run, why would she stick around Reynier? Why not move on? Had he missed something? Did she see something else that spooked her? Was it him?

"Look," he said, "I'm not trying to make you more uncomfortable. But I need to know who—or what—I'm dealing with. You're staying in my grandmother's house—and you're welcome, you can't live in a damned cave. But, honestly, I need to know I can trust you not to rob her blind." He sat back, and watched her, silently taking in every detail of her reaction.

She squirmed slightly, her fingers wrapping firmly around the stem of her glass. She sipped the last drops of wine and set it back down. Without looking at Dave, she picked up her napkin and refolded it.

"You're stalling," Dave said, trying hard not to show his frustration. "Talk to me. I'm not your enemy."

Maurelle tapped her chin with her finger as she looked at Dave. Then it was as though a dark shadow fell across her eyes like an eclipse. She turned her head away, and looked around the crowded bistro, then back at Dave. "We can't talk here. Not about this. Please."

Dave finished his wine. "I guess I can wait. But not too

long."

Romain reappeared, setting the hors d'oeuvres in front of them, and Dave breathed in the heavenly scent. He hadn't realized until now how hungry he was.

"Bon appetit," Maurelle said, and Dave repeated the phrase, while he refilled both of their wine glasses.

As they ate and talked, they kept their conversation light.

"What's England like? I've always wanted to see the country but haven't gotten around to it. Did you live in London, or in a more rural area?"

"London. Though my grandparents lived in a small village in the West Country. They passed away years ago."

Dave nodded.

"Do you miss England?"

"I haven't been away long," she said. "Only a few weeks. Still, I do miss some things. Well, as you know already, I miss sleeping in a bed, and of course bathing indoors."

She laughed. Looking up at Dave, a light danced in her eyes, and Dave caught his breath. He couldn't believe how beautiful she looked.

"And do you have someone special you miss," he asked, "a husband or boyfriend?"

Maurelle sipped her wine. "I do not."

"No serious relationship?"

"Once. We lived together for two years—until I caught him cheating on me with another woman."

Dave thought of Simone again. "How long ago was that?"

"A few months," Maurelle said, looking at him squarely.

She appeared to be waiting for more questions, but Dave didn't say anything. He swallowed another bite of food, pondering this new information. Could that be it? He was pursuing her after the break-up?

"I'm divorced," he offered. It was part her fault but more my fault, if I'm being honest."

"It must have been hard, especially if there were children involved."

"No children."

She leaned forward, her elbow on the table, and rested her chin on her palm, studying him. "You didn't remarry?"

Dave shrugged again. She was trying to turn the tables on him. He decided to change the subject. "Do you—or did you—have a job?"

"That seems like a different lifetime," she whispered. "I left my job. I'm not sure what I will do now."

"What kind of work did you do?"

She hesitated. "I was a school teacher. I taught English Literature. But that's over."

He smiled. "I'm a published author, but you wouldn't think it if you listened to my editor. He complains that I need to go back to school and learn more about grammar. Admittedly, I'm not the best writer, but luckily for me people buy my books anyway."

Maurelle laughed. "What kind of books do you write?"

"Mystery and crime novels. I've thought of trying another genre, but my agent says I should stick to what I know."

She looked at him quizzically, and opened her mouth to speak, but she closed it when Romain appeared with their main course.

"Is there anything else I can get for you, Monsieur?"

"I don't think so. How about you, Maurelle?"

She shook her head.

"I think we're fine," he said. Romain left, and Dave turned his attention back to Maurelle. "You were about to say something?"

"Oh, I was wondering about your writing. What makes you write the kind of stories you write?"

"I used to be a police detective back in Chicago. I quit several years ago."

Dave knew he'd struck a nerve when her face blanched. Now he was sure she'd been spooked yesterday by the gendarmes. It wasn't an ex-boyfriend pursuing her.

"Why did you leave the police force?"

"Long story. I don't want to bore you with it. I guess I'd rather save that for another day too." He tried from then on to talk about trivial things, knowing that he would get the answers he needed in due course. For now, he would be patient. But damn, that was going to be hard. And then he would have to figure out what to do. He damned well didn't want another Diana Lewis situation.

Later, as they made their way out of the popular bistro, they bumped into Paul Lepage and a group of friends.

Paul said, "Bonsoir," and then gave Maurelle an appraising look after which he smiled knowingly at Dave. Dave gritted his teeth and hoped that this encounter wouldn't make the gossip network, but deep down he knew it would.

After brief introductions, Dave marched away, with Maurelle practically jogging in order to keep up.

BACK AT THE house, they stood awkwardly in the living room, neither of them speaking. Maurelle finally broke the silence. "Thank you again for the dinner. It was the best I've had since I came to France."

"You're welcome. And thank you for spending the evening with me. Would you like something to drink? I'm sure Grand-mère has some wine around here."

"No thank you. It's still early, I know, but I'm quite tired. If you don't mind, I'd rather go to bed."

"Okay. Good night. Sleep well."

"Good night."

As she climbed the staircase, she felt his eyes boring into her back. She had to force herself to keep her pace slow and steady. When she reached the landing and was out of his view, she dashed to her bedroom, shut the door firmly behind her, and pressed her back against it as if she were bracing it from falling down. Her heart thudded hard and tears trembled on her eyelids. So much for her quiet dinner, several hours of sleep, and an early morning flit before anyone else awoke. Dave had postponed his trip. Translated, that meant, 'If you leave again, I'll come and find you'.

Maurelle closed her eyes and sagged until she was sitting on the floor. She drew her knees up to her chest and bent her head forward, resting her forehead on her knees. Feeling the strain of the day drain whatever energy remained, she pulled herself up and dragged her body over to her bed. She removed her shoes, pulled back the bedcovers, lay down without bothering to undress, and covered herself with the bedcovers.

Unable to quiet her mind, she took several deep breaths and settled back against the pillows, staring up at the ceiling. Watching the moonlight and shadows dance about like a theatre production, she thought about the shows and plays and ballets she'd enjoyed watching with her boyfriend or with her mother in London, from the Tricycle Theatre to Sadlers Wells, from the Globe to the Electric Cinema.

She eventually drifted in and out of sleep, but her memories and her nightmares intertwined so that she wasn't sure which was worse—sleeping or lying awake. In her latest nightmare, she was still in London, in a room that at first looked like her bedroom but which she knew was the Old Bailey. Dave was questioning her relentlessly and causing her to break down and finally confess to make him stop.

She woke up and jerked to a sitting position, trembling and

covered in perspiration. After throwing off her covers, she lay back down, her eyes wide open but still seeing the images as if she were back in the nightmare. Stop it, she told herself. It's your subconscious mind playing with you, seizing Dave's background and weaving it in with everything else.

But that knowledge didn't really help.

She struggled to empty her mind, but the dream's images wouldn't go away, and she began shaking again. She didn't know what time it was, but she sprang out of bed, grabbed her duffel bag, and started pulling out things that she could leave behind. Once the bag was lightened, she slung the strap over her shoulder, glanced at her sleeping bag, and decided to leave it behind. Carefully, she opened her door and peeked into the dark hallway. Stepping out the door, she made her way down the stairs as quietly as possible. One step squeaked. She jumped, then froze and listened. No lights came on. She continued downward. At the bottom of the stairs, she looked toward the kitchen. No sign of anyone. She headed for the front door and crashed straight into something.

Horrified, she stepped back, her mouth gaping open.

Dave was staring at her, though she couldn't see his expression in the darkness. She braced herself, fearing his anger, and knowing that she deserved it after everything he'd done for her.

CHAPTER ELEVEN

"GLAD YOU'RE UP already," Dave said in a conversational tone. "I'm starved. How about you?"

Maurelle was too surprised to do more than nod.

"Why don't you go on into the kitchen? I'll take your bag back upstairs and meet you there."

Before she could say anything in response, Dave grabbed the bag out of her hand and started up the stairs. Stopping on the second step, he turned to her. "You promised me that you wouldn't disappear during the night."

"I—I'm sorry," she said.

He stared at her for a moment before continuing up the stairs.

Maurelle closed her eyes. She could dash out the door without her bag, but what good would that do? She needed her money. Besides, he would only find her and bring her back. Resigned, she turned and headed toward the kitchen in this house that she was beginning to loathe. She flipped on the light switch and gazed around the room. A display of copper pots and dried flowers were perched on a shelf above the range. Assorted everyday cooking utensils hung from hooks below the shelf, and ornately patterned tiles in earth tones formed a backsplash directly behind the stove. The whole cooking area might have been described as charming had she been in a more receptive mood. She felt a hand on her shoulder and jumped.

Dave said, "Sorry. I didn't mean to startle you."

"I didn't hear you come in."

He motioned for her to sit at the dinner table, while he turned on the faucet to get water for the coffee pot.

Maurelle sat down, again looking at more of the kitchen decor, from the shiny walnut cabinetry and the elegant table made from the same wood to the intricately appointed chairs caned in green, tan, and black stripes. She had only vaguely noticed the furnishings during the tense lunch yesterday, but seeing them now, she decided the whole room had a kind of French country air, yet was current and could even be described as gourmet classy. The smell of the coffee now brewing added to that atmosphere.

When Dave sat down next to her, she cringed inwardly, expecting his anger to spill out.

"I hope you slept well," he said. "Coffee's nearly ready. Would you like some?"

She nodded, and studied his face, noting the creases in his forehead, the warning cloud that he seemed to be struggling to reign in.

"Dave," she whispered, "I truly am sorry. I appreciate what you've done for me. But I don't want to be a burden nor do I want you or your grandmother getting entangled in my problems."

He looked into her eyes as if he were trying to read her mind and Maurelle fought against the impulse to look away.

"You're not a burden. At least not yet," he said. "But please don't try to leave without talking."

"All right, I won't. I promise"

He gave her a smile and stood, returning a couple of minutes later with two cups of steaming coffee as his grandmother suddenly fluttered into the room.

"I smelled coffee."

Dave smiled and handed one of the cups to her. He went back to the coffee to pour another cup.

"When I've finished my coffee, I'll prepare my specialty," Fabienne said. She faced Maurelle squarely. "Crêpes. I hope you enjoy them. Strawberry confiture?"

"I'm sure I'll love them."

"Grand-mère is the best cook in the village. Everyone was disappointed when she sold her café, but I'm lucky. I still get to eat her scrumptious creations."

Fabienne blushed and wagged her hand toward him. "My grandson exaggerates."

"Thing is, Grand-mère knows darn well that she can out-cook everyone around here, including Jeannette, who thinks she does everything best."

Fabienne set her cup down on the table and walked over to the refrigerator to gather the ingredients for her crêpes.

"Is there anything I can do to help?" Maurelle asked.

"No, no, you relax. I'll take care of everything."

Half an hour later, as they began their meal, Maurelle said, "Dave was right. These are delicious."

Fabienne beamed, and Maurelle couldn't believe the change in her. Perhaps she'd misjudged the elderly woman. Of course, she told herself, it might also be Dave's presence that made the difference—either in herself or in Fabienne. Throughout breakfast, everyone chatted and laughed, and Maurelle felt an unexpected lightness that she expected would be short-lived.

DAVE WHISTLED WHILE he cleared the breakfast table, then filled the sink with warm, soapy water and scrubbed the dirty dishes. With Maurelle in the bathroom taking a shower, and his grandmother upstairs straightening up, Dave had time to think about recent events.

Last night, after Maurelle had gone to bed, he'd waited up for his grandmother to come home. When she returned from her evening out, they talked long into the night, mostly resolving their earlier impasse. He explained that he couldn't walk away and not find out what was going on with Maurelle—was she a victim, perhaps being pursued by someone who wanted her dead, was she a runaway from an abusive situation, or was she a criminal?

Fabienne admitted that she still disapproved of his involvement with the girl, but she agreed to play hostess for a while because it was important to Dave. And besides, she shared his curiosity, if not his desire to play detective.

As for Maurelle, Dave had expected another escape attempt, and though he'd hoped he was wrong, he had taken the precaution of sleeping in the living room after Fabienne went upstairs to bed.

Even with Fabienne's assurances that she would be more congenial, Dave was pleasantly surprised in the improved relationships between the women. Both were trying to get along. Fabienne had even invited Maurelle to use her washer and dryer, which made Maurelle so happy that she rushed upstairs, returning moments later with her bag full of dirty clothes.

A sudden noise behind him made Dave turn around. Fabienne had returned from upstairs, where she had gone to make her bed. She smiled, "Well, at least I'm getting something out of this. It's about time you help with the dishes."

"You know, I did try to help around the house when I first got here and thought you were dying. But you wouldn't have it. You kept pushing me out the door to see Simone. I should have suspected subterfuge then." Dave chuckled as he shook his head.

She waved her hand at him. Almost as an afterthought, she said, "If you aren't too busy this afternoon, would you drive me to Vendome? Coralie said she'll loan you her car."

He frowned. "Why do you need to go there? I went to Vendome for you yesterday."

"I have an appointment at the hospital."

Dave stared at her in bewilderment. "Okay, now I'm confused. Didn't you admit to me that you aren't ill?"

She waved her arm again. "It's nothing serious. Routine tests that I scheduled more than a month ago. Coralie was going to drive me, but her employee, Robert, called in sick and she has no else to cover for him in the store. I could cancel, I guess. Of course a woman my age can't afford to miss too many doctor appointments."

Dave rolled his eyes when Fabienne wasn't looking. So she was playing the guilt card again.

He sighed. "All right. What time is your appointment?"

She clapped her hands together and smiled. "Two o'clock."

"I'm sure Maurelle won't mind getting out of the house for a while," Dave said, smiling benignly.

Her face turned pink and she clenched her jaw, but said nothing.

THE SCENIC DRIVE to Vendome proved more pleasant than Dave had expected. At first Fabienne pouted because he had brought Maurelle along, but later she surprised him by behaving herself and even acting friendly.

Fabienne's routine tests include a mammogram, EKG, and bone density test. While Fabienne was undergoing the tests, Dave and Maurelle sat in the waiting room and chatted and continued to get better acquainted. But they both carefully avoided the hot topics.

Before returning home, the trio did some light shopping. Afterward, Dave found a pleasant restaurant where the three of them lounged under a red and white umbrella on a terrace and talked about music, movies, and books while they ate a light dinner. Dave watched Maurelle as she relaxed, talking and laughing with Fabienne. He was amazed at the change in her. After her shower, she had styled her hair in a French-braid down her back, and dressed up in a white sleeveless blouse that nicely showed off her tanned skin, and a sky blue skirt that danced around lightly in the gentle summer breeze. But it wasn't only her appearance that had changed over the past few days since he first saw her in the general store. She seemed calmer, more confident, and almost happy; though still she glanced round as though searching for or wanting to avoid someone.

When they returned to Reynier in the early evening, Dave dropped Fabienne and Maurelle off at the house and drove Coralie's car back to her house.

Afterwards, hiking back to Fabienne's, he pondered what to do for the rest of the evening. He really needed to spend time alone with Maurelle so that they could talk about her situation. But he admitted to himself that it wasn't the only reason. He felt at ease with her and simultaneously on edge, excited in a way he never was with Simone. As he opened the arched door, a scraggly long-haired tan terrier similar to the one the other day outside the bakery, pounced on him, and he stumbled backwards, surprised.

"What the hell?" Dave straightened up and looked around, but didn't see anyone. Bending down, he scooped up the young dog and strode into the kitchen where he found Fabienne and Simone sitting at the table drinking coffee and talking.

When they saw him, Simone stood and walked to him languidly. Leaning forward, she kissed him on both cheeks. "I see you've met our little guy. He's been abandoned and I brought him for you."

She smiled innocently, but Dave wasn't fooled.

"I don't need a dog."

"But I thought you liked animals," Simone said, "especially dogs. I thought you would be delighted."

"Well, you thought wrong," Dave said. "It's not that I don't like dogs. I had a dog for many years. But I can't take care of a pet right now. So, I guess you've got yourself a dog."

Simone pouted and put her hand on her hip. "I just—"

"Simone, I'm going back to Chicago soon. What do you expect me to do with the animal then?"

She shrugged. "I—we, Fabienne and I—hoped you might stay here longer."

Without another word, he spun on his heel and stomped into the living room, nearly smacking into Maurelle.

Maurelle looked surprised, but said nothing.

He grabbed her hand. "Come on. Get your shoes on. Let's go for a walk."

She hurried to the front door where her sneakers and her sandals lay. After a short hesitation, she grabbed the sandals and, hopping on one foot at a time, wiggled into them quickly.

"Where are we going?"

"I haven't the foggiest idea," he said, chuckling. "I needed to get out of there. Did you see the dog?" He walked past a few houses and past the chateau. Café Charbonneau, which was closed at this hour, was coming up.

She nodded, giving him a sideways glance. "Was the woman Simone?"

"Didn't my grandmother introduce you?"

"No," she said, quietly. "When she arrived, there was a lot of activity. They laughed and played with the dog. I watched for a few minutes, trying to stay out of the way, but went upstairs until just before you arrived." She glanced at him as he paused and kicked at a rock. "You should probably be there with them, don't you think?"

"I'm too angry right now."

Maurelle looked confused.

"It's a long story. Suffice it to say I don't enjoy being treated like a little boy."

A small smile touched her lips. "I have a hard time picturing you as a little boy."

Dave grasped her elbow and led her off the road near the café and onto the path leading to the troglodyte houses.

"Where are we going?"

"Do you remember the cave I told you about—the one with the fossils?"

She nodded. "I thought you made up that story."

"I want to take you there, if that's okay. If I'm going to be treated as if I'm a kid, I'm going to act like one."

Laughing, Maurelle rushed ahead, but he soon passed her by, with a quick look over his shoulder. He stopped, waited, then turned and climbed a narrow steep winding path. Near the top, he reached down and took her hand to help her navigate a particularly steep section of the path, scratching his arm on a thorny vine in the process. After a couple of more minutes of walking along a section of wall, he stopped and pushed away a mass of overgrown brush branches, and revealed a small cave opening. "Sorry it's so overgrown. It's been a long time since I was here last." As he let go of the branches, they fell back in place, allowing very little light to filter beyond the cave entrance. He moved the branches aside again, only this time he secured them behind a rock jutting out at the side of the entrance to let in more light, but it was still rather dark inside the cave. "Too bad I didn't think to bring a flashlight."

"It's not so bad," Maurelle said. "Your eyes will adjust quickly."

"I forgot that you're accustomed to caves," Dave said. He drew a circle in the tufa dust on the floor and then found a suitable rock to sit on while he chose his next words carefully. "I'm drawn to you, Maurelle. I can't say that I entirely understand it, but there's something about you that makes me want to know more. Don't get me wrong. I'm not exactly hitting on you. I just need to understand what's going on with you."

She sat next to him quietly atop her own rock, hugging her knees to her, with her long skirt draped over her legs, nearly touching her feet. He could barely see her face in the shadowy darkness, but he thought he detected a tremble in her body; from cold or from fear he couldn't tell.

After a moment, Dave took a deep breath and exhaled. In the softest voice he could manage, he asked, "What happened to you, Maurelle? What are you running from?"

She was silent for a while. Finally, she whispered, "Murder. I am wanted for murder."

CHAPTER TWELVE

THE CHATTER OF natterjack toads outside the cave grew louder, filling the sudden silence that had fallen between Dave and Maurelle with a muffled hammering sound. Dave used to love listening to them in the early evening when he was a kid. Tonight, their chattering grated on his nerves. He and Maurelle were sitting near the cave entrance, with only a trace of moonlight peeking through. She was closer to the entrance than he was. But he had the advantage since he faced the weak light filtering through the cave opening and could see her silhouette—her face turned slightly toward the exit, her chin quivering.

"Murder," Dave said, finally.

Her skirt rustled as she squirmed and tried to stand up. Dave half rose, leaned forward, and pulled her back down.

"I'm not here to judge you. Please talk to me. I'll help you if I can."

"You can't help." She pushed his hand away.

"I know that people get themselves into trouble. It doesn't mean they're bad people. Let me help, whatever the problem is."

"No. I really must leave now."

Dave took hold of both her hands and held them tightly together. "Look, I wanted to help you even though I guessed you were on the run. You ran away the other day when the gendarmes arrived in Reynier. Should I call them or take you to the Gendarmerie and let you answer their questions instead of mine? Is that what you want?"

"You're threatening me?" She tried to pull her hands from his grasp, but he held fast.

"I'm no longer a cop, but that doesn't mean I can sit back and do nothing. You're hiding from gendarmes and were living in a cave. Now you tell me you're wanted for murder. I need to know a lot more about what's going on. Tell me, or tell the gendarmes."

He heard a sharp intake of breath, then felt her body slump down in defeat.

"I don't really know where to begin," she said, her body trembling. Dave let go of one of her hands and placed his arm around her shoulder.

"Is it too cold in here?" he asked. "We can go somewhere else if you want."

"No, it's all right." She sighed, and pushed her side-sweeping bangs out of her eyes. "I just don't know where to begin," she repeated.

Dave wished now that he'd picked somewhere else to talk, somewhere warmer and with enough light that he could see her face and body language better. Perhaps he should have picked the old church on the hilltop. It wasn't cold outside and with the church's roof gone, the moonlight would have provided enough light. Too late now.

"I had been living with my boyfriend for almost a year," she began, "until I found him in bed with another woman. I had to move out of our flat. The lease was in his name because he lived there long before I moved in with him. Having no family left, and no really close friends, I had nowhere to go, so I checked into a hotel near my job. It was very expensive. I tried everything to find another flat, but nothing affordable was available in the area. During lunch one day, one of my colleagues, a friend in the English Department, told me her sister, Elizabeth Raybourne, who was recently divorced and in need of another source of income, was looking for a boarder." Maurelle paused a moment, the air again growing quiet except for the sound of the toads and crickets outside and a mouse scurrying around further into the cave.

"Go on."

"At first it seemed fine. But she had a teenage son, Jared, who was a pupil at the school where I worked. He wasn't one of my pupils and I didn't really know him." She hesitated, taking a deep breath. "He seemed bright but he told me his grades in maths and science were slipping. He asked me for help, and though they weren't my subjects, I began tutoring him at the house. A couple of months later, I heard teachers talking about him in the common room. They said that his grades were slipping in all subjects, and he wasn't trying."

Dave shifted, and stretched out his legs which were beginning to cramp. "What's a common room?"

"Oh, that's where teachers meet, take their breaks, and eat lunch."

"Ah. We call that a faculty lounge or staff room in the U.S. Okay, go on."

"I spoke to his aunt, my friend, about what I'd heard and she confirmed it. When I confronted him, he said he loved me. That's when it hit me that he'd used the tutoring as a way to get closer to me. Of course I told him I didn't share those feelings. I told him we couldn't become involved romantically. But he refused to accept it."

She was silent again.

"What happened then?"

"I stopped tutoring, of course. I avoided him altogether. But he wouldn't leave me alone. I watched the ads for flats constantly after that, and I finally moved out a couple of weeks later, when I found a suitable flat."

"I've heard similar stories back in the U.S." He didn't add that usually the teacher had actually been sexually involved with the student. She hadn't actually said she wasn't, but . . . . He shook his head slightly; it was hard to stop thinking like a detective.

Maurelle sighed. "Probably not like this case. Three weeks after I moved out, his mother found him dead in his bedroom. Someone had murdered him."

Dave was glad now for the darkness that shielded the surprise that must be written on his face, but he remained silent.

"It was all over the news," she said. "The police came to my flat while I was out shopping, one of the neighbors in my building informed me. From the very beginning, they were seeing me as a suspect, without even having talked to me. Then a former neighbor, an elderly man who lives across the street from the family, called. He suggested I should get away – he'd heard they were about to arrest me."

"Why did they think you did it?"

"There had been whispers at school, whispers of an affair. The school's governing board found out and suspended me from work until they could investigate. They suspended Jared from school also. The thing is, I had a key to the house while I lived there, but I gave back the key when I moved out."

"And you could have made a duplicate."

"Yes."

"Did you do it?" he asked abruptly. He wasn't expecting a confession, but he needed to spark a reaction.

"The police assumed I did." She showed almost no emotion.

"What kind of evidence did they have?"

"I have no idea. All I know for sure is that I didn't do it."

He rubbed his face and sighed. "If that's true, why did you run?"

"I got scared. I've heard too many stories of innocent people being convicted on circumstantial evidence and lies."

"But running away was a huge mistake."

"I know that now," she said. "I've even thought about going back and turning myself in, but do you know how scary that is?" She shrugged. "It was stupid, instinctive. If they were already thinking, from the start of the investigation, that I'd killed him, what must they think after I ran away? Wouldn't they automatically convict me?"

He moved away from her, feeling suddenly sick. He wanted to believe she was innocent. He knew she was a terrible liar. But he wasn't the best judge anymore. Once, he had believed he could always tell—plenty of officers got that way, sure they knew who was guilty and who was innocent. He'd found out the hard way that he didn't always know, and it had cost him his job. The silence that developed between them was like a dense fog, enveloping everything in its path and making him feel like he was drowning.

Angry at himself but unable to maintain control, he blurted, "I should have known. Grand-mère and Simone warned me about you. I'm a trained detective."

Maurelle didn't respond.

"My only explanation is that I tricked myself into believing I knew you." He chuckled dryly, without humor. "I don't even know your name. It's not Maurelle," he said, "that's for damn sure." He pushed his hand through his hair. "I knew you were in some kind of trouble, but I convinced myself that it wasn't anything serious." He stood abruptly, cracking his head with a loud thunk on the low ceiling for the second time in two days. "Ow, damn it!" He clapped his hand to his head, rubbing it. Pulling his hand back, he bent forward, turned slightly to his left, and carefully edged his way around Maurelle until he reached the cave opening. He ducked out and left, leaving her alone with her anguish.

Ten minutes later he entered his grandmother's house, stormed up the stairs, and walked straight into Maurelle's room. He grabbed her bags and carried them away.

"What's going on?"

Dave swung around. His grandmother stood outside her own bedroom, watching him. He sighed and felt some of his anger slip away. Instead of taking the bags to his room, he had another idea.

"Let me put these away, first, and then we can talk."

GRIEF THREATENED TO overwhelm Maurelle, but she bit her lip and suppressed it, closing her eyes and steeling herself. She sat alone, unable to move or even make a decision about what to do. The conversation had gone wrong like everything else she'd ever done. She'd shamed her mother, blown it with her boyfriend, messed up her job, messed up her life. She closed her eyes and pictured Jared—his long legs, slender body, blue eyes and blonde hair. Young enough to look innocent, old enough to get into trouble—and to drag her with him. The head teacher had questioned her about the relationship, having heard the rumors—who hadn't by then? She knew she had to stop it all, otherwise her life would be ruined. After the murder, she had to escape. What choice did she have? Ha. Her life was ruined anyway.

Her tears, unbidden and unwelcome, flowed freely until eventually worn out, she slipped into a fitful slumber.

She awoke lying on the hard cave floor, her face caked with white limestone dust that had formed a paste-like mask that itched. At first wiping at the mask half-heartedly with one hand, she soon gave up and focused instead on her situation. The mouse that had been rummaging around earlier, startled her momentarily as it darted past her into a crevice. Maurelle shook her head. *I'm just like that mouse.*

Earlier in the day when she had sat in the hospital with Dave, and later at the café, chatting about normal things, movies and music and books, she had almost felt light-hearted and optimistic, having lulled herself into thinking her troubles were disappearing and that maybe, just maybe, she could stay in Reynier.

Her naiveté had once again caused her to let down her guard. She would never be free, let alone carefree and happy. Her only option now was to go back to Fabienne's, somehow sneak in, and grab her duffel bag. After that she would vanish, change her name again, and change everything about her appearance. This time she would cut her hair, change the color, rent a flat, and work out of her home where she wouldn't have to deal with the public. Maybe she could teach English somewhere, private tutoring. Oh right! Scratch that.

She forced herself to get up and clean her face as best she could.

Peeking out of the cave, she was relieved to see no gendarmes waiting to cart her away. She slowly made her way back into the village and to Fabienne's house.

She stood facing the front door and wondered what time it was. Had they gone to bed? The streets were deserted, and most of the windows of the houses were dark, including this one. Placing her ear up to the door she listened, hoping the dog wasn't there to betray her. Not hearing anything, she carefully turned the doorknob, pushed the door inward as quietly as possible, and glanced around. Silently, she stepped through the threshold, leaving the door slightly ajar to expedite her escape. Although the living room was dark, light fanned out of the kitchen, making her stiffen. She held her breath and moved slowly toward the stairs, placing her left hand on the baluster. She froze when a male voice, Dave's, drifted out of the kitchen. She heard her name, which produced in her an overwhelming need to know what Dave was saying.

She quietly edged closer to the kitchen entrance, almost knocking over a vase with an umbrella in it in the process.

"How could I have been so stupid? I convinced myself that I was drawn to her because she needed my help, but that wasn't entirely true. I needed to prove something to myself."

"Why is this crime important to you? Do you think she killed that boy?" Fabienne asked.

"Damned if I know. But I don't want any part of it. I'm done with helping women like her. I'm done with helping people hide from justice. And I'm done with the judicial system that half the time doesn't work. People getting off on technicalities, while others get convicted of crimes they didn't commit. Dirty cops, bosses controlled by politicians, money speaks louder than truth, I'm really sick of it all."

"It isn't always that way, surely," Fabienne said.

"Enough of the time."

"What has that got to do with Maurelle?"

"Everything."

Confirming her fears, Maurelle wheeled around and tiptoed up the stairs to the bedroom she'd stayed in.

She opened the door and peered inside. She dared not switch on the light but luckily the moon outside was full, casting enough light through the sheer window curtains to let her see around the tiny room.

Carefully, she moved toward the chair in the corner of the room where she had left her duffel bag. In the darkness, she stubbed her sandaled toe on the edge of the bed's walnut footboard and almost cried out in immediate pain, but caught herself in time. When she reached the chair, the bag wasn't there. She scrambled frantically about, searching every inch of the room and the wardrobe and even under the bed, though she knew logically it wouldn't fit. It was gone. She dashed out of her room and into Dave's room, rummaged through his wardrobe, and emerged five minutes later empty-handed.

She stood in the hallway, debating whether to search Fabienne's room. But when the grandfather clock downstairs chimed, her heart jumped, sending her instead flying down the stairs and out the front door. She didn't bother closing the door behind her.

She didn't look back. Maurelle ran blindly through the shadowy streets, past the café, past the general store, past the post office, without a destination in mind. All she knew for sure was that she couldn't stay another minute in Reynier. She was an outsider here—everywhere. And without her money and belongings, she had nothing. She had earlier considered dumping the duffel bag, knowing that she could replace most of the contents. But she would have taken her bumbag which contained her pendant and the guidebook she was going to use to plan where she'd go next. She would have taken her identification documents—just in case. Most of all, she would have taken her cash, which could have bought her the basics for survival and maybe could have allowed her to rent a shabby flat in some remote place where no one would care whether she fit in or not.

CHAPTER THIRTEEN

DAVE CLOSED HIS eyes as if that would shut out his thoughts. He reopened them when his grandmother sighed. Fabienne was sitting in the chair across from him, and her wrinkled face and drooping body made him regret all over again dragging her into his problem. "Why don't we call it a night?" he said gently. "We aren't going to resolve anything now. I'm too damned tired and confused."

Fabienne yawned and nodded. She stood slowly and picked up her bifocals from the dining table. Strands of her white hair fell loose from her chignon and strayed into her face like bees fluttering around a flower, making her use her hand to swat them away.

Dave thought of his grandmother's beloved roses that she grew in her garden; she too was a delicate rose, only she had wilted a little tonight because of stress and lack of sleep. If he hadn't been so focused on her appearing too well to have cancer, he might have noticed sooner how much she'd aged and how vulnerable she now was. Even five years ago, she'd been more energetic. He thought back to the day she, Connie, and he had walked the three-and-a-half miles to Belvidere on market day, stopping periodically to rest. They had shopped for hours, eaten lunch, and walked back home again. Fabienne had been tired, but not much more so than he and Connie. Now, Fabienne got tired simply walking through town on those big shopping days.

That thought made him walk over to her and wrap his arms around her. Feeling closer to her than he had since his arrival here, he whispered, "Thank you, Grand-mère. I'm sorry to burden you with my problems. I didn't—"

He wanted to say more, but he choked up. He hadn't felt this way since his break-up with his wife, and he wondered how much he had been holding back.

"You can talk to me anytime," Fabienne said. She patted him on the shoulder, leaned back, and looked him in the eyes. "I'm sorry I'm such a busy-body. I gave you a hard time about that girl, and you were only trying to help her. You couldn't have known what she was hiding."

Dave opened his mouth to say something, but she held up her hand, shushing him.

"I know you, dear boy. I know that you beat yourself up because you let down your guard and trusted. But you shouldn't worry. You still have your instincts intact. Your problem is that you also have a good heart and a desire to believe the best about people, even though you've seen more than your share of bad people through your police work. That's part of what made you a good detective."

He wanted to believe what she was saying, but he'd always prided himself on his instincts, his objectivity and his bulldog attitude toward finding the truth, until . . . . He shook his head. He wasn't sure anymore that he possessed any of those qualities.

"But I have a lifetime of experience," Fabienne continued. "I don't have all the answers you need but I will listen. I may give you advice, if I can. Do with it what you will."

Dave smiled, kissed her cheek, and hugged her again, stroking her hair.

"Grand-mère, I'm sorry I've been mean and difficult lately. Here I am a guest in your home, and I've been behaving like a spoiled little boy."

"It's nothing," she said, shrugging hers shoulders. She wagged her hand at him as she moved toward the living room. "I was wrong too."

Dave grinned. "I wish I could say that makes my behavior acceptable, but I can't really do that. I've been a stubborn fool."

Fabienne stopped and spun around to face him. "Well, I can't imagine where you get that from," she said.

Dave chuckled. He followed her into the living room and bumped right into her when she stopped abruptly.

"Did you leave the door open?" she asked.

Following her gaze, he saw the wide-open door.

"No, it wasn't me." He switched on the lights and searched the main level of the house. Finding nothing, he said, "Wait here. I'll look upstairs." Before he left, he looked at his grandmother's ghostly white face. "Don't worry," he added, patting her hand reassuringly. He dashed up the stairs, switching on every light and searching the second floor, room by room. When he was done, he ran back down the stairs and headed toward the back door.

"Where are you going?" Fabienne called.

"She's not here. You should go on up to bed. I'm going to get something out of the cellar."

A few minutes later, he arrived at the tiny cave in the back portion of the house, a cave similar to the ones many residents had in their houses. As with most of these, it was used for storage. He flipped on the lights and pulled out the duffel bag that he'd hidden earlier, leaving the sleeping bag. When he re-entered the main house, he locked the doors so Maurelle couldn't sneak back in.

"Is that hers?"

"I thought you were going to bed. Everything is fine. Maurelle must have come back to get this, but she's gone now."

"Are you going after her?"

"I'm going to bed," he said.

Relief spread across Fabienne's face. She kissed his cheek before climbing the stairs to her room.

Dave picked up Maurelle's sneakers which he found near the front closet and put them in the duffel bag. Afterwards, he switched off the lights and climbed upstairs, closing his bedroom door behind him. He put the bag down on his bed and sat down. Taking a deep breath, he unzipped the bag and began unpacking it, laying her clothing in neat stacks on his bedspread.

After her clothes, shoes, and handbag, he found a fanny-pack with her necklace tucked inside, along with some coins. Digging deeper in the duffel bag, he found a cloth toiletry bag with deodorant, shampoo, make-up, perfume, and dental floss. Loose in the duffel bag were maps, a guidebook, two magazines, and three paperback romance novels. He set those items on the floor near his feet. Next, he found two small purple flashlights and he shook his head, smiling. The kind of flashlights he would expect her to have. His hand hit the bottom of the bag, but something wasn't right. He glanced at the outside of the bag and then the inside. It had a fake bottom.

He ripped it apart and found some loose items: an expensive looking man's watch and a small box containing what appeared to be childhood trinkets. Beside those were a zippered bag and a wallet.

His jaw tightened involuntarily as he studied the driver's license inside the wallet: Maura Barrington, 11 Willoughby Crescent, London, England; Date of Birth: March 5, 1986. Well, at least she hadn't lied about her age or where she was from, but that didn't make him feel better.

Thumbing through the wallet, he found two credit cards in

her name and five- hundred-and-thirty Euros, roughly equivalent to seven-hundred-twenty-five U.S. dollars. Tucked into a side pocket, he found three wallet-size photos that appeared to be childhood photos of Maurelle, and two more photos of a man and a woman. Her parents?

He set down the wallet on the bed and picked up the small zippered bag, running his hand over the soft worn-leather. Slowly, he unzipped it and pulled the sides apart to get a good look at the contents. Cash. Lots of cash. He picked up the thick straps and counted. Nine altogether. Automatically, he examined the front and back bills in the first strap. They were English pounds. His years of training had taught him how to spot counterfeit bills and these looked real. Thumbing through each strap, he verified that each consisted of £20 notes. He counted the first strap: one hundred notes totaling two thousand pounds. Assuming each strap was the same, which it appeared based on the thickness and weight of them, he was staring at eighteen-thousand pounds, equal to roughly twenty-seven-thousand U.S. dollars.

So much money. It looked as though she was prepared and hadn't simply left in a panic. Had she planned it all? But then why simply come to France and hide in a cave? It made little sense.

SIMONE SAT ON her sofa with the dog lying halfway over her lap, continuously using its nose to demand she pet him. No matter how many times she pushed him away, he kept coming back for more. The disgusting matted hair on the animal was in dire need of scrubbing and combing, but she wasn't about to do it. After she got rid of him, she would need to fumigate her home too.

"Maman, please, can't you keep the dog?" Simone asked.

"No. Serge is allergic to dogs. Besides, I thought you were giving it to Dave."

"I tried. He doesn't want him."

"Why can't you keep him? He'd be good company for you."

"You know I don't like animals. I should never have adopted him. Giving this mutt to Dave backfired terribly. I think now he's angry with me."

Coralie said, "Give him a day or two. He'll get over it."

"I don't know. He left Fabienne's this evening with that woman. He left me standing there gaping like a . . . a . . . I don't know what. It was humiliating. And she's much prettier than I remember from the other time I saw her." Simone looked toward the door, wishing Dave would come to his senses and ring the downstairs bell to let her know he was waiting at the bottom of the stairs to be let in. Instead, he was probably gazing into that damn woman's eyes and listening to her every word as if she was the only person in the world.

"Do you love him?" her mother asked.

Simone looked down at the dog. "Love? I don't know. I'm tired of being alone. You have Serge. I have no one. I'm not desperate enough to be one of Jonas Lefevre's mistresses."

"Do not say such things. Do you hear? You will find someone. What about Zacharie Gardinier over in Belvidere? He would be a good catch. I'm sure he is interested. He was eager to talk with you when we saw him in that restaurant. Do you remember? It was about a month ago. I don't know the name of the restaurant."

"Zacharie is all right, I suppose. I was hoping for someone more . . . sophisticated."

"Then don't give up on Dave. Not yet. But don't forget you're thirty-five and still single."

Simone groaned inwardly and wanted to scream. Did her mother—and grandmother, for that matter—have to keep reminding her of that? Maybe it was time to move back to Paris. She might have been lonely in Paris, but at least there she wasn't treated like a visitor, a newcomer. Shouldn't the fact that her mother grew up in Reynier have made Simone immediately part of the community? Even buying Fabienne's café and running it hadn't made her many friends.

"Maman, you're forgetting that I was married once."

"I'm only trying to help you, dear. Maybe you should try another approach with Dave. Make him see you as wife material. I remember Fabienne told me that his marriage broke up because he wanted children and his wife didn't."

Simone's mouth flew open and snapped shut again. "I'm not that desperate!"

"You could practice with the dog. Show Dave that you can be loving and nurturing."

Simone grimaced and didn't answer. At that immediate moment, she thought, being alone wasn't that bad. At least she didn't have to do what other people demanded. The dog sat up and looked into her eyes. He leaned in and licked her face, making her smile in spite of herself. At least somebody cared about her feelings. Maybe with a good bath, he could stick around.

CHAPTER FOURTEEN

AFTER A NIGHT in the woods southeast of Reynier, Maurelle realized she was in a far worse position than she had thought. Not only was she without money and without maps, she was also without decent shoes. Her feet, clad in flimsy and painful sandals, were blistered and raw.

She had hitchhiked before, without any incidents or problems. But her recent experiences had taught her to expect the worst, especially when she couldn't even trust herself. Last night, when Dave had asked her to grab her shoes and walk with him, she could have been practical, chosen her gym shoes and been comfortable. She could have gone upstairs, changed out of her skirt, and into jeans. But she hadn't. She wanted to look pretty and feminine—for him.

She closed her eyes. It was useless to dwell on things she couldn't change.

Her best chance for finding a ride would be to head to the main road, away from the isolated country lanes like the one on which Dave had found her. Of course, more traffic meant greater risk of being caught by law enforcement. And that meant being sent back to England. But what other choice did she have?

Maurelle turned toward the main road in hopes of catching a

ride. She stopped at a creek along the way and scrubbed her face with the cold water. It was well after sunrise when she finally reached the road. All she wanted was to get a ride. The chance to also get a bit of rest filled her with anticipation and a spurt of renewed energy as she breezed along the rough pavement. Of course, nothing was ever easy and this was no exception, as most of the traffic was heading in the other direction. Even the few cars going in the right direction shot straight past her. She continued walking until she reached the edge of Belvidere.

With feet aching horribly, Maurelle sat down on a grassy mound alongside the road to rest, her legs stretched out in front of her. She closed her eyes, soaking in the sunshine, wishing she could catch up on sleep, even if only for a few minutes. Her eyes popped open at the sound of a vehicle approaching and slowing down. It was a loud vehicle, which told her without looking that it wasn't one of the cars Dave had borrowed.

Slowly, she turned her head and glanced over her shoulder. A green pick-up truck had stopped on the side of the road near her. She leapt up and rushed to the vehicle.

A rather handsome man with black hair rolled down the passenger window. He regarded her quizzically. "Bonjour, Mademoiselle. Perhaps we met before, no? You look familiar?"

Her heart thudded and she felt sick. Did he recognize her from the news? "I—I don't think so."

He studied her, making her want to run in the opposite direction. Suddenly his face split into a wide grin. "I know. Dave Martin introduced us outside the bistro the other night. Where are you headed? And why are you out here alone? Did you and Dave have a fight?"

As panic coursed through her, she struggled to maintain composure. Thinking fast, she said, "I remember. You're a friend of Dave's, yes? Anyway, I was on my way to Vendome. I hiked here, planning to take the train from Belvidere to Vendome. But someone snatched my handbag. I really should have been more attentive, especially since I had heard about similar problems in the area recently."

"That's awful. Did you report it?"

She nodded, hoping that he wouldn't ask for details.

"Well now, come. Get in." The man reached over to the passenger door and opened it. "I'm on my way to Vendome to pick up supplies for a remodeling project I'm working on for a customer. Your company is more than welcome."

She climbed into the truck. He would probably tell Dave about this as soon as he had the chance. She sighed. The damage was already done.

"I'm Paul. Paul Lepage," the man said. "I apologize. I don't remember your name."

"Maurelle." She looked away, out of the window, trying to dissuade him from further conversation.

"After I run my errands," Paul said, "I can pick you up and drive you back to Reynier. Maybe we could have lunch together."

She continued to gaze out the window, pretending she was interested in the scenery as she deliberated on how to respond. She was hungry, but she didn't dare stick around. "That's kind of you. But I have a busy day planned."

"Well, you're going to need a ride back, aren't you? And if you and Dave aren't together anymore, you can stay at my place."

"Thank you," Maurelle said, "but I'm meeting someone." She hesitated, glancing back at Paul. He had a friendly manner, though his piercing green eyes made her feel as if he was undressing her. "I'll get a ride back to Reynier, I'm sure."

To her relief, he nodded and returned his attention to the road. But moments later, he resumed the conversation.

"Are you meeting Dave? Does that mean you are still together? That you're still staying with him and Fabienne, I mean."

She merely shrugged, not trusting herself to speak.

Although the rest of the drive was quiet and seemingly peaceful, Maurelle kept her body braced for action—as though he might grab her and force her to return to Reynier, or worse. She would jump out of the moving vehicle, if necessary.

As they entered Vendome, she kept a lookout for recognizable sights that she hoped would help her get her bearings. When they'd passed the hospital where Fabienne had received her medical tests yesterday, she relaxed a bit. From the hospital, lovely red-brick sidewalks lined the street and colorful gardens of red, pink, yellow, and white flowers brightened the roadside leading up to the river which they were about to cross. The short bridge resembled a drawbridge over a castle moat. She immediately recognized the castle-like entrance to the old town center—the old gate house of St. George, an ivy-covered building composed of two large crenellated and machicolated towers connected by a pavilion that topped the archway through which the road tunneled. After Fabienne's tests, they had also passed through that gate, ate at a lovely outdoor café near Parc Ronsard, and strolled in the lush park along the riverfront.

The truck passed through the gate and drove past centuries-old tall and narrow buildings, which now housed restaurants, cafés, shops, and offices.

"Where should I drop you off?" Paul asked while they were stopped at the first traffic light.

She hesitated until she recalled reading that the town's greatest monument was the old abbey-church of the Trinity, which seemed like a good 'meeting place'. "Oh, the Eglise de la Trinite, if that's not too much trouble," she said.

"No problem. We're actually close. It's right near the town square, Place Saint-Martin." He pointed to the left, and Maurelle could see the spires of the massive gray stone abbey in the distance. A few turns later, he pulled up.

"Thank you, Monsieur Lepage. I am grateful." She smiled sweetly, and pulled the door handle to get out.

"You're most welcome, Maurelle. I'll give you my mobile number. Call me if you need a ride—or anything. I would love to take you out to lunch or dinner. And you are welcome to stay at my home for as long as you like." He pulled out a piece of paper from a notebook on the floor of his truck and jotted down the number.

He handed the paper to her. "I hope you'll call. Oh, and by the way, it's illegal to hitchhike in France. I don't want you to get into trouble."

She nodded, smiled, and tucked the piece of paper into her blouse pocket more to humor him than anything else. Even if she had coins for making a phone call, which she did not, she wouldn't be calling him or anyone else. Silently, she climbed down from the truck and shut the door behind her.

After Paul drove away, she walked toward the main road again, hoping to find another ride soon. Traffic was extremely heavy here, which gave her hope but also increased her risk because a local Gendarmerie was located here.

As she strolled along the red-bricked sidewalk near the abbey, smells emanated from nearby restaurants and cafés, making her stomach growl. She tried to ignore them. She turned onto St. Martin Square and continued to the minor road, which she knew would eventually lead her back to the main road.

By the time she finally reached the main highway, she chastised herself for not asking Paul to let her out at Parc Ronsard, which would have saved her time and energy, both of which were in short supply. Although the brief rest in the car had helped her feet temporarily, they now ached even worse than before. On top of that, the bright sunlight and intense heat was unrelenting.

A car slowed down behind her, making her step into the dirt beside the road and turn around. Holding her breath, she watched the brown Peugeot pull up closer and stop. The driver rolled down his window. "Bonjour, Mademoiselle. Do you need a ride?"

Maurelle nodded.

"Where are you going?" he asked. His eyes were sharp and assessing.

"South. As far as Spain eventually," she blurted without thinking. She bit her tongue, wondering if maybe she should have given a closer destination.

"I can take you part of the way."

She hesitated, studying him carefully. He was attractive in a distinguished sort of way and reminded her of one of her former college professors. He wore what appeared to be a dark blue Armani suit with a pale gray shirt and tie. His hair was dark brown streaked with gray, his mustache neatly trimmed. She couldn't see his eye color behind his dark sunglasses. Overall, he looked polished, refined. Safe?

"Guess I should introduce myself. Pierre Auberge here," he said. "I'm on a business trip for my company. Only going as far as Limoges, but I can at least get you a little closer to your destination."

Maurelle vacillated. She wanted the ride, but she felt uneasy. Auberge looked respectable, and she'd accepted rides from strangers before. She had even gone home with Dave who, although she'd bumped into him a few times, had also been a stranger. Of course, that hadn't gone particularly well, she reminded herself. Taking a step backward, she twisted her foot slightly and the strap of her left sandal scraped over one of her blisters. She bit her lip to keep from crying out in pain.

"Merci, Monsieur." She hoped she was making a wise decision as she slipped into the car, sat down in the front passenger seat, and smoothed her wrinkled skirt.

DAVE AWOKE BLEARY-EYED and disoriented. As he glanced around his bedroom, he saw Maurelle's bag lying on the floor, her belongings stuffed inside haphazardly, her clothes spilling out. The previous night came flooding back, and he didn't want to get up and face a new day. After a few minutes, however, his mind refusing to be controlled or focus on anything except Maurelle, neither could he handle lying in bed doing nothing.

Groaning, he sat up on the edge of the bed, rubbed his face, feeling the stubble of beard growth. As he stretched, he realized he'd fallen asleep in his clothes, which were now so badly wrinkled from his tossing and turning that he wasn't sure they would ever be wearable again. Finally, he stood up, opened his wardrobe, and pulled out a pair of dark gray dress slacks and a light gray shirt. As he dressed, he, transferred his wallet, coins, and keys to the clean pants. Reaching into the last pocket, his fingers brushed up against his plastic comb. Suddenly he saw in his mind Maurelle sitting on the rock, combing her hair.

He rubbed his eyes to try to stop the vision, but the memories wouldn't stop. He saw Maurelle sitting in the grass next to the pond stripped bare and vulnerable, saw her sitting at the outdoor café in Vendome laughing and talking with him and his grandmother, saw her across from him in the bistro with her face glowing in the soft light. God, he wished he could rewind the clock and erase last night.

He combed his unruly hair as best he could, picked up his dirty clothes, and walked downstairs. The smell of fresh-brewed coffee lured him to the kitchen, but he resisted the urge and made a pit stop in the bathroom and shaved first.

Ten minutes later, he entered the kitchen and poured himself a cup of steaming coffee. Fabienne padded into the room in her slippers. She scooted back another chair and sat down, but he didn't acknowledge her. He wanted to be alone in his misery.

"What are you going to do now, David? About the woman, I mean." He shrugged. She rose and walked over to the oven. Grabbing an oven mitt, she opened the door, the smell of fresh croissants filling the room.

The aroma lifted his spirits, reminding him briefly of summers spent here helping his grandmother knead bread dough and cookie dough. Neither bread nor cookies ever lasted a full day because Dave and his grandfather would always polish them off within hours. He watched her as she reached in, pulled out the golden pastry tray, and set it on the stove top.

As if sensing his attention, she pulled off her oven mitt, tossed it on the counter, and turned to face him. "Do you think she'll come back?"

"Damned if I know." He looked away. He really didn't like admitting, even to himself, that he was not in control of the situation.

Fabienne placed the croissants on a platter and carried them over to the table. When Dave didn't move, she reached out and placed one on his plate.

He covered her hand with his. "I'm sorry for being snippy. It's not your fault I'm in such a lousy mood."

The remainder of breakfast passed with relatively few words between the two, Fabienne leaving Dave to his thoughts and Dave's thoughts continuing their torment. After breakfast, Dave rearranged Maurelle's belongings in her bag and hid the duffel bag back away in the cave cellar until he could decide what his next step should be. He was torn between going straight to the Gendarmerie in Belvidere and going to look for her to bring her back to the house. The gendarmes could hunt for her. They'd probably find her, but was he ready to do that? He massaged his neck and shoulders, trying to ease the tension in them. On the other hand, was he willing to continue harboring a murderer, if that's what she turned out to be?

His only other option, he decided, was to find out more details about the case. Now that he had names, he could search online for news reports. But when he tried to get on the neighbor's unprotected internet, it was down. He saved the document that he'd prepared with the names Elizabeth Raybourne, Jared Raybourne, and Maura Barrington, as well as Maura's address and date of birth. Tucking his computer under his arm, he left and walked down to Café Charbonneau. It wasn't his first choice by any means because it would be a struggle to keep nosy customers—and Simone—from looking over his shoulders.

Simone smiled as he entered, and strolled over to his table with a cup of coffee.

"Good morning," she said. "I was hoping you would come in."

"Thanks for the coffee."

She glanced around at her customers, before sitting down at Dave's table. "I'm sorry about last night. I guess the dog wasn't a good idea."

"That's okay."

"You aren't angry with me?"

"No. We're fine."

The bell on the door jingled and four people walked in.

"I'll talk with you later." Simone left to wait on them.

Dave opened his computer and typed in his password. He was ready to work. He took a sip of coffee while he waited for the internet. Nothing happened. What the hell? No internet access. It wasn't like this never happened back in Chicago, but at least there he had more options. Seeing that Simone had finished with her customers, Dave waved at her and she returned to his table.

"Sorry to bother you with this, but your internet isn't working."

"I know. I've already called the provider. They're doing routine maintenance which they say will take another two hours."

"Do you know where I can find Wi-Fi that is working?"

"You might try the big library in Vendome. My car is in the shop today, but I'm sure my mother would be happy to loan hers to you. She's working in the store all day."

"Thanks." He took a couple more sips of his coffee and then departed.

As he walked to the general store to speak with Simone's mother, Coralie, he thought about the library. He could probably print out articles there, which was a big help since he hadn't brought a printer on his trip. They would have actual newspapers, as well, and if he wasn't mistaken, there was a Gendarmerie in Vendome.

After he obtained the keys to Coralie's car, he went back to Fabienne's house and instructed her to keep her front and back doors locked while he was away.

When he arrived at Vendome, he parked in the parking lot at Parc Ronsard and strode toward the town hall in St. George Gate House. There, he was informed that the local Gendarmerie was next door in the sixteenth-century turret. The library was across the street and a few doors down. He thanked the receptionist and headed to the library.

As he entered the library, several people looked up from what they were doing to stare at him, but quickly resumed their own activities. Dave proceeded to the main desk to enquire about using a computer.

A pleasant, middle-aged woman in a dark blue suit said, "Yes indeed, we have computers available for our customers. You'll need to log in with your library card number."

"Uh, I don't have a library card. I'm visiting my grandmother in Reynier and she doesn't have internet access. I was hoping to use the internet here."

"Well, I can give you a one-time guest pass." She took out a card from behind the desk and handed it to him. "Use the number on here to log in. Our technology section is over there."

He turned his head, saw the overhead sign, and thanked her.

When he reached the technology section, all of the computer desks were occupied. He began to think he was being prevented from finding out more. As he was about to leave, a man departed, giving Dave his chance to slip into the vacated spot. His search for British newspapers produced numerous links. He didn't even need to type in the names Elizabeth Raybourne or Maura Barrington. Each paper had an article about the case, and most of the articles included what Dave figured must be the worst photographs of Maura that they could find. One looked like a mug shot with one eye half closed as if she were drunk. Another showed her in jogging clothes with her hair looking like a ratty mess. A photo of her in a party dress and kissing a young-looking man had the caption: 'Party girl with a passion for young boys'. One paper had a shot of her more respectably dressed, but apparently turning away from the camera like a criminal being led into court.

Some of the facts in the reports fit with what Maurelle had told him, but there were bits that didn't fit, such as the part about why she and her boyfriend had broken up and why she had to move out. An article showed a quote from him: 'I broke up with Maura because she was very intense. I can't believe she would kill someone, though.' Several teachers from the school said that Jared was a good student, and one cast doubt on Maura's claims to his mother that she was tutoring him—why have an English teacher tutoring maths? Another article quoted the victim's mother as saying, 'Jared had his whole life ahead of him and that woman took it away from him. I should never have rented a room to her. I thought the school would have done a better job of checking potential employees' backgrounds before hiring them.'

The opinion pieces were even worse—but for one which commented on the presumption of guilt and the way that it was being assumed she had run away because of guilt. The writer explained how circumstantial the public evidence was, taking each point in turn.

After an hour of reading news articles online and in print, Dave left the library and headed back to the parking lot where he'd parked. As he unlocked the car door, his cell phone rang. Though he wasn't in the mood to talk to anyone, he answered, thinking that it might be his grandmother calling.

"Bonjour, Dave. This is Paul Lepage."

"What's up? I didn't know you had my cell phone number."

"I didn't. I called Fabienne and she gave it to me. Sorry to bother you, but I wanted to make sure that you didn't have a problem meeting up with your lady friend."

"Huh?"

"I dropped her off a while ago. She said she was meeting someone, and I assumed that someone was you."

"Who are you talking about?"

"Maurelle Dupre."

Dave's mouth opened wide. He glanced around as though expecting either her or the police at any moment. "You saw her? When was that? Where is she?"

"I saw her about twenty minutes ago. As I said, I gave her a ride."

His heart was pumping harder. "Where did you drop her off?"

"La Trinite in Vendome."

She was here in Vendome? "I'm confused," Dave said. "Why

was she with you?"

"I found her walking along the road. She was hitchhiking after her handbag was stolen in Belvidere."

Dave quickly ended the call, thanking Paul, and stuck his cell phone back into his pocket, only to pull it right back out. He sat there in his car, debating. What the hell was he supposed to do? What was the right thing?

After several minutes, he made a decision. Whether it was right or wrong, he couldn't say, but, regardless, he was in too deep to stop now. He made a quick call to Coralie, and was relieved when she told him he could use the car all day, if needed. He called his grandmother, too, to let her know what was happening.

CHAPTER FIFTEEN

MAURELLE LEANED BACK and closed her eyes, finally relaxing after ten minutes of idle conversation. The tan leather seats felt luxurious to her tired body, and the cool breeze blowing at her face was heavenly. Lulled by the steady motion of the car, she couldn't keep her eyes open.

She jolted awake, realizing something had changed. As she looked ahead, she saw they'd slowed down and were getting off the highway. "What's happening?" she asked.

"I need to look for petrol."

Entering a small town, he turned right and stopped at the next intersection. A few moments later, he pulled into a petrol station on the right-hand side of the road. Pierre got out and proceeded to fill the tank, conversing with the attendant as he waited. When he finished, he opened his car door, but stood looking around the station as if waiting for something or someone.

She hadn't noticed anything particularly worrisome in his behavior, and yet somehow she'd been less nervous riding with Paul Lepage—maybe because Paul and Dave were friends. Two weeks earlier she'd hitchhiked with a farmer. He had been elderly and nearly toothless, but that didn't stop him from talking and joking. She'd actually laughed with him and enjoyed his company, probably because he reminded her of her former neighbor, Ian Waitley, who used to make her laugh as they sat in his living room eating biscuits and talking about their other neighbors.

Pierre discarded his suit jacket and tie, tossing them into the backseat. He slid back into the driver's seat and unbuttoned the top button of his dress shirt. Before he turned the key, he looked in the rearview mirror and combed his hair.

Returning to the highway, he quickly resumed driving speed, set his cruise control, and then turned on the radio, but seemed unable to settle on a station. "We'll stop in the next large city. It'll be close to noon by the time we get there—time for lunch, yes?"

Maurelle nodded. She was hungry, but she didn't have money for lunch and she didn't want charity from the man. Annoyed by the constantly changing music stations and the question of what to do about lunch, she was unable to relax. She gazed out the window at the forest they were passing through. Should she continue riding with Pierre or take off on her own at the next stop? After resting, she might manage on foot for a while.

As if reading her mind, Pierre turned off the radio and looked at her, one eyebrow raised. "You're traveling awfully light for someone on her way to Spain."

She cleared her throat, preparing to speak, but words wouldn't come. Shrugging, she turned and gazed out the window again, hoping he wouldn't ask any more questions.

"Looks to me as if you're running away from someone," Pierre said. "A boyfriend, maybe. Did you have a lover's quarrel?" Maurelle ignored him. "It's a shame that a pretty young woman like you should be all alone," he said. "I wouldn't let you take off like that if you were mine." Still she said nothing. "I would keep you to myself."

With each passing road sign and kilometer, her anxiety rose. "I want to get out now," she said, trying to keep her voice calm and level. "Please stop the car."

He slowed down slightly, and she sat up straight and reached for the handle. He turned off the main highway onto a narrow road with woods nearby.

"I have a friend," he said, "who has a little cabin hidden away in this area. I'm sure I can find it. He won't mind if we use it for a while."

Oh God! Oh God! Could she open the door and jump? Actors did it in movies all the time. But, that wasn't real. They used stunt doubles and tricks. In reality, she would probably end up with a few broken bones and be completely helpless.

A couple of minutes later, Pierre turned onto an unpaved road. As he drove, the car's tires stirred up plumes of dust which entered the vents and caused Maurelle to cough. He came to an abrupt halt. From what she could tell, they were in the middle of nowhere. At once she opened the door and ran for the woods. She barely reached the first trees when she tripped over a rock and landed face first in the underbrush. As she struggled to get up, he was upon her, holding her down, crushing her ribs, and knocking the breath out of her.

She shoved her palms into the hard soil and screamed. It didn't help because he slammed her face into the ground. Her nose and mouth were filling with dirt and making it difficult to breathe. Kicking and squirming, she somehow managed to raise herself up and take a gulp of air and along with it gained a second wave of strength.

She pushed backward with all her might, tipping Pierre off her back. As he fell sideways, he attempted to regain footing, but stumbled and tripped on a fallen tree branch. Maurelle, taking advantage, scrambled up and bolted. Moments later, he caught up to her and tackled her to the ground. In desperation, she screamed, kicked him and clawed at him. He threw his body on top of hers. His weight on her ribs and stomach held her imprisoned, throwing her into a frenzy of terror.

When she tried to rise up, he wrenched her shoulder so that she cried out in pain.

"Shut up," he told her gruffly, and shoved her down hard.

She turned her head and searched for something, anything that she might use as a weapon. Lying in the dirt and moss to the right of her head was a thick piece of tree branch that had broken off a tree. As she reached out for it, she realized it was out of her grasp.

Pierre shifted, moving one of his hands away and easing the physical pressure on Maurelle. She looked at him and realized he was unzipping his trousers. She twisted and contorted her body, grabbing onto the fallen branch with her right arm and swung it at Pierre's head.

IN HIS SEARCH for Maurelle, Dave drove along the congested highway, scanning the landscape and periodically swearing to himself out loud—at her and at him. What the hell was he doing searching for a fugitive, a murder suspect fleeing from the police, especially after he'd sworn not to let anyone dupe him again? And worse yet, he was doing it in a borrowed car with a broken air-conditioner. He should turn the car around and go back to Vendome, walk right into the Gendarmerie, and—

And what? Tell them he was tracking a woman who was wanted in connection with a murder in England? Send them after Maurelle and wash his hands of her?

In his mind's eye, Maurelle's innocent face, with its big blue eyes appeared. He smacked the steering wheel with his hands. Damn, damn, damn. He couldn't do it. He couldn't believe she was guilty without proof. He couldn't believe she was innocent without proof either. If he was going to help her—and that was a big 'if' right now—he had to remain objective.

He looked at the car clock. He was driving Coralie's car and couldn't keep imposing on her generosity. If he didn't find her by sunset, he might as well give up because it would be next to impossible in the dark. By morning, her trail would be cold. That gave him less than half a day.

Ten minutes later, Dave again wanted to scream as he sat in the hot BMW, waiting for emergency workers to clear away a traffic accident. Weaving in and out of traffic, trying to get past the bottleneck the accident had created, it took another ten minutes before he cleared the congestion. Just then, out of the corner of his eye, he saw something running in the field up ahead. He craned his neck and tried to make out whether it was an animal or a person, but it was still too far away to make out clearly. A memory of the last time he had searched for Maurelle flashed through his mind.

Dave held his breath and slowed down the car as he strained to see the runner more clearly, a move that nearly caused another accident. A car horn blare made him jerk his attention back to the road in time to see a disgruntled driver behind him swerve into the passing lane, yelling some profanity at Dave as he drove by.

He carefully turned his attention back to the runner, closer now but still a blurry figure. As he drew nearer, he could make out the runner as a woman with long hair, loose and flowing behind her like the mane on a wild stallion. He pulled off the road, jammed on the brakes, and parked in the grass. He vaulted from the car and ran toward her, catching her in his arms as she tripped and fell toward the ground.

Maurelle was sobbing and shaking uncontrollably as he held her, stroking her hair. When she calmed down, Dave led her back to the car and helped her inside. He squatted down next to her seat and searched her face, trying to figure out if she was all right. Prudence dictated he give her a bit more time and distance before attempting to ascertain just what had happened.

He rubbed his hand through his hair and stood up. He closed the door, went around to the driver's side, and climbed in. As he started up the engine, in a hoarse voice, she blurted out, "No! We can't leave."

Startled, he looked at her. "I don't understand."

"I hit him," Maurelle said. "I—I don't know if he's. . . ."

"You don't know if he's what?"

"Still alive," she whispered, the color draining out of her face.

"Christ, Maurelle, what did you do?"

She buried her face in her hands and cried, her body shaking.

Dave sat still, not touching her, not knowing what to think. His heart was racing. He took a deep breath, clutching the steering wheel. Slowly, he turned to look at Maurelle. "Tell me what happened. Who are you talking about? What man? Do you mean Paul Lepage?"

"No. Not Paul. Paul gave me a ride, too, but he was kind. This second man who gave me a ride told me his name is Pierre Auberge. He's probably twenty years older than Paul. I don't know him. I couldn't keep walking—not in sandals, anyway." She wiped her tear-streaked cheeks, and cleared her throat. "He gave me a ride. At first, he seemed all right but he somehow made me nervous. He started talking oddly, and when I asked him to let me out, he refused."

Dave pursed his lips, thinking about hitchhiking-related incidents he'd dealt with back in Chicago. Those incidents had become his cases because they'd left behind murder and rape victims. Hell, Diana Lewis and Johnny Kincaid had kidnapped some of their victims by picking up hitchhikers.

"Go on."

"When he slowed down, I jumped out of the car and ran, but he followed. He attacked me, and pinned me down to rape me," she whispered. "I fought him, found a broken tree branch, and hit him over the head. I got up and ran until you showed up."

"How long ago did this happen?"

"I don't know. Not long ago—perhaps ten minutes ago. "

"Can you take me to him?"

She nodded.

"Are you okay? Did he—hurt you?"

She tensed, shaking again momentarily, but said, "I'm all right. Just scratched and shaken."

Dave wasn't entirely convinced that she was okay, but he needed her to take him to this man, first. He'd deal with Maurelle later.

She led him to the turn-off and then to the unpaved road. He stopped the car and she led him into the woods, stopping occasionally to look around to get her bearings. Each time, like a trained hunter, she would carefully choose her path, which surprised Dave.

She reached an area in the woods where she stopped and pointed a few yards away.

"Are you sure this is the place?"

"I recognize that gnarled tree over there," she said, pointing to a particularly knotted, half-dead magnolia. "And here is the broken tree branch that I hit him with."

She picked up the branch and handed it to Dave, and he turned it over, noting a damp patch that looked and felt like blood.

"Well," Dave said, "obviously he survived, since I don't see him here. Do you have any idea where he left his car?"

She shook her head, momentarily looking bewildered.

"It can't be far away." She pivoted around, looking as if she was trying to get her bearings and then she stopped. "There," she said, pointing.

As they approached the road, Dave heard a car engine. He spotted a brown Peugeot speeding away around the bend, heading toward the highway. Feeling a mixture of anger and relief, Dave turned around to look at Maurelle. Judging from the look on her face, she'd seen it too. She stood still, her face pale as an ice statue.

CHAPTER SIXTEEN

MAURELLE PULLED THE bedcovers over her head and tried to get back to sleep, but her stomach growled, forcing her wider awake. She groaned, threw off the covers, and opened her eyes, letting in the pinkish-gold light coming through the pink sheer curtains. Glancing down at the unfamiliar blue flannel nightgown she was wearing, she felt disoriented but as she turned over and looked around the cozy room bits and pieces from yesterday's events came back to her.

Dave had helped her back to the car. He barely spoke as he drove back towards Reynier. She thought he was taking her to the Gendarmerie, but she had been too tired and worn-down to care. Somewhere along the way, she drifted into a half-sleep and awakened only when he stopped the car. When she saw Fabienne's house, her heart sank and yet at the same time she felt comforted, her body relaxing.

Dave had whisked her upstairs and helped her to lie down on the bed, with Fabienne standing nearby watching, anxiety etched in her wrinkled face. Turning to Fabienne, Dave said something, though the words were a blur in Maurelle's mind. Later, a woman who had introduced herself as Sandrine Fortier, a nurse and friend of Fabienne's, examined her and told them that Maurelle had bruised ribs and a bruised right shoulder, but was otherwise unharmed physically. Sandrine had given her an herbal remedy, which enabled her to sleep through the night for the first time in several days, but now left her foggy.

She tried to sit up, intending to get out of bed, but sharp pains jabbed at her upper torso, causing her fall to back on the soft duvet. Determined, she tried again, this time preparing herself for the pain and bracing herself with her arms.

When she managed to sit on the edge of the bed, she was surprised to see her duffel bag on the chair in the corner of the room, in the exact spot where she had left it. Confused, she wondered if she'd somehow overlooked the bag when she'd previously left empty-handed. She wobbled over to the chair and unzipped the bag. Her clothes were neatly folded as she'd left them, only not in the same order. Digging down to the bottom, she pushed the contents out of the way and lifted the false bottom. It was empty. Frantically, she searched through the main compartment. Her clothes, toiletries, books were all there—the things she didn't care about.

She threw the bag onto the floor and sat in its place on the chair. What had Dave done with her cash and identification? Reaching down, she pulled the bag back to her and yanked out a pair of jeans, a gray blouse, a bra, and knickers. After dressing and combing her ratted hair, she opened the door and stepped out of her room, smacking right into Dave.

He grabbed her arms to steady her. "I was coming to check on you. How are you feeling?"

"Better." She wanted to ask about her money and ID, but decided to not confront the topic immediately, hoping for a good, *please let there be a reasonable*, explanation.

"Good. Are you ready to eat something?"

Maurelle nodded.

They walked together down the hallway. At the top of the

stairs, Dave took hold of her arm and carefully led her, like one would a small child, down the stairs and into the kitchen. He pulled out a chair for her at the table, where an omelet plate was already waiting.

"Thank you," she said.

Fabienne handed her a steaming cup of coffee, which she gladly accepted. Dave and Fabienne sat at the table, and after a quick round of 'bon appetit', they all ate together, then shared the task of cleaning up the kitchen.

"Well, I'm off to see Jeannette," Fabienne said, surprising Maurelle.

Maurelle and Dave watched her from inside the kitchen, where they had a clear view of Fabienne as she hastily donned her shoes, grabbed her handbag, and left. As soon as the door closed, Dave turned around. "We need to talk."

She nodded. Without thinking, she stiffened her shoulders, forgetting her bruised right shoulder, the movement instantly sending lancing pain through her.

Dave was watching her intently and must have noticed her flinch in pain, but said only, "Let's go in the living room."

She nodded, and walked with stiff dignity into the living room.

DAVE SAT IN the chair across from Maurelle. "I need to know the details about the case against you." He paused, searching for the right words. He'd rather not sound like he was conducting an interrogation if he could avoid it. "It must be difficult for you. I can't imagine all that you've been through. I'd like to believe you and help with your problem. I'm trying, but we need to trust each other a little, first. You didn't even tell me your real name. I had to find that out on my own."

Her body stiffened. "You went through my duffel bag. You

took my passport and wallet—and my money."

Dave leaned in. In a controlled voice he said, "You are in no position to take such an attitude with me. You are the criminal here, not me."

She drew back as though he'd slapped her in the face. "I'm not a criminal."

"You're guilty of running away from a murder investigation. That alone makes you a criminal. I'm trying to figure out whether or not you're guilty of anything else."

"I would never kill anyone. I would never steal either. I'd rather starve than stoop that low."

"You nearly killed a man yesterday."

She opened her mouth, closed it and re-opened it, without saying anything. She sank back against the sofa back. "That was self-defense." She paused. "I'm sorry. I know you want to help."

"I did take your things," he admitted, "but I don't want them. Let's just say I'm holding onto them for now—until I – until we decide what needs to be done."

She nodded.

"Talk to me, Maurelle. Let me in, please. Tell me what happened before and after the murder. How long ago did this happen?"

He actually knew when it happened, and where. He knew the victim's name and age, his parents' names, where his body was found, and some of what had led up to the murder. He'd found out a lot of details in news articles online. But he needed to hear it from Maurelle. More importantly, he needed to watch her body language and listen to her voice. He needed to read her the way he'd read hundreds of other suspects.

"It was about five or six weeks ago, I think," she said. "I'm losing track of time. I already told you some of it. The victim was Jared Raybourne, a sixteen-year-old pupil. It was rumored that I was involved with him. But I wasn't—not ever. Not romantically." She looked straight into Dave's eyes. "He wanted us to be, but I refused and told him to leave me alone."

"But he didn't?"

"No. He persisted. I had no choice but to move out of the Raybournes' house. Elizabeth didn't want me to leave—she needed the extra income. But she wouldn't do anything about her son's obsession."

"Why did she need the income? Why did you rent from this woman?"

"She needed money to help cover her mortgage. I needed a place to live, and she needed money, so she offered to let me rent the room which helped both of us."

He nodded, and leaned forward. "You talked to her about Jared?"

"Yes. I tried that first, before I decided to move out."

"What did she say when you talked to her?"

"She said that her son was merely going through adolescence, and that it was common for teenagers to develop crushes on their teachers. He would quickly get over it and move on. She assured me it wasn't a problem, and that I shouldn't worry."

"But he didn't?"

"No. Even after I moved out he continued chasing me, sending me emails, calling me on my mobile. He even told his friends and classmates that I was his girlfriend. I changed my phone number and my email address, but he somehow got the new ones."

She stopped and closed her eyes.

Dave patted her on the hand, prompting her to continue.

"Jared had emotional problems. I wish I'd known sooner. I could have referred him to the school's counselors who might have helped him. I had been teaching for a few years, but lacked experience in that sort of problem—crushes and infatuations—

which was a good thing, and yet that meant I didn't know how to deal with it."

"What did you do?"

"I talked to Pauline, Jared's aunt."

"And that didn't help?"

"Not really. She told me she had a pupil like that years ago, and it passed without incident. It usually did, she said, but she wasn't convinced this one would blow over. She talked to her sister about Jared, but she couldn't get through to her either."

"What happened next?"

"Over the next couple of weeks—this was after I moved out of the house—Jared was spreading rumors around the school. The headmaster heard about it and talked to me. I was placed on suspension, pending a hearing. I believe Jared was suspended from school, but I'm not certain."

She fell silent.

Dave again reached out and covered her hand with his. "It's okay. Take your time and tell me what happened."

"As I said, I told you much of it when we were in the cave. Most of the rest is kind of a blur. I was so stunned by Jared's death that I don't think my brain really registered everything."

"If I remember right," Dave said, "you told me that people immediately considered you the prime suspect. Is that correct?"

Maurelle nodded.

"But you weren't there in the house that day?"

"No."

"Did you have an alibi? Where were you the night of the murder?"

"That's just it," Maurelle said. "I was at home, alone, watching the telly. No one could verify it. I'm a homebody. I don't go out on lots of dates or to parties or out with friends."

Dave nodded. "Did Jared have any enemies? Or maybe a girlfriend his own age?"

"I don't know about enemies. He had a girlfriend, Penny Miller, but they had already broken up."

"What else do you remember? Tell me more about his mother."

"She said he was reacting to his parents' divorce and that he would get over it. That lots of children go through emotional upheavals when their parents fight or get a divorce."

"She found him dead?"

She nodded. "The news reports said that she found him on the floor in his bedroom the morning after the murder."

"If she was at home, how could she not have heard anything? How could someone come into the home and murder him without her waking up?"

"All I know is what I heard on the television and read in the newspapers. They said that Elizabeth had been out for the evening. When she got home, it was late and she went to bed straight away without seeing her son."

"Seems odd that a mother would not check on her son when she got home. Did the police rule out the mother as a suspect?"

"I can't imagine a mother doing that to her own son. What reason could she have?"

Dave said, "I've seen everything. People do things that boggle the mind. Were you close friends with the mother?"

"No, not really," she said. "She wasn't the easiest person to get to know. She was a little bit strange."

He quirked his eyebrows, questioningly. "How so?"

"I don't know how to explain. She was moody, often depressed. I suppose that's normal right after a divorce. The ex-husband was sometimes difficult from what I could tell, and that didn't help."

"What caused their divorce?"

"I don't know. The ex-husband has a girlfriend, but I don't know if that relationship began before or after the divorce."

"Did the two women get along with each other?"

"No. Definitely not, from what I could tell."

"What did Elizabeth do when she wasn't working?"

"She spent a lot of time in her bedroom, or sometimes she went out and left her son alone."

"Was the kid involved in drugs or gangs?"

"Not that I know of. I didn't see or hear anything to suggest that."

"Did the police consider anyone else a suspect: the ex-girlfriend, one of the parents, a neighbor, a classmate?"

"I don't know. As I told you last night, I left at the beginning of the investigation."

"Who else might have killed him? Do you know anything about the family, their friends, the boy's friends, his enemies?"

"Only a handful of people ever visited the Raybournes while I was there—Jared's aunt and uncle, his father, his father's girlfriend, and a few neighbors."

"Who are the neighbors?"

"Well, there's Nick and Jenny Hallowell from a few doors down, Ian Waitley from across the street, Rob Carsters from the next street over, and Sally Kavanaugh from the corner house."

"What about next door? Didn't they get along with those neighbors?"

"They were polite to each other, but they didn't really associate."

"What are their names?"

"Alice Rickards lives on one side and Judy Winston lives on the other side."

"Were any of them questioned? Were they suspects? Did they hear or see anything?"

"I don't know. I'm not sure who else, besides me, were considered suspects. All I know for sure is that someone," she said, her voicing choking up, "stabbed Jared with a knife." Her eyes filled with tears. Her voice broke for a moment. Pulling herself together, she said in a calm voice, "I couldn't do something that horrible. Hitting Pierre with that fallen tree branch, thinking that I might have killed him, nearly devastated me, and that was out of self-defense. Pierre was going to rape me. I could never intentionally, and in cold-blood, murder someone." She looked straight into Dave's eyes. "I'm not a bad person," she said, her eyes filling with tears. "I'm certainly not a saint, but I couldn't do something that despicable."

Dave reached out and pulled Maurelle close, embracing her while he stroked her hair. She relaxed into him, her tears dripping down her face.

TWENTY MINUTES LATER, while Maurelle showered, Dave sat in the kitchen, tapping his fingers on the table and studying the six newspaper articles he'd printed from the internet while he was in the library.

If he traveled to London, he could poke around and see what else he could find out, but first he needed a cover story, a logical explanation for his interest in the case. He couldn't pretend to be a friend of the family, since the police in London could easily verify that with the Raybourne family. Dave knew too well that he had to be particularly cautious. If he drew too much attention, he could risk giving away the fact that he and his grandmother were harboring a fugitive. That certainly wouldn't help Maurelle's situation and it could land all three of them in jail. It might anyway, whatever the outcome.

Maurelle walked into the kitchen, looking refreshed with rosy cheeks and damp hair.

Dave smiled and quickly tucked the papers back into the folder. "You look as though you're feeling better."

She nodded and sat down next to him.

"I was thinking about a plan." He was about to say more, but was interrupted by the doorbell. "I'll be right back."

He strode to the living room, opened the front door, and was surprised to see Simone and her new dog.

"Bonjour," Simone said. She held out her arms and wrapped them around Dave, kissing him on the lips, almost dropping the dog leash in the process.

Dave embraced her, while raising his brows slightly. "I thought you would be working."

"Ah, well, I do get the occasional day off," Simone said, smiling and pulling on the dog's leash. "Bono needed a walk—oh, I guess you don't know. I gave him a name. I haven't seen you since, well, you know." She glanced around him, and added, "Is *she* still here?

Dave gave her a quizzical look.

"The little stray you found."

"If you mean Maurelle, yes. She is still here," Dave said dryly.

"Who is she anyway? Have you found out what she's doing here?"

"As you said, she's a stray, a runaway. I'm trying to help her out."

"Does that mean she'll be leaving soon?"

He shrugged.

Simone pouted and then brushed his arm with her hand. "Well, aren't you going to invite us in?"

He stepped aside to let her and the dog inside.

Simone gave Dave a sideways look. "Since it doesn't look like we're going on travel anytime soon, I bought us two tickets for the theatre next week. You will go with me, won't you?"

"Yeah, sure, I guess."

She smiled and let go of the leash, turning Bono loose. Eager for attention, the playful pup sprang at Dave, who patted the dog's head. Bono still wanted more. He jumped, trying to get Dave to pick him up. Instead, Dave squatted down and the dog placed his paws on Dave's knees. Dave reached out and cupped the dog's face in his hands, which sent the dog into a frenzy of licks.

Dave chuckled and Simone laughed, clapping her hands delightedly.

When he finally stood back up, Maurelle was standing in the archway between the kitchen and living room, watching them with an unreadable expression.

Simone turned and looked in the same direction.

Dave winced. He suddenly felt like an awkward teenager.

He cleared his throat. "Have you two been introduced?"

"No, we haven't, Cheri. Not formally."

After Dave made the introductions, each of them stood waiting for someone else to break the silence. Dave rubbed the back of his head. He had an idea. "Why don't we have some lunch? I'm not much of a cook, but I'm sure I can throw something together."

"No, no," Simone said, "I'm a much better cook than you. I will fix lunch."

Dave held up his hand. "This is your day off. Sit and relax. I insist. I'll take care of everything." He retreated to the kitchen, stopped, and peeked back in. "You girls can get acquainted."

He didn't wait for a reply. Good God! How had he gotten himself into this situation? Though he didn't enjoy cooking, he would do his best to stretch out the chore for a good, long time.

Dave managed to cobble together a salad that he thought Fabienne would be proud of, though of course it couldn't compete with her specialty salad. He rejected thumbing through her cookbooks, thinking he shouldn't try anything fancy. He settled on making Monte Cristo sandwiches, which had always been one of his favorites.

When he nearly had everything ready, he heard a loud commotion, followed by a dog barking and a female screaming, "No!" He rushed into the living room. As he anxiously surveyed the room, he asked, "What's going on?"

Simone was standing in front of the grandfather clock, and Maurelle was kneeling down near the back edge of the clock where it butted up against the wall. Bono had his nose and one paw stuffed in between the clock and the wall, his tail wagging ferociously.

Maurelle turned her head and looked up at Dave, pleadingly. "He's got a mouse. He trapped it behind—or underneath—the clock and he's been battering it. Please don't let him kill it. Can you get it away from him?"

Dave raised one eyebrow. He glanced over at Simone, who was watching with amusement, and he was suddenly curious about what he had missed before this. He reached down and grabbed the dog's collar, pulling him out of the way, then kneeled down and looked behind and underneath the clock.

Maurelle said, "Mice don't usually run out in the open when people are around but this one did. It ran across the room, right by the couch where I was sitting. It actually scurried over my feet. The dog was on Simone's lap, across from me, and, well, he saw the mouse and chased it behind here."

Dave smiled, but didn't turn his head to look at her. The mouse, caught underneath the massive piece of furniture, with its rear and long tail sticking out, reminded Dave of the wicked witch crushed underneath Dorothy's house in the Wizard of Oz. The part of the body that Dave could see was smashed, he guessed by the dog.

Kneeling on the wooden floor, he pulled back and looked into Maurelle's pleading eyes. "I'm sorry. It's too late." Dave pulled out the dead mouse and stood up. The dog jumped and tried to get it from his hand, but Dave held it up higher, out of the dog's reach. Maurelle and Simone watched as he carried it from the room.

Out of their view, he carried the mouse outside in the backyard and placed it in an empty planter to dispose of later. He went back inside and washed his hands in the kitchen sink. Before he turned off the water, he splashed some water onto his face, blotting it off with a paper towel. Reluctantly, he went back into the living room.

Maurelle was standing next to the clock, her face bleak with sorrow. Dave walked over to her and hugged her. Simone, who was holding Bono, was sitting on the edge of the couch. "I'm probably the world's worst chef. I won't blame you if you decide to bail on lunch," Dave said, "but, if you're willing to brave it, lunch is ready."

To his surprise and dismay, both women followed him into the kitchen. He had hoped that Simone might tire of the present company and leave to visit friends or family, but she also had a stubborn streak.

During lunch, their conversation was awkward, making Dave as uncomfortable as he'd expected. On several occasions, he noticed Maurelle looking embarrassed, Simone looking pouty, or the dog looking ready to leap onto someone's lap because no one was paying him attention. At least no one was feeding their food to the dog.

He was not cut out to play host. While married, his ex-wife had thrown parties and dinners which were always successful. But Dave had never bothered after the divorce, convincing himself that it was out of laziness, and not out of lack of know-how. Eventually, he'd discovered that hosting was a learned skill or a natural talent, and for the first time, Dave wished that Fabienne had been here to chatter happily. He wouldn't even have minded her gossiping in this situation because she could have turned the whole affair around and made it fun.

CHAPTER SEVENTEEN

STANDING IN THE kitchen, Maurelle smiled politely. "Au revoir. It was nice to meet you, Simone." Normally, she would have added that she was looking forward to getting to know her better, but she couldn't bring herself to say those words.

Simone nodded and smiled. Taking hold of Dave's hand, she said, "You are going to walk me to the door, aren't you?"

After a glance at Maurelle, Dave escorted Simone into the living room. Bono ran ahead, yapping excitedly. Maurelle breathed deeply, and slumped back down onto her chair.

Throughout the afternoon Simone had delivered subtle jibes and sneers that were obviously meant to diminish Maurelle in Dave's eyes. The only thing that prevented Maurelle from despising Simone was that the derogatory comments were deserved for the most part. She'd already sunk about as low as she could go.

"I'm sorry about Simone," Dave said as he returned to the kitchen.

Maurelle looked up and tried to smile.

"She can be sweet, but she can be difficult, too." He sat, leaned toward her, and placed his hand over hers. "I hope she didn't give you too hard a time." He paused, as if waiting for her to fill him in on the highlights of their conversation. What was she supposed to say? The sophisticated and beautiful Simone had talked about her life before she'd moved to Reynier; an amazing life as a fashion model in Paris and married to a prominent photographer. Maurelle's ordinariness had been so obvious that it might well have been stamped on her forehead.

She shrugged finally. "She talked about Paris, mostly."

Dave raised his eyebrows. "Apparently, from what I gather, she had a pretty good life there when she was younger." He paused, studying her with a curious intensity. "Did she tell you why she left Paris?"

"No."

"Her career took a nose dive when she reached her early thirties. Models that age aren't in high demand. When her career turned sour, I guess her marriage did, too. So, a year ago, she moved here and bought my grandmother's café."

Maurelle looked at Dave, pondering the implications of this new revelation. "I didn't know that. She made it sound so—different."

Dave nodded knowingly. "She doesn't want people to know those details. She only talks about the good times and the glamour. I only found out about them from bits and pieces I gathered during conversations."

"I wish I'd known that sooner," Maurelle said softly. "Knowing the back story might have made listening to her success story a bit less brutal."

"Well, if it helps any, I think she's jealous. She's threatened by you."

"But she shouldn't be," she said. "I could tell that although you've only known one another for a few weeks, you have a bond due to your families' connections."

Dave sighed. "You're right about the family connections. Our grandmothers have been lifelong friends. They grew up together in a small village, and moved to Paris together as teenagers. They moved to Reynier a few years later when they were both married and starting families. I suspect they want Simone and me to marry and, of course, live here. I guess I went along with it for a while. Not the marrying part, but the dating. But —"

"Are you in love with her?"

"No. I am definitely not," Dave said, quietly. "It would be great if I was because it would make everyone happy. But I'm not."

"But she's in love with you."

"I'm not sure about that. Simone is lonely, and doesn't have many candidates for a boyfriend or husband. You've been here long enough to see how few available men there are in this town. Anyway, I've involved myself in a situation that doesn't have an easy solution."

"Maybe if you go on that trip around France with her, you'll feel differently."

"I don't think so," Dave said. "I told her upfront that I didn't want a long-term relationship. She and I went out a few times and enjoyed each other's company. I never expected anything more. Besides, right now I intend to see what I can do about your situation, if I can."

"What can you possibly do about it?"

"I thought I could travel to England and poke around a bit. Maybe I can find out what's happened in the investigation. I might even figure out what really happened."

"Don't you have to get back to your work? I'm keeping you away from that, too."

"No, I've finished my latest book. It's in the publisher's hands, so I have time off for a while. I started my next book but have plenty of time to work on it."

Memories of the conversation she'd overheard two nights ago flashed through her mind. "I—I overheard you talking to your grandmother about your . . . disillusionment."

"You heard that?" He said, looking sharply at her. "That must have been when you came back to the house to look for your bags."

She nodded.

He remained silent for a few moments, and finally shrugged, suddenly looking like his grandmother. "I can't promise anything, but I'm willing to go to England and see if I can help—if you can look me in the eye and swear to me that you are not a killer and not in any way connected to his murder. Can you do that?"

She nodded, looked him directly in the eye and repeated his words, denying any connection to the killing.

"Okay. I'll do what I can, but I'm warning you now that I'm going to be objective and keep an open mind. We'll discuss the case in detail before I leave and I'll take thorough notes that I can use once I get to England. There, I'll investigate as much as I can. I won't ignore evidence if I find something that proves you've lied to me. Is that understood?"

"Yes. I wouldn't expect you to do otherwise."

"I need you to stay here with my grandmother while I'm in England. I don't want to go there and put myself in jeopardy, only to have you running off again."

"Would it be better if I went with you and turned myself in? You could investigate properly, and it would put you at less personal risk, wouldn't it?"

"It might. I admit I considered that option, but that could easily prove disastrous. My trust in the U.S. justice system is on shaky ground, and I'm not certain the U.K. system is much better. For now, I'd rather keep you here out of harm's way, as long as you can promise me you'll stay put until I return."

"I promise. And Dave, thank you for believing in me."

DAVE SAT NEXT to Fabienne on the couch, filling her in on what had transpired during her four-hour absence. He told her about his morning talk with Maurelle and the awkward visit and luncheon with Simone.

"I wish I had been here for the luncheon," Fabienne said, nervously rubbing her hands together. "A man should never get himself caught like that, between two women. At least if I had been here I could have turned it into a lighter affair."

"I agree. I missed you more than you know. I really stepped into that one."

She gave him a sly smile. "Well, sweet boy, you certainly have gotten yourself into a mess. You didn't want to listen to me, did you? Thought you knew everything. But you didn't really know what getting yourself mixed up with two women meant. Ha!" When he didn't comment, Fabienne pursed her lips and sat back against the cushions with her arms folded.

"Oh, and by the way," Dave said, suddenly remembering the dog's encounter, "there's a dead mouse in one of your containers in the backyard."

Fabienne looked at him puzzled.

"Simone's dog killed a mouse underneath the grandfather clock."

She shook her head. "That little mouse has been giving me grief for months. Good dog and good riddance."

Dave said, "I'll dispose of it later. And, you might want to watch what you say about it around Maurelle. She was quite upset about the mouse being killed and wants me to bury it."

Fabienne suddenly leaned forward and looked squarely at Dave. "It's time you choose between those women. It's obvious you can't keep sleeping with both of them."

"Grand-mère! Shame on you. I'm not sleeping with either of them!"

'Mon oeil," Fabienne said as she pulled her lower eyelid

down slightly with her index finger, indicating that she didn't believe him.

Dave stood up and towered over her. "I have never slept with them."

Fabienne smoothed her dress and pulled a loose strand of hair out of her eyes before continuing. "Well, I hope you're telling the truth." She paused, looking down at her hands that were now resting in her lap. "I've come to like Maurelle, as far as I know her, but you must realize you can't expect a real relationship with her. Even if you help her and she is found not guilty, can you ever really be sure she didn't kill that boy?"

"Did I say I wanted a relationship with Maurelle?"

Fabienne didn't answer. He turned toward the stairs.

"Where are you going? We aren't finished talking, are we?"

"We can continue this conversation later, Grand-mère. And you owe me an apology. Right now I need to talk with Maurelle." He moved toward the stairs, but stopped at the foot of the staircase. "Please don't talk to Simone about any of this, okay? Things are complicated enough right now."

Fabienne nodded, raising both of her hands up in the air in a gesture of defeat.

Upstairs, Dave knocked on Maurelle's door. "May I come in?"

She stepped back, holding the door open for him to enter.

"I need to know something," he said. "What do you intend to do if you are cleared of the charges?"

Her eyes widened. "I don't know. I never allowed myself to consider that possibility."

"Why not?"

"Because I didn't think it was possible. I'm innocent, but I never expected anyone would believe me or help me."

"You didn't expect me to save you?"

She raised her eyebrows. "Why would I expect that? I was

trying to get away from you because I thought you would be horrified if you found out my secret. I thought you would turn me in. Isn't that what police do, even if they are no longer police?"

He didn't answer, but stepped forward and slowly pulled her close to him, clasping her body against his and kissing her. When he finally moved his lips from hers, he gazed down into her surprised eyes. She didn't back away. Without thinking he pulled her roughly against him, causing her to cry out in pain.

He let go, and looked at her in surprise.

"I'm still quite sore from yesterday."

"Oh, God. I'm sorry. I forgot about your bruises." He hesitated. "Before I go to London, I'll call some friends back home. Maybe they can help. Anyway, I don't want you to give up. We'll figure this thing out, together."

Maurelle wiped away tears that had suddenly formed in her eyes.

"I've got a lot to do to get ready," Dave said, "and I'll need your help. As I said earlier, we'll need to make a list: names, addresses, anything that might be useful, okay?"

"It's not too late for you to get out of this."

"That's not going to happen. I believe you and I'm too damned stubborn to let it go. You shouldn't waste your breath trying to talk me out of it."

"But—"

Dave smiled. "Don't even try. Once I've made up my mind, there's no turning back. You can ask my grandmother about that. I'm more stubborn than she is."

Maurelle frowned. "Take some of my money. You'll need it."

Dave's eyebrows arched in surprise. "Oh yeah, I completely forgot. I'll give you your things back before I leave, but you have to promise you won't run away again. I don't want to do all of this for nothing. Promise?"

"I promise."

"But I don't need your money," Dave said.

"Please take it. I already owe you so much. Besides, it's already in pounds which will save you a lot of trouble."

"Well, I guess that's true. We'll figure out the details before I leave." He paused, suddenly thinking about her duffel bag. "I am curious about something. Two things, actually. First, the large amount of cash, but second, I can't figure out why you're carrying around an expensive-looking man's watch."

Maurelle squared her shoulders. "I withdrew the money from my accounts right before I ran. I didn't know if I would ever return, and I needed money to survive—until I could get a job. I didn't realize how difficult it would be to find work without proper identification." Her voice cracked suddenly. "As for the watch, it's a woman's watch. It belonged to my mother. It was her only gift from my father. She held onto it until the day she died. I guess now I hold onto it in her memory."

Dave nodded. "Don't you think she might have considered you also a gift from your father?"

She shrugged her shoulders and looked down at her feet. "If she did, I can only imagine that she wouldn't feel that way now."

He wanted to say something supportive, but he was at a loss. Finally, he pulled her into an embrace, and whispered, "Why don't we see if we can change that, okay?"

She nodded, and he leaned back, looking into her eyes. "I guess we'd better get to work."

AS DAVE LOOKED through the case notes on his computer and the newspaper articles he'd printed out, he still wondered if he was making the right decision. Did he really want to take on a case that he had no business getting involved in? Didn't he have enough problems of his own? Then he thought about his kiss with Maurelle. What had possessed him to do that? Of all people, he should know that wasn't a good idea.

He sighed and closed his eyes. Maybe what he should really be doing is going back to Chicago before getting further involved. But in his heart he knew he could not let it go.

CHAPTER EIGHTEEN

DAVE TRIED TO resist second-guessing the rightness of his decision to go to London. He'd made the decision and would follow through on it. He simply had to know the truth, but he wondered what he would feel and do if the truth turned out to be other than he expected. After what had happened in his police career, he knew he was pursuing this in part to prove to himself that he could still read people. And he needed to verify his own good judgment He also knew that this obsession was more than just proving his capabilities. There was a heavy emotional investment. If Maurelle indeed killed Jared Raybourne, his faith in himself, in humanity, and especially in women, would be shattered, not to mention how it would affect his growing feelings for her. Could he love a murderer?

Fabienne and Maurelle kept saying they were worried about him getting into trouble in London. All he could do was assure them he would be cautious. He just hoped his investigative skills weren't as rusty as he expected.

"Let's go over the names again," Dave said as he and Maurelle sat together on the sofa. "Tell me about the next door neighbors. How well did you know them?"

"Mrs. Rickards was sick and was in and out of the hospital. I think we only spoke to each other once or twice. Mrs. Winston, on the other side of the Raybourne house, was a retired widow, and from what I gather, was fairly well off. She was gone quite a bit, traveled often. It's funny. When she was home, she was interested in another retired neighbor, the man across the street, Ian Waitley. Spent a lot of time preening, getting her hair done, putting on makeup, that sort of thing, trying to get him interested. But he would run and hide whenever he saw her heading his way."

"Why was that?"

"He told me she was too old, which was comical, actually, because he was a year older than her, and he knew it. A few of his neighbors, including Mrs. Winston and I, attended his sixty-first birthday party a month earlier—and at the time she'd announced that she was about to celebrate her sixtieth birthday. He was sometimes forgetful, and people thought he was bit batty. I thought he was funny and nice, just eccentric."

"How do you know she wasn't lying about her age?"

"Because later someone tried to deliver flowers to her, but she wasn't home. The delivery man brought them to the Raybourne house. I was the only one home. I accepted them, and watched for her to come home. When I carried them over to her house, she told me the flowers were from her grandson and she showed me the card that came with them. It said "Happy Sixtieth Birthday, Grandma."

Dave laughed. "Okay. What about the Hallowells?"

"Nick and Jenny Hallowell were good friends with Peter and Elizabeth Raybourne, from what I heard—at least, before the Raybournes divorced. Jenny would sometimes invite them over for dinner or drinks and to play cards, but Elizabeth would trash Peter, or Robin, or both of them all evening."

Dave jotted down notes on a pad of paper. "Who is Robin?"

"Oh, she's Peter's girlfriend."

"Did she have an affair with Peter? Is that what caused the break-up of the marriage?"

"I don't know."

"How did the Hallowells react to Elizabeth's negative talk about her ex-husband?"

"I heard them trying to defend Peter one night, which made Elizabeth angry. They tried to tell her that they were still friends with him. She didn't seem to want to hear it."

"You mentioned Rob Carsters and Sally Kavanaugh."

"They were both around Elizabeth's age. I think Rob was interested in Elizabeth after her divorce. He would drop by the house and invite her out to dinner or a movie sometimes. She always said no, that she wasn't interested in dating. Then he would say that he was only being neighborly, that he wasn't making a move on her. I think he was. It's a shame she wasn't interested. He seemed like a nice man."

"Was he a family friend? Did he know Peter and Elizabeth?"

"I don't know."

"And Sally Kavanaugh?"

"She was a friend of Elizabeth. Sally would come over sometimes to try and cheer her up. Most of the time Elizabeth would say she didn't feel like talking, but once in a while they would go out for the evening or Sally would eat dinner at the house. Usually, if she did, they would order take away because Elizabeth hated cooking."

After each of their talks, Dave transferred his notes and the pointers Maurelle was giving him into his laptop computer and studied them. The more details he got, the more he wondered how he would accomplish all the work, especially in a short period of time. Thorough investigations could take months, even years. Investigating in a city that was unfamiliar to him would be difficult, but doing it alone, especially when he'd always worked with a partner was daunting to say the least. He wondered what his old partner, Greg Saunders, was doing. Greg was one of the few people he still trusted. The last time they'd spoken, Greg had complained about lack of adventure in his life. Dave dialed Greg and they chatted for a while, catching up on what they'd both been doing lately. Finally, after talking for an hour, Dave told him he was going to England to do research for a book.

"I'm jealous," Greg said. "France, and now England. Why do you get to go on all the exciting trips?"

"Well, that's part of the reason I called. I was wondering if you have any vacation time coming. I remember you saying how bored you were and how you needed a good vacation."

"Yeah, I have three weeks of vacation available. The boss has been pushing me to use some of it. Just don't have any place to go or anyone to go with. How pathetic is that?"

"How would you like to go to England as my guest?"

"Your guest? Does that mean you're paying?"

"Yeah, it does."

"What's the catch?"

"As I said, I'll be doing research, and I'd like your help with it. I'm sure there will be time for sightseeing, too. The other thing, it would need to be now. I'm getting ready to leave in a few days."

"Why do you need me? What kind of research is it?"

"I'm unofficially looking into a murder case that's similar to what I have in mind for a mystery novel I'm working on. I'm out of practice investigating. You might see something that I overlook. Besides, we always worked well together. You were my right-hand man."

"Are you considering going back into police work?"

"No. I'm strictly a writer now. I'm hoping to get some realistic details for my book, and to tell you the truth, it's a good excuse to visit England. Always wanted to visit."

"Me too. Okay. I'm in. Well, assuming I can get the vacation time quickly. I'll have to talk to the boss and get back to you."

Two days later, Greg called back. "It'll be great seeing you again and seeing England. I still don't know why you're interested in investigating a case you aren't getting paid to investigate, but that's your choice. Personally, I get enough of this stuff. I wouldn't do it for free."

"Would you rather not be involved?"

"No, I wasn't saying that, buddy. Hey, I get a free vacation out of it. You're paying, you said."

"Yeah, I'm paying. You're sure you're okay with working on your 'vacation'?"

"Sure. As long as I get to do some sightseeing, too. And some nights out in the pubs."

"It's a deal."

Dave made reservations for himself and Greg at the hotel Maurelle recommended, bought airline tickets, and called Greg to give him the details.

Knowing that he would have help in London assuaged his worries, but not entirely. His main concern, he told Fabienne and Maurelle, was that he not let anyone, including Greg, become suspicious that he was in contact with Maura Barrington.

ON THE LAST night before his flight to London, Dave took Maurelle back to the bistro for dinner. While they dined, they each talked about their childhoods, their schools, their parents. When he told her that his parents had sent him to visit his grandparents in Reynier every summer when he was young, she said, "Didn't they come with you?"

"No. They would put me on an airplane with a flight attendant to look after me."

Her eyes widened. "Weren't you frightened?"

He shrugged.

"How old were you when you started coming here?" she asked.

"Well, I must have been about six. I'd finished kindergarten. Now that I think about it, the first visit was scary, not because anything bad had happened, but because my parents had argued for days before they put me on the airplane. My mother cried, and said flying was dangerous. She didn't want to put her only child in harm's way, but my dad said it was perfectly safe. In his words, 'the boy needs to learn to be a man'."

"Oh, that sounds tough. What did your father do for a living?"

"He was a police detective. I guess that's part of why I became one. What about you? You said your mother was a professor, and you became a teacher? Did she push you into it?"

"No. I naturally gravitated toward teaching, though it wasn't easy for me because I'm somewhat shy. Are you and your father alike?"

"I suppose we are. Although I'm not sure I would put my own child on an airplane alone at such a young age. It was a good flight. I remember staring out the window at the clouds and at the miniscule farms and roads. The stewardesses talked with me, gave me headphones to use for listening to music and watching movies. One thing that was a bit scary was meeting my grandparents for the first time."

"You didn't even know them?"

He shook his head. "They picked me up at the airport. It took a few days for us to get acquainted, but by the time I returned home, I felt as if we'd always known each other." He stopped suddenly, nearly adding 'until she lied to me and I found I couldn't trust her.'

THE FOLLOWING MORNING Dave gathered his things

together and prepared to leave. Maurelle, watching him as he opened the door, said, “Be careful. I’m worried about you.”

He kissed her gently on the lips and pulled her close to him. When he let go of her, he reached down, picked up his duffel bag, and looked over at his grandmother who was standing in the kitchen doorway, watching him anxiously. He strode over to her, and gave her a big hug. “Take of yourself, Grand-mère. I love you.”

“You keep out of trouble, dear boy. We don’t want you getting yourself arrested over there.”

“I’ll be careful. And remember what we discussed. Don’t tell anyone about Maurelle’s situation. Promise?”

Fabienne nodded, wringing her hands nervously. “You can trust me.”

Dave nodded and looked at one woman and then the other. “Don’t tell anyone anything about where I’m going or what I’m doing. I can’t stress that enough. If anything goes wrong on either end, we could all be in serious trouble.”

Maurelle said, “It’s not too late for you to change your mind. You don’t have to go. You don’t have to jeopardize yourself or your grandmother.”

“I told you I’ve made up my mind. Grand-mère and I have talked it over. She’s willing to take a chance, too. I’m only trying to reiterate to both of you the need for secrecy.”

Fabienne said, “We’ll be careful. Promise.”

A car horn sounded outside. Dave dashed to the front door. He opened the door and picked up his bag. “My ride’s here. I guess I’ll see you both as soon as I can. Take care of each other.” He waved and started out the door to where the taxi was waiting.

Maurelle rushed over to him and gave him a quick kiss.

She and Fabienne stood together in the open doorway, waving as he climbed into the taxicab.

After he left, the two women strolled to the general store to buy groceries. After taking their purchases home, they headed out again. This time, Maurelle went to the cheese shop while Fabienne visited with her friend Jeannette. Maurelle had offered to buy the groceries earlier but Fabienne wouldn't let her. Now was her chance to surprise her with a gift basket of cheeses and crackers. She entered the cheese shop and greeted the clerk. While she waited in line, she studied the assorted cheeses within the glass case.

"Well, hello there, Maurelle," a voice from behind said.

She turned around abruptly and found herself face to face with Paul Lepage.

"Bonjour," she said.

"I've been hoping we might bump into each other again," Paul said. "Maybe we can have lunch together."

Her face grew hot. "Oh yes. I owe you a debt of gratitude for giving me a ride. Unfortunately, I've already made plans for lunch."

"All right. How about dinner? Tomorrow, around seven o'clock?"

"I—I can't," she said.

Paul stared at her. He opened his mouth to speak, but before he got a chance, the clerk said, "May I help you, Mademoiselle?"

"I think he's talking to you," Paul said. "It looks as though we'll have to continue this some other time."

Maurelle nodded. She whirled around and promptly stepped toward the glass case.

That evening, when Fabienne went into the kitchen to prepare dinner, Maurelle followed. While she watched, Maurelle would gather up things that Fabienne asked for. It made Maurelle feel better and made her feel as though she wasn't entirely a useless burden.

"How did you learn to cook so well?" she asked as she stirred a pot.

Fabienne looked up at her and gave her a rare smile. "I've always loved cooking. My mother and grandmother were the best cooks I've ever known, and they taught me, as I taught my own daughter, Eloise."

"Eloise? Is she Dave's mother?"

"Yes, she is," Fabienne said as she kneaded soft dough. "She met an American in Paris while she was attending the university. She married him after a couple of months. It was much too soon, and I tried to tell her so, but—" She gave Maurelle a sideways look.

"Did it work out?"

She shrugged. "They're still married after all these years."

"Then why do you think they moved too fast?"

Fabienne didn't answer right away. She kneaded the dough harder now, pounding it with her fists. When she finally spoke again, she sounded sadder.

"Eloise gave birth to Dave while she and her husband Edward were still at college. She had to leave school to take care of the baby. It wouldn't have been so bad if they'd moved here. Claude and I could have helped. But no. Edward wouldn't hear of it. He wanted to return to the U.S. Wanting to be near his own parents, he packed up the family and moved back. St. Louis," she said, pronouncing it as though it was French.

"Do you see her often?" Maurelle asked, taking a bite of cheese from a dish on the countertop.

"No. Never," Fabienne said, wagging her hand. "Once Dave was old enough, she and her husband would send Dave back here to spend his summers with us." After she placed her ready dough into a pan and shoved it into the oven, she turned to face Maurelle. "I shouldn't have let her see that wretched man. He turned my Eloise against me, he did. All I have now is my grandson."

"I'm sorry. Is that why you want him to move here?"

Fabienne stopped in the middle of kneading dough. "Where did you get that idea?"

Maurelle felt her face flush as she said meekly, "From Dave."

"He told you that?" Fabienne asked as she stood there, now with her hands on her hips. "Did he say anything about Simone?"

She didn't answer.

Fabienne smoothed her hair back out of her face, and finally said, "Simone is the granddaughter of my best friend, Jeannette. Simone is pretty. I thought Dave would like her. Jeannette's daughters are here. Coralie in Reynier, Brigitte in Orleans. Both of her grandchildren live in Reynier, too, now." Fabienne looked suddenly sad and tired, making Maurelle want to hug her; she didn't dare risk it for fear the woman would push her away. "They all include me in their family activities, almost as if I were one of them, but it's not the same as having your own family," she continued. "I was hoping Dave and Simone would make a good match because it's easier to be in-laws with friends than with strangers. I thought that Dave would move here with her, instead of whisking her away as his father did with my Eloise."

"I know what it's like not having a family around," Maurelle said. "It's the saddest thing in the world."

Fabienne's eyes suddenly filled with tears. Maurelle decided to take a chance. She moved closer to Fabienne and wrapped her arms around her. To Maurelle's surprise, the older woman squeezed her gently and stroked her hair.

"I'm sorry I haven't been a good hostess to you."

"You have nothing to apologize for." Maurelle stepped back and looked Fabienne in the eye. "I really didn't think I would ever again be among friends, that I would be able to trust people. You and Dave have made that possible."

Fabienne turned her head and studied Maurelle. "Why didn't

you seek help from your friends and family when you got into trouble?"

"My best friends, from my school days, moved away—one to Japan, one to the Australia, and one to the U.S.—within a few years after we all graduated from university. My newer friends were closer to my former boyfriend than to me, so when we broke up, I drifted away from them. As for my family—my father actually lives in Paris with his wife and their children. At first, I thought I might go to him for help. But—"

Fabienne looked at her questioningly, prompting her to continue.

"He didn't marry my mother. He didn't want her or me." She paused as emotion shook her voice. "My mother died two-and-a-half years ago. Cancer. She would have been horrified at my . . . situation. I could never have imagined I'd be glad that she isn't here to see what's become of me." Her voice cracked again with emotion as she whispered, "I miss her so much."

Now Fabienne reached over and hugged Maurelle, patting her on the back as if she was a child.

CHAPTER NINETEEN

DAVE THREW HIS carry-on bag over his shoulder and strode through the crowded Heathrow terminal, looking for signs that would direct him to public transportation stations for the London Underground, overland train, or city bus. Maurelle advised him that any of those would be preferable to renting a car and trying to maneuver on his own through London.

Finding the Tube turned out to be relatively easy since the underground system was linked to the terminal by moving walkways. But reading and understanding the underground map to where he wanted to go proved more difficult. He finally figured it out and from Terminal 2 he took the Picadilly Line to King's Cross and walked the rest of the way to the Hallworth Hotel where he and Greg would meet. He found it without problem and checked in. Entering his room, he dumped his bag onto the bed. The room, while rather old and perhaps not top of the line, appeared to be spotless and well appointed. He sat down on the edge of the bed. It was perhaps a bit too soft, but okay. He got up again and checked the TV, which also seemed in good working order. Time for a shower and change of clothes. He took a leisurely shower, dressed, glanced at his watch, and called down to the front desk to inquire if Greg Saunders had checked in. The clerk put his call through to Greg's room but there was no answer. He lay down and closed his eyes. A few minutes later, his telephone clanged so loudly that he woke up and nearly fell off the bed onto to the floor.

"Hello," Dave said.

"Cheerio, mate."

Huh? What the hell? Dave sat up, rubbed his head.

"I'm glad to hear that you made it here, old man," the voice said again.

"Is that you, Greg?"

"Were you expecting someone else?"

Dave laughed, stretching and relaxing his shoulders, and realizing that the trip had created a bit of stress. "It's good to hear your voice. I take it that you're here in London, too."

"Yep," Greg said. "Ready to meet for drinks and dinner?"

"Sure."

"I've already checked around," Greg said. "The pub across the street looks good."

"Okay. I'll meet you there—in say, fifteen minutes."

"Sounds like a plan."

DAVE STEPPED INTO the pub and stopped for a moment, glancing around in the dark for his friend. The pub was rather charming with bare stone walls, large open hearth fireplace, intricate stained glass windows and lamps, and massive wooden beams overhead. In fact, he mused, it looked a bit too charming, like some film set in a spy movie, but the atmosphere was definitely a big draw; the place was packed.

Greg sat at a corner table, waving his hands to get Dave's attention. Dave smiled, nodded, and made his way through the throng of tables and patrons. When he reached the table, Greg stood and greeted him with a handshake and a quick hug.

"Good to see you, buddy. It's been a while." Apparently noticing that Dave was looking at the other guy sitting at the table, he added, "This is my old friend, Nigel James. He's a local. He and I lost touch with each other after he moved back here. But after I talked to you, I decided to call him up."

Nigel stood and shook hands with Dave. "I've heard a lot about you. Greg has told me many stories of your adventures on the force. Sounds like you two had some good times."

"We sure did," Dave said.

Nigel said, "Greg started without us. I guess he can stay and guard our table whilst you and I go up to the bar to order."

When they returned, a brunette woman was leaning her arms on the back of their booth, talking with Greg. She flashed a smile at them when they approached, handed a piece of paper to Greg, and left.

Dave said, "What was that? Did she already give you her phone number? You know what, you're still as much a hound dog as ever."

Greg grinned and stuffed the paper into his shirt pocket. "Are you seeing anyone? We didn't get around to discussing that sort of thing on the phone last time we talked."

"Well, I've been writing, traveling, visiting family."

"Uh huh, and?" Greg asked. "Come on. Involved with anyone?"

"I've been seeing someone," Dave said. He told him briefly about Simone, hoping that would satisfy him.

Greg said, "Why is it that you have all the luck with women?"

"Huh, look who's talking," Dave said, "Are you trying to say you don't, after the little incident we just saw? You jump around from woman to woman. You always have, as long as I've known you."

Greg laughed. "I recently broke up with someone so of

course I'm already looking around!" He glanced after the brunette, who was now sitting at a table with two other women.

Dave and Nigel chuckled, then Dave asked the question he'd been wanting to ask. "So, how do you two know each other?"

Nigel said, "What? You mean Greg didn't tell you? I lived in the U.S. for two years and worked with him."

"Yeah," Greg said. "He joined our precinct about a year after you left. He suckered me into introducing him to my sister, Kelly. You remember her, don't you?"

"Sure."

"It was love at first sight, me and Kelly," Nigel said. "Before long, we were living together. We even got engaged."

"What happened?" Dave asked between sips of beer. "Did she move here with you?"

"No. She came to her senses and dumped him, that's what happened," Greg said, patting Nigel on the back.

"Sad but true. After that, I came home and asked for my old job back."

"He's a police detective here," Greg said, "but he isn't working on the case you're interested in."

Dave nearly choked on his drink. He'd told Greg not to share anything about their plans with anyone. So much for trust. Regaining his composure, he said, "Do you have any connections with the inspectors on that case?

Nigel said, "No. My dad's been a detective for forty years. I may be able to inquire through him."

Dave nodded.

"I don't mean to put a damper on things, but I still don't know why you're interested. Greg couldn't really explain. If you want my help, I need to know why you want the information and what you plan to do with it."

"I'm exploring the case as part of research for a novel I'm writing."

Nigel sat back against the pub bench. Finally, he said, "Do you expect me to believe that?" Nigel shook his head and in a coolly impersonal tone said, "You'll have to do better than that. I'm not stupid and I'm certainly not inclined to help someone who can't be straight with me."

THE DAY AFTER Fabienne began teaching her how to cook some of her best French dishes, Maurelle felt as though she had gained not only a cooking instructor, but also a friend. After her latest lesson, the two women munched on the scrumptious creations together, chatting and laughing like old friends. Afterward, Fabienne suggested they plant flowers around the site where Dave had buried the mouse a couple of days before, endearing herself even further to Maurelle. They spent the entire afternoon procuring suitable plants at the town garden shop, planting the flowers, and puttering around the backyard garden.

"You're good at this," Fabienne said. "Have you done much gardening?"

"My mother had a lovely garden when we lived near Oxford. I would help her plant flowers and shrubs. We put in paths and fountains and benches. I started helping so I could spend more time with her, but I discovered that I really enjoyed the work."

"You lived near Oxford? Did you attend Oxford University?"

"No, but my mother was a lecturer at one of the colleges there for many years. She eventually accepted a position at London University, and we moved. I was twelve at the time. Being in the city, we had a smaller home and not much yard for a garden."

"Was your mother sad about that?"

"Not really. She soon met a man, a semi-retired professor, and he got her interested in travel. They took long trips over the summers to Germany, Switzerland, Italy, Denmark, and weekend trips to the countryside or to Scotland. I'm glad they had that time together. He passed away from leukemia six months before my mother died. A month after he died, she learnt she had cancer, too. So I'm very glad they had that time together."

"Did you travel with them?"

"Not usually. I was at boarding school, at first, and then at University. After that, I was working."

When they finished with their gardening and went back inside the house, the telephone was ringing.

"That must be Dave," Fabienne said as she rushed to answer the phone, with Maurelle following closely.

After hanging up, Fabienne shoulders sagged. "That was Jeannette calling to remind me that we're invited to a dinner party at her house tonight. I'd completely forgotten."

"You mean you are invited, don't you?"

Fabienne shook her head. "She said both of us."

"I can't go. If Simone is there, it will be miserable. She and I don't really get along."

"Don't worry about Simone. Jeannette knows you two don't like each other. She's assured me that Simone has other plans for the evening. You'll like Jeannette once you get to know her. Why don't you go upstairs and do whatever you need to do? While you're doing that, I need to run to the store to get a small gift for our hostess. I won't be long."

"What should I wear?"

"I'm changing into my best dress when I return from the store. You should wear that lovely skirt and blouse you wore the other day."

"HELLO FABIENNE," SOMEONE called from behind her. "I've missed seeing you in the café."

Fabienne swung around as Simone stepped onto the sidewalk near the doorway to the florist shop, apparently having crossed the street moments earlier. "Oh, yes, I've been quite busy lately. Sorry."

"Grand-mère misses you, too."

"I know. I talked to her earlier today. I'm going to her dinner party tonight. That's why I'm out and about. I need to buy a gift to take."

Simone nodded and looked as if she wanted to say something; then she shrugged.

"Well, good day, Simone."

Fabienne turned to go into the shop.

"Wait. How is Dave doing? I haven't heard from him recently."

"He's fine. Very busy. You know how it is."

Before Simone had a chance to answer, Fabienne waved, smiled, pulled open the door, and dashed inside the florist shop. She wished she didn't have to be curt, but she was afraid the younger woman would engage her in more conversation. Gossip was a hard habit to break, she'd discovered, and Fabienne worried she wouldn't be able to control her tongue if Simone managed to get her caught up in some juicy chitchat.

MAURELLE DRESSED IN her best skirt and blouse, and went downstairs to join Fabienne, who had already changed clothes and was fussing with a bouquet composé.

"What do you think of this?"

"It's lovely. I'm sure she'll be pleased."

As they headed out the door, Fabienne said, "The guests will be Jeannette's daughter and her boyfriend, Jeannette's grandson, and a few friends of the family. Be friendly but it's probably best if you let me do most of the talking. I know how to deal with them, especially with Jeannette."

Maurelle nodded. Keeping quiet suited her fine.

Along the brief walk to Jeannette's house, Maurelle enjoyed the light evening breeze and the smells of foods that drifted through the open windows of neighboring homes, making her grow hungrier by the minute.

When they arrived, Fabienne handed Jeannette the gift, which elicited the inevitable "Oh, il ne fallait pas", which Maurelle translated as, "Oh, you shouldn't have." Jeannette, dressed in an expensive looking dress that made everyone else look under-dressed for the occasion, ushered her guests into a sitting room that almost made Maurelle gasp. She would never have expected such a luxurious room from the outside appearance of the house.

Jeannette offered them an aperitif while she placed the bouquet of mixed flowers into a waiting vase. Then, looking around, she leaned in and asked, "Where is David? Didn't he come with you?"

"No. The dear boy is away on business. He had to meet with his editor or agent, I'm not sure. Something about his latest book. I'm sure he wouldn't have missed your dinner party if he could have avoided it. You understand, yes?"

"Of course," Jeannette said, motioning toward the couch, her diamond-studded bracelet dangling from her wrist for everyone to see. "Please, please sit. I'm glad you and—what was your name, again?"

"Maurelle Dupre."

"I'm glad you could come, too, Maurelle."

A moment later, Paul Lepage, along with a tallish middle-aged woman whom Maurelle didn't recognize, came out of the kitchen.

"Oh, you're here," the woman said, rushing over to Fabienne. Bending down and kissing her on one cheek and then the other, she said, "Bonsoir. I'm so glad you could come." She turned, straightened up, and looked down at Maurelle. "I don't believe we've met."

Jeannette said, "This is Maurelle Dupre. She is staying with Fabienne." She quickly added, "And this is my daughter, Coralie Charboneau."

"I'm delighted to meet you, Madame Charboneau." Maurelle knew, of course, that Coralie was Simone's mother because Fabienne had told her, but she was surprised how alike they looked—the same golden blonde hair and gray-blue eyes. Coralie looked more like Simone's older sister than her mother.

Coralie glanced around the room, and asked, "But where is Dave?"

"Unfortunately, he is away on business," Jeannette said, waving her hand as she spoke.

Coralie looked surprised, but before she could respond Paul stepped forward, kissed Fabienne on both cheeks, and looked at Maurelle.

Jeannette looked abashed. "Please forgive me. Mademoiselle Dupre, let me introduce my grandson, Paul Lepage. His mother is my youngest daughter, Brigitte."

Maurelle said, "We have met, actually."

"You have?" Jeannette and Fabienne said, simultaneously.

"Well, yes." All eyes focused on Maurelle, and she almost stumbled over her words. "Dave introduced us, though he didn't tell me he was your grandson." She looked from Jeannette to Paul. They didn't really resemble one another. Jeannette's red hair, which was obviously dyed, gave no hint as to whether she originally had blonde hair like her daughter and granddaughter or had black hair like her grandson. She held her breath, hoping he wouldn't mention the hitchhiking incident.

Paul nodded, but didn't comment.

Jeannette cleared her throat. "We're waiting on a few more

guests. They should be here momentarily."

While they waited, Maurelle caught Paul staring at her from across the room. He nodded, then turned and walked away.

Ten minutes later, more guests arrived and introductions were made: Coralie's boyfriend Serge, Sandrine Fortier, Jonas and Lillian Lefevre, and Charles and Helene Gavalda. Maurelle remembered Sandrine, the nurse who had attended to her after the hitchhiking incident, but neither of them mentioned it.

After everyone had an aperitif, Jeannette escorted her guests into the dining room, and assigned seats to her guests. Maurelle noticed Jonas Lefevre watching her from across the table and down several spaces. Before they could begin the meal, the doorbell rang and Jeannette excused herself, returning moments later with Simone in tow.

Maurelle's mouth dropped open involuntarily. She quickly snapped it shut, hoping no one had noticed. She flashed a look at Fabienne who looked equally surprised.

After another round of greetings, Simone took a seat at the dinner table.

"Simone had a previous engagement, but it was cancelled. She's going to join us."

Simone raised her eyebrows and asked, "Where is Dave?"

Jeannette said, "He's out of town, on business, isn't that right, Fabienne? Or is he out of the country? You didn't really say?"

Before Fabienne opened her mouth to answer, Simone made a clicking sound of disapproval with her mouth. "He left without telling me? He didn't even say au revoir?" She paused, and her face clouded over. "I bought tickets for us to attend the theatre together in Vendome for tonight. He didn't even call to tell me he couldn't make it."

"I'm sure he simply forgot in his haste. He'll be back," Fabienne said. "Something came up unexpectedly. His work, something about his book, you know."

Simone pouted, stood up, and turned on her heel. Almost as abruptly, she stopped and turned to face the dinner table. "She did this," she said quietly, glaring at Maurelle.

Maurelle felt her own face grow hot as all eyes focused on her. She couldn't think of anything to say to help the situation.

Jeannette stood and positioned her arms on Simone's shoulders. "I'm sure that Dave will be back soon." She rubbed her granddaughter's shoulders, and continued in a soothing voice, "Fabienne has told me that she is the one helping Maurelle now—not Dave. Don't be upset. Please come and sit. Dinner is getting cold."

Simone didn't move or say anything. The room was quiet and everyone's eyes now focused on Simone and Jeannette.

Finally, Simone broke the silence this time as she glared at Fabienne. "I don't believe that Dave is away on business. He told me that everything was going great with his latest book, and that he didn't need to go back to Chicago or to his publisher in New York any time soon."

"I told you that it was unexpected, Simone," Fabienne said. "He couldn't have known ahead of time."

"You're lying," Simone said. "The way you lied to get him here. He told me about that. I know what a liar you are."

Fabienne's face turned bright red and she wagged her hand at Simone. "You ungrateful . . . ! I should never have introduced you to my grandson."

"I think he's doing something for her. I've been thinking about what you told us last week, about her being in trouble with the law. He's gotten himself involved, hasn't he?"

Not waiting for Fabienne to answer, Simone said, "Of course he would. That's the detective in him." She squinted her eyes, causing little wrinkles to gather around her nose. "So, what has Maurelle done that would make Dave leave here without taking her along? Why would he need to keep her hidden?"

Fabienne gathered her napkin in her hands and twisted it.

"Out with it," Simone demanded. "If you won't tell me, maybe I'll make a call to the Gendarmerie Nationale."

"You wouldn't dare," Fabienne said. "Dave would never forgive you."

"Then he is hiding her from the gendarmes!" Simone stood with her hands on her hips, satisfaction plastered on her face.

Fabienne clapped her hand over her mouth, and sank back in her chair. Suddenly, she scooted her chair back and stood. "We should go," she said.

CHAPTER TWENTY

AFTER DINNER WITH Greg and Nigel, Dave excused himself and went back to his hotel room. The last thing he wanted to do was to go "pubbing" with them. *Damn Greg.* He knew Dave wanted to keep a low profile. What had made him think that bringing a local detective in on the investigation would work? Of course the guy would want to know why he was interested in the case; no cop in his right mind would blindly help them.

He pulled back the covers on the bed, undressed, and laid down. Hoping for a distraction from his worries, he turned on the television, but he switched it off ten minutes later. His mind dwelled on the newspaper articles he'd read and his conversation with Nigel until he eventually nodded off to sleep. Dave slept fitfully, tossing and turning all night, dreaming about Maurelle in a British courtroom with judges wearing white wigs. By the time he awoke, he wondered if he'd made a serious mistake coming here.

He dragged himself out of bed, showered, and dressed quickly, giving himself no time for second thoughts. He pulled out a London map and public transportation guides, studying them to develop a plan for the day. He would go to the

Raybourne home first, where the murder had occurred, and check it out from the outside. With any luck, he might get a chance to speak with neighbors. Also, somewhere along the way, purchasing a disposable phone or a phone card would be prudent.

With plan in hand, he exited his hotel room, pulling the door shut and locking it. As he turned to leave, he came face to face with Greg who was rushing along the narrow hallway.

"Hey, buddy," Greg said. "Glad I caught you before you headed out. We need to talk."

Dave grunted.

"Sorry about last night, but you've gotta understand. Nigel isn't going to stick his neck out for you if you won't tell him what this is all about. He can't trust you; he doesn't know you like I do."

"I know. I got that. I'm sorry I dragged you into this. I'll go it alone on this one. Enjoy your stay here in London."

"Hey, I didn't say I wouldn't help. But I don't think Nigel will unless you open up."

"That's not going to happen. You know me well enough. I don't trust easily, not anymore." He looked away.

"But you expect everyone else to trust you," Greg said, raising his hand. "That's not exactly fair."

"I have my reasons."

"Let's get some breakfast and talk, okay?"

"I'm not really in the mood."

"Come on. You owe me a breakfast considering I flew all the way here because you asked me to."

"All right. We can go to the coffee shop next door."

Ten minutes later, after ordering coffee and pastries, they carried their purchases to a table and sat down.

"Look, you know darn well that you wouldn't stick your neck out for anyone without knowing what you were getting yourself into. That includes me. I trust you, buddy, but I need something. After all we've been through together, you know I trust you. But even I need to know why you're so interested in this case."

Dave rolled his shoulders, looked around uncomfortably, then stared at the floor.

"Back when we were partners, you did everything by the book—at least up until the end. You would have made anyone asking for help on a case outside your jurisdiction jump through hoops before you'd get involved."

"Okay, but I can't tell Nigel," Dave said. "He may be the one person who could help because of his connections, but he could as easily bring everything crumbling down."

"Oh, God," Greg said. He looked at Dave in concern. "You know the suspect, don't you?"

Dave shrugged, shuffling his feet nervously.

"Is she this 'Simone' that you told us about?"

"No. I was seeing Simone before I met her."

"Oh, man! Please don't tell me you're involved with the suspect."

"I didn't know about the case when I met her. I want to make that clear."

Greg looked at him as if he thought Dave had lost his mind, but he didn't say anything.

"Look," Dave said, "I'm going to keep an open mind and look at all the evidence I can find before I make a judgment. I don't know if she's guilty or innocent, but I need to find out."

"So where is she?" Greg asked.

"I can't tell you that."

"What if she's using you? What if she's guilty?"

"Then I'll find out and turn her over to the police. I'm not going to help her get away with murder if she is guilty. I already told her that."

Greg was silent for a few moments, obviously weighing what Dave had revealed to him. Dave hated putting his friend on the spot like this, but he seemed to have little choice except to come clean with Greg about Maurelle. Unfortunately, Greg was just too good a detective and saw through his apparently weak subterfuge.

"Okay", Greg said. "Although I'll probably be sorry for this, I'm still willing to help. I see now why you didn't wanna tell Nigel. Man, you really know how to get yourself into a mess."

Dave said, "Thank you for trusting in me." Greg looked like he was going to say something, but Dave raised his hand to hold him off. "I know it's a lot to ask of you. For now at least, it's better for you if you do not know her whereabouts and we stick to my cover story about my doing research for a novel; plausible deniability and all that. I asked you here though because I've been out of touch with police work for too long. I need your expertise and your insights. I can't confide in Nigel for obvious reasons, but I have been thinking about other potential help. I read some newspaper articles last week. Most were slanted against the accused, but there was one which commented on the presumption of guilt and the way that it was being assumed she had run away because of guilt. The writer showed how circumstantial was the evidence as known to the public, taking each point in turn."

"So, what are you thinking?"

"Maybe we could start by talking to the journalist. He might consider working with us?"

"That might work. Do you remember the journalist's name?"

"K. L. Hill. The article was an opinion piece and said that he was a freelance journalist."

"Have you looked up the guy online?"

Dave said, "No, I haven't tried yet."

"Okay, so what do you need me to do?"

"I'm still concerned that I was wrong in asking you to come here. I didn't think it through properly."

"Why do you say that?"

"With each bit of information I give you, you become more at risk. It's bad enough that I could go to jail for protecting her. I certainly don't want you in trouble, too."

"Look Dave, I'm a big boy and can make my own decisions. You were honest with me. While I don't know if this woman is innocent or guilty, I'll reserve judgment on that score once we get the facts. But I am curious now, too, and I want to help you find the answers you need—as long as you don't let your feelings for her cloud your judgment."

Dave said nothing, but after a few moments nodded and lifted his hands in a gesture of surrender.

"So, where do we start?"

"Scene of the crime, if we can. Hampstead. I want to check out the neighborhood where the murder took place. I was planning to go this morning."

"Do you have the address?"

"Yeah. She gave me the address as well as names and other details. We can snoop around the neighborhood and maybe talk to neighbors."

"Sounds like a plan," Greg said, smiling.

BACK AT THE house, Maurelle and Fabienne sat in the kitchen, talking and worrying long into the night, neither of them hungry, both of them tired. They had rushed home from the quarrel, missing the dinner and regretfully embarrassing their hostess which, after the scene with Simone, had been unavoidable. Both women felt extremely uncomfortable about the incident and both were worried about what Simone would do.

Finally, Fabienne said, "We should try to get some sleep. I'll talk to Jeannette in the morning. I hope she and Coralie talked some sense into Simone."

Maurelle tried to fall asleep, but she tossed and turned, her mind fixating on one worry after another, trapping each one in a mind-web that grew ever wider. Finally, she managed to thrash it away long enough to catch a couple of hours of sleep before she awoke and began the whole process again. Hoping to surprise Fabienne by making the morning coffee, she hastened downstairs. But halfway down, the scent and hiss of coffee brewing greeted her.

"Good morning," Maurelle said, trying to sound cheery. "I wanted to make coffee and breakfast for you this morning."

Fabienne waved her hand. "That's sweet of you, but I couldn't sleep. I needed to do something useful."

"Same for me. I'm so sorry that I put you in this situation."

"Don't you go blaming yourself for Simone's actions. If you want, you can help me with the omelets. We should try to go about our usual business until a reasonable hour. When it's time, I'll call Jeannette and find out what happened after we left."

"What can I do to help?"

"Here, you can chop up the ham into tiny pieces while I grate the cheese."

Half an hour later, the omelets made, they finished eating, and sat sipping coffee. Fabienne looked at the clock. "I suppose I should call Jeannette. She should be up by now."

Maurelle stood up. "While you do that, I'll clean up in here."

A few minutes later, Fabienne hung up the telephone. The expression on her face sent chills through Maurelle.

"What's wrong?"

"Jeannette says she can't talk to me right now. She'll come by the house as soon as she can get away."

Maurelle bit her lower lip. "That doesn't sound good, does it?"

"No. I guess we should try to keep busy until then." Fabienne bustled around the kitchen, storing away the washed dishes while Maurelle swept the floor. Fabienne wasn't whistling or humming her favorite songs the way she usually did, and Maurelle became increasingly concerned.

The doorbell rang, making both women jump.

Fabienne wiped her hands on her apron, and rushed into the living room with Maurelle trailing behind.

'Bonjour," Jeannette said. "I'm sorry it took me so long to get here." She looked nervous.

"What happened after we left last night?" Fabienne asked.

"Simone calmed down, eventually, and we ate our dinner—cold. It was my worst dinner party, ever."

Maurelle moved closer. "I'm really sorry about messing up your party. If I hadn't gone, everything would have been fine."

Fabienne wagged her hand. "Oh, non! It wouldn't have made a difference."

"She's right about that," Jeannette said. "Simone would have shown up, anyway, and she was angry—not at you, in truth, but at Dave. He didn't tell her he was leaving. He stood her up and she lashed out at the two of you."

"So, everything's better now?" Fabienne asked.

Jeannette bit her lip, her face reddening. "Well, no, I'm afraid not. This morning Coralie came over. She told me that she'd gone to Simone's café for coffee and Paul was there."

Fabienne raised her eyebrows, her bifocals slipping precariously on the bridge of her nose. "What happened?"

"Well, Paul got into an argument with Simone. Apparently, he told Simone that she should call the Gendarmerie Nationale, but she refused, saying that whether or not Dave loved her, he was still her friend and she would lose him for sure if she turned in Maurelle. Anyway, Paul stormed out, saying he would make the call as soon as he returned home. She took off after him, and begged him not to call but he ignored her."

Fabienne's face went white, and Maurelle felt her heart race.

"Why would he do that?" Fabienne asked.

"He thinks Maurelle is hiding something. He also said that he, as the only male in the family, owes it to his cousin to look out for her."

Jeannette paused and took a deep breath before waddling over to the couch and sitting down. "Simone sent Coralie to my house. She asked me to call Paul and see if I could talk him out of it, but his phone was busy. When I finally reached him, the deed was done. He told me that the Gendarmerie Nationale will send gendarmes here to investigate. They are in Belvidere. They could arrive any time."

"Oh dear God! What are we supposed to do now?"

"You must send her away," Jeannette said. "I don't know what she's hiding, but if you're caught harboring a criminal, you could be arrested."

Fabienne turned to face Maurelle. "Gather your things. We must get you out of here. I'll pack a bag, too."

Maurelle started up the stairs, and was halfway up, when it suddenly dawned on her that Fabienne had said she would pack a bag, too. She paused and turned around, her hand on the railing, and listened to the two women in the living room.

"Can you talk Coralie into loaning us her car so we can get away?"

Jeannette looked flabbergasted. "Mon dieu! You can't drive! Have you lost your mind?"

Fabienne motioned toward the stairs. "She can."

"You don't have to leave with her. Dear Fabienne, I never meant that you should go away. You can tell the gendarmes that you didn't know about the girl's problems until last night. You can tell them that she took off during the night and you don't know where she went."

Fabienne shook her head hard. "I'm going with her. Dave wouldn't forgive me if I didn't. Besides, I trust her. Now, are you going to ask Coralie to loan me, us, the car?"

Jeannette pouted. Her face looked red as a tomato even from Maurelle's vantage point midway up the stairs.

After a brief pause, Jeannette said, "All right. But on one condition: I'm going with you."

"Are you crazy? Why would you want to put yourself in the middle of our problem?"

"Well, first of all, you're my oldest and dearest friend, and second, no one has taken me on a road trip in years and I am not about to miss my chance, and third, who on earth will look after you if I don't?"

Fabienne suddenly burst out laughing and crying at the same time, and the two women hugged.

Maurelle stared in disbelief. It was bad enough that Fabienne wanted to go, but Jeannette? Jeannette didn't even like her.

"I'll pack my things," Fabienne said to Jeannette. "I guess you better get busy, too. We don't have much time."

CHAPTER TWENTY-ONE

DAVE HAD ALREADY mapped out the tube route to Hampstead, but Greg had other ideas: he wanted to ride on one of London's famous double-decker buses.

"The tube will be faster," Dave said.

"Not necessarily. Nigel says the buses here are better than in Chicago."

After making inquiries, the men discovered they could catch the bus at Euston, which wasn't far from their hotel. By the time they reached their destination, Dave had to admit he had enjoyed the ride. The top deck gave them a great view of the city along the way.

They exited at Flask Walk, Hampstead's pedestrian mall, a kind of an alley of specialty shops, chic boutiques, and the ubiquitous pubs. From there, they walked through the residential area.

When they passed Hampstead tube station and the Finchley Road station, Greg said, "I guess we should have taken the subway after all. Would have saved us a lot of walking."

Dave chuckled. Greg had always been hardheaded. "Next time. Walking around the area was a great way to get ourselves oriented."

Ten minutes later, they reached Willoughby Crescent, the cul-de-sac where Maurelle had lived for several months. Number eleven, the Raybourne home, was a purplish brown brickwork house of average-size for the neighborhood, two-stories tall, square, with the middle one-third of the face pushed out about two feet to make a bay window. The five front windows, all mullioned, were trimmed in white.

"Damn," Dave said. "I wish we could get inside and look around."

"You thinking of breaking in?" Greg poked at his friend.

"No, of course not. Just thinking."

He turned around and looked at the neighbor's house across the street and the houses on either side of the Raybourne house. "What do you say we head over to Ian Waitley's house and ask him a few questions?"

"Who?"

"A neighbor. I have a list of names, addresses, and phone numbers."

"Ah, okay."

Since no one was home, they went to Alice Rickards' house. No one answered there either.

"Now what?" Greg asked.

"The house on the other side. Judy Winston."

Dave rang the doorbell and waited. After a few minutes, he turned to leave at the same moment the door opened. A gray-haired woman said, "May I help you?"

"Sorry to bother you," Dave said. "Are you Judy Winston?"

"I am."

"Well, my friend here is a detective from the U.S. and I'm a writer. He's helping me do research for a book I'm working on, a book set here in the U.K. and with a similar plot to the Jared Raybourne murder case. We hoped we might talk to neighbors and ask questions to get some insight."

She looked from one to the other. "What sort of questions?"

"Just general background."

"Did she go to America, then?"

Baffled by the leap she had taken, Dave opened his mouth but didn't answer.

Greg said, "No, although there may be an American connection."

"You'd better come in," she said, looking past them into the street. She led them into her living room. "Would you like some tea?"

Greg said, "That would be nice."

She smiled. "Please sit and make yourselves comfortable. I'll be back in a jiffy."

Five minutes later, barely long enough to boil water for tea, she returned carrying a silver tray with three cups and a plate of cookies. She handed them each a tea cup. Dave took a sip. It was coffee.

"Please have some biscuits," she said, holding out the tray of cookies for them.

Dave realized then that 'biscuit' was the British word for cookie. He took one and nibbled it. Greg took two.

She said, "I've always wanted to write a book. My daughter says she'll help me write my memoirs when she has time. But I suspect I'll be long gone before that happens." She chuckled.

Dave studied the woman. Her short gray hair looked as if she'd come straight from her hairdresser, and although her pale blue eyes looked tired, she seemed younger than sixty, remembering Maurelle having indicated her age.

"What do you want to ask me?"

Dave said, "Well, where were you the night of the murder? Did you see anything suspicious?"

"Dear me, no. I was on a trip to see my daughter and her children in Edinburgh. I got home a week after the murder. I must say, when I heard about it, I was in shock. Murder right here in our quiet little neighborhood! I thought I'd moved away from the high crime areas. The estate agent assured me this was a safe area. But we've had one thing after another—and finally murder. I'm afraid to go to sleep at night."

"What other kinds of problems has the neighborhood had, Mrs. Winston?"

"Graffiti, thefts, vandalism. That sort of thing. Some of us think it was that boy who was responsible for most of it."

"That boy? Do you mean Jared Raybourne?"

She nodded. "We haven't had any trouble since he was killed."

"Who do you think killed Jared?"

"Me? Well, I wouldn't know really. I mean . . . I wasn't here, after all, and I didn't know him. Gangs, I suppose."

"You haven't heard anything?"

"I've heard reports on the news, of course. Who hasn't? And in the newspapers. The boy's parents are certain it was Maura Barrington—she rented a room from Elizabeth Raybourne."

"Do you know Maura?"

"I met her. She was nice, but kind of shy."

"Do you think she killed Jared?"

Judy Winston shrugged. "It's hard to imagine, but I suppose people can be pushed to extreme action. If anyone could push someone, it was that boy. It's a good thing I'm not home much, because someone—maybe Jared—vandalized my home once, and I can tell you if I'd caught him vandalizing it again, I might have been pushed to throttle the little so-and-so myself."

Dave and Greg exchanged glances, and then Dave asked, "Did he have a lot of enemies?"

"Oh, I wouldn't be the least bit surprised. Gangs, I expect."

"Can you think of anyone else in the neighborhood who might be willing to talk to us and answer our questions? Anyone who knew Jared or the teacher?"

"There's Brittany Stevas. She's a pupil at that school. I don't know if she had any classes with Jared. I do know she was in one of Maura's classes. Her mother told me that, right after the police began questioning everyone."

She gave them the address. They thanked her for her help and left.

At the Stevas's residence, Dave rang the doorbell. A young woman with long blonde hair answered.

"Hello," Dave said. "We're looking for Brittany Stevas."

"I'm Brittany." She was slender and wore jeans and a tee-shirt with 'Plan B' on the front.

"Sorry to bother you," he said. "A few minutes ago we spoke to one of your neighbors, Judy Winston. She suggested we come here and talk to you. I'm a writer, and my associate and I are conducting research for a book."

"You're Americans?"

"Yes, we are," Greg said, moving up one step so that he was now standing next to Dave on the porch.

"I plan to visit the U.S. someday. What part of the country do you come from?"

"Illinois," Greg said. She frowned, then shrugged as though it meant nothing to her.

Dave said, "Mrs. Winston told us that you went to school with Jared Raybourne and that you knew the schoolteacher, Maura Barrington. Is that correct?"

She eyed him speculatively. "Why do you want to know that?"

"As I said, I'm a writer. This might be the sort of thing to get dramatized, you know?"

"Wow, I wouldn't have thought the case was important enough to be on American television."

Dave smiled. "Oh, we didn't actually hear about it until we

got over here. We've spoken to an inspector from Scotland Yard and he told us about some interesting cases in the area, this being one of them."

She nodded, seemingly satisfied with his answer.

"Jared and I went to school together, but we weren't in the same classes."

"Did you hang out together outside of school?"

"Nooo waaay." She shook her head. "I may have spoken with him two or three times the whole time he lived in the neighborhood."

"How long did he live here?"

"I dunno. Maybe five or six years."

"What about the teacher? Did you know her?"

"Yes, she was my English teacher."

Greg asked, "Do you believe she killed Jared Raybourne?"

Brittany shook her head. "No, but there are plenty of people who think she's guilty. I guess we might never know."

Dave asked, "Why is that?"

"She disappeared. Some people think she ran, others think the killer got her, too."

"What about the boy's mother? What do you know about her?"

Brittany shrugged. "Don't really know hardly anything about her. I never met her. I saw her sometimes in the street, you know? That's all."

Dave asked, "What about your parents? Do they know her? Are they friends?"

"I don't think so. I mean, they talk occasionally, but I wouldn't call them friends or anything." A dog started barking and ran up to her from somewhere in the house. "Sorry, I better get going." She grabbed hold of the dog's collar and pulled him back.

Greg smiled. "Thanks for talking with us, Brittany."

She started to close the door, then pulled it open again and shouted at them as they were walking away. "Hey, if you're really interested, you might talk to Ian Waitley, the old man across the street from the Raybournes. He's always looking out his windows. Gets on my nerves, you know? Like he's perving. He has eagle eyes and sees more than anyone else round here. Don't get me wrong, though. Ian's all right for an old guy. He's funny and we talk sometimes."

LATER, IN THE afternoon, Dave searched online for K. L. Hill and found numerous articles written by her, and a few about her. K. L. stood for Kate Louise Hill. She was a fifty year old journalist who had at one time, according to one article, worked for a big newspaper, but went out on her own because she apparently disagreed far too often with her bosses; the writer of the piece hinted that this was more due to her than to her editors.

He found her website and read everything that was posted. Her photo looked younger than fifty, but he figured it might be an old photo. He clicked on the contact link, and sent her an email. An hour later, while Dave sat in a pub with his laptop on the table next to his meal, Kate sent a reply. Yes, she would meet with him tomorrow at noon. Her office was in her home in Putney.

CHAPTER TWENTY-TWO

MAURELLE CARRIED HER bags downstairs and stood facing the front window, though she stayed hidden behind the curtain. The house was quiet except for the ticking of the grandfather click. A man walked past the window, and she held her breath, waiting for a knock on the door. Nothing happened. Her instinct pressed her to flee now, but that's what she always did and it hadn't worked out. She'd also promised Dave she wouldn't disappear while he was investigating in England. And what about Fabienne who was placing herself in harm's way for her?

Maurelle turned around and glanced at the stairs, then stared at the front door. Fabienne was still in her bedroom gathering things for the trip. When Dave made her promise not to leave, he certainly hadn't anticipated this turn of events. Would he want her to stay and let the gendarmes take her into custody? Would he want her to drag his grandmother into hiding? Either way, Fabienne could be at risk for harboring a criminal. And what of Jeannette? So far, she was not involved at all. Taking her away from Reynier could get her into trouble as well.

"I'm ready," Fabienne said.

Turning abruptly, Maurelle watched the older woman pad down the stairs, dragging a suitcase that looked like it was at least fifty years old.

"Here, let me get that for you," Maurelle said, rushing up the stairs.

"Thank you, dear. Jeannette should be here any minute. Would you mind helping me water the newly planted flowers? We don't want them to die while we're gone."

Maurelle set the bag down in the living room. She closed her eyes, took a deep breath, and for the umpteenth time hoped she was making the right decision; her track record wasn't good. "Of course. Maybe Coralie will agree to come over and water them periodically while we're away."

"That's a good idea. I'll ask her."

After watering the plants, they stood together, looking out the front window and waiting for Coralie and Jeannette. The silver BMW pulled up and Fabienne clapped her hands.

Coralie was already getting out of the car when Maurelle opened the front door. She looked up at them and waved. As the duo assembled their luggage and struggled out the door, Coralie placed a hand on Fabienne's shoulder and said, "Maman tells me she insists on going with you. Are you sure you want to do this?"

Fabienne nodded.

"I don't know how much mother told you, but I'm going with you as far as Orleans. If anyone asks, Simone will say that Maurelle took off on foot during the night, and that the three of us have gone to visit my sister, Brigitte, in Orleans." Looking at Maurelle, she said, "I'll get out at my sister's. Brigitte is expecting me. She'll drive me back in a week or two. You can continue on from her house."

"You told Simone?" Fabienne asked, holding her hand on her chest. "Can we trust her?"

"She's sworn that she'll stick to the story. I don't think she would betray her own family."

Fabienne eased her elderly frame carefully into the car.

"Does Simone know that it's not true?"

"She does. But she doesn't know where you're going. For that matter, mother hasn't told me."

"And what about Brigitte? How much of this does she know?" Fabienne asked.

Coralie pulled away from the house and drove down to the main road. "I told Brigitte simply that I'm visiting her for a week or so, while you are going on vacation elsewhere. She doesn't know anything more."

The drive to Orleans went by quickly, with everyone chattering, and Maurelle almost forgot that this wasn't actually a pleasure trip but a criminal getaway. When Coralie pulled up outside Brigitte's house, everyone climbed out of the car and met with Brigitte who was standing near the road watching them. Coralie took her own bag out of the trunk and closed the lid, then stood by, watching her mother and Fabienne out of the corner of her eye. They were talking excitedly as they stretched their legs.

After the women said their goodbyes and the trio climbed back into the car, Fabienne and Jeannette both opting for back seats, Coralie handed the car keys to Maurelle. "Drive carefully. And keep a close eye on those two. They are old and fragile, but they can still get themselves in trouble."

Maurelle smiled and nodded.

Coralie added, "For some reason unknown to me, they appear to trust you. I hope they're right in doing so."

"I won't let you or them down, I assure you. I appreciate everything that you're doing."

Coralie nodded. "Be careful, all of you, and don't forget to call me when you get to wherever it is you're going."

Maurelle had been wondering all morning about their eventual destination, but she didn't ask. She wondered, too, how the older women would get back home and how Coralie would get her car back since the two older women didn't know how to drive.

As she stuck the key into the ignition and started the engine, the enormity of the situation hit her hard. Since she—being from England—had to sit on the wrong side of the car and drive on the wrong side of the road, this wasn't going to be an easy drive regardless where they were going. It didn't help that her companions didn't know the least bit about driving, from what she could tell. "Where are we going?" she asked.

Jeannette said, "Follow Fabienne's instructions for now. She knows how to get us out of Orleans. We'll tell you more when you need to know." She leaned back in her seat and folded her hands in her lap. As Maurelle's eyes locked with Jeannette's via the rear-view mirror, Jeannette's mouth twisted into a smug smile and Maurelle gritted her teeth, wishing the redhead hadn't insisted on tagging along.

Following Fabienne's instructions, she drove south from Orleans, and to her relief she adapted quickly to the difference in driving. She was also pleasantly relieved to find that Fabienne was good at map reading.

At the city of Bourges, Jeannette asked if they could stop for lunch. During lunch Fabienne spread the map over the table and pointed out the route they would take to the Languedoc-Rousillon region of France.

"Where are we going?" Maurelle asked. "Do you have a destination in mind?"

Jeannette said, "Saint-Julien-du-Tarn."

Looking closely at the map, Maurelle found the town, which seemed even more isolated and remote than Reynier, potentially making it a good hiding spot. But getting there involved driving over rugged mountainous terrain, which might not be so easy. After studying the route a few minutes more, she decided she would make it work somehow. What choice did she have?

She folded the map, and sat listening to the older women chat excitedly. Apparently, this was a great adventure for the two. When there was a lull in conversation, she asked, "How did you find this place? I mean, what made you decide on Saint-Julien-du-Tarn?"

"Oh, dear me," Fabienne said, looking flustered. "Let me see. My husband, Claude, inherited his parents' house there." She paused. "Heavens, that would have been just about thirty years ago now. It's hard to believe it was that long ago. Anyway, after that we would go there often on holiday, usually bringing Jeannette and her husband, Charles. Those were the good old days."

"Oh, you are so right," Jeannette said. "Do you suppose the village has changed over the twelve years since we were there last?"

"It's hard to know. I'm afraid many of our friends may be gone. And of course no one has lived in or even visited the house in years since we stopped going there after Claude became ill. I pay an agent to check on the house once a year, you know, but it will not be wonderful. I hope we can clean it up enough to stay for a week or two until we hear from Dave."

Maurelle frowned. "How are we going to hear from Dave now that we're on the move?"

Fabienne's eyes widened. "Oh, dear. I didn't even think about that. What are we going to do?" She wagged her hand at no one in particular. "We can't go back, we can't call Dave, and we won't have any way for him to call us when we do get to Saint-Julien."

Jeannette asked, "Where is he? Can't you call him on his mobile phone?"

"We can't call him," Fabienne said. "It's complicated. He didn't take his regular mobile. In England, he's either going to buy one of those disposable phones or a phone card that he can use from his hotel room phone or any public phone. We don't know his number, and he instructed us not to call his hotel."

"He could call Coralie and then we could—" Maurelle stopped herself. "He can't call Coralie, either, can he? He doesn't know she's in Orleans. That means Simone is the only person he might be able to reach, who knows what is happening."

Jeannette said, "Perhaps when we get to Saint-Julien, I could call Simone and let her know where we are."

Fabienne's eyebrows shot up. "No. I don't think that's a good idea."

"Then what are we going to do?" Jeannette asked.

Maurelle said, "I don't know. Well, maybe we'll figure out something after we arrived in Saint-Julien."

DAVE SIPPED HIS morning coffee and watched as Greg flirted with the one of the women working in the coffee shop. Today, they would go back to Hampstead and try again to talk to more of the neighbors before meeting with Kate Hill. Dave still needed to buy a disposable cell phone or a phone card, although he didn't have any real news to share with Maurelle and Fabienne. No sense telling them about the meeting with Greg's detective friend; it would only worry them. He probably wouldn't tell them about Kate Hill either. It was too soon to know if that connection would be useful.

An hour later, when they exited the tube at the East Finchley station, Dave paused outside a Post Office.

Greg said, "What's up?"

"I need to get a phone card or disposable phone."

Greg looked at him curiously, and a moment later said, "Oh, yeah. You've gotta call *her*, right?" He smiled and jabbed his friend in the shoulder. Dave queued up and then, immediately after getting the disposable phone, went into the phone box outside and closed the door to give him privacy and quiet. Before dialing on his phone, he glanced at Greg waiting outside and found him watching a pretty woman swing her derrière as she walked into the Post Office. Dave pulled out a paper with his grandmother's phone number and dialed. The phone rang and rang. He sighed. Probably at the café. He had a busy day ahead, which meant he would likely have to wait until evening to try again. He felt a bit irritated and even slightly worried, though he told himself both emotions were irrational.

Arriving at Ian Waitley's front door, Dave rang the doorbell and tried to put his grandmother out of his mind.

A white-haired man opened the door a few inches and peered around. "What do you want?"

Dave said, "Are you Ian Waitley?"

"Who wants to know?"

"I'm Dave Martin and this is my associate, Greg Saunders. We're writing a newspaper article and conducting research for a book. We'd like to ask you some questions regarding Jared Raybourne and his family. May we come in?"

Ian opened the door wider, stuck out his head, and glanced up and down the street. Having apparently satisfied himself that nothing more appeared to be going on, he opened the door and motioned for them to enter. "Sorry about that. Awhile back we were bombarded by news crews with cameras. They were a nuisance."

Dave asked, "Are you Ian Waitley?"

"That's right."

"We met one of your neighbors yesterday, a school girl. She says she knows you—Brittany Stevas."

The old man's eyes lit up. "Such a lovely girl, she is."

"Brittany suggested that we talk with you."

"Well, why didn't you say so afore?"

He led them down the long hallway and through the living

room with a navy blue sofa, a red recliner, a green recliner, and a wood coffee table that had been painted turquoise. On the lime green walls hung bright deco paintings.

Finding the décor particularly without a theme, as well as unattractive and worn, Dave said, as an opener, "Your home is quite colorful."

Ian turned his head to look back at Dave, and smiled.

"It used to be drab in here. Too depressing. Wanted a bright and cheerful house—though I go outdoors whenever I can. I prefer the outdoors. Always have. Gardens, fresh air, freedom."

"It certainly is bright in your house." Dave heard Greg cough slightly and saw him turn his head away from Ian to hide his expression, revealing what he really thought of the gauche room.

Ian opened the glass door off the dining room. "You gents can have a seat outside. Be back with tea and biscuits presently."

Ian's white hair was unkempt, and his alert blue eyes darted back and forth as he flitted around with amazing agility. Dave remembered Brittany's description of Ian's eagle eyes and he agreed that the avian description fit not only his eyes but his whole appearance and behavior as well. There was something essentially bird-like about the man, though it seemed to him more sparrow-like than eagle.

While Dave and Greg sat on thick cushioned lounge chairs on the bricked terrace, awaiting Ian, Dave looked around at an adjoining small yard. There were gardens filled with beds of daylilies, orchids, and assorted annuals, a small newly mown carpet of grass, an elderly apple tree without fruit at the moment, an intricate bird bath, and a white wooden bench positioned in shade under the tree. Near the fence several pink bougainvillea swayed in a gentle breeze, reminding him of Fabienne whose favorite plant of all was the bougainvillea. Dave decided she would very much like this garden.

Greg was sitting next to Dave, his arm resting on a small side table, looking bored.

The glass door opened and Ian flitted over to the table. Dave smiled, wondering how the guy could manage that appearance without spilling the tray he was carrying. Ian promptly poured out tea and handed a cup to each of his guests. He sat down eying Dave and Greg. Dave took that as his cue to begin.

"Brittany told us that you were the eyes of the neighborhood. How did you get that reputation?"

"Nearly always home. Retired. Got nothing much to do. Besides, started having some problems around here. Somebody needs to watch."

"You seem keen on gardening, like my grandmother."

He beamed. "It's a hobby I like. I'm always starting new projects, new gardens. Used to be all grass back here, but I keep goin'. Soon, won't be any grass left."

Dave noticed some new patches of grass by the tree and a small bed of freshly earth. Some branches of the tree had recently been trimmed and were in a neat pile near the fence. "What's your next planting project?"

"I'm thinking about more flowers. At first I wanted more bushes, but they're difficult to keep trimmed up. I had to get a neighbor to help cut those branches off my tree. Flowers are easier."

"You mentioned some trouble in the neighborhood. What kind of trouble?"

He shrugged and poured cream into his tea, then stood up suddenly. "I forgot me biscuits." He sprang back into the kitchen and practically flew back to the terrace with a plate of biscuits, unwittingly reinforcing Dave's image of him.

Greg chuckled and shook his head.

"That girl, Brittany," Ian said as he set down the biscuits in front of the men, "is the sweetest girl in the neighborhood. Of course, Maura used to be the sweetest—that was until the whole dreadful murder."

"Does that mean you think she murdered Jared?" Greg asked as he stole a look at Dave.

"Now, did I say that?" He gave Greg a reproachful look. "Don't go puttin' words in me mouth."

"Sorry," Greg said. "I'll be more careful."

Dave laughed, and Greg raised his hands in a gesture of giving up.

Ian said, "Maura went away, that's why she's not the sweetest girl here anymore. I tried to tell those policemen, I did, that she wouldn't kill nobody, but they treated me like a senile old man who didn't know nothing."

"Did you see anything that night?" Dave asked, leaning forward. "Do you have any idea who killed Jared?"

The old man's face lit up and his hands trembled, shaking his teacup so hard that he nearly spilled the dark liquid. "Well, finally there's someone asking the right questions of me. Them coppers were too busy to talk to me, they were."

Dave smiled, though inwardly he hoped the police weren't right about the old man. "Go on."

"Well, I'll be telling you. After Maura moved out, there was comings and goings aplenty at that house."

Dave looked at Greg, and back at Ian. "What do you mean? Who was coming and going? How was it different?"

"The dad would come at odd hours, sometimes staying 'til dawn. Sometimes, I would see the dad's girlfriend, Robin, and Elizabeth arguing outside in the shadowy lawn. And that Elizabeth—she's an odd bird, that one."

"How so?"

"She kicked her husband—that be Peter Raybourne—out of the house, divorced him, she did, because of that girlfriend of his. Elizabeth's a bitter woman. But then, she starts dolling herself up and trying to win the loser back. Make sense to you?"

Dave frowned, wondering how it all fit together. "Do you think the Raybournes were getting back together?"

Ian shrugged, tapped the side of his nose, and smiled.

"Are they together now?" Greg asked.

The old man shook his head. "No, sir. Peter blames Elizabeth for the death of their son."

Dave squinted as he looked over at Greg and back at Ian. "Peter thinks his ex-wife killed Jared?"

Ian shrugged. "Maybe, maybe not. All I know is their boy had problems. After the murder Peter said Elizabeth should have taken the boy to a psychologist long ago."

Dave took a deep breath, thinking, and let it out slowly. "How do you know all of that?"

"Robin told me."

"You're friends with her?"

"I guess so. She sometimes came by to drop off Jared after he'd spent a weekend with her and Peter. I'm outside often, tending my front garden. She'd come by and we'd chat a bit. She needed to blow off steam and I was there, willing to listen."

"When Peter stayed all night, do you think he was there to be with Elizabeth or with their son, Jared?"

"I can't see through walls," Ian said, raising his hands.

Greg leaned forward now, looking straight at Ian. "Did Maura visit after she moved out? Did you ever see her coming or going?"

Ian hesitated, then shook his head, saying, "Nope, she wouldn't come near that place. She wanted nothing more to do with that boy."

"She told you that?"

"Aye, she did. She had tea here with me several times. Last time was a few days after she moved out."

"Was she ever romantically involved with Jared like people

say she was?" Greg asked.

"Never. She wouldn't get involved with that little gobshite. She treated him as if he was the little brother she never had—until she realized he was obsessed with her. That changed everything."

"What do you mean?" Dave asked.

"I mean, she left. She told me he tried to pick the lock on her bedroom door once, while she was sleeping. She woke up and made him go back to his room. She told me she had to barricade the door after that. Two days later, she moved out."

"Who do you think killed Jared?" Dave asked again.

"How should I know? I got me hunches, mind you, I do, but I can't tell you who done it. Not for sure, anyway."

"Go on," Dave said. He hoped Ian might have something concrete, but he doubted it.

"Well, I've been thinking it was Elizabeth or Robin."

Greg looked at Dave, while pointing down at his watch.

Dave said, "We really appreciate your talking with us. Unfortunately, we have an appointment we have to rush off to. Would you mind if we call on you again?"

Ian pursed his lips together, and nodded. "Any time you gents want. Good to have some company sometimes."

Dave and Greg took last sips of tea, put their cups down on the table and stood to leave. Ian led them back through the house, giving them one more look at the rainbow décor. After shaking hands with Ian, and thanking him profusely, they left and hastened back to the bus stop in time to catch a double-decker headed toward South London.

As they found seats Dave asked, "So, what do you think?"

"He doesn't seem to think Maura did it, though he didn't have any reasons other than she was a friend and is kind to animals."

"Do you think it's odd that he seems to know everything that goes on with his neighbors?"

"Nah. He seemed friendly enough, just lonely. And bored. I remember how it was when my dad first retired. He nearly drove my mother crazy. Eventually, he found some other retired guys to hang around with. I think he likes to feel he's at the heart of it all, though I wonder what others really feel about him." Greg chuckled. "From what I've seen of the neighborhood, there aren't many people home during the day, like he said. I can imagine him watching for them to come home so he'll have somebody to talk to."

"Yeah, you're probably right. Guess that makes sense," Dave said. "

SIMONE GROANED INWARDLY when two uniformed gendarmes walked into her café. She'd been expecting them, of course, but after an hour she had begun to hope Paul hadn't followed through on his threat.

One of the men walked over to the counter where Simone was standing.

"Excuse me, Madame. Are you the patronne, Simone Charbonneau?"

"Yes."

"I am Officer Roland of the Gendarmerie. I need to ask you some questions about a young woman we believe is going by the name Maurelle Dupre. Have you met this person?" He showed her a photograph.

Simone nodded.

"Paul Lepage told us that she is hiding in Reynier and staying in the home of Fabienne Laurent. Do you know anything about that?"

"I think she was staying there, temporarily."

"Was? Does that mean she has gone?"

"My grandmother is a good friend of Fabienne. Fabienne told her that Maurelle took off on foot during the night. Last night, I mean."

The gendarme studied Simone for a moment, and then said, "Why would she suddenly leave?"

"We all attended a party last night. Unfortunately, it didn't go well. We had an argument. I threatened to call the gendarmes—you—on her. She and Fabienne left the party early. I suppose Maurelle got scared and ran away."

"And what is she hiding?"

Simone shrugged.

"You must know something if you told her you planned to report her."

"I don't really know anything about her. I was angry and suspicious."

"Why?"

Simone sighed. "She was hiding out in one of the caves for a while when she first arrived in Reynier. Who does that?"

"Monsieur Lepage mentioned the same thing. Why did Madame Laurent take her into her home?"

Simone licked her lip. "Do you have a grandmother, Officer Roland?"

"Yes."

"Then perhaps you know how lonely they can get. I think Fabienne felt sorry for the girl and thought she could help her out and also have a temporary companion."

He thought about it a minute, and nodded. "Do you know where we can find Madame Laurent?"

"She was upset about losing the girl. My mother and grandmother were going on a trip to Orleans to visit my aunt. They invited her to go with them."

"When did they leave?"

"This morning."

"I'll need the name and address, please."

Seeing no choice, Simone gave him the information. As he turned to leave, she said, "Officer Roland."

He turned back to face her. "Yes?"

"Maurelle isn't really in trouble, is she? This is only a misunderstanding, yes?"

"I can't say. We believe she may be a suspect in an ongoing investigation."

Simone watched as he and the other gendarme left the café. As soon as the door closed behind them, she glanced at her wristwatch. She wasn't sure whether to hope the women had already made it out of Orleans and were headed wherever it was that they planned to hide, or whether to hope she could warn her mother and prevent them from going. The officer hadn't said what kind of investigation it was. To be on the safe side, she picked up her mobile from behind the counter and dialed her mother's mobile number.

"They've already left," Coralie said, after Simone told her what she knew. "I'm sure they'll be fine."

As Simone hung up the phone, Lillian Lefevre rushed into the café. "Simone, have you heard the news?"

"What news is that?"

"The gendarmes are questioning people about that woman. You know, the dark-haired stranger. They say she's a murder suspect from England. Jonas went on the internet after we heard that and he found out her real name is Maura Barrington. Can you believe it? I knew there was something strange about her."

"What did you tell the gendarmes?"

"I didn't tell them anything. I don't like them. Never have. Let them find her on their own. That's what I say. And plenty of others feel the same way."

Simone felt goose bumps on her arms. For the first time, she wished she'd tried harder to find out more about Maurelle. If only she'd asked Maurelle more questions when they were at Fabienne's for lunch.

CHAPTER TWENTY-THREE

PUTNEY WAS A district in south-west London, located in the London Borough of Wandsworth, and about five miles southwest of Charing Cross. Forty minutes after leaving Hampstead, Dave and Greg arrived there and exited the Tube station. Looking for Kate Hill's house, they walked through the neighborhood that Dave had mapped out, but they still ended up lost. Finally, they asked a man in a business suit and obtained directions.

From a short distance, the house was a large two-story red-brick with white trim. On closer examination, Dave noted a row of eight small windows gabled out from the roof; an attic, he guessed. Closer up, a four foot brick wall backed by much taller shrubs, perhaps six or seven feet tall, gave the house privacy. A black iron gate attached to the wall was open to the driveway where a black Mercedes was parked. Everything about the place spoke money.

Greg said, "Looks like we're in the wrong line of business." Dave agreed. They walked into the courtyard and up to the front door, and Dave rang the bell.

A tall woman, looking slightly older than in the photo on her website, answered. She had shoulder-length curly brown hair, kept tidy, and wore a modest amount of makeup, a stylish suit, and flat shoes.

After the cordial introductions, she said, "Let's go into my office, shall we?"

As they followed her to the back of the house, Dave stared out the large picture window overlooking the River Thames. "Your home is lovely," he said. "And what a spectacular view."

"Thank you. It was my parents' house. I inherited it a few years ago. Some people might have sold it for a profit, but I love this house and the town. I wouldn't trade them for anything."

"This is our first visit to Putney. It's a remarkable looking town. I can see why you like it here."

"Are you interested in boating?" she asked, pausing to look out at the river. "Since the second half of the nineteenth-century, Putney has been a major centre for rowing in England. We have more than twenty rowing clubs here." She sighed and turned to face Dave. "My husband—he passed away six months ago—was an avid rower."

Greg said, "I used to belong to the crew team when I was in college."

She smiled. "You should check out the clubs while you're here, if you have the time."

"We saw a lot of stately buildings here," Dave said, "and quite a few magnificent-looking houses, or should I say mansions. Quite impressive."

"Oh, you are right. This area became highly desirable to wealthy city-dwellers back in the 1890's, and they began moving in. They weren't exactly welcomed at the time. The locals called them 'outsiders'.

Dave nodded.

"We also have one of the oldest cricket teams in London—Roehampton Cricket Club. It was established in 1842. I don't suppose you play, do you? Being from America, I mean."

Greg chuckled. "No. We don't have cricket there. At least not that I'm aware of."

"You do know who J. P. Morgan is though, don't you."

"Sure," Greg said.

"He was made an honorary member of the club in 1900."

"Interesting," Dave said.

She laughed. "I am pretty much quoting from an article I wrote a couple of months back for the local paper. I know nothing about cricket really."

Dave and Greg followed her into an impressive study, apparently turned into an office. Lined with bookcases, it looked more like a library. They sat in overstuffed burgundy leather chairs across the desk from Kate.

"Well, shall we get down to business?" she said. "In your email you mentioned a criminal investigation you wanted to discuss with me. Which investigation, and why me?"

Dave said, "Greg is a detective from Chicago. We used to be partners until I left the force to become a writer. My newest mystery novel will be set here in the London area. That's partially why we're here—to look around, gather information, take notes, as well as sightsee. I've been reading local newspapers, and came across a case that appears similar to my storyline. I figured that by researching the case, I could get some good details that I can use. I'll change the names, and such, of course."

She leaned back and studied him.

Finally, she said, "Okay, why me?"

"Most of the articles I read were somewhat biased. Yours were more objective."

"What's the case?"

"The Jared Raybourne murder."

She raised an eyebrow. "That's an interesting case, I'll grant you that. It seems the victim had some problems that no one wants to talk about. They're more focused on this school teacher,

Maura Barrington."

"Do you know why?"

"She had gained a reputation, with whispers flying around Westglenn Comprehensive for a few weeks before the murder. When people heard that Jared had been killed, they automatically assumed she'd done the deed."

"Was there any proof of an affair?" Greg asked.

"Proof, no. Innuendo, yes. Mostly by way of emails and voicemail messages." Kate looked at Dave, and said, "Even if she did have an affair with the boy, that doesn't necessarily mean she killed him. That's what I've been saying. Most people don't want to listen. I can't exactly blame them. After all, she did run away."

Dave nodded. "Will you help us?"

"I'm not sure what you want me to do."

"As a local journalist, we thought you might get us interviews that we can't get on our own, such as with the victim's family. We've spoken to a few neighbors, but trying to talk to parents, and other relatives, and to school officials and students could be tricky. Perhaps if you were to make the introductions and say that we're working together on a story . . . ."

She chewed on the top end of a pen, while she studied Dave. Finally, she said, "Let me do a bit of checking up on you two and let think about it. Where can I reach you? Through your email? Give me your phone number too."

IN THE EARLY evening, while Greg stayed at the pub where they'd eaten dinner, Dave walked back toward the hotel among a crowded mass of people rushing about, most likely on their way home from work or their way out to eat. Although he'd tried calling his grandmother several times during the day, he hadn't been able to reach her. He was feeling disconsolate and growing ever more concerned. His phone rang and he pulled it out of his pocket, almost dropping it in his haste. He answered on the second ring. It was Kate Hill.

"First," she said, "the woman, Maura Barrington, lived in close proximity to the boy. Second, she claimed she'd tutored him, but people are saying that's a lie. Third, people say he was in love with her. Fourth, she was under investigation by the school's governing board and they were getting ready to question the pupil."

"I know all that," Dave said. "What I want to know is what I haven't read in the newspapers. What are the discrepancies in the case? What is true and what is false or misleading? I need to ask questions."

"Why are you really interested in this case?"

"I told you already. It's research. You're a writer. You know how we need to gather information. It's in our blood."

She didn't answer, and Dave wondered if he'd lost the connection.

"You're right about one thing,' she said finally. "It is in our blood to gather information. I did some checking into your background. You didn't just leave your job in Chicago to become a writer. You were more or less forced out. I know about the Diana Lewis case."

Dave sat down on a bench near a bus stop while pedestrians walked briskly past.

"You let a woman manipulate you into trying to prove her innocence," she continued. "She almost got away with it, but your Chief of Police saw what was happening. He saw that you were becoming obsessed with her and pulled you off the case. The way I see it, you fell in love with Diana Lewis. That makes me wonder what really brings you here. Why are you asking questions about an ongoing investigation in which the prime suspect is a beautiful woman on the run?"

"It's not that simple," he said. "Yes, I made a mistake in believing Diana, but I was never involved with her. I wasn't attracted to her, and I was married. The reason I helped her was that I thought she was a victim, that she'd been kidnapped by the other suspect, a man named Johnny Kincaid. She swore that he'd forced her to watch while he kidnapped other young women and killed them, that she'd tried to escape many times, but couldn't."

"He didn't really kidnap her?"

Dave didn't answer right away. He hadn't talked to anyone about the case since he left the force—not even his parents.

"Kincaid did kidnap her when she was seventeen," he said. "She was one of his first victims. Some strange attraction between them followed, and he decided to keep her alive. Over time, she fell in love with him and began working alongside him—until he got caught. By then, she was twenty-two, and had participated not only in luring the women to places where he could grab them, but also in killing some of them. She pretended she had nothing to do with it, that she was simply a victim. She played on my trust and used me. She thought I wouldn't dig too deep, that I wouldn't see her as capable of being involved."

"Why did you believe her?"

"I don't know. It drives me crazy. I thought I was smarter than that."

She didn't say anything for a moment.

"What about the Jared Raybourne case? What's really going on?"

"I'm trying to find out whether Maura Barrington is guilty or innocent."

"So you know her."

He didn't answer.

"If you find out she's guilty, then what?"

"I'll turn her over to the police." Kate's silence was punctuated with Dave silently kicking himself, recognizing this as a repeat of the conversation he had had with Greg, and realizing his cover story must be particularly lame. *I really suck at lying.*

"Okay. I'll help you. But on the condition that I get the exclusive on whatever story comes out of this—and if you promise to turn her over to the authorities if she turns out to be guilty. Come by my house in the morning, ten o'clock, and we'll go over the case."

AFTER THEIR LUNCH stop, Maurelle, Fabienne, and Jeannette returned to the highway and headed toward Saint-Julien-du-Tarn. The sky had been clouding over, but so far no rain had fallen.

Soon Maurelle was driving in a gorge, flanked by rocky bluffs and steep drop-offs. She didn't dare talk as she scaled the mountain. Dizzying bends forced her to slow down and lean forward, cautiously navigating the tight curves and drop-offs. Once she was more accustomed to the drive, the tight curves were less problematic and she managed to take in the panoramic view unfolding.

"It's beautiful in this region. Truly wondrous," she said. All during their journey, she had admired the increasingly wild terrain of chestnut forests interspersed with ancient villages and dotted with farmhouses surrounded by mulberry orchards. But the majesty of the current scenery truly left her in awe. She said as much to Fabienne and Jeannette.

"Oh, you haven't seen anything," Fabienne said, "until you see the scenery at Saint-Julien. Magnifique! It's tucked at the foot of sheer cliffs on the left bank of the Tarn River."

"Not far from Sainte-Enimie," Jeannette added.

Fabienne said, "I really do love Saint-Julien. I didn't realize until now how much I miss that ghostly village." She laughed then, and so did Jeannette.

This comment drew Maurelle's attention. "What do you mean by ghostly village?"

"It's true, I'm sorry to say," Jeannette said, confirming her best friend's description. "The town itself always seemed drab as a black and white movie from way back when we were born, all the houses a dreary gray with matching roofs, white ghostly linen hanging out to dry on clotheslines."

Fabienne piped in saying, "There's not much in the way of amenities, businesses, and such there either. At least there wasn't back when we visited."

"Oh, you are so right," Jeannette said. "You probably think Reynier has little to offer, Maurelle, but at least it now has a wine shop, a post office, a furniture shop, a hotel, and a decent restaurant. Saint-Julien has merely the basics. But I suppose it may have grown since we saw it last."

"I really did enjoy visiting there though," Fabienne said. "It may not be the loveliest village, but what it lacks in man-made beauty, it more than makes up for in natural beauty."

"Yes," Jeannette said. "But do you remember the old Roman bridge that crosses to the beach on the right bank of the river?"

"Oh, I had completely forgotten about that. I tell you, Maurelle, it's not a good thing, this growing old. Your brain starts to go, right along with your joints and your hair. Dave thinks I'm a liar when in fact half of my supposed lies are really only my forgetfulness."

Jeannette laughed at that.

Fabienne said, "I do remember that we used to go boating, the four of us, in the river. We would swim and lay on the beach and soak in the sun. My favorite pastime on those sunny outings was gazing across the river, taking in the view of the village, watching the small cascades gush out of the cliffs through the terraced gardens and arched garden walls."

"Oh," Jeannette said excitedly, "and I loved to go to the

town square in the centre of the village and wade through the stream that meandered right through the middle."

She stopped and Fabienne asked, "What's wrong?"

"Well, I guess the man-made things in town weren't quite as drab as I first remembered," Jeannette said, smiling.

"I told you that our brains don't work as well as they used to, didn't I?" Fabienne said, laughing.

"Your village sounds delightful," Maurelle said. "I can't wait to see it." For the first time in months, she was actually looking forward to something instead of looking behind her.

"We should be there in another hour, I think," Fabienne said, "though I would rather you slowed down a bit. If it takes longer, I won't mind."

Maurelle glanced over at Fabienne who was nervously twisting her hands in her lap, and she let up her foot from the gas pedal, slowing down enough to allow the older woman to relax, but not enough to impede traffic. Drops of rain had begun to splatter the windshield, and though the drops were intermittent, she herself was getting nervous.

Maurelle was reasonably comfortable driving on the wrong side of the road now, and was getting used to driving through a winding gorge. She didn't mind driving in heavy rain either. But the dreadfully real possibility of combining all three was jangling her nerves.

An hour later, while searching for signs that would tell her where to turn off the main road to get to Saint-Julien, a deafening thunder crash startled all three women, causing Jeannette to scream, and nearly making Maurelle swerve off the slippery road. Maurelle gritted her teeth and grasped the steering wheel as she craned her neck, trying desperately to see through the increased torrential downpour. *Just what we need. Why can't anything ever be easy?*

She wiped away beads of perspiration forming on her

forehead. After another fifteen minutes, she saw a signpost that listed Saint-Julien-du-Tarn, which meant they were at least on the right track and nearing the town.

"We're getting close," she said.

"Oh, thank God," Fabienne said, clasping her hands together. "I have never been so frightened." She leaned forward toward Maurelle, and added, "It wasn't because of you, dear. You did a wonderful job. We—Jeannette and I—were frightened because we were reminded of something, a horrible experience we shared years ago."

"What happened?" As Maurelle listened, she set the windshield wipers to a slower setting. The rain had reduced its intensity from fire-hydrant gushing to fountain spraying.

"It was sixty-three years ago," Fabienne said. "It's silly that we should be scared of a bad storm after all this time, really."

Jeannette picked up the story from there. "We grew up in Candes-St.-Martin in the Indre-Loire region. You knew that we grew up together, didn't you? That was before we moved to Paris."

"Yes, Fabienne told me," Maurelle said, thinking how wonderful it was that these women had maintained their friendship throughout their long lives. She, herself, had good friends when she was in school, but they'd all gone their separate ways.

"Well, there was a horrible storm on our way to school one day," Jeannette said. "My older brother was driving us in our family truck. The road was slippery like today, the visibility terrible. Anyway, he lost control of the truck and slid off the road, crashing into a tree. After that, neither of us have had any desire to drive."

"Oh, I'm so sorry. Was anyone hurt in the crash?"

"My brother died. Fabienne was in a coma for two weeks because of a bad concussion," Jeannette said. "I only suffered bruises and a broken arm."

"How terrible. I'm really sorry. I should have found a place to stop and wait for the storm to pass."

"No, no," Jeannette said. "We made it through fine. Anyway, we are looking forward to getting to Saint-Julien. You did the right thing, continuing through the storm. Don't feel bad."

Fabienne said, "That's right. Actually, you are a much better driver than my Claude ever was. If he had been driving through this storm, Jeannette and I would have huddled on the floor so we couldn't see what he was doing. Charles would have split his side howling with laughter at us."

Jeannette broke out laughing and Fabienne joined in.

Maurelle was glad to hear the women laughing again. She doubted that she was a better driver than Claude had been, since she didn't have a great deal of experience considering that she mostly used public transportation in London. She figured they were only being nice, but it made her feel better anyway. And at least the three women were getting along now.

WHEN DAVE RETURNED to his hotel room, he pulled out his phone and dialed his grandmother's phone number. Still no answer. He missed Maurelle and really wanted to talk to her, not only to let her know what was happening, but also to ask her some more questions about the Raybourne family.

He tried calling several more times throughout the evening while he watched television and scoured the internet for anything new. When he still couldn't reach them, he called Jeannette's and Coralie's phone numbers.

No answer there either. Seeing no other option, he dialed Simone's number.

CHAPTER TWENTY-FOUR

AS THE RAIN began to abate, daylight returned, providing frequent glimpses of sheer cliff walls bordering the roadway on her right, glistening with moisture, and faint misty shadows of more distant cliffs and mountainsides, once again dividing Maurelle's attention between her driving and the awe inspiring scenery.

"Oh look," Fabienne blurted in excitement, pointing ahead. "We're coming to the first tunnel. That means we're close to Saint-Julien."

Jeannette tapped Maurelle on the shoulder. "Dear, you'll need to turn on the headlights. I don't like the darkness. These tunnels are close together, one after another and they're pitch-black."

Maurelle switched on the headlights and was happy to have been warned. Jeanette was indeed correct. These tunnels were very narrow, curvy and long, carved through the mountain's core, without any electric lighting. Driving without lights would have been really spooky, not to mention more than a bit dangerous. A few minutes later, after they exited the final tunnel, Fabienne had her made a sharp right turn onto a narrow road posted to be the turn-off leading to Saint-Julien.

Ten minutes later, after they drove through the final tunnel, they made another sharp turn to the right and followed the narrow road going into Saint-Julien.

"Oh, there it is," Fabienne said, clapping her hands together as they approached the village.

Maurelle smiled. Everything looked fresh and beautiful after the cleansing rain. The clouds had floated away, leaving a clear view of mid-evening sun and a faint breeze delivering the pleasing scent of summer freshness. They drove into the tiny village, which looked, at least to Maurelle, like a smaller version of Reynier. The hill behind it, however, was far more vertical, which meant the houses and businesses butted right up against a straight rock wall. On the opposite side of town was another shorter jagged vertical wall that dropped down to a roiling river below.

Fabienne said, "It's been a long time."

"It certainly has," Jeannette said. "Too long. How could we have thought it drab?"

"We won't have electricity or water at the house, but tomorrow we can buy propane for the stove, bottled water for drinking, and oil lanterns or candles for light."

Maurelle popped in. "Shouldn't we stop at the general store then and pick up something for tonight, if not for lighting, at least snacks and drinks?"

"No. It's too late, past seven already. The shops close early here. Tomorrow we'll buy what we need. I'm too tired, anyway, to go shopping. I just want to rest."

Worried, Jeannette said, "Dear me, we should have brought things with us."

"I know, but we didn't have time," Fabienne said. She clicked her tongue, apparently annoyed at Jeannette who leaned back against the seat, pouting. "Maurelle, you should follow the main road. It'll go up an incline at the town edge. That's where you'll find my little house."

Maurelle nodded. As she drove, the road turned and angled up, becoming narrower and almost hidden under a tunnel of tree branches, making her worry that she would run right into the rock wall. Her fears quickly vanished when the road ended in front of a lonely stone cottage, half-hidden amid overgrown bushes and situated directly in front of the rock wall.

"Oh, Fabienne whispered, tears streaking down her face. "I can almost see Claude standing by the door, waiting for us."

Maurelle stopped the car and they all climbed out. As Fabienne and Maurelle walked across the weed-filled yard, with Jeannette right on their heels, Maurelle put her arm around Fabienne's shoulder. The older woman instinctively pulled away slightly, but then looked up and gave a small smile.

Spears of light pierced the overgrown canopy in places, providing spotty illumination and allowing the three to find the front door, which was painted light chocolate to match the shutters covering the windows on the outside. Some of the paint had peeled off the door and shutters, revealing a dwelling in severe need of care.

"I hope you remembered the keys," Jeannette said, between huffs of breath as she trudged up the path to the door. "Wouldn't that be our luck if you left them back in Reynier?"

"Well, I'm forgetful but I'm not that senile yet," Fabienne snapped. When they reached the front door, Fabienne dug through her handbag, looking for the keys. "Well, I know I put them in here," she mumbled.

"Ha," Jeannette said, "not senile, she says."

A second later, Fabienne yanked out the keys and waved them in the air defiantly.

Her hands trembled as she tried to stick the key in the lock, and Maurelle sensed that strong emotion rather than feebleness was to blame for Fabienne's clumsiness.

The key eventually entered the lock but did not want to turn.

Several tries later, with much key jiggling and grunting, Fabienne was able to get the lock to work, and she pushed the door open. It was too dark to see much inside.

Jeannette said, “Help me open the shutters. We need as much light in here as we can get.”

After they pulled open the outside shutters and secured them, the three women entered the house. In the foyer, they stopped and gasped. The sharp contrast of outside light shafts splaying higgledy-piggledy around the foyer and living room gave the house an eerie feel. Maurelle eased forward and ran a fingertip along the top of a bookshelf. A decade worth of dust blanketed everything. She gazed up to the ceiling and shivered, following the thick cobwebs that dangled from it like stalactites. Mouse droppings littered the dusty wooden floorboards and furnishings. For a moment, she was back in her lonely cave with only its resident mouse for companionship. On second thought, the cave was decidedly cleaner and preferable.

“Well, I think we should get to work,” Fabienne said. “We should have brooms and mops and such in the closet.”

“I’ll bring in our things from the car,” Maurelle said.

“That’s a good idea, dear girl.”

Jeannette glared at Fabienne “I thought you were tired. You said you wanted to rest.”

“N’importe. I’ve got a surge of energy. How could I not, now that we’re here?”

AN HOUR LATER, as the sun was setting, the three women sat in the living room admiring the transformation. Fabienne had found a few candles salted away in a cabinet, behind stale half eaten soda crackers, so there was at least going to be minimal lighting available. Surprising everyone when Jeanette tried the faucet, there was actually running water. Maurelle decided her earlier comparison to her cave may have been hasty after all. "You know," Jeannette said, "this is like coming home. Thank you for letting me come with you, Fabienne. And you, too, Maurelle."

In the soft flickering candlelight, Maurelle studied the two older women. Jeannette closed her eyes for a few minutes, her lips curved up in a smile. Fabienne sat next to her on the couch, her hands folded in her lap, still clutching her dust rag, a faraway look in her eyes, the same kind of look Maurelle had seen in her own grandmother's eyes years ago, when she, her mother, and grandparents had visited her grandmother's childhood home. Maurelle felt a satisfaction knowing that she'd inadvertently made this emotional journey for Fabienne and Jeannette possible, and yet she still couldn't shake her worries, couldn't forget that this was no mere pleasure trip.

Jeannette sprang up from the couch, screaming, and causing Fabienne to jump up, too, and clutch her chest.

"What's wrong?" Fabienne shrieked.

"A mouse!"

Fabienne looked across the coffee table at Maurelle and burst out laughing. "Well, I think we have acquired a pet. Better leave some bread crumbs out on the kitchen floor for the poor thing."

Jeannette glared at Fabienne as though she thought she was out of her mind, but Fabienne smiled and sat back down, folding her hands in her lap.

"OH, THANK GOD you're home!" Dave said when Simone answered her phone. "Where is everyone? I've been trying to reach Grand-mère for two days."

She didn't say anything. Dave wondered if he'd gotten a

wrong number. "Simone?"

"Yes," she said. "Where are you?"

"I'm on a business trip. Didn't Grand-mère tell you? Where is everyone?"

She was silent again, making Dave want to scream at her. Instead, he clenched his jaw and waited. Rain pelted against his hotel window and people walking down the hall past his room were laughing. On the other end of the phone, though, the silence was deafening. Finally, Dave said, "What the hell is going on, Simone? I've spent the past two hours calling people—my grandmother, Jeannette, Coralie. No one answered their phones. Where did everyone go?"

"You left me without saying a word. We had a date. I bought us tickets to the theatre. You didn't bother to cancel or to even say goodbye."

"Huh? What are you talking about?"

"I dressed up for our date and waited for you to arrive to take me out. Do you have any idea how embarrassing it was to be stood up? And I wasted all that money on tickets that we didn't use."

"Simone, I'm sorry. Something came up unexpectedly. I should have had the decency to call and cancel, but with everything I had to do to get ready for my trip, I completely forgot about our date. As for saying goodbye—well, there wasn't time."

"You can cut the act, Dave," Simone said, with a bitter edge to her voice. "I know that you're trying to help Maurelle—or should I say Maura Barrington—get away with murder."

"What?" He felt as though she had slapped him across the face, and he nearly fell off his chair. He recovered quickly. "Okay, first of all, I'm not helping anyone get away with murder. I am trying to find out exactly what happened. That's what I do. I guess you were right about one thing—I am still a detective deep down."

"Of course you are, Cheri," she said, cooing at him. It was something that he used to find attractive about her. Now it seemed phony. What bothered him, too, was her desperation and insecurity. She didn't need to be that way. While her physical attractiveness and sophistication were superficial, created and honed for and by her modeling career, yet not enough to keep him interested, they were certainly enough for some men.

"And how do you know about Maurelle?" he asked, his stomach churning suddenly. "What happened?" He heard her sigh this time, and braced himself for the worst.

"I only found out after the gendarmes arrived. I didn't call them. I wouldn't betray you. You must believe me."

"Then how did they find out she was in Reynier?"

"Someone called them. It wasn't me. But, well . . . I guess it was sort of on my behalf."

"What the hell did you do?"

"It wasn't me. I swear. It was Paul. I tried to stop him. Maman and Grand-mère tried, too."

"Oh, Christ," Dave said. "Why would he do that? And what do you mean it was sort of on your behalf?"

She was silent again.

"Simone, please tell me. What happened?"

"Paul was upset that you stood me up, and he knew it had something to do with Maurelle. We all did. He came to me and told me he'd put together some clues—my God, she was hiding in a cave! He also told me she was hitchhiking last week and he gave her a ride. He didn't know who she really was or what kind of trouble she was in, but he figured that if he called the gendarmes, she would run away. Anyway, he thought that he was doing me a favor because with her out of the picture, and you available again, you might return to me. He meant her no harm, really, and he was only looking out for me. You know how protective he is."

Dave bent forward and closed his eyes. "Paul's created a huge mess."

"He knows that now, and he's sorry about it."

"Where is Maurelle?"

"I don't know where she is. That's the truth. The gendarmes don't know either, if that makes you feel better."

"Where is my grandmother?" he asked as calmly as he could.

"I . . . well, I was told that she and my grandmother were going with mother to Brigitte's." She paused. "The Belvidere gendarmes notified the Vendome and Orleans gendarmes, but they only found my mother. No one seems to know the whereabouts of the others."

Dave didn't say anything as he tried to comprehend what she'd told him. Finally, he said, "So you're telling me that Maurelle and two elderly women are what—hitchhiking, hiding in caves, walking through the woods—what?"

'They took mother's car. The gendarmes are looking for the car and for all three women. I think they're calling our grandmothers hostages. You see, Maman either had to tell them that she and Grand-mère and Fabienne were all aiding a fugitive, or simply say she didn't know what had happened."

"What?"

"I—I'm supposed to notify the gendarmes if I hear from you, Dave."

"What's that supposed to mean? Are they going to arrest me too?"

"I don't know," she whispered.

"Do you have any idea where the women might have gone? Please tell me, Simone."

"I wish I did know, but I don't. And neither does Maman."

After he hung up the phone, Dave pounded his fist into the desk in his hotel room, sending shooting pains into his knuckles.

He couldn't have imagined his day getting any worse, and yet it had. Kate Hill had told him she would help with the investigation, but the fact she knew about his past and about his knowing the suspect was unsettling as hell—and now this! He concluded that there wasn't going to be any point in trying to sleep tonight.

He picked up the phone again and dialed. "Hey, Greg. Did I wake you?"

"Na, I was watching the TV. Did you know they show topless women on TV here?"

Dave didn't laugh. "I was wondering if you'd meet me downstairs in the bar. Something big has come up, and I could sure use a friendly ear."

"Of course, buddy. That is, if you're buying."

TWO HOURS AND three beers later, Greg said, "Sounds to me like you need to go back to France. I can stay here and continue working the case."

"I can't. From the way Simone talked, I'd probably be arrested if I showed up in Reynier or Orleans."

Greg took another swig of beer. "What if I went instead? You could stay here. I haven't seen Maura or whatever you call her. I don't have any real connection. I can poke around and talk to your friend, Simone."

"Hmm, that's not half-bad. What kind of cover story would you use?"

"I could say that I'm your old partner from the police force, which is true. I'm on vacation, traveling about Great Britain and Europe, and you invited me to visit you in your grandmother's hometown before I left home."

He got up then and walked over to the bar, returning a couple minutes later with two more beers. "I could show up, expecting to find you and your grandmother. When they tell me that you've left, I can pretend that you must have forgotten about inviting me."

"That actually sounds plausible," Dave said, taking a leisurely swallow of draft. "You're pretty good at this."

Greg laughed. "Yeah, scary, isn't it?" Both paused to think about this new proposal and down a couple more sips of their beer.

"I think that could work, assuming that you can speak French," Dave said. "You're sure you wouldn't mind?"

"What's to mind? I look at it this way—I get to travel, see France, and meet this Simone that you've told me about. So we're clear, she isn't your girlfriend any more, right?"

Dave laughed, seeing Simone turning her charm on Greg, and Greg dishing it right back at her.

"She's all yours, pal," Dave said. "I can't wait to find out how you two get along. You've gotta promise to keep me posted on your investigation and on your flirtation."

Greg gave Dave a sly look. "And if I find Maura? Is she your girlfriend, or isn't she?"

Dave hoped his friend was kidding, but not taking any chances, he said, "She is off-limits."

Greg laughed. "I saw photos of her online. She's pretty. I hope Simone is as pretty."

"Didn't I tell you? Simone is a former model."

"Well, then, it really sounds like a plan," Greg said, laughing heartily. Raising their mugs, they toasted each other and their new plan. "I guess I better try to get a few hours' sleep before I shove off. Can you give me details in the morning, say nine o'clock?"

"You bet," Dave said, finishing off his beer.

"By the way," Greg said as they reached the hotel's staircase, "I do speak French, though admittedly I've never gotten a chance to use it for real. Studied it in high school and college. Obviously it's been a while, but hopefully it'll come back to me, at least enough to get by."

Dave smiled and patted him on the back, "You'll do fine." The two entered the hotel and the elevator to Greg's floor, just below Dave's. Before Greg stepped into the hallway, Dave said, "I don't know what I would do without you, Greg. I'm sorry I didn't keep in touch much over the past few years."

"Yeah, me too. My fault too; I wasn't any better keeping in touch. But at least now, we can catch up. Maybe you'll even decide to come back to the police force after we're done with all this."

Dave nodded and his friend disappeared down the corridor toward his room.

CHAPTER TWENTY-FIVE

AT BREAKFAST, DAVE filled Greg in on everyone he would likely meet in Reynier, and then talked about his grandmother and her friends.

"Your grandmother sounds like a real character. I hope I get to meet her, though it doesn't seem likely if what Simone said is true."

"Simone is a bit calculating, but I don't think she would lie about something that big, especially knowing I am already unhappy about what she did."

"Yeah, it must have been difficult for her to tell you what happened. What about her brother?"

"Huh? She's an only child."

"Oh, I guess the guy was a cousin or something?"

"Paul." Dave shrugged. "Yeah, he's her cousin. I guess I'd call him a friend—we've known each other practically forever, but I don't always like the guy. Quiet, somewhat lazy and moody, but a damn good artist. He could probably go places if he applied himself."

"Sounds like my brother and my relationship with him. What about Simone's mother? You said she went with Maura—I mean Maurelle."

"Only as far as her sister's house in Orleans. Supposedly, Maurelle stole Coralie's car and took off with my grandmother and Jeannette."

"Well, if she really is guilty of murder, she might be desperate enough to take hostages, and two elderly women would be easy targets." As Dave gave him a look of protest, Greg held up his hand. "I'm just sayin'."

Dave looked down at his coffee mug. Greg was supposed to be supportive and at least try to be open-minded enough to consider Maurelle innocent. Apparently, he was more willing to believe in gossip—like most people. Perhaps sending him to Reynier was a bad move, but what else could he do?

After breakfast, Dave walked with his friend to the Tube station.

"Good luck, buddy." He patted Greg on the back, then shook his hand. "Call me when you can, and give me updates."

"Will do." Greg smiled, waved, and fed his train ticket into the automated slot. When the ticket popped back up and the gate banged open, Greg removed his ticket and passed through the gate.

As Greg disappeared, Dave again hoped he was doing the right thing sending him to France. Of course his decision meant that he would be working solely with Kate Hill.

LATER THAT MORNING at Kate's house, Dave sat in her office drinking coffee while she read aloud from a document she'd obtained from a 'source', whom she wouldn't name. The report began with the basics in information-gathering—the five W's and one H, as they were known in journalism and police investigations: who is it about, what happened, when did it happen, where did it take place, why did it happen, and how did it happen? It was written in clear, simple English the way police reports were written.

"According to witnesses, when Maura broke up with Jared and moved out, he was devastated. He wouldn't let go. He got into fights at school. Eventually the school's governing board became involved. They placed Maura on suspension, pending an investigation and a hearing." Kate paused, and took a deep breath, letting it out slowly. "People claimed they believe she killed Jared so that he wouldn't be able to testify at the governing board's hearing, and thus she wouldn't lose her job."

"That's all circumstance and hearsay," Dave said.

"Yes, but it is also logical. Several credible witnesses, including the head teacher at the school, said that Jared had confided in them."

"Have you actually seen the case files?"

"No," Kate said, "but I spoke with a detective on the case when I was working on my pieces for several newspapers."

"So far, I haven't seen or heard any evidence that there really was a relationship between them. She says not." He shook his head. "Is there any way that we can get a look at the evidence? Maybe we would pick up on something that was overlooked, especially since I've spoken with Maura."

"Hmm." She leaned back in her chair. "Perhaps. Not the actual evidence, but I know people who might be able to get me copies of some of the paperwork about it. I've been in this business a long time and have quite a few friends who owe me favors."

"Thank you. That would be great."

After she made three phone calls, they ate a light lunch together in her kitchen while they waited.

"Do you miss being a police officer?"

"Sometimes. But definitely not the politics. The investigation and finding the truth I miss."

She nodded.

"You already know quite a bit about me from your queries," Dave said, "but what about you? Why did you go freelance?"

"I needed to write facts. My bosses were more interested in opinion pieces even when they seemed to lack facts. I want people to think for themselves, draw their own conclusions."

As they ate, they continued to chat about perspectives and the work that brought them to their current situations. About forty-five minutes from the first call, the phone rang. The fax machine beeped and started printing.

They returned to her office. The fax machine was humming as it continued to spit out paper. An itemized list of evidence collected at the scene was unsurprising. He had seen hundreds of files such as this in his career: fingerprints and hair strands collected from Jared's room (including Maura's, Jared's parents, and the father's girlfriend, Robin, none of which proved any of them were there on the night of the murder), unidentified clothing fibers, blood spatter evidence, two puncture wounds on the victim's neck, etc.

Kate handed him copies of photographs, body diagrams, witness statements, and emails sent from Jared's computer to Maura.

By the time he finished reading the medical examiner's report, toxicology report, dental charts, and death certificate, Dave could see why Maura couldn't necessarily be ruled out as a suspect, but didn't find anything that actually pointed to her guilt.

Dave said as much to Kate. "You know, there's a ton of circumstantial evidence, but I still haven't seen any proof, anything that makes me believe Maura is guilty of murder—or for that matter, even of having an affair with a pupil."

"I'm inclined to agree that there is no hard evidence, but short of having the crime on video, what evidence do you need? She did have access, motive, and she ran. The police have witnesses who are willing to testify against her."

"But didn't the investigators look at any other suspects? I didn't find much of anything to suggest they even considered anyone else."

"Who do you think they should consider?"

"How about the parents? Or the father's girlfriend, for instance?"

"They didn't have motives. They did have alibis."

"Greg and I spoke to some neighbors of the Raybournes. One in particular was helpful. He knows the family, he knows Maura and he thinks—"

"Who are we talking about? The old man across the street?"

Dave nodded.

"The detectives I've talked to told me that old man doesn't know anything, and they described him as senile. The detective said he told them nothing that could be verified and his story pretty much contradicts what everyone else said."

"But it is because he is old, is a busy body, stays at home and watches the neighborhood that he sees everyone who comes and goes in that house," Dave said. "Also, Maura confided in him."

"Did she tell you that? Did she suggest you talk to him?"

"She mentioned him. So did another neighbor, Brittany Stevas. Look, Ian Waitley told us that he believed Elizabeth was trying to win her husband back. He said Peter Raybourne had been spending a lot of time at the house before the murder. So, wouldn't his girlfriend, Robin, have a motive as well?"

"If Elizabeth had been the victim," Kate said, "then, yes, I might believe that. But what possible motive could Robin Sutcliffe have had to kill her boyfriend's son?"

Dave ran his hand through his hair and stared at the papers scattered over Kate's desk. "Okay, you got me there. But I'm sensing now that I may have been wrong about where you stand. I chose you to work with because I thought you were impartial, that you hadn't made a judgment yet. If anything, from your article it seemed like you were on Maura's side."

"Then you misunderstood. I wrote the piece you read as journalism, to be different, to take a counter view and get people to stop making assumptions. Surely you must know how it is."

He slumped into his chair. "I do. But now it seems to me like you are the one making assumptions, leaping to conclusions without solid facts."

Kate opened her mouth to protest, but then apparently thought better of it. After a few moments, she said, "All right, I concede that I may have made hasty conclusions about Maura's guilt without sufficiently exploring other suspects." She looked round at all the papers laid out. "I'm still interested – there might be a good story. Let's proceed down that avenue and see if there are others with motive and opportunity. Can you tell me who, exactly, you think killed him?"

Dave sighed. "Well, what if Robin Sutcliffe killed Jared because he was the bond threatening to bring Peter and Elizabeth back together?"

"That's actually a possibility I hadn't thought about—unlikely, but I would be interested in talking with her and the parents with that in mind. This is all good human interest anyway, so I can pursue it. Any others you want to interview?"

Dave twisted his mouth as he contemplated. "Yes, I'd like to speak with Elizabeth Raybourne's sister and with Jared's former girlfriend. I think her name is Penny Miller. I guess after that, I want to meet again with Ian Waitley."

"Why do you want to talk with the crazy man again?"

Dave raised his eyebrows, puzzled. "Why do you call him crazy? Have you even met him?"

Kate shrugged. "No, I haven't actually met him, but that's what others have told me. Ah. Jumping to conclusions again, aren't I. I guess we'll only find out for ourselves by talking with him."

Dave told Kate about the cover story he and Greg had given the neighbors with whom they'd already met.

"Yes, let's stick with that," she said. "We can add that I'm working on more articles. That should work fine." She gazed at him for a moment. "There are stories here for me. I don't mind the work. But maybe there is something more?"

"I can pay . . . ."

"No, I don't want money—well, it's always pleasant, but I don't want your money."

"What then?"

"An exclusive interview with Maura. And I get to write the story."

Dave thought of Maura gazing at him and trusting. "Okay," he said. He decided not to tell Kate that right now he would have promised anything. He also decided not to tell her at that moment he had no idea where Maura was. "I will ask her and do my best to convince her. That's all I can promise."

AN HOUR LATER, Dave and Kate sat in the light blue waiting room outside Elizabeth Raybourne's office in the Callowise Advertising Agency in Soho.

Finally, a woman who was around Dave's age and dressed in a stylish gray suit appeared. Her resemblance to Jared as he appeared in photographs was quite remarkable—same blue eyes, light blonde hair, and high cheekbones. Dave also thought of Simone. The woman's face was made-up, and she looked attractive, and yet there was something about her that put Dave off. He couldn't pinpoint what it was.

"I'm Elizabeth Raybourne," she said.

Kate stood and extended her hand. "Kate Hill, freelance reporter. I spoke with you earlier. This is my associate, Dave Martin."

Dave, who had also stood up, stepped forward and shook her hand. "Good to meet you."

She looked at him but didn't say anything.

Kate said, "Dave Martin is studying the differences in the investigative methods in the U.S. and U.K. for a book he's writing."

Elizabeth nodded, then looked directly at Kate. "Do you have some news? It's been a while since any reporters have been round. I was beginning to think they'd given up on the case. The police haven't been in touch for a while either." She hesitated. "It's like no one really cares."

"I'm afraid nothing new to report, yet. If you don't mind, though, we'd like to ask you a few questions about your son. This is all quite unofficial. Would you have a quiet place where we might chat with you?"

She pursed her lips and motioned them toward her office. Once they were inside, she closed the door behind her.

"Please have a seat," she said as she sat down stiffly behind her desk.

They had decided beforehand that Kate would do the questioning. Dave would take notes.

"First," Kate said, "we would like to offer our condolences. It must be incredibly difficult for you, and we really do want to help find your son's killer."

She nodded, her posture easing a bit.

"The police reports indicate that you discovered your son's body?"

She nodded again, placing her hand on the top of her desk. Dave noticed that her nails had been chewed down to the point they were probably painful.

"You found him on his bedroom floor. You had come home late the night before, but didn't find him until morning. Is that correct?"

"Yes."

"The post-mortem indicates he had been dead for hours before you found him. How is it that you didn't see him when you arrived back home?"

Elizabeth sighed. "I've already been through all this. As I told the police I went along the hall directly into the kitchen and made tea, then went straight up to bed. It was late—and quite dark." Her shoulders slumped. "I was tired and wanted to go to bed since I had to get up early for work in a few hours. I didn't bother turning on lights."

"You didn't check on your son?"

"He was sixteen. I didn't think it necessary, and he would have been furious. There was no sound, so I knew . . . guessed he was asleep."

"What happened in the morning?"

"I followed my normal routine." She paused and looked at Kate. "I got up, took a shower, and dressed for work as usual. After that I went into Jared's room to make sure he was up and getting ready for school before I made coffee and toast. But . . . he wasn't in his bed. His bed hadn't been slept in either. That's when I looked round his room and saw him . . ." She stopped, swallowing hard, ". . . lying on the floor in a pool of blood."

Kate nodded and glanced over at Dave. "Were you and Peter getting back together before the murder?"

Elizabeth looked surprised.

"Why would you think that? I wouldn't get back with him. He's not good enough."

"Why was he spending a lot of time at the house? He spent nights there."

"Who told you that?"

Kate shrugged.

"It's wrong. We weren't getting back together," Elizabeth said, straightening her back.

"Then why was he there so often?" Dave asked.

Elizabeth turned so that she was facing Dave, a faint look of puzzlement on her face as though she hadn't expected the question to come from him in such an assertive way. She sighed. "He was Jared's father. Of course he would visit."

"At your home? Didn't Jared spend time at his father's new home?"

"Sometimes. But Peter was living with someone."

"Did Jared get along with his father's girlfriend?"

Elizabeth tensed her shoulders. "You'll have to speak with Peter and Robin about that."

"Did Peter ever spend the night at your house after the divorce?"

"That's none of your business."

"Sorry, how did Jared deal with the divorce?"

"He didn't like it. Most children don't, and I suppose he had the usual reactions—anger, aggression, fear, confusion . . . hurt. He complained sometimes."

"Did he act on those feelings?"

"Jared had changed drastically over the last year. He did get very down and seemed to obsess about things sometimes. He had an argument with another boy at school, and Jared kept on about it for weeks. Then all this with . . . her . . . . He sometimes did mean or hurtful things, too." She glanced from one to the other.

"Like what?"

"I forget. It's not really important anyway."

"It could be. Try to think of some of the things he did."

She hesitated, looking angry briefly. "All right. After Jared's girlfriend broke up with him, he would call her sometimes in the middle of the night and hang up. It was a childish prank. He didn't mean any harm. I found out when her father called me and complained."

"What did you do?"

"I talked to Jared and he stopped the calls. Really, this is not important, unless you think Penny murdered my son. She doesn't seem capable of murder, if you ask me. Besides, she broke up with him, but I don't think she hated him in the end. They were just kids and made foolish mistakes."

"Are you sure he stopped?"

She nodded.

"Did Peter help you with your son?"

"Not enough."

"Why do you say that?"

"This is all Peter's fault. If he hadn't had an affair, none of this would have happened!"

"None of what would have happened?"

"All of it! The divorce, the woman renting a room from me, Jared's problems. The murder." She glared at Dave. "If it hadn't been for him my son would still be alive!"

CHAPTER TWENTY-SIX

MAURELLE WOKE UP as the first hints of morning sun peeked through her bedroom window. For a moment, she didn't know where she was and believed herself at home, her childhood home. The moment soon passed as remnants of sleep faded and everything returned to her. She stretched and sat up, then tossed off her covers. A shiver followed. Apparently, it was downright chilly in the morning at this altitude. She sprang out of bed and rushed to her duffel bag to get out clean clothes, but stopped short, remembering she'd unpacked the bag last night.

She dressed warm and went into the narrow hallway, hoping that Fabienne and Jeannette were still asleep. As she padded down the hall passing each of their rooms, loud snores escaped through both open doorways. She snickered to herself and carefully tiptoed on down the creaking stairs.

Strolling along the village's main street toward the bakery she'd glimpsed the night before, she breathed in the sweet scent of mature trimmed bougainvillea hugging intricate arbors, enticing entrance to mountain cottages. Outside the bakery, the sweet scents of cinnamon, bread, and coffee drew her in. A stout elderly woman with platinum hair and a heavily flour-stained apron covering her checkered dress looked up at her, startled.

"Bonjour," Maurelle said. "Are you open for business?"

"But certainly," the woman said. "What can I get for you?"

Maurelle studied the assorted breads and pastries, which looked wonderful, making her mouth water, especially since dinner the previous night had consisted of an unsatisfyingly miniscule quantity of fruit, crackers, and juice they'd bought along the way to snack on in the car. "I would like three each of your croissants, and un chausson aus pommes?"

"May I get you anything else?" the woman asked.

Distracted momentarily, Maurelle studied the baker, wondering her age. The woman's face was plump, with skin pulled tight, resembling animal skin stretched over one end of a bongo drum. Even without wrinkles, though, faded blue eyes, dark age-spots on her skin, and knotted veins in the backs of thick legs suggested an age close to Jeannette's and Fabienne's.

"Oh, I want a loaf of your pain de compagne. Three large coffees, too." Maurelle smiled and pulled out her wallet.

Moments later, the woman filled three paper coffee cups, and wrapped up the bread and pastries, all the while stealing peeks at Maurelle. "What brings you to our little village, if you don't mind my asking?" she asked, carefully placing the cups in a tray and food into a sack.

"Uh . . . my family owns a house on the edge of town," Maurelle said. "They haven't been back here and years and, well, they figured it was time to visit again."

"The Laurent house?" the woman asked, eyeing Maurelle curiously.

"Yes, that's it. How much do I owe you?"

"It's on me. Is Fabienne with you?"

"Yes, she is. She's sleeping and I wanted to surprise her and Jeannette with breakfast."

"Jeannette is here, too? How splendid! After their breakfast, would you please ask them stop in to see me? We must catch up."

"I will. And thank you so much for these. Who should I say sent them?"

"Oh, pardon. I am Nathalie Bardot."

Maurelle departed the shop and rushed back to the house. She wasn't sure how long she'd been gone, but figured no more than half an hour. When she opened the front door, she was startled to see Fabienne standing at the top of the stairs, looking sternly down at her.

"Oh, there you are. We thought you'd run away again."

Maurelle held out both her hands, one with a tray of coffees, the other with a bag. "I've brought breakfast. I hope you're hungry."

"What a dear girl you are," Fabienne said, clapping her hands together, traces of her former stern demeanor disappearing. When she reached the bottom of the stairs, she said, "Did you see that, Jeannette? I told you she wouldn't desert us."

Maurelle spun around. Jeannette stood in the kitchen doorway, pouting and with her arms folded.

"You should have waited for us," Jeannette said. "We would have liked to go out."

"I'm sorry," Maurelle said as she walked over to the couch. "I wanted to surprise you both, to do something special because you've both been so good to me."

She set the items down on the coffee table. "I brought your favorite—un chausson aus pommes."

Jeannette's face warmed into a smile. Uncrossing her arms, she glided over to the couch. "I do love those, you know, although no one makes them as good as our Fabienne."

Maurelle nodded. "Oh, I nearly forgot. I met an old friend of yours, a woman named Nathalie Bardot. She gave us all of this at no charge. She said she's looking forward to catching up with you."

"She's still here?" Jeannette asked. "I hadn't really expected that our old friends would still be around. I thought practically everyone we knew back in those days would have moved away or passed on, didn't you, Fabienne?"

"Oh, I do hope that Cecile and Vincent are still here. Do you think we could look them up later?"

"Well, I don't see why not," Jeannette said. "We should talk to Nathalie first though. She can catch us up on village gossip, to be sure."

Fabienne, who sipped her coffee, set the cup down at looked at Maurelle. "What did you tell Nathalie about us, dear?"

"I told her that my family owns a house on the edge of town and that they haven't been back here in years. From that, she figured out that I was with you, Fabienne. I hope you don't mind my calling you my family. It was presumptuous, but I thought it would sound believable."

"Of course I don't mind," Fabienne said. "When we talk to the locals, we'll use that. We'll tell them that you're my grandson's wife."

At the unexpected words, Maurelle's hand involuntarily jerked and coffee splashed over the cup's edge. She was getting to know Fabienne, certainly, but the older woman could still surprise her.

After the delicious breakfast, the women made a list of things they needed from the store and headed out together. They bought groceries, more cleaning supplies, and candles. After they took those back to the house, they went back to buy more things. When Fabienne and Jeannette found some of their old friends, Maurelle offered to continue the shopping alone, giving them time to visit. She didn't mind being on her own a bit. In fact, although she enjoyed their company, at times she also found them a bit overmuch.

For a time she sat on a bench beside the stream that ran

through Saint-Julien and breathed in the scent of flowers and fresh mountain air while she listened to the rippling water and thought about her strange, almost surreal situation. London seemed a long way away and with each passing day that distance grew somehow. Dave would be finding his way around the city by now. Was he enjoying the Tube, the pubs, and the local food? She glanced at the hill and was reminded of Reynier. What was happening back there? Were the gendarmes now swarming the area? What had Simone told them?

How otherworldly these small villages were compared with London; quiet, calm, peaceful. So why did she miss home? She looked toward the road that led out of town and part of her wanted to go, and yet at the same time she didn't. Was it England she missed, or Dave? What? Now where had that thought come from, foolish girl? She found she wished she could show him around the places where she'd grown up, her mother's former home and grave site. She closed her eyes, and tried to picture her mother's face. Instead, she involuntarily saw Jared's. She shivered, and stood up abruptly, shaken.

Continuing her walk, Maurelle found the general store and bought a phone card and more essentials for the house, careful to buy no more than she could carry each trip. She didn't want to use the car unless absolutely necessary.

Late in the afternoon, Maurelle, Jeannette and Fabienne strolled out of the town's one café after eating a sumptuous dinner. They strolled across the street to a pay phone, where Jeannette called Coralie at Brigitte's house.

"Well, what did she say?" Fabienne asked. "Did she have any news? Has she heard from Dave?"

"Coralie couldn't talk. I don't know what's going on, but before she hung up, she whispered that the gendarmes are looking for us and for the car."

Fabienne raised her eyebrows and glanced over at Maurelle.

She put one hand on her forehead and the other on her chest. "Tant pis! We'll cover our tracks, that's what we'll do. We'll hide that damned car so they won't find us."

Maurelle nodded, and the three women hurried back to the house. After looking around the grounds, they found a good hiding spot amid some wildly overgrown bushes behind the house.

"Who would have thought it would pay off to let the bushes grow wild?" Fabienne said. "I used to worry about neglecting this place."

Maurelle moved the car into place and covered it with additional branches. Fabienne and Jeannette carefully erased the car's tire tracks in the dirt with brooms.

Toddling back inside the house, Fabienne grabbed onto Maurelle's arm for support. When Maurelle glanced at the older woman, she saw how pale her face was and that she was huffing and struggling to catch her breath.

Fabienne said, between breaths, "I haven't been this happy in years. Let's pray the gendarmes don't go and ruin it."

"Are you all right?"

"Yes dear, I'm fine. These bones are just not used to this much excitement is all," Fabienne said, not convincing Maurelle at all.

DAVE AND KATE left Elizabeth Raybourne's office in Soho, walked to the train station, and boarded a train that would take them to Euston where Peter Raybourne and Robin Sutcliffe lived. Dave followed Kate to seats in the middle of the car. As the train began moving, Kate said, "What did you think of Elizabeth?"

"She was lying, or at least hiding something. She at least knows more about her son's activities than she was letting on."

Kate smiled. "She answered too much and seemed mainly keen on attacking her ex-husband."

"I agree." Dave paused a moment, reflecting on points of the interview with Elizabeth, then continued. "After we talk with the ex-husband, I think we should talk with her again, in her home this time. I really need to have a look inside the house. I doubt we'll see much, but at least we'll get a second chance at her, and you never know, maybe we'll get lucky."

Departing at Euston station, they walked several blocks to Peter and Robin's house. After introductions, Robin Sutcliffe showed them to the living room and sat down in a stuffed chair across from Dave and Kate who were sitting on the sofa. Robin had neat straight brown hair down to her waist, parted in the center. She had brown eyes behind wire-rim glasses. Her eyes reminded Dave of an ex-girlfriend, eyes that were intelligent and watchful. She told them that Peter wasn't home from work yet, though she expected him momentarily.

Kate said, "We know you've already given a statement to the police, but we'd like to ask a few questions. First, could you tell us about your relationship with Jared? Did you two get along?"

Robin shrugged. "We didn't really talk much."

"Why is that?"

She fidgeted, seemed nervous, twisting strands of her hair between her fingertips.

"He blamed me for his parents' divorce. It's understandable, I suppose. But I didn't seduce Peter. It just happened. I tried to convince Jared of that. He wouldn't listen."

"How did you and Peter meet?"

"We worked together at Castle Magazine. It's a publishing company. Peter is an editor. I was his assistant. I primarily researched and verified data."

"You used past tense. Does that mean you are no longer

working there?"

"That's right. Our personal relationship was against company policy. Either Peter or I had to quit."

"Were you involved while Peter was still married?"

"Yes, but that wasn't the problem. He couldn't be my boss."

"How did they find out about your relationship?"

She shrugged.

Kate glanced at Dave. He said, "Did Elizabeth or Jared tell them?"

Robin took a cigarette out of a packet on the coffee table, lit it up, and took a puff.

"I can't really say."

"Did you and Jared ever argue?" Kate asked.

She lowered her eyes, then said, "No."

"What about his mother, Elizabeth? What's your relationship with her?"

Robin looked up, her eyes full of anger, taking the cigarette and placing it on an ash tray. "It's no secret that she and I don't like each other. I'm sure you've already heard. Have you talked to her already? What did she say about me?"

"One of Elizabeth's friends told us that you and Elizabeth argued several times before Jared's murder. Is that true?"

"We argued because she was trying to get Peter back. She would make up excuses to call him over to the house." She retrieved the cigarette and took another nervous drag, blowing smoke into the air.

Dave interjected. "Who do you think murdered Jared?"

"Peter thinks it's either Elizabeth or that woman, the teacher who rented a room from Elizabeth."

"But what do you think?"

"Elizabeth could have killed him. She's an alcoholic, you know. Jared disapproved of her drinking, and the two of them fought about that all the time."

"Are you sure she's an alcoholic? That's a pretty big claim."

Robin took another drag and stubbed the unfinished butt out in the ash tray. "She was often drunk. That's part of what drove Peter away. He would stay at work later than necessary frequently so he wouldn't have to go home and deal with her."

The front door opened, and a man's voice called out to Robin.

"I'm in the living room," she answered. When he appeared, Robin went to him and kissed him, made the introductions, and explained why they were there. Peter Raybourne watched her walk out of the room, then sat in the spot she'd vacated.

Peter's hair, the color of wet sand, was a darker shade of blonde than his ex-wife's and their son's, and was wavy. He looked older than Elizabeth, certainly older than Robin. Dave tried to recall the man's age. He'd read it in one of the reports or an article. Forty-one or forty-two.

"Robin told us you used to be her boss," Kate said.

Peter nodded.

"Did she leave the company?"

"Yes."

"How long ago was that?"

He shrugged.

"Where's she working now?"

"I don't see why you're asking," he said with an edge of truculence.

"We're trying to get to know the main people in your son's life."

"Why? We already know who killed him."

Dave noticed a slight twitch in Kate's jaw.

Kate said, "Who do you think it was?"

"I've already been through this with the police." He leaned forward with his arms resting on the chair's arms.

"But not with us."

"And I still don't see why I should talk to you." He sighed. "All right. I'll say it again. The schoolteacher, Maura Barrington, had a key since she'd previously rented a room in that house. And she had a motive. The school officials told us she was under investigation of an affair with Jared."

"And you believe they had an affair?"

He walked over to the fireplace, picked up a framed photograph, and stared at it briefly before handing it to Kate. "He was a good looking boy. It's not surprising, really, that she could fall for him," he said.

"Have you met her?" Kate asked, avoiding the obvious affirmation.

"Briefly."

"She is attractive, too, isn't she? Is it possible that he had a schoolboy crush on her and that she didn't really have an affair with him?"

Peter shrugged.

"Is it possible that he was obsessed with her and that's why she moved out of the house? That he spread rumors about her because he wanted it to be true?"

Kate handed the photo to Dave. It looked fairly recent. Jared was dressed in school uniform, his hair groomed and his expression cocky. Jared was slender and good-looking. A slightly older woman might be attracted to him, as distasteful as that seemed to him. Maura had denied that. Dave looked up at the fireplace mantel at another photo, a picture of Peter and Robin. She didn't appear to be much older than Maura. Dave handed the photo back to Peter, who was still standing.

Peter sat back down, the frame in his lap, and leaned toward Kate. "Even if that was the case, that he was obsessed with her and made up everything, she still had motive."

"How is that?"

"She was under investigation by the school's governing

board. Wouldn't she save her job if Jared was gone?"

Dave said, "Not really. Jared's murder only added to the suspicions, not made them go away. Also, if that was true, she would have stayed here and fought the allegations, wouldn't she, if she was so desperate to keep her job?"

Peter looked deep in thought. "I don't know. But if she didn't kill him, then who did?"

"Did your son have any enemies?"

Peter shrugged. "I won't lie to you. He went through some difficulties after his mother and I split. He got into fights in school. He was accused of vandalism at school and around the neighborhood. I can't tell you who he might have angered." He stared at them with an oddly defiant expression. "Look, I think I have given you enough time now. I will expect to see anything you write before it is published." He stood, and waited for them to follow suit.

After Dave and Kate left the house, Kate said, "Do you want to go to Elizabeth Raybourne's house tonight, or wait till morning?

"I'd really like to talk with her now, if you don't mind."

She reached into her handbag and pulled out her phone.

Dave said, "Wait, why don't we surprise her, not give her a chance to turn us down?"

She nodded and dropped the phone back inside.

They took the train from Euston to Hampstead, then made the familiar trek to the neighbor.

At the Raybourne house, Elizabeth did indeed look surprised when she answered the doorbell.

"What are you doing here?" she asked.

Dave detected the smell of alcohol on her breath. Maybe Robin was telling the truth and it wasn't simply malice on her part.

Kate said, "We need to ask you a few more questions."

"Then make an appointment at the agency." She started to close the door on them, but Dave stuck his foot in between the door and the jamb.

"We really need to talk now. We've just come from your ex-husband's home."

She pursed her lips. "Give me a minute to tidy up." She closed the door.

Dave looked at Kate and shrugged. He wasn't sure what Elizabeth would do.

Elizabeth returned a few minutes later, hair combed. She opened the door wide and led them into the living room. "Please have a seat." She motioned toward the beige sofa. Dave glanced around and peeked through the kitchen doorway. An empty glass and an uncorked wine bottle sat on the countertop.

Elizabeth sat in a chair beside the sofa, her hands wrapped together in her lap.

Kate said, "How would you describe your son's mental condition immediately prior to his death?"

Her eyes widened. "I—I don't know. I'm not a doctor."

"But you're a mother. You told us that your son wasn't happy about your divorce, and he had been acting out."

"Peter wanted to take Jared to a psychologist, but Jared refused, saying he would do something dreadful if we forced him to go."

"Do you think he meant suicide?"

"No, he wouldn't kill himself. I'm certain of it."

How many times had Dave heard that from the families of people who had taken their own lives? Rarely did a parent or spouse believe their loved one would resort to suicide. Was Elizabeth one of those who refused to believe, or did she know her son well enough? And if she didn't think he would kill himself, what did she mean by 'do something dreadful'?

He glanced at Kate, waiting for her to ask the questions he

wanted to ask.

"What did you do when he threatened to do something terrible?"

"We let him believe we would hold off, but he overheard us discussing it one night. He came in and flew off the handle, raging at both of us. After that, well, we didn't really know what to do. All we could do was keep an eye on him. You know, try not to leave him home alone if we could help it."

"What were you afraid he would do?" Kate asked. "You said you didn't believe he would harm himself."

Elizabeth shook her head, hesitating and chewing on her lower lip.

"You mean you thought he might hurt someone else?" Kate asked.

She shrugged, suddenly looking close to tears.

"I'm a bit confused here. Just now you said you were trying not to leave him home alone. Then why did you leave him alone that night if you were worried he might do something? He was home alone the night of the murder, was he not?"

"Yes," Elizabeth said, in a shaky voice. "The one time we left him alone, he died."

"You haven't answered the question. Why did you leave him alone that night?"

"Because my career was on the line, that's why! The agency was struggling in the bad economy. Roger Newton—he's my boss— was desperate to acquire a client, Fournier Industries, which could save the company. He planned a dinner party with the heads of Fournier as guests of honor. Roger made it quite clear that it was my duty to attend the party and snag the client. If we landed the client, he promised me a promotion and a raise. But if I failed, my promotion and raise wouldn't happen. He intimated that I might even find myself jobless. I really had no choice. When Maura Barrington moved out, I lost the rental income. I needed the job and the raise."

With the mention of Maura, Dave decided to broach that subject. "Did you know Maura well? Do you really believe she killed your son?"

"I barely knew her, but who else could have done it?"

"Do you believe that she was having an affair with Jared before she moved out?"

"I don't know," she whispered. "She told me once that he had made advances toward her. I didn't think much of it at the time."

"Could Jared have instigated the rumors?" Dave asked. "Could it be that he wanted a relationship and that when she refused, he started spreading rumors to get back at her? Or maybe he really believed there was something going on between them when there wasn't."

She leaned back in her chair, looking defeated. "I suppose that's possible."

"If true," Dave said, "then maybe she didn't kill him either. So, the question is—who might have had a grudge against your son? Who might he have angered?"

Elizabeth shook her head, her eyes now filling with tears.

Changing the subject, Dave said, "We heard that you and Robin Sutcliffe quarreled several times before the murder. Can you tell us what you argued about?"

"Who told you that? I wouldn't dream of seeking an argument with Robin. We don't like each other, but we tried to get along as well as possible for Jared's sake."

"You never quarreled with her?"

"It's none of your business!" Elizabeth looked away. There was a silence, and then she finally shrugged. "She complained sometimes, but I wouldn't say we argued. She—she disliked Peter's spending so much time at the house. But we were civil to one another."

Dave recalled Ian Waitley's words and Robin Sutcliffe's words, both of them contradicting what Elizabeth was currently saying. "Why was Peter spending so much time here?"

"Because of Jared's problems." Elizabeth seemed defeated, answering mechanically.

"Did Robin know that?"

"Yes. Of course she did. It didn't really help, though. She thought that if Jared needed his father, he should spend time at their house, where Peter wouldn't have to see me. I could understand that."

"And did you suggest that to your son?"

Elizabeth nodded. "He refused."

"What was your last conversation with Robin—before Jared's murder—about?"

Elizabeth sighed. "Robin accused me of taking advantage of the situation to get Peter back home. She thought that I was in some way causing, or perpetuating Jared's problems, to get Peter to come around more often."

"Were you?"

"Of course not!" She stood up abruptly. "Now, look, I have work to do. I've given you more than enough of my time."

They both rose and turned to go.

"Will. . . ." Elizabeth began. "Will you let me see what you've written before it's published?"

Kate looked back at her and smiled. "Of course."

As they stepped outside, Dave turned around. "One last question," he said. "Does Robin have a key to this house?"

Her mouth gaped open, then closed. "I—I don't know. Peter has one. Jared once told me he keeps it on a hook by the front door of his house."

ON THE TRAIN ride back to Kate's house, Dave said, "Don't

you wonder why they're all so ready to talk to us?"

"The power of the press. People complain about it, but they always want to talk. If they don't, it usually means they have an exclusive deal with another paper."

"Maybe," Dave said.

"What else?"

"Professional criminals get good at saying nothing. But amateurs want to be clever, or they want to find out what the investigators know. They can't keep away from it. Then you get the innocent ones with their own agenda.

Kate said, "Like what?"

"Like getting someone else suspected, or even convicted. And not necessarily the guilty person."

CHAPTER TWENTY-SEVEN

THE FOLLOWING MORNING Maurelle stretched off remnants of sleep and wondered what time it was, since the sun wasn't peeking through her curtains yet. She got up and looked out at a gray cloud-filled sky that overnight had settled over Saint-Julien. She turned from the window and dressed. By the time she padded downstairs to the kitchen, Jeannette was already setting out plates.

"Breakfast is my treat today," Jeannette said as she busily sliced fresh bread.

Maurelle poured herself a cup of steaming coffee. It burned her lips when she took a sip and she decided to let it cool a bit before repeating. "Have you seen Fabienne this morning?"

"No, the poor dear was awfully tired last night. I thought it best not to awaken her." Jeannette sat down and set plates of bread on the table. "She over-did things yesterday, I'm afraid."

"I did no such thing!"

Maurelle swung around. Fabienne was standing in the doorway, looking paler than last night. Dark bags under her eyes made her look as if she hadn't slept in weeks. Her hair was disheveled, her clothes wrinkled.

"Don't go treating me like some kind of invalid," she said as she shuffled across the cold stone floor. "Just because I get a bit winded doesn't mean anything."

"You are the most stubborn old woman I know," Jeannette said. She held out a cup of coffee to Fabienne who crossed her arms for a moment, but then reached out and accepted the cup. "Of course we're worried about you. Did you forget to take your medications yesterday?"

Fabienne attempted a stubborn pout, but her face crumbled. "I left my medications at home. Right before we left, I searched my handbag for my keys to this house. When I couldn't find them, I dumped everything out on my bed. I found the keys, but my bottle of pills must have rolled off the bed. I was in such a hurry that I didn't notice."

"Oh dear," Jeannette said. "We have to go back for them."

"No!" Fabienne said. "I won't hear of it. That would be ridiculous and far too dangerous. I'll be fine. Don't go making this a bigger deal than it is."

Jeannette shook her head at Fabienne, then looked at Maurelle as if seeking her input, which surprised Maurelle since Jeannette usually acted like her opinions didn't matter.

The two grandmothers were the same age, but Fabienne looked older; her color really wasn't good today, and probably hadn't been for days, only Maurelle had been too distracted to notice. There was a grayness to her cheeks, and her eyes seemed dulled. Her missing those pills might not be the only problem. Maurelle's grandfather had died of a heart attack back when Maurelle was a teenager. He'd exhibited similar symptoms.

"If we can't go back, we need to get you to a doctor," Maurelle said.

"No! I don't need a doctor. I'm telling you I won't leave here."

"We'll find a local doctor," Maurelle said. "Surely they have one somewhere in the area."

"If I don't feel better in a day or two, I'll consider seeing a doctor. But not yet."

"All right. We'll give you one day. In the meantime, you are going to take it easy. Jeannette and I will take care of you. Right, Jeannette?"

"That's right. You're going to sit down, and let us treat you like a queen."

Fabienne nodded, but her mouth was a thin line.

By the end of breakfast, the sun was already breaking through, and the temperature was rapidly climbing. The day promised to be warm. Maurelle scurried into the town square to the shop where she'd seen rocking chairs for sale. She selected two wicker rocking chairs and paid for them with cash.

"Would you like some help putting these in your car?" the sales clerk asked.

"Uh, actually I don't have a car." The lie came automatically because she didn't want the vehicle seen. "I'll need to carry one home, and come back for the second one."

The clerk, a young man, looked at the older man who worked there. The man nodded, and then the young man said, "I'll carry the other one for you."

"Thank you, that's very kind," Maurelle said.

At the house, she set both chairs outside near the front door, and then went inside to get Jeannette and Fabienne. She ushered them outdoors.

"These are for the two of you."

Fabienne clapped her hands together and then hugged Maurelle, kissing both her cheeks.

"What a dear girl you are," Fabienne said. "Now we can sit outside and enjoy the fresh air and watch our friends. How lovely!"

"Oh yes," Jeannette said. "This is wonderful. Now our friends will know we're here, and more of them will come visit. I should go inside and prepare refreshments."

"No you don't. I'll take care of that," Maurelle said. "Both of you just relax and enjoy."

Maurelle didn't wait for an answer. She rushed into the kitchen and rummaged through the large cooler that they had filled with ice and assorted meats and cheeses. She quickly made up finger sandwiches, which she set out on a serving platter. On a second platter, she placed a jar of sun tea and six teacups. She carried a large folding table outside first, and set it up. It took two more trips to bring out everything, but when she was done, Fabienne smiled and began humming.

Maurelle tiptoed away. She glanced back once and smiled tenderly at the two women pouring tea and chatting. In the house, she sat down on a stuffed chair by the front window and began reading a book that she'd bought the day before. Occasionally, she would look out and watch the two women as they conversed with locals who popped in now and then.

They spent the whole day that way. In the late afternoon they brought the trays inside and the three of them set out for a stroll to the only restaurant in the village for an early dinner. They were enjoying their meal, but all were still subdued. Though Fabienne tried to make bright conversation, she seemed to avoid any mention of Dave.

Jeannette said, "Where do you think Dave is right now?"

Maurelle glanced at Fabienne across the table from her. The older woman's mouth tightened and her forehead creased with worry lines. Maurelle said, "He's probably enjoying the sights. It really is a lovely city."

Fabienne's expression relaxed, and Maurelle was glad, though her own fears lingered. Somehow, they needed to find out what was happening. Maybe Simone had heard from him. Forty minutes later, after finishing their dinner, they strolled back toward home. As they approached the cottage Fabienne slowed down and started wobbling. Maurelle grabbed hold of her arm to steady her.

"Are you all right?"

Her face was ashen. "I think I'm in trouble."

Maurelle checked Fabienne's pulse. "We need to get you to a hospital. Jeannette, can you help me get her to the car?"

Fabienne's eyes widened and she grabbed Maurelle's arm. "You can't do that. You can't risk getting caught. I'll be fine. Help me back to the house. I'll go to bed straight away. You'll see."

Jeannette shook her head, looking panicked. "Maurelle, talk some sense into her!"

"Fabienne, I know you're trying to protect me, but it comes down to taking a chance of getting caught versus running the risk of losing you. It's obvious you need medical attention. I won't take no for an answer."

"I won't allow it, and you know how stubborn I am."

"Well, now you're going to find out how stubborn I can be."

"And where do you think you're going to find a hospital around here?" Fabienne asked, giving a weak smile.

Maurelle and Jeannette each put an arm around Fabienne and walked the last fifty yards to the cottage. As they arrived at the front door, Jeannette said, "Nathalie will know. We should ask her."

Maurelle nodded. "I'll find Nathalie. Will you stay here with Fabienne?"

"I'll run away," Fabienne said. "You can't keep me here. You're as old and decrepit as I am."

"That's what you think," Jeannette said. "We had to practically carry you back to the house. You think you're going to run away? Now that I'd like to see."

While Fabienne pouted, Maurelle slipped quietly out the door.

Ten minutes later she returned with Nathalie, who said, "We have a doctor in Saint-Julien, now. He's good. Dr. Maison can handle most emergencies, except for major surgeries, and he has evening hours twice a week. He'll work later if necessary. If he says you need hospitalization, he'll know where the best local hospital is located. Come with me." She hesitated, then added, "Can you walk, Fabienne, or shall I bring the doctor to you?"

"I can walk," Fabienne snapped. "I don't know why everyone insists on treating me as though I'm an invalid."

Outside, Fabienne shrugged off help from Maurelle and Jeannette until they'd gone only a block. She stopped and leaned forward, bracing herself with her hands on her knees. Without saying a word, Maurelle and Jeannette stood by her side and when she straightened up, they each put an arm around her waist and supported her as they continued another block to the doctor's office.

Nathalie stayed in the clinic's waiting room, while the other three women sat in the doctor's consultation room. Dr. Maison asked Fabienne about her medications and medical history. Maurelle was surprised to hear that Fabienne had a stent placed in each of two arteries last year and had been taking an anti-platelet drug to prevent heart attack or stroke.

The doctor explained that his initial tests would include an electrocardiogram, blood tests, and chest x-rays and then led Fabienne into the exam area.

Maurelle paced in the waiting room. It was eerily quiet, unlike the hospital where her mother had undergone treatments. Here, there were no other patients, and only one nurse that they could see, although Maurelle occasionally heard faint voices coming from the exam area, probably the doctor and the other nurse she'd seen when they'd first arrived. Jeannette dozed off in her chair, her head tilted back slightly against the wall. The phone rang, and the nurse answered it, speaking softly. For all Maurelle knew, she could be speaking to the gendarmes. They could burst through the front door of the clinic any moment. She chewed on a fingernail and stared at the clock above the door. Forty-five minutes had passed since Nathalie left, but she calculated that with the tests, they'd been in the clinical for nearly three hours. She'd read—or at least browsed—all of the magazines in the waiting room.

The door opened, and the doctor and Fabienne came out together, both sitting down near Maurelle and Jeannette.

"Madame Laurent wanted me to give her the results with all of you," Dr. Maison said. Turning to Fabienne, he said, "I didn't find any evidence of an abnormality or damage. Your blood tests were fine, and your blood pressure and heart rate appear to have stabilized. You may have had a new blockage that reopened on its own, or perhaps a spasm in one of the coronary arteries. It could also have been as simple as overstress, caused by worry over having forgotten you medications. Since we don't know for sure, and we don't have the necessary test equipment here in this clinic, I would like to send you to the hospital for a more thorough examination."

Fabienne said, "Do I have to go to the hospital now? Can't I wait?"

"I will put you on a beta blocker and give you a new prescription of your medication that you left at home. We can see how that works."

"Oh, thank God," she said, clapping her hands together.

"Don't get too thankful yet. As I said, you'll need more tests when you get back to your home. You'll need rest, and you must reduce your stress level. It is still possible that you have a blocked artery, especially considering your history."

"Oh, I hope not," Fabienne said, squeezing Maurelle's hand.

"Pardon, Madame. No need to worry right now. Get your prescriptions filled and get some bed rest for a couple of days. I'll come by to check on you."

Maurelle said, "Are you sure she doesn't need to go to the hospital tonight?"

"I would prefer to send her there now, but it's not absolutely necessary."

"Where is the nearest hospital?" Jeannette asked.

"It's forty-five minutes away from here."

Fabienne looked at Maurelle and Jeannette, and asked, "What should I do?"

Jeannette said. "Let's see how the medicine and rest go. You didn't have any problems while you were taking your medicine."

Fabienne nodded.

THE BELL ON the café door jingled and Simone looked up. A tall man with curly brown hair stood inside, a few feet from the door, looking lost. He was holding a small suitcase. Simone set down the coffee pot she was holding and walked over to him.

"Bonjour. May I help you?" she asked.

"Uh, yes, I'm looking for Simone Charbonneau." He spoke in French, but his pronunciation was atrocious, and his accent was thick. American?

"I'm Simone. What do you need?"

He scratched his head with his free hand. "Well, this is going to sound strange, but I came here from Chicago to visit my friend, Dave Martin. He invited me a couple weeks ago. But I can't find him. He gave me an address, his grandmother's house. I went there several times and no one is around. I finally talked to a neighbor who told me I should check with you. Said you might know where I can find them."

"I wish I had good news for you. Something came up, and Dave had to leave unexpectedly. His grandmother left, too."

"Oh, no. He must have forgotten to call me. Thanks. I don't

really know what I'm supposed to do now."

"You could stay at Chateau de Reynier until he returns. It's just down the street from here."

"Thanks. My taxi driver dropped me off in front of the house. It didn't occur to me to have him wait. I'm kinda stuck here."

"Why don't you sit and have something to eat? My employee will be here any minute. After she arrives, I will walk with you to the chateau."

"Thank you. That would be wonderful. And I actually am starved." He sauntered over to one of the tables, plunked his suitcase down on an empty chair, and sat down.

"How do you know Dave?" Simone asked.

"I'm sorry. My name is Greg. I'm his old partner from the police force. I'm on vacation, and I've been traveling around Great Britain and Europe. Dave and I send emails back and forth. He invited me to visit him if I had time before I went home."

"I thought you sounded American. How long had you planned on staying?"

"That depends." He flashed Simone a dazzling smile that transformed him into the most charming man she'd seen in a long time.

CHAPTER TWENTY-EIGHT

IN THE LATE morning Kate met Dave at his hotel and from there they travelled together by train to Westglenn School north of Euston. They'd decided not to schedule an appointment because that might put the Headmaster on guard. Surprise could work to their advantage. Whether or not that was true in this case remained to be seen.

As they exited the Tube station, they discovered that the blue sky had grown overcast with heavy clouds. A block from Westglenn the rain began pelting them. Kate covered her head with her handbag. They quickened their pace, practically running outright, and ducked inside the school building moments before pea-sized hail accosted the roof, windows, and neighborhood. Their rather wet and bedraggled appearance brought smirks from a number of students.

In the main building they snagged one of the students and asked for directions to the Headmaster's office. Dave and Kate waited inside the doorway while the Headmaster's secretary talked to a young, nervous-looking boy. When he left, looking even more worried, Kate approached the secretary's desk.

"May I help you?" she asked. She was a young woman with a friendly looking face.

Kate introduced herself. "We are here to speak with Headmaster Fowler." The woman got up and went into another office, then returned in a few minutes. "Mr. Fowler can see you now."

Fowler, a middle-aged man wearing a navy blue suit and vest, stood up behind his desk and shook their hands as Kate introduced herself and Dave.

He smiled and reseated himself. "Please have a seat. How may I help you?"

Kate explained why they were there.

His expression darkened, and Dave worried they might not get his cooperation. The phone rang. He excused himself to take the call, giving Dave time to study him and the surroundings. Fowler had brown hair, which was thinning on top. His face was pale, with deep wrinkles, likely a sign of his responsibilities and profession. The observation made Dave wonder how the scandal may have affected him personally. The man's office appeared typical of what one would expect of a headmaster. There were two white walls that were accented with a couple of unimpressive paintings and two framed degrees. The other two walls were covered in a fine oak wainscot, perhaps worn a bit from the years, but impressive all the same. The headmaster's desk was organized, but piles of paper spoke of many hours of work yet to complete. There was a photo on the desk, but as it was facing away, Dave assumed it was of a wife, kids, or perhaps other family member or members.

He hung up the phone a moment later and Kate said, "Could you tell us about your former employee, Maura Barrington?"

"She was an English teacher, fairly new, still learning. This was her first teaching assignment. She worked here for four years."

"Was she a good teacher, a good employee?"

"She was basically efficient. The children seemed to like her. Pupils in her class did well."

Kate said, "Were you surprised when you heard the rumors about an affair with a student?"

He didn't answer right away, seeming to think about it. "She was attractive. Probably too attractive."

"Why do you say that?"

He shrugged. "Sometimes she seemed a bit too friendly."

Kate said, "Was she ever romantically involved with a school employee?"

Appearing uncomfortable, he said, "I can't really answer that." He put his hands together, steepling his fingers. "Let me make something clear. I believe in cooperating with the press. But these days one must always take into account public opinion. But there must be limits. I am sure you understand."

Kate nodded. "Of course, our apologies. If it's acceptable, we would like to speak with a pupil, Penny Miller. We understand she was Jared Raybourne's former girlfriend."

"I'm afraid that is out of the question. Our pupils have already been questioned by police and that was difficult enough. I'm sure you understand."

"We'll be discreet and—"

"I really can't allow that. Now if you'll excuse me." He began shuffling papers around on his desk.

"Mr. Fowler, if I may, what does your governing body think about Jared Raybourne's murder?" Dave asked.

Fowler's hands froze in mid-air as he looked at Dave. "This is something no school wants."

"Has it hurt the school's reputation?"

Fowler rubbed the top of his head. "Parents were shocked, of course. It hasn't been easy reassuring them. Our students are perfectly safe here. Security is tight." He nodded and looked at them seriously. "I would like that stressed, please. This did not take place on school property nor during school hours. This is a safe place."

Dave thought about their arrival in the building. They'd walked right in and no one had stopped them or questioned them. "Does your governing body believe Jared's murder was connected with their investigation?"

"I don't know what you mean."

Dave said, "With the allegations of an affair, the board was going to conduct a hearing to find out whether it was true. Some people believe Maura Barrington killed Jared to keep him from testifying at that hearing."

Tight lines formed around Fowler's mouth. He didn't speak for a minute, then he said, "I don't have anything more to say. Now, if you don't mind . . . ." He gestured towards the door.

On their way out, Dave stopped at the secretary's desk. "Could you tell us what time school lets out?"

"Three-thirty."

"Thanks. Is there a restaurant or café nearby?"

"Yes. Bailey's Café is just round the corner. Further on, there are several cafés."

"Is Bailey's popular?" Kate asked.

"I suppose with teenagers, anyway. It can get pretty noisy, though, in the late afternoon."

Dave and Kate made their way to Bailey's and found a booth. Dave went to the counter and ordered coffees. When he returned to the table, Kate asked, "What did you think of Headmaster Fowler?"

"He was certainly very nervous and defensive."

"I suppose that's understandable," Kate said. "The scandal happened on his watch. That can't be good for a man in his position."

Dave nodded.

They talked now and then while eating lunch. Afterwards,

they read newspapers as they waited for school to let out. Dave set the alarm on his watch for a quarter past three, giving them plenty of time to get back to the school before dismissal time.

When students began trickling out of the building at three-thirty, Dave and Kate were on the scene asking if anyone knew Penny Miller. Several knew her, but they didn't know where she was. As the crowd thinned out, a boy pointed to a girl with long dark hair, coming out of the front door.

Walking up the steps, Kate asked, "Are you Penny Miller?"

"Yes." She pushed hair out of her eyes the way Dave had seen Maurelle do on numerous occasions.

"I'm Kate Hill, a journalist. This is my associate, Dave Martin. We're investigating Jared Raybourne's murder and were hoping we could talk to you."

Penny's blue eyes also reminded Dave of Maurelle's, though musing that Penny's eyes lacked Maurelle's sparkle and allure. Catching his mind wandering, he chided himself.

"Yeah, whatever."

"Perhaps we can talk for a few minutes at Bailey's Café. Do you know the place?"

She nodded.

They walked to the café and took a seat in the same booth where they'd sat earlier. Dave bought three coffees and carried them to the table. They had decided in advance that Kate would ask the questions.

Kate asked, "How long did you and Jared date?"

"I dunno, maybe four months."

"Why did you break up?"

Penny glanced down at her hands, which were folded in her lap. When she raised her eyes again, she didn't look directly at Kate or Dave.

"He was nice and thoughtful when we first went out, but he changed. It was almost like he'd turned into a different person."

"When was this?"

"About two months after we started dating. His parents had just split up. He was angry about it. After that, I got scared sometimes being around him."

"What did he do that scared you?"

"He would pick fights with me and with other people. He was moody and mean and suspicious. I saw him kill a bird once by smashing it with a bat, and he smashed someone's mailbox with a shovel. He didn't have a driving license, but he took his mum's car out for a joy ride and made me go along with him. While we were out, he hit a dog and left it in the road. That's when I told him I didn't want to see him anymore."

"Did he get angry with you over the break-up?"

Penny nodded. "He told his friends that he broke up with me because I was sleeping around. It wasn't true."

"Was he ever involved with any other girls here? Maybe a classmate?"

"Maybe. I don't know."

"Did Jared have any enemies that you know of?"

"He wasn't popular. People didn't much like him after he changed. But that doesn't mean someone would kill him, does it?"

"Did you know the teacher, Maura Barrington?"

"Sort of. I was in one of her classes."

"What was she like?"

"Nice. I liked her. Most of the kids did. She wasn't strict."

"Was she a good teacher?"

"She was all right. She made her classes interesting."

Kate said, "Do you believe she had an affair with Jared?"

Penny shrugged. The door of the café opened and a group of kids walked in, laughing and talking. She stood up. "I gotta go."

Dave and Kate watched her leave, then glanced at each

other.

Kate said, "Let's split up, shall we?"

Dave nodded. He approached two teenage boys. One was a slender boy with eyeglasses and the other was an overweight pimple-faced boy. They were sitting at a table. After introducing himself, Dave asked if they'd known Jared Raybourne.

The slender boy, who identified himself as Ray Wills, said, "Yeah, we knew Jared. Grew up with him."

"Were you still friends?"

Ray glanced at his friend. He looked back at Dave and shrugged.

"Was he popular?"

"A lot of kids disliked him. 'Course some of us admired him."

"You admired him? Why?"

Ray stared at him as though he thought Dave was stupid. "Because he got to hook up with that teacher. She was fit. Worth dying for, you know?"

"What do you mean? Do you think she killed him?"

"'Course she did. If he'd told everything, she would have lost her job for sure. That's what everyone says."

Dave found another student, Jenny Hayes, and asked her similar questions.

"I saw Jared and Ms. Barrington sitting together eating lunch one day," Jenny said. "Another time, they were whispering together in the hallway and looking, well, you know."

"Couldn't they have been discussing school?"

"He wasn't in any of her classes. Besides, he was one of the best-looking boys in this school. Dreamy blue eyes and blonde hair. It's not surprising that she would be attracted to him. I heard she wasn't that much older than Jared."

"Do you know Brittany Stevas?"

"Yeah, she's in some of my classes."

"Were she and Jared friends?"

"I don't know."

Dave looked around for Kate. She was talking to a group of middle-aged women. Not wanting to interfere, he scanned the café for more students. Kate was now standing and preparing to move away from the women. He stood by and waited for her. "Any luck?" he asked.

She touched his arm. "Let's go. We can talk on the train."

It was late afternoon, approaching rush hour, and the train was already packed with bodies of all ages. Dave and Kate found two empty seats together near a young woman with three children, including a baby. Dave hoped the baby would sleep during the train ride.

As the train began moving, he said, "The kids think she and Jared had an affair. They believe she killed him to keep him from testifying so she wouldn't lose her job. His death didn't help her in any way. She obviously didn't kill him to save her job."

Kate closed her newspaper. "She may not have gone there intending to kill him. Maybe she just wanted to talk him out of telling the board the details of their relationship. This is how I see it: They quarreled, she went to leave, he yelled after her, she got angry, went into the kitchen and grabbed a knife, went after him, and stabbed him. A typical crime of passion."

"Why do you assume that simply because of what those kids said? What do they know? They have no real experience."

"I talked to a couple of the teachers, too. They told me that Maura Barrington was quiet and gentle, and sometimes it seemed she wasn't tough enough to be a teacher. In fact once, shortly after she qualified, she completely lost control of a class. It got so bad that one day she lost her temper and threw something across the room. A pupil said she had thrown it at him, but another teacher had been going into the room at that point and said it was just a piece of chalk and it hit the ceiling—it was accepted that it was an accident. Still, she left the school for a while soon after, and said she was going to take time out to look after her mother who was dying."

Dave sat silent, thinking, for the rest of the ride.

BACK AT KATE'S house, they searched through more emails and faxes that had come through. Somehow, Kate had gotten copies of Jared's school records, which showed he was an average student. Nothing, however, seemed to move them forward.

Frustrated, Dave ran his hand over his hair and said, "Let's take another look at the police reports, particularly anything involving Raybourne family friends and neighbors."

"We've already looked at the murder report." She pulled out a piece of paper, put on her glasses, and began reading out loud.

Dave closed his eyes, tuning out most of it since it was the same report he'd already read.

"On the morning the victim was found, police went to the flat where Maura Barrington lived. She, having recently moved out of the victim's home and being a potential witness, was wanted for questioning. Upon discovering she'd fled from London, the police issued a bulletin alerting the public to be on the lookout for her."

He opened his eyes. She'd run away before she was ever questioned and was only considered a witness at that point. He thought back to the many times she'd run away: when she was flustered in the general store, again when she saw the gendarmes, and when his grandmother and Jeannette had intimidated her at lunch. And what about when she'd supposedly been attacked by the man who'd given her a ride? Did she always panic when cornered? Or was she always running away because she was guilty?

Dave frowned. Up until now, he'd convinced himself that no one could ever manipulate him again, that he knew how to spot the Diana Lewis' and he wouldn't fall prey. The evidence was telling him otherwise. His grandmother had also succeeded in fooling him, and now Maurelle . . . .

As he'd done on numerous occasions, he continued the debate internally with himself. Was he an idiot? Did he really know what he was doing? What was his motive for getting involved? Part of him wanted to hand her over to the police and let them sort it out. Another part wanted to just walk away and have done with it. Yet another part wanted . . . what? To find the truth no matter what it took or where it led?

Realizing that he was not going to fare any better with this internal argument than he had on prior occasions, he looked at Kate and asked, "Can we look at other crimes committed in the area? Maybe we're missing something. Maybe it was a random murder or a break-in. What about a case of mistaken identity, or maybe someone from school had a grudge against Jared? Or just maybe, his murder is linked somehow to something else."

"All right. We can do that, but I doubt we'll find anything more."

BY EVENING, DAVE and Kate were bleary-eyed and hungry. Dave suggested to Kate that they take a break and grab some dinner at a local Indian restaurant Kate had pointed out earlier in the day, saying it was a favorite of hers. During dinner, not being able to break habit, they discussed a couple of vandalism reports, a couple of drug-related arrests, several Peeping Tom reports, and a cat killing report that had never really developed into a real case. They decided to visit some more of the neighbors the next day.

After dinner, and after seeing Kate off, Dave went back to

his hotel, hoping that he would get a call from Greg. He waited up until midnight, vaguely watching TV, but after dozing off three different times, he gave up and went to bed.

CHAPTER TWENTY-NINE

DAVE AWOKE ABRUPTLY to the buzzing of his hotel room telephone. He almost knocked over an alarm clock when he reached for the phone. "Hello?"

"Cheerio, mate," Greg said.

"Hey, you made it to Reynier."

"Yep," Greg said. "Met your Simone, too. She's pretty and sexy and flirty the way you described her."

"Sounds like you two hit it off, if she's flirting already," Dave said, rubbing his eyes and the stubble on his face, trying to fully wake up.

"Oh yeah. So how goes the investigation?"

"Long story," Dave said. "We're slowly moving along, though we haven't got a suspect yet. At least nothing concrete. Right now, I'm more interested in what you found out."

"Well, I'm heading to Orleans this morning with Simone. We're going to visit her mother at Simone's aunt's house."

"Does that mean Simone knows you're working with me?" Dave felt a flash of alarm. "I thought you were working this on the down low."

"Don't worry, I am. She told me that she was going to visit her mother, and I asked if I could tag along, seeing as how I had nothing better to do. I played up the fact that you ditched me the way you ditched her. She seemed to like that."

"Thanks. I sound like a real nice guy. Anyway, that certainly sounds like Simone," Dave said, chuckling. "Does that mean you're already . . . getting friendly?"

"Jealous? I thought you weren't interested in her anymore."

"I'm not. I'm curious. I didn't think even you worked that quickly."

"I haven't made a move on her—yet," Greg said. "But that might change."

"Yeah, sure. While you're staying in her aunt's house with her mother down the hall. Fat chance." Dave grinned, imagining Greg in a house with those women, and he was suddenly thankful that it was Greg going there and not himself.

"Yeah, you've got a point there, old man." He laughed and added, "Oh well, maybe when we get back to Reynier."

"Have you found out anything about Maurelle and my grandmother?"

"Only that the police have been asking lots of questions around this village. Most people aren't talking to me, probably because I'm a stranger."

"What about Paul? Simone said he's the one who called the gendarmes."

"From what I heard, he told the gendarmes that Jeannette Devlin has two cousins who live in Paris. He thought that's where they would go to hide." He paused for a second, and before Dave had a chance to comment, added, "Oh, I almost forgot. The gendarmes also discovered that Maura's or Maurelle's father lives in Paris. That gives them two possible hiding places in the same general area."

"Hmm," Dave said. "Actually, that might be a good thing. I don't think they would go there. Maurelle would steer clear of Paris."

"Hope you're right. Anyway, I'd better go. I'm supposed to meet Simone in fifteen minutes. I'll call when I can."

"Hey, before you go, how did you get all of this information if no one knows that you're working with me and nobody's talking to you?"

"Easy," Greg said. "This whole damned village is a gossip mill because of all the excitement. Everyone's talking to everyone else. All I have to do is eavesdrop. Apparently, the police were the only people around here who couldn't get an earful, so they left."

Dave chuckled. "Yeah, that sounds like Reynier."

KATE HAD PERSONAL errands to run in the morning. She told Dave she would meet him after lunch in Hampstead. Dave grabbed a quick breakfast before sitting himself in front of the hotel lobby computer to do some research on the internet. When he finished, he took in a bit of sightseeing in London proper, eventually ending up in Hampstead, where he ate lunch in one of the pubs.

In the early afternoon Kate phoned Dave and picked him up outside the pub. They drove to Willoughby Crescent and parked on the street, about a block from the Raybournes' house.

"Where should we begin?" she asked. "Any idea which neighbors know the Raybourne family?"

Dave glanced at his notes again. "Alice Rickards is the next door neighbor, but she's in a nursing home right now. I called and tried to talk with her. Her caregiver, who lived with her, told me that Alice had gone into the hospital the day before and wasn't home at the time of the murder. Greg and I already spoke with the neighbor on the other side, Judy Winston. She also wasn't home at the time of the murder. She did tell us a little about Jared's bad behavior, vandalism, etc. Ian Waitley was home, as far as I know. I guess I'd like to speak with him again."

"What about other neighbors?"

"Sally Kavanaugh lives there, on the corner," Dave said, pointing at a house. "She's a friend of Elizabeth's, but she wasn't at home when Greg and I were here last, so we should talk to her if we can. Also, I was told that Nick and Jenny Hallowell from a few doors down were friends with Elizabeth and Peter. There's another friend, Rob Carsters. He lives on the next street over."

"Very cozy. All right. Let's try Sally Kavanaugh, first, and then make our way around to the others."

Sally Kavanaugh looked at them skeptically, until Kate showed her a business card. "Oh, I know who you are. I read an article of yours in the paper a while back. I guess I can answer a few questions."

She invited them inside, and showed them into the living room. As Dave sat down on a sleek black leather sofa, he looked around at a large number of black and white photos covering the walls.

"I'm guessing you're a photographer," he said.

"Yes, I am."

"They're lovely photographs," he said, indicating the walls. "Do you have an exhibit going?"

"Thank you. I did. I hope to have another in a few months. Some of these are from the last exhibit."

Dave nodded as he looked around the room again, carefully viewing studies in isolated alleyways, lonely people, and bridges over the Thames River, all captured very artistically. All of the pictures were framed in shiny black or white frames.

"This is all your work?" he asked.

"Mine, yes, but these are not all of them. I have many rooms full of photographs. Make yourselves comfortable and look around more if you'd like while I bring some coffee, tea, and biscuits."

While she was in the kitchen, Dave and Kate walked around most of the ground floor of her large house. Nearly every wall was covered with her photography. One room held nude photos. This caused Dave to wonder about Sally. She was around Elizabeth's age and attractive, shoulder-length pitch black hair, sleek and shiny. Would a sixteen-year-old be interested in her?

Back in the living room, they sat down as Sally returned with a tray.

"Are you interested in photography, Mr. Martin?"

He picked up a biscuit and a cup of hot coffee, took a sip, and replied. "Actually, I am. My mother is an amateur photographer. I think she's always wanted to make a career of it."

"I love my work," she said.

Kate sat quietly sipping a cup of tea, apparently comfortable playing the observer this time and letting Dave take the lead, because Sally seemed to prefer conversing with him.

"Your photos are quite artistic, including the nudes. Ever photograph your neighborhood or neighbors?"

"Maybe." She flashed a smile at Dave, and touched her chin. "I guess I do occasionally. But if you're asking if I ever photographed Jared, the answer is no."

Dave nodded. "How well did you know him and his family?"

"I'm friends with Elizabeth. We used to have a cozy group of neighbor friends back when Peter and Elizabeth were still married. We used to get together for dinners and to play cards. We took turns at different houses."

"How did she take the divorce?"

She sighed. "Elizabeth was devastated. Guess that's not really surprising, is it?"

"No. When I divorced I started drinking too much."

"Yes— well, yes, that can happen."

"Did you ever go to her house after the divorce?"

"Sure. Several times for dinners, though we more often went out."

Changing the subject after taking a bite of biscuit and washing it down with another sip of beverage, Dave asked, "Did Jared have any friends in the neighborhood?"

"Not that I'm aware of." She sipped her tea and peered over the rim in a flirty kind of way, bright pink fingernails with glittery stars on them sparkling and enticing. "Well, now that you ask, possibly Brittany Stevas. I saw them together a few times."

"When was this?"

"Over the last few months before Jared . . . well, you know."

"What were they doing?"

She was silent and looked deep in thought. After a few moments, she said, "I'd completely forgotten about this until you brought it up, but the last time I saw them together, they were having an argument in the street. It must have been a few weeks, a month maybe, before his murder. Oh, you don't think . . . ."

Dave said, "Do you remember anything else about them?"

Sally shook her head and sipped her tea.

Dave said, "What about Robin Sutcliffe? Do you know her?"

"Hah. I certainly do. She was Peter's assistant, and not a very good one from what I've heard. But there, I'm just gossiping, I don't really know. As Elizabeth told it, Robin was afraid she'd lose her job, so she started making advances on Peter. Well, you know the rest. That woman broke up the marriage."

"Elizabeth blames Robin for the breakup?"

"Of course."

"Did Elizabeth or Peter confide their problems to you?"

"Elizabeth, yes. Peter, only once or twice."

"Did you actually meet Robin?"

"Yes, once at a dinner party. That was right before the break-up."

"What did you think of her back then?"

She shrugged.

"Then how do you know about Robin?"

"Elizabeth liked to talk. That was months ago, mind you. I wasn't sure what to actually believe about Robin, until I saw her and Jared together at the movie theatre."

Dave set his cup down and asked, maintaining calm, "When was that?"

"I don't remember."

"Was Peter with them?"

"No. And they looked pretty cozy, too. Even shared a drink from the same straw."

"Did you tell Elizabeth?"

She nodded.

"What did she do?"

"They had a big blow-up, Elizabeth and Robin, I mean. Robin wasn't allowed at the house after that. It caused problems between Elizabeth and Jared, naturally."

"How do you mean?"

"Elizabeth resented him. He was too much like his father. I think he was a lot like Elizabeth, also, but she didn't see it. All she saw when she looked at him was Peter."

"Are you sure about that?"

"She rang me and wanted to go out for drinks. She ranted for hours about Robin and Jared and Peter."

NICK HALLOWELL DIDN'T seem at all reluctant to invite them inside. He called out to his wife, Jenny, who met them at the door, wiping her hands on her apron. "You're just in time for refreshments," she said. "My cake is cooled off and the tea is finished brewing. Go ahead and show these folk around, why don't you, Nick, while I'm in the kitchen."

"Sure, thing, love." He smiled, then turned to Dave and

Kate. "Follow me. My wife and I love to have guests, in case you hadn't noticed."

He led them into the parlor and waved his hand. "Here in our parlor you can see some of our artwork and artifacts from around the world—Africa, Asia, you name it—we've probably been there."

"What kind of work do you do?" Kate asked.

He gave a blank look for a moment, and then said, "Imports. This isn't a hobby. We own a store where we sell these and others like them. We sell online, too."

Kate nodded.

Dave thought of Jeannette Devlin whose house was filled with antiques. As they walked around from room to room, Dave was impressed. These were obviously people with good taste.

Back in the parlor Jenny had set out a feast of tea, cake, biscuits, and even fresh strawberries. She poured four cups of tea. "Oh, Mr. Martin, you are American, yes?"

He nodded.

"Forgive me, we are out of coffee, I hope tea is okay? Please help yourselves to the food." She filled her own plate with a little of each offering. Dave and Nick followed suit, but Kate merely smiled and shook her head.

Husband and wife sat together on the sofa. Dave and Kate took the two side chairs.

"Can you tell us about your relationship with Elizabeth and Peter Raybourne?" Kate asked.

"We used to get together for card games once a week at different locations," Nick said. "Sometimes we met at their house, sometimes here, or at the Randolphs' house, Sally's, Ian's, or even Rob's. The Randolphs moved away about four months ago."

Jenny said, "That's right. We thought it only fair to switch off. That way, no one got stuck hosting and cooking every time.

Of course, all of that was before the divorce."

"What happened after the divorce?"

"We tried to stay friendly with both Elizabeth and Peter," Nick said. "Peter was okay, but Elizabeth made it difficult. She was bitter and would gripe about Peter and his girlfriend every time we got together. Kind of ruined the evenings for us. Eventually, by group agreement, we stopped inviting them."

"Did you go to her house?"

"Yes. A few times. For cards and dinners—like before."

Jenny said, "I do miss her. We used to be close. It's so sad."

"What was her relationship with her son? Did you notice any changes in their relationship after the divorce?"

Nick and Jenny exchanged glances. Jenny said, "The few times we saw Jared, they argued."

"Do you know what they argued about?"

Nick said, "Just usual teenager-parent stuff as far as we could tell. I remember when my parents divorced. I was around the same age. My behavior was rather atrocious. It was a phase. That's all."

Jenny shook her head. "Call it what you want, but their relationship wasn't good. I wouldn't have allowed his behavior if he'd been my son."

"What about Robin Sutcliffe's relationship with Jared? Did you ever see them together?"

Nick said, "I think we only saw them together once or twice. That was when Peter invited us over to his new home for dinner. Jared walked out in the middle of the meal. Poor Peter was embarrassed."

"Why did Jared do that?"

"We don't know. He and Robin were whispering together in the hallway, and then he left."

"How long ago was that?"

Nick shrugged. "Maybe a month or two before he was

killed."

"Did you know Maua Barrington, the woman who rented a room from Elizabeth?"

Jenny said, "Maura, yes, sort of. She was there when we went to Elizabeth's house for dinner. We only spoke briefly. She seemed nice, quiet."

"Did she eat dinner with you?"

"No. She only came out of her room for a few minutes."

"Was it a large dinner party?"

Nick shook his head. "Only the two of us, a few other neighbors came, and Elizabeth's sister and brother-in-law."

THEY LEFT THE Hallowells' house shortly after and walked over to the street where Rob Carsters lived. Kate pulled up her jacket collar to ward off the wind, which had become rather chilly.

Dave zipped up his own jacket. "Did they ever find the murder weapon?"

"I don't think so. The post-mortem report indicated it was probably a kitchen knife, but the weapon hasn't been recovered."

"Are any knives missing from the Raybourne house?"

"Elizabeth couldn't tell the detectives," Kate said.

"Why is that?"

"Apparently, she didn't cook much. She didn't really know how many knives they had."

Dave frowned. "The Hallowells said she invited them over for dinner. Who did the cooking?"

"That, I can't tell you," Kate said. "Though it seems like a good question." She glanced sideways at Dave.

Dave said, "I have another one for you. Why did the inspectors assume someone used a key to enter the house?"

"I can't answer that either," Kate said. "All I know is that they said it didn't look like a break-in."

"Yeah, well, that doesn't mean he didn't let someone in. For that matter, he could have left the door unlocked, maybe for his mother or maybe out of laziness. Who knows?"

Rob Carsters didn't answer his door, and when Dave and Kate turned around to leave, they almost bumped into a man who was walking a collie up the sidewalk to the front door. The dog pulled on the leash and the man let go.

Dave reached down and petted the dog who was wagging its tail and lapping up the attention.

"He likes you. Were you looking for me?"

"That depends. Are you Rob Carsters?"

"I am." He pulled a key out of his jacket pocket, walked past Dave and Kate and up the steps, and unlocked the door. He turned around to face them, obviously waiting for them to say something.

Dave introduced himself and Kate. The man nodded.

"Come on in. I don't have anything to offer you. I've been running errands off and on all day. No time for domestic stuff."

"That's fine," Kate said. "We would like to ask you a few questions about your neighbors—especially the Raybourne family."

"I expected as much. I bumped into Brittany Stevas. We walk our dogs in the same park."

"Were she and Jared friends? Did they ever go out on dates?"

He shrugged. "I can't keep up with all the kids—who they like or don't like, who is dating who, who just broke up. I gave up trying a long time ago."

Dave said, "What do you do for a living?"

"I'm a science teacher. If you remember back to your high school days, I'm sure you'll understand what kids and dating are like."

"Where do you work?"

"Westglenn."

Dave studied him more closely. Young, maybe early to mid-thirties, brown hair, brown eyes, athletic build. What had Maurelle told him about Carsters? She thought the guy was interested in Elizabeth, but she wouldn't go out with him. Why hadn't Maurelle mentioned that he was a teacher at her school?

"Did you know Maura Barrington?"

Carsters nodded.

"How well did you know her?"

"We went out a couple of times. Nothing serious."

Avoiding Kate's eyes, Dave said, "Why did you stop going out?"

"Seemed like a nice woman, but we didn't really have much in common—other than teaching and neither of us wanted to talk shop."

Kate said, "Were you surprised by the rumors of an affair?"

He shrugged again, and sprawled his legs out the way Jonas Lefevre did back in Reynier when Dave visited him.

"Was there a lot of that kind of thing going on in the school? Student-teacher romances?"

"Like I said, I gave up on following that stuff—whether it's students or teachers or a mixture."

Dave finally dared to look at Kate. She had apparently been watching him, and a look of something verging on pity flashed in her eyes before she turned her attention back to Carsters.

"There must be a lot of talk amongst the faculty."

"It's not my business."

Again, Carsters reminded him of Jonas. A laid-back, devil-may-care attitude. Could he get away with murder? He wondered about Carsters and Brittany Stevas and their rendezvous in the park.

Kate flipped a page in her notebook. She looked up and met

Carsters' eyes. "You were friends with Elizabeth and Peter, is that right?"

"Yeah."

"What happened after the divorce? Did you maintain those friendships?"

"With Peter and Robin, yes."

"But not with Elizabeth?"

"Not much."

"Did you two have a disagreement?"

He shifted in his seat.

"What happened between the two of you?"

"Nothing happened. It's just not easy staying friends with both of them."

Outside, on Rob's front porch, Kate whispered, "I sure would like to know what he isn't telling us about his relationships with Maura and Elizabeth."

MAURELLE AND JEANNETTE took hold of Fabienne's arms and helped her walk back to the stone cottage, though Fabienne kept resisting. "I don't need help. I'm feeling better." As the house came into view, it struck Maurelle how warm and inviting it now looked. The light chocolate-colored shutters that had been tightly shut when they'd first arrived were now pulled back, and flowers graced the window boxes. Yesterday, with Fabienne fretting about the flowers she'd left behind, Maurelle had gone back to the store and bought more. She planted them, while the older women sat in their rocking chairs and watched. Two neighbors, having noticed the open shutters and flowers, had come over and cut back some of the overgrown bushes and brush. One of the neighbors, Lucien, told them that they had started performing this ritual at least twice a year in the hopes of stopping further encroachment into their adjacent lands.

Jeannette and Fabienne, after ensuring that the men didn't uncover the hidden car, had gushed over both and sent store-bought pastries home with each of them. Maurelle smiled as she remembered Fabienne closing the door behind him as they left and confessing how embarrassed she was that she hadn't baked them something from her own kitchen.

Fabienne looked backward as they neared the cottage. "Can't we stop at the café for coffee?"

Jeannette said, "I'll go pick up your prescriptions and bring you a coffee."

"No. I want to visit with our friends."

"Not going to happen," Maurelle said. "You're going home and straight to bed. No argument."

"But I feel much better now."

Maurelle opened the front door and pointed upstairs. "Dr. Maison gave orders. You're to take it easy for a few days, and I intend to enforce those orders. Jeannette and I will bring you your meals in bed. If you behave yourself, we'll allow visitors. Clear?"

Fabienne stomped up the stairs with Maurelle following. When she reached her room, she sighed and climbed into bed, pulling covers around her. Although Fabienne's curly white hair affirmed advanced age, Maurelle decided she looked every bit the naughty child. Funny how in such a short time they'd done such a complete turnabout. It was barely a week ago that Fabienne and Dave had stood by her bedside, treating her as though she was the child.

Jeannette appeared moments later with a cup of coffee from the kitchen. "I'll be going out for a while. Maurelle and I decided that I should call Coralie and let her know about your incident. Maybe she'll be able to pass a message to Dave. Or maybe she'll have news for us. Either way, I need to call her."

Fabienne nodded.

WHEN JEANNETTE RETURNED an hour later, she brought several locals, people from Jeannette's and Fabienne's past. They were all introduced to Maurelle, but their names soon escaped her. Three hours passed before Maurelle had an opportunity to ask Jeannette about the phone call.

When she finally was able to corner her in the small kitchen, Jeannette told her, "Coralie was shocked about Fabienne's illness. She couldn't talk much because the house was full of people. She did tell me though that Simone was there. Oh, and Simone brought a man. I think she said his name was Greg. He's an American friend of Dave's. That's probably a good thing, don't you agree?"

Maurelle's heart leapt at the mention of Dave. She figured that Dave had met with Greg in London as planned and had subsequently heard about their new predicament. And Dave, knowing he couldn't very well show up right now with the gendarmes looking for them, had sent Greg to France in his place.

She smiled at Jeannette and hugged her, whispering "Thank you, Jeannette. I'm sorry that you and your family are stuck in the middle of this, but I'm glad that you're here in Saint-Julien with us."

Jeannette patted her on the back. "So am I, dear."

CHAPTER THIRTY

AS THEY LEFT Rob Carsters' house and walked back toward Willoughby Crescent, Kate said, "I don't know what to think anymore. That man feels sleazy to me, but it doesn't mean he would kill someone, does it?"

Dave said, "No. I wonder, though. If he was interested in Maura, and thought Jared was a rival, might he have been driven to it?"

"The thought had occurred."

"It seems plenty of people could have had it in for Jared. I'm not ruling out Maura Barrington, but my money is on Robin Sutcliffe or Elizabeth."

"Why do you say that?" Kate asked.

"It sounds as though Robin had a brief fling with the boy, or she wanted to. Maybe the mother found out, and they argued. At least two neighbors have mentioned a blow-up between them. Now suppose the ex-husband, Peter, didn't know about it, and someone threatened to tell him. I'm thinking Jared or Elizabeth."

Kate looked deep in thought, then said, "Could be either of them. Robin might have gone to the house to talk to either Jared or his mother. Who knows? My guess is that Robin and Jared got into an argument and in the heat of the moment, she stabbed him. Of course, Elizabeth could have turned on Jared and killed him because she saw him as a younger version of her husband, coming on to Robin. She might have resented him and could no longer cope."

Dave nodded assent.

As they turned the corner onto Willoughby Crescent, Kate added, "On the other hand, what if Peter did know? What if someone had told him and he confronted his son about Robin? They fought and Peter stabbed him."

"You're right. That's another good possibility," Dave said. Approaching Ian Waitley's house again, Dave saw the curtains move in the front window. Ian was watching them. Not surprising, since they'd already heard he watched the comings and goings of everyone. If anyone had seen the killer, it was most likely Ian.

When Dave knocked on the door, Ian peeked out the same way as he'd done the previous day, as if he didn't already know who was there.

Ian opened the door a crack and nodded his head in Kate's direction. "Who's she?"

Remembering that Greg had been with him on his previous visit, Dave said, "This is Kate Hill, a freelance journalist I'm working with."

Kate stepped forward and handed her business card to Ian. After glancing at it, he opened the door for them to enter and tucked the card in his pocket.

Dave spotted a wooden coat rack in the corner next to the door. Several hats, a cardigan sweater, and a light jacket with a logo on it hung from the hooks. Dave moved in nonchalantly to get a closer look at the logo. It was a circle with a picture of a restaurant or pub on it. Next to the coat rack was a bench, under which was a pair of scuffed sneakers.

Ian led them through the long hallway and into the living

room. "Make yourselves comfortable."

Kate sat in a rocking chair across from Dave.

"I should be offering you tea," Ian said, standing behind the sofa.

"That won't be necessary," Kate said. "We've recently had some." Ian sat down on the sofa. "Dave tells me that you've been keeping an eye on the Raybourne house."

He didn't respond.

"He said you see everything that happens around here. That made me wonder if you were home on the night of Jared Raybourne's murder. Perhaps you might have seen something." He shrugged. Kate pursed her lips and glanced at Dave.

"Mr. Waitley," Dave said, "did you see anyone go to the Raybourne's house on the night of Jared's murder?"

Ian abruptly rose and said, "We need something to drink. I'll be right back."

Kate leaned toward Dave. "He's stalling."

Ian returned, balancing a tray with a pitcher of lemonade and three glasses. He set the tray on a table next to the couch and poured the liquid into each and handed them to his guests.

Dave took a sip and said, "Did you see anyone at the house, Mr. Waitley?"

Ian squirmed, uneasy, slurped his lemonade rather loudly, and finally said, "All right. If you must know, I saw a woman."

"Why didn't you tell the police?"

"I mentioned it to one copper, barely out of nappies, he was, took no notice."

"Could it have been Maura Barrington?"

"No."

"You must have some idea of who it was."

He crossed his arms, uncrossed them, and rearranged a stack of magazines on the coffee table in front of him. "Robin Sutcliffe, it was" he said finally.

"You're sure about that?"

He nodded.

Dave looked out of the window at a lamppost across the street, lighting the area near the Raybourne driveway.

"What time was it when you saw her?"

He shrugged. "Early evening, but I remember it was already dark out, well, except for the streetlamp and it being a full moon that night. She was in the shadows some of the time, of course, but I could see well enough."

"Had she driven to the house? Did you see her car?"

He tilted his head, momentarily thinking. "No, I didn't see any car. I don't expect she did. She often rides the train and walks from the station. It's common around here."

"How long was she there? Did you hear any arguing?"

He shrugged again.

Taking a different approach, Dave said, "What do you know about Robin and Jared?"

"Oh, I know plenty about that boy."

"Like?"

The old man's face lit up. "He was a menace, he was. And mad as a loon. Well, I'll be telling you. He spray-painted the school one night. Oh, nobody could pin it on him, but I know it was him."

Kate looked at Dave. Why hadn't they heard anything about that? Dave wondered.

"What makes you think it was him?" Kate asked.

"I seen the paint cans through the door of their shed," Ian said. "It weren't but two days after the school incident, it was."

"What else did he do?" Dave asked.

"He killed Abby and Josephine."

"What?"

"My moggies."

Dave drew his eyebrows together in confusion. "I'm sorry.

What are moggies?"

"Cats, moggies be cats!" Ian said, rolling his eyes at Dave. "Abby and Josephine were my companions for fourteen years, they were. My girls—my own Wilhelmina's kittens. Of course she's long gone. My poor moggies."

"Ah," Dave said. That was the cat killing they'd read about. He leaned forward. "Why would Jared kill your cats?"

"He was an evil boy," Ian said. "He—" The old man snapped his mouth closed. He looked out towards the garden as though drifting off into his memories.

"How did Jared kill Abby and Josephine?"

"He . . . he cut their heads off."

Dave noted Kate's sudden intake of breath before asking, "With what?"

"I don't know," Ian said. "I couldn't get anyone to investigate their murder. The coppers treated the case as petty and not worthy of their time because the victims were just cats, is what they said."

Kate glanced over at Dave, signaling him to stay quiet. Then she calmly prodded Ian to continue. "Why would he do that?"

Ian's eyes darted between Kate and Dave as though he were trying to decide whether to answer. Finally, sotto voce, he said, "He was trouble, that's what. We argued sometimes and we didn't like each other."

Dave squinted, looked over at Kate and back at Ian.

Kate asked, "What did you argue about?"

Ian shrugged. "I don't recall. But ask around, why don't you? Everyone argued with that boy because he picked fights. Ask old Mrs. Winston. I'm sure she can tell you some stories. Ask Brittany Stevas. Ask the Headmaster over at the school."

"How did Peter and Jared get along? Did they argue?"

"Peter's a pushover. Takes a lot to rile him up."

Kate said, "What about Maura Barrington? Did she argue

with Jared?"

"She wouldn't kill nobody. I tried to tell the coppers, but they wouldn't listen."

"What makes you so sure? Almost anyone could kill, given the right circumstances."

"Maura's too nice and too gentle. She might kill in self-defense, but not for the reasons people are saying."

"Don't you think she might have considered it self-defense because she would have lost her job?"

He shook his head rapidly. "No, she couldn't even kill a spider or a mouse. She's a softy. I suppose if a wild animal was attacking her, she might fight back and try to kill it, but she wouldn't unless she was sure it was going to kill her."

Dave thought about the man who had given Maurelle a ride near Vendome.

"Did Jared ever threaten her that you know of?"

He shrugged.

Dave said, "Do you know anyone who had a grudge against him?"

"You go ask the Headmaster. I'd tell you to ask Jared's parents, but they wouldn't tell you the truth. They know."

LATE AT NIGHT, after Fabienne and Jeannette were asleep, Maurelle got out of bed and tiptoed down the stairs. Thinking about Fabienne's illness and Dave's absence was keeping her awake.

She sat on the sofa, tucked her legs underneath her body, and asked herself what Dave would want her to do. Before he left for England, he'd made it clear they couldn't call each other, but wouldn't he want to know about their changed situation? Wouldn't he want to know about his grandmother? She'd considered calling him several times since they'd left Reynier and had held back because she didn't want to worry him. It was different now that she had some good news. Fabienne was on the road to recovery.

She went back upstairs, got dressed, and pulled from her bag the piece of paper with Dave's hotel name and its number. Downstairs, on the kitchen counter, she grabbed the phone card they'd bought. It should still have enough minutes left on it.

The streets were darker than she'd expected, filled with spooky shadows, with only a sliver of moon and the stars to guide her to the phone booth near the general store. She paused halfway between the cottage and the store and glanced up at the sky. Back in Reynier, she'd been amazed sometimes at the amount of stars. Here, with a clear sky and virtually no lights anywhere in town, the sky was sensational, bright with starlight, like being in an observatory, only much better. She picked out the Big Dipper and Little Dipper the way she'd done with her mother when they were on a holiday, then smiled.

When she reached the phone booth, she pulled out the piece of paper from her pocket and dialed.

The desk receptionist answered and at first was reluctant to put her through until she said it was a family emergency. There was a far off buzzing, and someone picked up on the second ring.

"Hello."

"Is that you, Dave?"

"Yeah." He mumbled something she couldn't understand, then said, "Who's this?"

"Uh, it's me. Maurelle."

Silence.

"Did I wake you?"

"Yeah."

"I'm sorry. I know I'm not supposed to call. I thought you should know what's happened."

"I talked to Simone. She told me what Paul had done, that the gendarmes were looking for you, so you had to disappear, and you took Grand-mère and Jeannette with you. I sent Greg to Reynier to check the waters and snoop around."

Maurelle hesitated. Did Dave sound angry?

"Yes, but that's not why I called. Your grandmother became ill. We thought she might be having a heart attack. She had some medical tests done this morning, but she's all right."

"What? What happened? I thought she'd made up the story about being ill."

"She had stents put in two arteries a year ago and was on heart medication, but she forgot her pills when we left Reynier. The doctor doesn't think there was any damage done. He put her on the same medication she was taking and she seems to be much better now, but she'll need to get checked out in a hospital when she gets back home."

"So, she lied to me about having cancer, but didn't tell me she had a heart condition. Just wonderful. Why does she do these things? Is she in a hospital now?"

"No. She's here at home, well, at our temporary home."

"And you're all safe?"

"Yes. Are you? Is—is everything going all right?"

"As good as can be expected, I guess."

Maurelle hesitated. "Have you found out anything helpful?"

"We're getting a lot of discrepancies. Which reminds me, while I have you on the phone, how well do you know Ian Waitley?"

"Not well. He's a strange man, but funny. I liked talking with him. Why do you ask?"

"What was his relationship with the Raybourne family? He seems to know a lot about their lives. Is that just from watching them?"

"Well, as I recall, he and the Raybournes moved into the

neighborhood around the same time, about four or five years ago. Jared would have been about eleven or twelve then. Ian told me he would sometimes check in on Jared while Peter and Elizabeth went out for the evening. He always seemed to need to help, wanted to be part of things. Apparently, back then he and Jared got along."

"But not later?"

"Not so much, I guess."

"Did Elizabeth and Ian get along?"

"I think so. I remember one time, this was shortly after I moved in, Elizabeth was sick. She'd had her appendix removed. Ian came over and cooked for her. He was like that, always willing to help out if he could. He was a really good neighbor."

"Did you ever hear Elizabeth and Jared quarrel?"

"Yes, several times, but I tried to stay out of it."

"Do you know what they fought about?"

"Everything. At least it seemed that way. It's not unusual for kids that age to push boundaries, so I didn't think much of it at the time."

Silence followed. She could hear Dave breathing. "Is something wrong?" she asked.

Instead of answering her, Dave asked, "What can you tell me about Rob Carsters?"

"Rob? Why do you ask about him? There's nothing really to tell."

He sighed loudly enough that she could hear, and her heart sank.

"Why didn't you tell me you dated him and that you two worked together?"

Becoming ever more anxious, she stammered, "I—I didn't think it was important."

"Another thing. You told me you were tutoring Jared, but people here are saying it's not true."

"Dave, it's true. Why would they say that?"

"Good question."

Maurelle hesitated. Unsure what to say, she asked, "What are you thinking, Dave?"

"We're still looking at all angles. It's a tough case. I wish I could tell you we've ruled you out as a suspect, but I can't. I should hang up now. The longer we talk on the phone, the riskier it is for both of us. You shouldn't call again unless it's really an emergency."

After she hung up, feeling devastated Maurelle sobbed and put her hands over her face, wishing she hadn't made the phone call. Everything seemed to be closing in on her again.

CHAPTER THIRTY-ONE

SITTING ON THE edge of the bed, Dave hung up the phone, groaned, and hung his head. He'd wanted to talk to Maurelle badly ever since he'd left France, and apparently he had succeeded. He'd wanted to give her good news, but she had caught him off guard, and the news about Grand-mère had upset him. The phone call left him feeling depressed and doubtful. Nothing she'd told him so far and none of the leads he had followed up on had given him what he needed to prove her innocence. Was he still playing the fool, letting himself be duped again? Was this like the Diana Lewis case all over again? He wanted to believe she'd called because of his grandmother, but what if that was just an excuse to find out what he'd found and to see if she needed to run again. There was also another darker thought that he didn't like to consider: Was Fabienne safe with Maurelle?

He eventually drifted back to sleep, but he awoke upset and more tired than before he'd gone to bed. All through the night he'd dreamt of his grandmother—lying in the hospital after suffering a major heart attack. In one dream the heart monitor had straight-lined. He'd dreamt of Maurelle, first rescuing his grandmother but in a later dream, causing her heart attack.

After showering and dressing, he dragged himself down the hotel hall to the staircase. He desperately needed coffee and something to eat. Kate would be picking him up outside the café across the street at nine o'clock, so he decided he might as well eat and wait in the café.

At the top of the staircase he caught sight of a red-headed man in a suit, walking up the stairs with his head bent. He seemed to be reading something in a folded-up newspaper as he walked. Dave mused that it didn't seem to be the smartest thing to do, but something about the man also seemed familiar. Dave took a step down, and at the same moment the man looked up. It was Greg's detective friend, Nigel James.

Startled, Dave stopped, grabbed the railing, and waited.

When Nigel reached the top of the stairs, he said, "We need to talk. I didn't want to do this over the telephone. Greg called me from this hotel on his first night in London and told me you were staying here, too. I took a chance you'd still be here."

Dave nodded and turned around. Nigel followed him to the hotel room. Inside, Dave sat on the edge of the bed and motioned to the chair and table nearby.

Nigel pulled the chair around, sat down, and crossed his legs, obviously appraising Dave in the way detectives do before they interrogate a witness or a suspect. Dave steeled himself.

"I know you've met Maura Barrington," Nigel said.

"You're making a pretty big assumption."

"It's not an assumption. The Met have been notified by the French. Since I've taken an unofficial interest, I heard of this."

"The Met was notified of what?"

"They said someone in Reynier called the gendarmes about a mysterious woman who was being harbored by an elderly woman and her grandson. Sound familiar?"

Dave shrugged.

"The elderly woman, your grandmother I've been told, has

disappeared and may have been taken hostage by the woman. The gendarmes, and now the Met, believe the woman is Maura Barrington. I'm afraid it all makes perfect sense to me now, considering your interest in the case."

Dave looked at the clock near the television. Kate would be at the café in thirty minutes.

"I want to know how you are involved. What do you know about this woman?"

"Look, I met her in Reynier. She was living in a cave. I invited her to stay in my grandmother's home and then found out she was running from the law here. She told me about Jared and tentatively convinced me of her innocence. I really don't know much more than you do. I came here to get answers. That's all."

Nigel put his fingers together steepled near his chin and looked directly at Dave. "You must realize that if Maura Barrington did murder Jared Raybourne, she may be dangerous. You may be putting others, your grandmother included, at risk. She could kill again if she feels threatened."

"I don't believe that. She wouldn't hurt my grandmother." Dave pushed the memory of his nightmare out of his mind.

"I hope you're right. As I understand it, the French police are narrowing in on her location. They'll make an arrest soon. My fear is that if Ms. Barrington finds out before they get there, she might do something drastic. If you're in contact with her, I need to know."

"I'm not."

"You never answered my other question. How are you involved?"

"I came here to solve the Jared Raybourne case. I figured that I'd either prove her innocent, in which case she would be free, or I'll prove her guilty and turn her over to the police."

"Then you know where she is."

Dave sighed. "She left shortly after I got here. I don't know where she is at the moment."

Nigel stood up and handed a card to Dave. "You know, I ought to arrest you for harboring a fugitive, but at the moment she is officially just wanted for questioning. As a courtesy to a fellow officer, and by the way, I am aware you are no longer on the force in the US, but being a friend of Greg, I will give you forty-eight hours before turning you in. But you must promise me that if you hear from her, you will call me immediately. And do not tell her about our conversation."

As soon as Nigel left, Dave closed his eyes. This was the last thing he needed. Had his hotel phone been tapped by the Met? Was she really guilty of murder? Damn. He needed to solve the case now and get back to France.

DAVE AND KATE arrived at Westglenn an hour later. On the drive over, he'd debated whether to tell Kate about his conversation with Nigel. He decided against it. He kept thinking about Maurelle, about her accident in the general store, her running away from the man who'd given her a ride and then attacked her. She wouldn't kill anyone, would she? He remembered what he'd told her on the phone last night: 'I wish I could tell you we've ruled you out as a suspect, but I can't'.

Kate asked him a few times if he was all right because he was extra quiet. The silence became overbearing, so she turned on the radio.

At the school students were arriving. Some milled about outside, talking and laughing.

"First, let's walk around the building," Dave said. "I want to see if there's any graffiti."

"You do know that it's probably a false lead. There wasn't a police report. The old man probably got it wrong or was just spreading rumors he'd heard."

Dave kept walking. He knew better than anyone how gossip spread. He walked across the grass and continued around the corner of the building. He stopped abruptly. Kate bumped into him.

White, orange, and yellow streaks of paint covered a quarter of the side of the building.

"Seems the old man knew what he was talking about."

"Indeed," Kate said. "I think we need to talk to Fowler."

Dave followed her back to the front of the building and up the concrete steps. He pulled open one of the double glass doors, holding it for Kate. They made their way through the crowded corridor toward the Headmaster's office. This time they knew exactly where they were going. But they stumbled upon Patrick Fowler in the corridor. He was facing them, and frowned when he saw them coming. He promptly finished his conversation with a man and woman, and approached Dave and Kate.

"I thought we were done," Fowler said.

"We need to ask you more questions, Mr. Fowler," Kate said. "Could we go to your office?"

He chewed his lower lip, then whirled around on his heel. They followed. His office was at the front of the building, off to one side.

"We heard there was a graffiti incident here a couple of weeks before Jared's murder."

He didn't respond.

"Why didn't you report it to the police?"

Again he didn't answer but stared out the window. After a moment, he turned and looked directly at Kate. "You must understand. We run a decent school here. We didn't want parents getting upset."

"Do you know who was responsible for the vandalism?"

"Yes, we spoke to the boy's parents. They assured us they would discipline him and would pay to have the paint removed."

"But the paint is still there."

He nodded.

"Who was it?"

He looked down at his desk and pretended to rearrange papers.

"It was Jared Raybourne, wasn't it?"

"It doesn't matter at this point."

"It could make a difference in solving his case. Why did he spray paint the wall near your office?"

He picked up one of the papers, and scanned as if reading, set it down and picked up another.

"Mr. Fowler?"

He sighed and set down the paper. "Fine. Jared Raybourne got into fights regularly during his last few months here. I lectured him many times. I called his parents in for meetings. I wanted to expel him, but the Governors and the education authority were reluctant. When I heard reports from teachers about an affair between Raybourne and one of our teachers, Ms. Barrington, I brought her in and discussed it with her. She denied the charges. When numerous parents contacted members of the Board, they finally opened up an investigation."

"So, you think Jared spray-painted the building in retaliation?"

"He was on suspension when it happened."

"And Ms. Barrington?"

"Maura Barrington was on leave of absence pending the Board's investigation and hearing."

"Did the Board ever investigate?"

"No. They were ready to begin when the Raybourne boy was murdered."

"Who do you think killed Jared Raybourne?"

"I don't know."

"You mentioned Jared got into fights. Did he have enemies?"

"Not really enemies from what I've heard. The fights were usually started by Mr. Raybourne."

He glanced at his watch. "Look, I'm sorry, but I have a meeting I must get to in a couple minutes."

"Okay, thank you for talking with us, sir," Kate said. "If you don't mind, we would like a word with one of your teachers. I believe she is the sister of Elizabeth Raybourne."

"Ah, yes. Pauline Wynn. She was already questioned by the police."

"I understand," Kate said, "but we'd like to conduct our own interviews. You understand, don't you?"

"This is not something I normally allow." Abruptly, he nodded and left the room.

While he was out, Kate said, "If you'd like, I'll have you conduct the interview while I take notes."

Dave nodded.

Fowler didn't return. Instead, a blonde woman appeared. She bore a remarkable resemblance to Elizabeth Raybourne, except that she was older and somewhat plumper.

Dave stood and shook her hand. "You must be Pauline Wynn."

"I am."

"This is my associate, Kate Hill. We're writing an article about your nephew's murder case. We would like to ask you some questions."

Kate shook her hand, sat back down, and pulled out a notebook and pen as she nodded to Dave.

Pauline sat down and gazed around the room, obviously nervous. She said, "I am not sure I am happy about this. We don't want anything sensationalized. It was bad enough from the beginning, and we're trying to stay out of the papers. Why should I talk to you? Who did you say you work for?"

"Ourselves; we're independent journalists. Look, we don't want to sensationalize anything, and you will be welcome to see anything we write before it is published. We just want the truth, we're not out to harm anyone," Kate said.

"You'll let me see before publication?"

"Absolutely."

She seemed to relax, though her hands were clasped together in her lap. Dave saw her knuckles were white.

"Well—what do you want to know?"

Dave said, "I understand you introduced Maura Barrington to your sister, Elizabeth, when she was looking for a place to live."

"That's right." Sitting with her legs crossed, Pauline shifted and reversed them.

"Were you and Maura friends then?"

"I suppose we were," she said. "Although we didn't socialize much outside of work, but we usually ate lunch together here."

"Why didn't you socialize outside of work?"

"Well, mostly because I have a husband and five children to look after. Doesn't give me much time to run around with the girls."

Dave nodded and rubbed his chin. "How did Maura get along with co-workers?"

"Mostly all right." Pauline shifted again and reversed legs again, apparently still uncomfortable.

"Can you elaborate?"

"She was the youngest female teacher—by quite a few years. The men liked her. Some flirted with her, but she only went out with one of them once or twice, as far as I know."

"How did the women teachers feel about her?"

"Well, that's a different story. Some liked her. I think some of them were jealous."

"Did they talk about her?"

"Everybody did. Rumors started a couple of months after she moved into that house. It was my fault. I never should have sent her there."

"Why did you?"

"She needed an inexpensive place to live, and my sister needed a lodger, needed the money."

"Do you believe Maura Barrington killed your nephew?"

She stared at him, saying nothing, and he wondered if she'd heard the question. He was about to rephrase it when she said, "I don't believe she did it. I don't think she had an affair with him either."

Dave pondered her statement. Although she sounded genuine, he wondered why she had hesitated. "Why haven't you spoken out in her defense?"

"I tried to stop the whispers about the affair, but people believe what they want to believe," Pauline said, twisting her hands as though trying to hold on to her composure. "Maura is young and pretty. People get jealous of women like that." She paused, looking down at her hands for a moment. "The other teachers wanted to believe the worst. I think some even fanned the flames, hoping that she would be fired and that would be the end of it."

"But then Jared turned up dead."

She nodded. "After that, there was no stopping the whispers. Gossip spread like wildfire."

"Who started the whispers of an affair, do you know?"

"Oh, I'm afraid that was Jared, himself," she said, suddenly looking disgusted. "He bragged to his classmates. It made some kids look up to him."

"You're sure of that?"

"I'm not positive, but two of my own children attend this

school. They told me about the story coming from him. It sounded like something he would do, too. Lots of boys do that kind of thing, boast about girls they have been with, and some do it about teachers, too. But Jared went further, and he kept on about it. ”

“What happened with Penny, his former girlfriend?”

“I think he scared her away. He became obsessive and controlling. He had been a bit strange all his life, but he became increasingly weird after his parents split up. He became truly frightening.”

“How do you know all this?”

“Penny is a friend of my daughter. I sometimes hear them talking.”

“Can you tell us any more about Jared’s behavioral change?” Dave leaned forward. Maybe they’d finally found the right person to talk to.

“Well, everything really happened within a short time. He started dating Penny in November. His parents broke up a couple of months later. Soon after that, Maura moved into the house. She told me she tried to keep to herself, minimizing her time there.”

“Why did she try to minimize her time there?”

“She said right from the start she didn’t really feel comfortable, especially with a male pupil under the same roof. She said she wouldn’t have moved in there if she could have found another place to live.”

“You and she were friends. Couldn’t she stay with you?”

“Oh, no, that wasn’t possible. Our home is way too crowded as it is. My husband and I live in a three bedroom house with our five children.”

Dave nodded, and gently said, “Go on.”

“I guess that after Jared broke up with Penny, he became . . . interested in Maura. More than that, the way the kids talked he became fixated. Maura said she felt sorry for him because he was depressed both about Penny and his parents. When he told her that his grades were slipping because of his depression, she agreed to start tutoring him. She didn't know how troubled he was. None of us did, at that point."

"Unfortunately, hindsight is always better," Dave said. "I understand some teachers said he was a good student."

"He was—in previous years."

"But that changed?"

Pauline nodded. "He was getting into fights here. Anyway, after all the rumors, things finally came to a head. Maura was placed on suspension from work, and Jared was placed on suspension from school." She stopped and took a deep breath, letting it out slowly.

"What happened then?"

"Right after that, someone spray painted graffiti on the building. Well, nearly everyone, myself included, figured Jared did it. Fowler called Elizabeth, Peter, and Jared to his office. Jared swore it wasn't him, but later Elizabeth found empty spray cans in their shed in the back garden."

"What was Jared's relationship with Robin like?" Dave asked.

Pauline opened her mouth, but hesitated.

"Mrs. Wynn?"

"I can't really say for sure. Elizabeth said she thought . . . well, she thought he and Robin might be involved. I don't know if it's true. She doesn't like Robin, you see."

"You think she may have been looking for something to blame on Robin?"

She shrugged. "I don't know. Perhaps."

"Do you know where Peter and Robin were on the night Jared was murdered?"

"Yes. Peter and Robin were in Cambridge visiting Robin's

parents. Peter told me it was the first time he'd met them. He said they spent the whole weekend there, spent some of the time touring the university. The police confirmed their alibi."

"Are you sure?"

She nodded.

"What do you know about their neighbor, Ian Waitley? Mr. Waitley claims that Jared killed his, Ian's, cats right around the same time as the graffiti incident."

"Ian was always friendly, but things got weird after the divorce. Ian tried to continue the friendship with Elizabeth, but Jared wouldn't have it. He told everyone that Ian was a pervert and a Peeping Tom. He warned Ian that if he caught the old man spying on his mother, he would be sorry."

Dave and Kate looked at each other. "How do you know this?" Dave asked.

"Elizabeth told me. She was there when Jared and Ian had a huge row in the driveway right after the graffiti incident."

"Did Jared catch him spying?" Dave asked.

"I have no idea and Elizabeth doesn't believe it."

Dave thought about the murder scene photographs. The blonde teenager lying on the floor with two knife wounds to the neck. "Do you know who did the cooking in your sister's household?"

Pauline looked blankly at him.

"We've been told that Elizabeth rarely cooks, and that she told the police that she doesn't know if she's missing any knives."

"Oh. Peter did most of the cooking while they were married."

"Who cooked after the divorce?" Dave asked. "Did Maura cook for them?"

"Maybe for herself and sometimes for Jared. Right after the divorce, family, friends, and neighbors invited them for dinner quite a bit, or they would bring over dishes. Later though, I know Elizabeth went out a lot, leaving Jared to fend for himself."

"Why did Elizabeth spend so much time away?"

"I guess she was trying to make a life for herself, you know, have a social life and start dating."

"And she forgot about her son?"

"I suppose she figured he was old enough to take care of himself," Pauline said, looking irritated for the first time in the conversation. It wasn't clear if she was irritated at the comment or at her sister.

Dave said, "Elizabeth told us that in the weeks before his murder she and Peter rarely left him alone because of his emotional problems."

"That was after the headmaster suspended him. Jared's friends, what few he had, avoided him. He argued with everyone around him and, quite frankly, hardly anyone could stand to be around him at that point."

"A friend of Elizabeth told us she drinks a lot. Does she have a drinking problem?"

She looked down at her hands folded in her lap, then back at Dave.

"No, of course not."

"Does she ever go out to drink? Do you know where she goes?"

"There's a pub only two blocks from Elizabeth's street. It's popular with locals."

"Kate, do you have any more questions for Mrs. Wynn?" Kate shook her head. Dave thanked Pauline for taking time with them, gave her one of Kate's cards, and asked her to call if she thought of anything else.

CHAPTER THIRTY-TWO

MAURELLE WENT BACK to the cottage, but she couldn't sleep because she was plagued with the feeling that Dave didn't believe her. She could bear almost anything but that. And if he didn't believe her, there seemed no point sticking around here. She probably should leave again and continue on her own. Fabienne was going to be fine. In fact with Maurelle gone, Fabienne's stress level would probably improve. She and Jeannette could manage here on their own for a few days, and Simone and Coralie could come and pick them up.

Her heart sank even lower as she contemplated leaving yet again. You let yourself get your hopes up, she told herself. Now you care for all of them, especially Dave, and it tortures you to leave all of them behind. But what choice do you have? Tomorrow night, once you're sure Fabienne is recovering all right, you have to say goodbye.

IN THE MORNING, someone knocked on the front door of the cottage. Expecting it was one of Fabienne and Jeannette's friends, Maurelle didn't hesitate to open it. But the sight of Dr. Maison holding his medical bag made her hesitate for a moment.

"Bonjour, Dr. Maison."

"I hope I didn't awaken you," he said.

She realized suddenly that the breakfast dishes were sitting on the coffee table and she wished they'd cleaned up instead of being lazy. A quick glance over her shoulder found Jeannette, who apparently had heard the exchange, rushing around the living room. She was picking up newspapers and the offending dishes. Jeanette disappeared into the kitchen and Maurelle said, "Won't you come in, please, Dr. Maison."

"I would normally have called, but since you don't have a phone here . . . ."

"That's perfectly all right. I suppose you're here to check up on Fabienne."

He nodded.

Jeannette came back into the living room for a moment, said her good mornings to the doctor, and then left the house. Maurelle led Dr. Maison up the stairs into Fabienne's room and waited in the hallway outside the door. She could hear muffled talking. A few minutes later the doctor stuck his head out the door and motioned for her to come inside.

"She's doing remarkably well," he said. "I am quite pleased with her recovery." He glanced from Fabienne to Maurelle, and added, "Looks to me like she has a good nurse. She tells me that you've made her stay in bed for twenty-four hours. Good for you."

Maurelle smiled. She remembered tending to her mother during her illness and though it had been difficult, she was glad that she'd done it. Her mother had been weak and fragile at the end, and yet she hadn't complained. She had talked about the old days, her childhood and growing up, her relationship with Maurelle's father, and her fear of raising a child alone. She'd patted Maurelle's hand and hugged her, tears filling her eyes as she said that she was so happy that she had her loving daughter.

"I'd say you have your hands full." He looked down at Fabienne and added, "I do believe you're ready to resume light activities, but I caution you to not overdo it."

At that, Fabienne almost leapt out of bed, grabbed her hand-knit sweater off a chair, and started to dash over to the door, then slowed down as she realized the doctor was watching and frowning. As she reached the door, she stopped momentarily and stuck out her tongue at Maurelle.

Maurelle shook her head and laughed and waved her on as Fabienne rushed like a child out the door and down the stairs, slamming the front door behind her as she took off, probably in search of Jeannette.

Dr. Maison coughed and said "Yes, I do believe you had your hands full."

Turning around, Maurelle said, "Thank you for everything, Doctor. I don't know what we would have done without you."

"I'm happy I could help her. Just try to keep her under some control for a few days."

When they reached the living room downstairs, Maurelle asked, "Would you like some tea before you return to the clinic?"

"Oh, I'm fine, thanks. I must be getting back."

She nodded, waiting as he continued toward the door, but then he stopped. He set down his medical bag on the side table and looked directly at her. "I did want to ask you something."

She tried to keep her face blank and not let him see her rising panic. He must have read something in the newspaper in one of the large cities.

"We don't get many visitors here," he said, "and although I often go to Florac on business, I rarely meet new people, especially, uh, beautiful women." He coughed nervously. "Uh, I wondered if I could take you out to dinner sometime. I would like to get to know you better."

Flustered momentarily by the turn of events, Maurelle

quickly recovered. "I'm flattered, but I—I'm married. I'm sorry." She didn't like lying to him, but Fabienne had already told people that Dave was her husband. She couldn't date the town's doctor even if she wanted to.

"Oh, I'm so sorry," the doctor said, his face reddening. "I didn't know. I shouldn't have asked you. Please accept my apologies."

"Of course," Maurelle said.

As he picked up his bag to leave, Maurelle felt sorry for him. "Dr. Maison, we would love to have you come to dinner tonight though, say around seven. We owe you our gratitude. It's the least we can do."

"Thank you. I would be delighted."

After Dr. Maison left, Dave's face instantly sprang into her mind; his grin, blue eyes, and sandy hair. She realized how she missed him and how she actually loved that little white lie. Her husband. For a second, she could see them at the altar, but the vision quickly evaporated. It could never happen. Their late night phone call flooded back to the forefront of her memory. Dave didn't believe. He wouldn't be able to clear her name. Did it matter? Even if Dave managed to clear her name, he wouldn't want her. The stigma of being accused of murder would never go away.

Maurelle busied herself with straightening the house, but her mind kept going to England and to Dave. What was happening with the investigation? Did he still believe in her, or was he sorry he'd gone to England? The uncertainty made it difficult to concentrate on anything else.

When she told Fabienne and Jeannette about the dinner plans, both women jumped in and said they would take care of the cooking and planning. All Maurelle needed to do was go buy the groceries.

That evening, the two older women practically smothered

Dr. Maison with attention. They talked about life in the village, the locals, and the good old days. Fortunately, he seemed delighted by the attention. Maurelle tuned out much of the conversation, continuing to think about Dave.

When Fabienne brought out dessert, Maurelle managed to pull herself back to the conversation as she ate.

"Are you going to our annual summer festival at the riverside park tomorrow?" Dr. Maison asked.

Fabienne clapped her hands together. "Yes, I can't wait. We couldn't possibly have come here at a better time. Saint-Julien's summer festivals are wonderful, from what I remember."

"I don't think it's a good idea for you to go, Fabienne," Maurelle said. "It's a long walk to the riverside park. I don't know if you're up to that yet."

Fabienne looked pleadingly at Dr. Maison.

"I think she can handle it," he said. "That is, provided she takes it slow and easy."

After the doctor left, Maurelle sighed. She realized she now couldn't leave until after the festival. It would break Fabienne's heart if she spoilt the event for her. But how much of a risk would going to the festival be?

DAVE AND KATE, upon finishing at the school, found the pub around the corner from Willoughby Crescent and ordered a beer for Dave and red wine for Kate. They sat at the counter and watched the bartender, a short middle-aged man with a limp and a prominent bald spot, put away clean glasses. Dave said, "I would expect you get a lot of regulars from the neighborhood."

"That we do."

"Do you happen to know Elizabeth Raybourne?"

He didn't look up, but kept working.

"What do you wanna know 'bout Elizabeth?"

Dave turned around toward the speaker. A lanky man with white hair was standing behind him, holding an empty beer mug.

"Can I buy you a beer?" Dave asked.

"I could use another pint." He proceeded to sit down on a stool next to Dave and pushed his empty tankard toward the bartender, who grudgingly filled it.

Dave reached out his hand and said, "Name's Dave, and this is Kate. You would be?"

The man said his name was John but gave no last name.

"Do you see Elizabeth in here often?" Dave asked.

"She's a regular. Why do you wanna know?"

"I heard about her son's murder. It must have been devastating. I can't imagine losing a child."

"Yeah, she took it pretty hard. Some of us had to take turns walking her home after the murder."

"Are there a lot of regulars? A big group that hang out together?"

He guzzled down the beer and held out his mug for a refill. The bartender looked at Dave, who nodded.

"Well, let's see. There's me, Tony, James, Chris, Joe, and occasionally Elizabeth. Oh, and Sally. Ian sometimes." He made a humorous face.

"Ian Waitley?"

"Yup."

"How often does the group come here?"

"Most nights for the blokes. Ask Johnny here. He can verify that, can't you Johnny?'

The bartender nodded and grinned.

"Tony and I come during the day sometimes, too. The night's when this place gets fun though. Games of darts, everybody laughing and clowning around. We would stay all night if Johnny and Judi didn't throw us out."

"Were you all here on the night of the murder?"

"Yeah, most of us."

"What about the women and Ian?"

He scratched his head. "Seems Sally was here, but Elizabeth had to work. Ian didn't come either. Like I said, they only come occasionally."

"Did Elizabeth's son Jared ever come here?"

"Maybe once or twice with his mum."

"Was he ever here while Ian was here?"

"You know, now that you mention it, I do remember one day, maybe a week or two before the murder, they were both here. I remember 'cause they got into an argument outside. Don't know what it was about. Jared left after that and Ian came back in all irritated. Took him a while to settle down."

A short time later, on the drive to Kate's house, Kate said "Ian says he saw Robin, definitely. Yet she was in Cambridge."

"So he must have seen someone else, mistaking it for Robin."

"Yes. But a woman, young, slim."

Dave said, "Maybe he didn't really see anyone at all, just wanted to be in the limelight."

"Let's see—Robin has a sound alibi, as do Peter and Elizabeth. In fact, everyone does except for Maura. As for motive, what parent would kill their sixteen year old son for such reasons? Even if he had an affair with Robin, and there is only weak innuendo for that, Peter would hardly stab him to death like that. Carsters might have been jealous if he was more infatuated with Maura than he suggests, so there is a weak motive—but still, to murder over it? And there's no other evidence pointing to Carsters. He might even have an alibi. Dave, sometimes if it is yellow and quacks, you just have to accept that it is a duck."

Dave gazed out the window at the cars and buses, but his mind was elsewhere. Something was bothering him. Where was the murder weapon? And something else he couldn't quite put a finger on was niggling at the back of his mind.

He turned to Kate. "We need to talk to Elizabeth again. A phone call would probably suffice."

She glanced at him, her brow creased.

"You want to tell me what you're thinking?"

"Not yet. Bear with me here, I'm trying to work something out."

The rest of the drive went by in silence.

Back at Kate's house, Kate looked up Elizabeth Raybourne's phone number and gave it to Dave. He dialed and put it on speaker. When she answered, he identified himself.

"Ms. Raybourne, the murder weapon was described in the post-mortem as a kitchen knife. It hasn't been recovered. We've been told that you aren't missing any knives. Are you sure about that?"

"I really wouldn't know. I don't cook much."

"Your husband did all the cooking?"

"Yes."

"But he didn't take the utensils when he moved out?"

"Only some of them. Robin already had a kitchen full of them. That's also another reason I can't tell if one of the knives is missing."

"But you had dinner guests at your home after the divorce, didn't you?"

"I did. Why do you ask?"

Dave scratched his head and looked at Kate before resuming. "Who cooked those dinners?"

"A neighbor, Ian Waitley, came over a few times. He used to be a chef back in Ireland. He's retired now, but he's still quite the gourmet. He used to cook for us occasionally when Peter still lived here, too. He was always, you know, wanting to help. Lonely, I suppose."

After he hung up, Dave sat very still. What was it Ian had said about his cats' murder? Various fragments of conversation drifting through his mind began to fall into place. Maura saying something about running . . . tins of spray paint . . . and something about flowers—no, it was something about gardening.

He stood and began pacing. "Can you get a background check on someone?"

They set to work, sending off emails to various contacts of Kate's. Before long, the replies began trickling in, some by email, some by fax.

Kate picked up one of the printouts, read it, and handed it to Dave. It said that on one occasion Ian had been fined in London for affray—but he had been attacked by another man.

Dave looked up. "What's affray?"

"A disturbance or fight."

He continued reading. Ian Waitley had a criminal record back in Ireland—several arrests for affrays and for armed robbery. He'd moved to England sixteen years ago after several cautions, mainly for indecent exposure and voyeurism. "So that's why he's 'retired' at such a young age."

Another reply came in. Kate read it and then abruptly left the room without saying anything. Dave, curious about the contents of the reply, drummed his fingers on the desk and waited, wondering what was going on.

A few minutes later, she returned. "Listen to this. Ian's wife, Wilhelmina, divorced him after he was arrested the first time. She took their two daughters, Abby and Josephine, and moved to Australia."

"Okay, I'm confused. Weren't those the names of his cats?"

"Yes, they were. I just got off the phone with Peter Raybourne. He confirmed that Ian had three cats with those names. The mother cat died of old age, but the younger cats were still alive when Peter lived across the street from Ian."

THE NEXT MORNING, while having breakfast with Kate, Dave called Greg's friend, Nigel James.

Nigel asked, "Where are you?"

"In a pub across the street from the Hallworth Hotel. Late breakfast.

"What did you want to discuss?" Nigel asked.

Dave tried to set out what he was thinking now. There was a house they needed to search. Despite Dave's desperation, Nigel was dismissive.

"We don't have enough evidence for a search warrant," Nigel said. "It's total supposition. There's far more evidence against Maura Barrington than anyone else. She had an affair with a student and she had a powerful motive. And she also ran."

"But—"

"Dave, I am sorry, but I think your time's up on this. Stay put. I'm on my way over to see you now."

"Now what?" Kate eyed Dave's look of frustration as he ended the call. He told her most of what Nigel had said. "You know, the worst part is, from Nigel's perspective, he's right. It could well have been Maura."

Kate didn't help his dour mood by saying, "We just don't have enough yet to go on."

Dave drank his beer and didn't answer. Nigel made it sound like the case was closed. If he was on his way over to see him and wanted him to stay put, he probably intended to question him—maybe even arrest him for harboring a criminal.

"I know," he said finally, "All we can do at this point is keep asking questions. Let's go back to Willoughby Crescent. If you don't mind, I'd like to leave as soon as possible."

They quickly finished their breakfast in silence.

On the long drive in Kate's car, something else continued to lurk at the back of Dave's mind. It was something Maurelle had said. What was it? All of a sudden he had it. It was back when they were in the cave on the night she'd told him she was wanted for murder. Someone had suggested to her that she run. Of course, she could have made that up as an excuse for her bad decision, but it seemed unlikely to him.

They parked in front of Ian Waitley's house.

Dave saw the curtains move inside the house as Ian peeked out a window, watching them as they walked up the steps.

Greeting them at the door, Ian said, "You're back again. Did you talk to the Headmaster like I told you?"

"We did. Thank you, we've learned a great deal. Could we speak with you again?"

Ian's face lit up and he sprang toward the living room like a little boy who was about to get a treat. Dave thought about the isolated residents of Reynier, who thrived on gossip, and it struck him suddenly that someone who made a habit of watching people would probably be eager for gossip, too. He could use that to their advantage.

"Hey, it's such a nice afternoon. Can we sit in your lovely garden again? Kate hasn't seen it yet."

"Ah, yes, of course! A pleasure!" Ian led them out on to the small terrace and waved them towards the wooden garden chairs.

Dave gazed out again into the lovely yard, newly mowed. The apple tree was freshly trimmed, the bird bath filled, the flowers in bloom. A wooden bench completed the picture.

"Make yourselves comfortable while I make some tea."

A few minutes later Ian returned with refreshments and set them on a round glass-topped table.

"Now, what would you like to talk about?"

IN THE LATE morning, Fabienne and Jeannette began preparing for the festival that would start at eleven o'clock.

"I'm still not sure about you going to the festival," Maurelle said.

"We're going, and that's that," Fabienne huffed, folding her arms together. "You should come, too. We know that you miss Dave, but you shouldn't sit around the house waiting and brooding."

"I suppose you're right, and it does sound like fun." Besides I need to keep an eye on both of you older women, she thought.

When it came time to go, Fabienne packed a couple of last minute items into their picnic basket and Jeannette carried it. Maurelle grabbed three folding chairs, and they set out along the ancient cobbled lane through town. As townspeople took to the street, they smiled and waved to relatives, friends, and neighbors.

Children ran ahead of their parents and grandparents, laughing and clowning around. Now and then, a mother would grab a child and reign them in to allow cars, some with boat trailers, to pass.

As they strolled along, Maurelle breathed in the fragrant air, filled with the scent of the many flowering bougainvillea, and allowed herself to enjoy the sun's rays bathing her face and her bare arms. The Romanesque architecture, especially notable in the centuries-old church with intricately appointed square belfry reachable only by an outside staircase, once again enchanted her.

She had heard Fabienne and Jeannette rave about the spectacular view from the other side of the river, and she was delighted that she would finally get the chance to cross the bridge to see the view for herself. She suggested they go across the bridge first, but the older women insisted they set up their picnic spot before the beach became too crowded. That made sense. They found a lovely spot near Jeannette and Fabienne's friends on the village side of the river, and set up their chairs. They chatted for an hour and then ate their lunch. Afterwards, more people arrived, and friends dropped by to introduce the three women to other friends and neighbors.

By late-afternoon, seeing that the women were in capable hands, Maurelle excused herself and walked across the bridge. She then followed a walking path toward the river, stopping at the top of the staircase that led down to the riverbank. She stood and gazed back at the village. Everything she'd heard about the view was true. Small cascades erupted out of the cliff's face and plummeted into small streams that meandered through the town square, finally merging and rushing through a stone archway, only to tumble again over another small cliff into the green river. People in colorful kayaks floated along the peaceful river, causing her to smile in appreciation of the canvas.

She descended the steep staircase and stood watching the kayakers, enjoying a refreshing mist from the nearby waterfall. After an hour, she went for a long walk along the river and enjoyed the peacefulness.

As evening approached, it started sprinkling and people began packing up. She climbed back up the stairs and gazed across to the beach and picnic area, looking for Fabienne and Jeannette. The crowd had grown considerably, and surprised Maurelle, who hadn't realized the village was that populated. Then she remembered the nearby villages, and she supposed people had come from all around the general region for the outing. She finally spotted Fabienne and Jeannette, scrambling to pick up chairs and picnic items to escape the rain, and yet they were laughing and looked completely contented, reminding her again of friendships she'd never expected.

With the rain increasing in intensity and pelting her now in earnest, Maurelle dashed back across the bridge. On the other side, swerving to avoid a dog chasing a Frisbee, she narrowly avoided a collision with a middle-aged man standing in the grass. She stumbled and landed hard on her hands and knees. She wasn't hurt, didn't feel pain from the fall, but she felt her face burn with embarrassment, until she recalled the day outside the bakery when Dave had crashed into her and called himself an oaf.

That fond thought turned suddenly sour and she almost started to cry. Why did she have to think of Dave right now? She was going to miss him and Jeannette and Fabienne. She hated the thought. She would miss Saint-Julien and Reynier and friendship and laughter. But her time was up. After everyone went to bed, she would have to do what she needed to do.

CHAPTER THIRTY-THREE

DAVE SAID, "YOU were right about the graffiti, Mr. Waitley. The Headmaster confirmed that Jared was responsible for it. We saw the paint. An awful mess."

Ian set down the tea pot and shook his finger at Dave. "I told you that boy was a problem."

"You were also right about the fighting between Elizabeth and Robin. I'll bet Peter has his hands full with those two women."

Ian chuckled and poured the tea. Kate was scribbling something in her notebook, and gave Dave a confused look, not knowing exactly what he was planning.

"You know, something else you told us was that you saw Robin Sutcliffe at the Raybournes' house on the night of the murder. But she and Peter Raybourne were in Cambridge, so it couldn't have been her." Ian shrugged and sipped his tea. "Did you really see someone?"

"I'm old. My memory might be a bit spotty."

Kate said, "Could it have been Maura Barrington that you saw?"

"Well, I guess, maybe."

Dave raised an eyebrow. Up until now, Ian had defended

Maura. "Ian, did you actually see someone or not?"

Looking flustered, Ian said, "The streetlamps were lit, but there were lots of shadows. I saw a woman. She looked like Robin. I guess they do both have long dark hair now that I think about it."

Dave grimaced and bit the inside of his mouth.

Ian, apparently trying to regain his composure, held out a plate of biscuits and Dave shook his head. Kate politely took one. Ian set the tray down and took another sip of tea.

"I was thinking about something on the way over here. Did you call Maura Barrington on the morning Jared's body was discovered and suggest she should run?"

Ian coughed and spurted out his tea.

"Are you all right?" Kate asked.

He nodded, cleared his throat, and said "Now why would I tell her to do that?"

"Why indeed?" Ian fidgeted with the plate of biscuits, avoiding Dave's eyes. It might not mean anything, but Dave decided to push him further. "You were defending her the other day, and now you say it could have been her you saw on the night of the murder."

"I'm an old man. I get mixed up. That's why them coppers didn't want to listen to me, you got it?" He set down the plate.

"Tell me, you said you saw the cans of paint Jared used—is that right?"

"Yes, clear as day, I—"

"In their shed. In their back garden." Dave leaned forward. "What were you doing there?"

"Yes, well, I was over there to borrow something. Wait, I forgot the biscuits!"

He stood and hurried it back into the house.

Kate leaned in and whispered, "I think you hit a nerve."

Ian returned moments later empty-handed with a tight

expression on his face. The anticipation and brightness he'd shown upon their arrival was gone. He remained standing, but began involuntarily twitching. He looked more than ever like a nervous bird.

Dave said, "You told us that Jared killed your cats—Abby and Josephine. I'm really sorry about your loss."

Ian sank back into his chair and moaned, "They were my life."

"I can understand that. My dog, Howie, was hit and killed by a car three years ago. It took me a long time to get over it." Ian nodded. "Where are they buried, Mr. Waitley?" They might have been cremated. Or thrown away with the trash; Dave had seen that before. But he remembered Maurelle and her dead mouse. If she had wanted to see that small creature properly buried, Ian would most certainly have done the same for his beloved pets.

Ian turned and glared at Dave. "Why would you want to know that?"

"If you think Jared killed them, don't you want a post-mortem done?"

"What difference does it make now? The boy is dead."

"I would still want it on record what he'd done if I were in your place." Dave kept a close eye on Ian, who seemed to be getting more and more agitated by the moment.

"Nobody cares. They're just possessions to most people."

"Where did you bury your moggies, Ian? Show them to us."

Ian stood up, his face knotted with anger. "You should leave now."

"Show me where they're buried, Mr. Waitley. They are there, aren't they, under the tree?" Dave pointed. "Those new patches."

"I'd like you to leave now."

"Or what? Will you call the police?"

He didn't answer.

"You have two patches over there that look as if they were

dug about the same time. You have a smaller one that looks even fresher. What's buried there, Ian?"

Dave picked up a shovel that was resting against the wall of the house, and started towards the apple tree. Ian rushed forward and tried to grab it away from Dave, but he was no match for the younger man. Dave shrugged him off and began digging in the first patch.

"No! Stop!" Ian threw himself on the ground, moaning incoherently.

Five minutes later, Dave squatted, reached into the hole, and pulled out a clear plastic bag. He opened it and held his breath. Inside was the remains of one cat, its head severed from its body. He laid it down and began digging in the newer, smaller patch. Soon he lifted out another bag. This time, inside was a large kitchen knife, still stained with blood. Dave carefully left the bag sealed.

Kate was standing nearby talking on her mobile phone. Moments later she stated "The police are on their way".

Dave picked up both bags and went to the last patch. He dug up another cat. When he looked up, Nigel was standing at the gate, watching.

"No! You can't take my moggies," Ian wailed.

Dave grabbed Ian's shoulders, glaring into his face, and he found he actually felt sorry for the old man.

"I couldn't protect my babies," Ian cried, "but I saw to it that that boy would never harm anyone again."

"Why did you bury the knife there?" Dave asked quietly.

"I figured it belonged to them," he whispered. "It was for them that I killed that hateful boy."

"Why did Jared butcher your cats?"

"He was jealous. He didn't want me looking at his mother, at Maura, at any of the women in the neighborhood."

"He caught you doing that?"

Ian's face flushed. "I snuck into the house one night and when Elizabeth came out of the shower, I watched her. She didn't see me and I never touched her. But Jared caught me sneaking out of the house."

Dave glanced at Kate. They both turned and saw two uniformed police officers appear behind Nigel at the gate. Nigel strode over to where Dave was standing.

"I came here half-expecting I would have to arrest you," Nigel said, shaking his head. "Even when I heard Waitley yelling, I thought you were trying some rough stuff to get him to talk. You've still got a few things to answer for. What made you think it was him?"

"Little things, really. As soon as Maura ran, the focus was on her. It was almost like a confession. He pushed her to go."

"He used her," Kate said. "I thought he liked her."

"Maybe he did, maybe he even convinced himself he was somehow helping her. But he was still prepared to see her convicted rather than go to prison himself. But there were other things, like the paint, which told me he snooped around, and his readiness to suggest other suspects. No one really noticed him. They thought of him as someone who watched, not as someone who did anything. Then his record in Ireland suggested a bit more than that. Lastly, there were his cats. That was the only time we really saw something of him, of what was underneath that rage." Dave looked at the flowers and the apple tree. "You know, when I first came here I saw these recently dug patches, and when I heard about his cats I immediately connected them with here, it was the way he glanced over here. But it didn't fit; there were two cats and three patches. That kept nagging at me, and finally I connected it with the murder weapon."

Kate nodded. "After all those tangles, it was the person least involved in their lives—none of the affairs and attractions and enmities really meant anything much, just typical small community stuff. Ian was always the extra man, the outsider."

Dave said, "Yes. I think he was always snooping, looking in through windows. And when you come down to it, he was the only one apart from Maura who didn't have any kind of alibi, he wasn't even at the pub. He didn't see anyone that night, no one but Jared."

BY NIGHTFALL THE media was blasting news of the arrest all over the television. Dave sat in his hotel room, watching a few of the reports. Tiring of it, he switched off the television. He sat with his eyes closed, and let the satisfaction of solving the case flow through his body. It was then that it dawned on him: he'd not only redeemed Maurelle, but also himself. He'd messed up the Diana Lewis and Johnny Kincaid case because he'd believed in the wrong person and let it cloud his judgment. This time, he'd believed in someone, but he hadn't let his personal feelings keep him from conducting a logical and thorough investigation. And his judgment had been right.

He smiled, opened his eyes, and took out his address book from his pocket. He looked up the phone number he had listed for Greg, and dialed.

When Greg came on the phone and heard Dave's voice, he said, "Hi, buddy. What's going on?"

"We made an arrest."

"You did? That's great! Okay, I'm dying to know, who did it? Come on, are you going to make me pry it out of you?"

"I'll tell you after I get to France."

WHEN DAVE ARRIVED in Orleans, Greg, Simone, and Coralie met him at the airport, and immediately bombarded him with questions about the case. After he briefed them, he said,

"Where are they?"

Greg said, "You're not going to like this. Right after you called, Jeannette called. She said they don't know where Maurelle is. She left a note for them saying 'she was going to do the right thing' whatever that means.

"What? You can't be serious."

"Afraid so, chum. We've got a long drive ahead of us. Are you up to it after your day of traveling?"

"Yeah. Where are we going?"

"Saint-Julien."

"That sounds familiar."

Coralie said, "Your great-grandparents used to live there. Fabienne owns their house. That's where they've been hiding."

"We're taking my car," Simone said. "It's going to be cramped."

"That's okay. I'm just eager to get there."

IT WAS A LONG drive and by the time they arrived in Saint-Julien, Dave was worn out. He felt much better, though, when he saw Fabienne and Jeannette sitting in rocking chairs on the porch and waving at the car.

Fabienne got up, rushed over, and hugged him as he stepped out of the car, nearly knocking him over in the process.

"I'm so glad you're home, dear boy" she said. "I've missed you."

Home, he thought. That didn't sound bad.

She looked up into his eyes. "Have you heard from Maurelle?" she asked. "We've been worried sick about both of you."

"How long has she been gone?"

"We went to the festival yesterday and it was a lovely day. But when we woke up this morning, she was gone. She left a note."

"Greg told me."

"Do you know what it means?"

"I have a hunch. Is there a Gendarmerie around here?"

Fabienne nodded.

"YOU HAVE A visitor. Come with me." Maurelle was lying on a cot and looked up at the guard, but didn't move since she assumed he was speaking to the woman on the other cot. "Are you coming?"

She raised up on an elbow and glanced at the woman on the other side of the small room. The woman was sleeping. "Do you mean me?"

"Yes. Come on."

She jumped up and watched as he unlocked the cell door. She followed him out, walking past three other empty cells. He opened another door and led her into a long gray corridor without windows or decoration. He stopped three-quarters of the way down and opened another door. Standing behind his broad body, she couldn't see anything and didn't know what was happening. He finally moved aside and motioned for her to enter. She hesitated, took a deep breath and walked in. There, sitting at a table, was Dave.

She stood frozen, unsure how to behave, her mouth gaping open. Dave got up and approached her. "I'm sorry," she said. "I know you didn't want me to turn myself in until you'd had a chance to investigate, but I had to do it. It was a mistake to run. I think they're making arrangements to send me back to England."

Leading her on in a mixture of amusement and irritation Dave replied, "Why now? Why turn yourself in while I was trying to solve the case? Didn't you trust me to know what I was doing?"

"Of course I did. I don't know that you trusted me though. Anyway, an investigation can go on for months, years even. It was wrong of me to let you go there and put yourself at risk. I was wrong to put your grandmother and Jeannette at risk. I can't undo any of that, I know. All I can do is—"

Smiling, he said, "Maurelle, it's over."

Her heart lurched, and all she managed to stammer was, "What?"

"The police made an arrest yesterday afternoon. It's a solid case now with concrete evidence and a confession."

Her eyes widened and her heart pounded. "It's solved. Are you sure?"

"Yes, I'm sure. The suspect is behind bars."

"Who killed Jared?"

"Ian Waitley."

"What!" Her mouth gaped open for a second. "Are you serious? He seemed so harmless." Dave nodded. "Why on earth would he do something that awful? He was kind to me and to almost everyone."

"Apparently, he was a Peeping Tom, and Jared found out. Jared threatened him, saying that if he didn't stay away, Ian would regret it. When Jared caught him in the Raybourne house, spying on Elizabeth, Jared killed Ian's cats. I guess killing Jared was Ian's revenge."

Shaking her head and moving to sit in one of the chairs, she replied, "I guess he was pushed over the edge. I guess you never know about people. He seemed so nice and funny, just a bit eccentric."

"Yeah, I feel a little sorry for the guy because, from what I can tell, Jared really did push him to it. But what I can't forgive him for is getting you to run. At the end, he was even prepared to claim he'd seen you go into the house that night. "

She got up and hugged him, squeezing him tightly, then

faced him. "Thank you for everything you've done. What will you do now? Are you going back to Chicago straight away?"

He stared into her eyes. "I'm not entirely sure. What about you? Will you go back to England, to teaching?"

She shook her head. "Will they release me from here?"

"Yes. It might take a few hours. They're working on it."

"I can't go back to teaching. The murder case may be closed, but once there's the accusation of an affair . . . ."

"I spoke to Headmaster Fowler and the inspectors," Dave said. "They're willing to let that go. It's over."

The way Dave was looking at her, she could tell he thought she was guilty of an affair with Jared. "I still won't return to teaching. If a teacher is accused of that, her or his career is basically over, whether or not it's proven. And even disregarding that, the stigma of being a murder suspect will stick. I don't know if I'll ever redeem myself. As for England . . . ." She shrugged, not knowing where she would go now. He didn't say anything, and she felt suddenly sad and looked away so he wouldn't see.

"I wouldn't be so sure of that," he said finally. "I thought the same thing, until recently."

She didn't know how to respond.

"Have you considered staying in Reynier or here in St. Julien?" he said.

"Well, I do like France."

"I did some checking on the internet while I was in London. There is this lovely troglodyte house for sale in Reynier. I saw photos of it on the web and I called up the estate agent. Believe it or not, I'm thinking of buying it and relocating to France." Maurelle smiled. "That is, unless you've had your fill of cave-dwelling."

She cocked her head. What was he saying?

"If you're done with caves, I could buy a normal house,

instead. And if you'd prefer Saint-Julien, I could talk to Grand-mère about buying her house. I'm not promising anything, but we could try living together and see what develops."

She reached up and kissed him.

Made in the USA
Middletown, DE
14 December 2014